Superstar Speedsters

Superstar Speedsters

Volume 1

Josh Zimmer

Copyright © 2021 by Josh Zimmer

All rights reserved. No part of this book may be reproduced in any manner whatsoever without written permission except in the case of brief quotations embodied in critical articles and reviews.

First Printing, 2021

1. Intergalactic Wars: Rise Of The Flame Order
2. Intergalactic Wars: Taking Down Sir Phantom
3. Crimson Fox: Jungle Warrior
4. Crimson Fox: Mouse Hunter
5. Crimson Fox: Wolf Hunter
6. Crimson Fox: Raccoon Hunter
7. Crimson Fox: Chipmunk Hunter
8. Crimson Fox: Squirrel Hunter
9. Crimson Fox: Jackal Hunter
10. Supersonic Warrior vs the Shopping Carts
11. Supersonic Warrior: Becoming An Superhero
12. Supersonic Warrior: Escape From Electric Industries
13. Supersonic Warrior: Fire vs Ice
14. Supersonic Warrior: Finding Love
15. Supersonic Warrior: Shattered Love
16. Supersonic Warrior: Consumed By Darkness
17. Supersonic Warrior: Taking Down The Darkness
18. Fire Slinger: Battling Through Post Depression
19. Fire Slinger: Despair
20. Spider Crusader: Destruction Of Zoomopolis
21. Acorn High School: Acorn Dragons vs Shallow Falls Bears
22. Pine Cone Academy: Hope vs Despair

CONTENTS

Section Break 1

Intergalactic Wars:
1. Intergalactic Wars: Rise Of The Flame Order
2. Intergalactic Wars: Taking Down Sir Phantom

1

In a galaxy far far away, the Crimson Wing was being boarded by the Flame Order. The Flame Order are bounty hunters that want to leave no one alive. Justin is a scavenger, and his crew were being killed by the Flame Order. The crew members laid in puddles of blood, while Justin hid behind the column. Justin held his blaster in his hand, and was shooting down the bounty hunters. The leader of the Flame Order, Commander Plasma, walked through the hallway. Commander Plasma walked behind the column, and shot Justin in the arm. Justin dropped his blaster on the ground. Commander Plasma said, "Don't bother picking up the blaster, you are a wasted piece of scum in the galaxy." Justin reached for his blaster. Commander Plasma stepped on Justin's arm. Justin screamed in pain! Commander Plasma took out his blaster, and shot Justin in the chest. Justin rolled on the ground, as blood poured from his chest. Justin slowly got up from the ground, and limped toward the escape pod. Commander Plasma followed Justin, and shot his blaster at him. Blaster bolts hit Justin's body, as he limped toward the escape pod. Blood dripped on the ground. Justin pressed the buttons on the panel, and activated the escape pod. Justin walked in to the escape pod. The escape pod started up, and launched from the Crimson Wing in to outer space. Commander Plasma and his troopers walked to their ships, and departed from the Crimson Wing. The escape pod crashed on to the sandy planet of Sandtopia. Droid scavengers opened the escape pod, and carried Justin to their crawler. Justin woke up on the droid scavenger crawler, and noticed that his body was patched up. Justin was surrounded by various droid models. The various droid models were beeping at him, and circling around him to scan his body. Justin got up, and explored the crawler. Justin grabbed a blaster from the weapon compartment, and some explosives from the explosives compartment. Justin put the explosives in to his bag. Justin walked to the front of the crawler. Droid Scavengers were patrolling the hallways. Justin shot his blaster at the droid scavengers, and killed them. The droid scavengers laid on the ground in puddles of blood. Justin walked in to the driver compartment, and grabbed the droid scavenger leader by its neck. The droid scavenger leader said, "Br-rrrrrrrrrr, let me go human!" Justin wrapped his arm around the droid scavenger's neck, and pointed his blaster at its skull. The droid scavenger leader was choking, and was gasping for air. Justin said, "You deserve to die, alien scum." Justin shot his blaster, and the droid scavenger leader's skull exploded. The droid scavenger leader laid on the ground in a puddle of blood. Justin took out explosives from his bag, and attached them to the crawler. Justin opened the door for the crawler, and jumped out of it. Justin rolled on the sand, and pressed the detonate button. The crawler exploded, as pieces and gears landed on the sand. Justin got up from the sand, and brushed the sand off of his clothes. Justin walked through the sandy wasteland, with the sun shining on top of him. Sweat was dripping from Justin's forehead, as he walked. Justin was wiping sweat from his forehead, when he noticed a small town called Sandville. Justin walked in to Sandville. Various aliens and droids were walking through the town. The security trooper stepped in front of Justin, and pushed him. The security trooper said, "I need your security card!" Justin said, "You don't need my security card!" The security trooper said, "You think this is a joke, I need your security card for you to walk in to the town." Justin said, "Security cards are useless to you anyways." Justin took out his blaster, and shot the security trooper in the chest. The security trooper laid on the ground, in a puddle of blood. Random aliens and droids ran away, and hid behind the wall, when they saw the chaos. The security trooper's communication device was blinking, as it sent a call for reinforcements. Justin stepped on the communication device, and crushed it to pieces, as he walked through the town. Security trooper carriers were rolling through the town! Justin walked through the town, and analyzed the tents. The tents were selling various snacks and supplies. Justin walked to one of the tents, and bought a apple with his currency. Justin ate the apple, as he walked through the town. Justin threw the remains of the apple in to the trash compartment. Security trooper carriers rolled in front of Justin, and stopped in the middle of the town. The doors of the security trooper carriers opened, and security troopers marched out of them. The security troopers surrounded Justin, and pointed their weapons at him. The security troopers said, "Surrender or be destroyed, human scum!" Justin took a grenade from his bag, and backflipped in the air. Justin threw the grenade at the security troopers. Justin landed on the ground, and the grenade exploded. Groups of security troopers laid on the ground in puddles of blood. Justin ran toward the security trooper carrier, and killed the groups of security troopers that marched out of it. Justin stopped at the security trooper carrier, and attached explosives to it. Justin ran in to one of the tents, and went behind the wall. Justin pressed the button on the detonator, and the security trooper carrier exploded. Justin smiled, as he walked in to the cantina. Justin walked to the cantina bartender, and ordered a drink. Justin grabbed his can of space punch, and sat in the booth. Justin drank his space punch, and analyzed the area. Various aliens and droids were enjoying their refreshments in the cantina. An smuggler names James sat in the booth next to Justin. James was talking with a anthromorphic cockroach. The anthromorphic cockroach said, "Bzzzzz bzzzzz, there is a bounty on your head. Prepare to be destroyed, human scum." James pointed his blaster at the anthromorphic cockroach and said, "You can't outsmart me, I am the smartest smuggler in the galaxy." James shot his blaster at the anthromorphic cockroach's chest. The anthromorphic cockroach laid on the ground in a puddle of blood. James got up from his booth, and walked to Justin's booth. James sat right next to Justin and said, "Hey kid, I haven't seen you before in this town." Justin said, "I am a scavenger, I am hiding from the Flame Order." James said, "The Flame Order are a bunch of bullies. Let me join your crew, I have a ship that can take you anywhere in the galaxy." Justin said, "Sure, The Flame Order won't stand a chance against us." James and Justin got up from the booth, and walked out of the cantina. Security troopers were patrolling the area! James and Justin were sneaking through the town, avoiding the security troopers. Security troopers were patrolling and scanning the area. James and Justin were bent down next to a fruit cart, when the security troopers analyzed it. The security troopers waved the security trooper leader to the cart. The security trooper leader walked over and analyzed each apple, by picking them up. The security trooper threw the apples on to the ground. The apples rolled toward James and Justin. Justin ate the apple! The security troopers set explosives on the fruit cart. The explosives detonated, and the fruit cart exploded. The security trooper leader pressed a button on his wrist, and more security troopers swarmed the area. The security troopers pointed their weapons at James and Justin. James and Justin got up from the ground. The security troopers shot their weapons at James and Justin. The weapons shot James and Justin in the chest. James and Justin slid backwards, as blood poured on the ground. James and Justin took out their blasters, and shot the security troopers. The security troopers laid on the ground. The security trooper leader grabbed his missile launcher, and shot a missile at James and Justin. James and Justin smashed in to the wall, and laid on the ground, with blood leaking from their bodies. The security trooper leader and the squad of security troopers walked over to James and Justin. The security trooper leader and the squad of security troopers electrocuted James and Justin with their electric batons. James and Justin got electrocuted, and closed their eyes. The security troopers picked up James and Justin, and hunched them over their shoulders. The security trooper leader and the security troopers walked to their ship. The ship departed, and flew to the space station. The ship landed on the space station. The security trooper leader, and the security troopers threw James and Justin in to a laser cage. James and Justin woke up in the laser cage! The security troopers were standing in front of the panel for the laser cage. James and Justin slammed their fists on the laser cage. The laser cage electrocuted James and Justin. The security trooper leader said, "Don't bother, our leader wants you to behave, so we don't have to exterminate you." James said, "Your leader must be scared to show himself in front of us." The security trooper growled and said, "Are you insulting our leader?" James said, "No, I am insulting your empire, you guys are so pathetic, if you think a laser cage counts as torture for humans." The security trooper presses a button on the panel, and electrocutes James and Justin. The security trooper said, "If you speak out of tongue again, you will be exterminated." Commander Plasma walked in to the room. The security troopers stepped away from the panel. James and Justin trembled in fear! Commander Plasma stared at James and Justin through his armored mask, and sent chills in to their bodies. Commander Plasma pressed a button on the panel, and turned off the laser cage Commander Plasma pulled James toward him with his powers. The squad of security troopers pointed their weapons at Justin. James was terrified in fear, while Commander Plasma held him in his grip. Commander Plasma took James to the interrogation room. Justin followed Commander Plasma, with the security troopers behind him. Commander Plasma walked in to the interrogation room, and threw James in to the cage. The security troopers pushed Justin in to the cage. The security troopers closed the cage. Commander Plasma pressed some buttons on the panel, and brought the space station's laser online. The windows opened in the interrogation room. The laser moved in to place. Commander Plasma set the destination in the laser settings. The laser pointed at Sandtopia. Commander Plasma pressed the button on the panel. The laser from the space station blew up Sandtopia in to space debris. James and Justin watched through the window in horror, as they trembled in fear. Commander Plasma laughed through his mask. James took out his blaster, and shot the panel for the cage. The cage went down, and the security troopers took out their weapons. Justin hid behind the cage. James shot his blaster at the security troopers. The security troopers laid on the ground in puddles of blood. James shot his blaster at Commander Plasma. Commander plasma dodged and reflected the blaster bolt back at James. James slid backwards, as the blaster bolt hit his arm. Blood poured on the ground, as James kept shooting his blaster at Commander Plasma. Commander Plasma reflected the blaster bolts with his vibroblade. James slid in to the wall, as the blaster bolts reflected back at him. Commander Plasma pulled James toward him, and kicked him in the chest. James slid backwards, and dropped his blaster. The blaster fell on the ground. The security troopers kicked the blaster away from James. The blaster slid toward Justin. Justin picked up the blaster, and put it in his bag. Commander Plasma walked toward James. James stepped backwards, and the security troopers pointed their weapons at James. The security troopers shot their weapons at James. James stepped forward as he got shot in the arm. Blood poured on the ground, while Commander Plasma walked closer to James. Justin took his blaster off of his belt, and shot the security troopers. The security troopers laid on the ground in puddles of blood. Justin put his blaster back on his belt. Commander Plasma sped toward James, and grabbed him by the neck. James struggled in Commander Plasma's grip. Commander Plasma smashed James in to the ground. James laid on the ground! Commander Plasma stabbed James in the chest with his vibroblade. James laid on the ground in a puddle of blood. Commander Plasma walked to Justin. Chills were sent through Justin's body, as Commander Plasma walked through the hallway. Justin grabbed his blaster off of his belt and said, "You're a monster!" Commander Plasma said, "Awwwwwww, the scavenger cares for his friend. You will be destroyed." Justin shot his blaster at Commander Plasma! Commander Plasma deflected the blaster bolts with his vibroblade. The blaster bolts hit Justin in the arm, as he slid backwards. Blood dripped on the ground, as Justin sped in to Commander Plasma. Commander Plasma grabbed Justin's arm, and kicked him in the chest. Justin rolled on the ground in to a shelf! Justin's blaster fell on the ground. Commander Plasma stabbed his vibroblade in to Justin's blaster, and shattered it to pieces. The shattered pieces of the blaster laid on the ground. Commander Plasma swung his vibroblade at the ground. Justin rolled on the ground, in to the shelf. The shelf shook, and a vibroblade landed next to Justin. Justin grabbed the vibroblade! A voice spoke in Justin's head. The voice said, "It's your destiny, Justin! Use the vibroblade and save the galaxy from Commander Plasma's reign of terror." Justin held the vibroblade across his chest, and was confident to swing it at Commander Plasma. Commander Plasma walked toward Justin, and swung his vibroblade. Justin swung the vibroblade, and it clashed against Commander Plasma's vibroblade. Justin backflipped, and kicked Commander Plasma in the chest. Commander Plasma slid backwards! Justin sped in to Commander Plasma, and grabbed Commander Plasma's arm. Justin threw Commander Plasma in to the panel. The panel exploded, and knocked out the power in the space station. The backup power generator went online, and the lights in the space station turned red. Commander Plasma laid on the ground. Justin swung his vibroblade at Commander Plasma. Commander Plasma defended himself with his vibroblade. Commander Plasma backflipped off of the ground, and swung his vibroblade at Justin's arm. Justin defended himself with his vibroblade. Commander Plasma said, "You're pathetic for caring about your friend. You are human scum for having feelings. Commander Plasma kicked Justin in the chest. Justin slid backwards, and sped towards Commander Plasma. Justin growled, and swung his vibroblade at Commander Plasma's chest. Commander Plasma slid backwards! Justin held his hand out, and used his powers to push Commander Plasma through the wall. Commander Plasma smashed in to the wall, and laid on the ground. Justin growled, and bent down in front of Commander Plasma. Justin swung his vibroblade at Commander Plasma's arm. Commander Plasma deflected it with his vibroblade. Commander Plasma said, "Fuel your anger, your anger is the path to unlimited power." Commander Plasma shoots lightning out of his hands, and electrocuted Justin. Justin steps backwards, and deflects it with his vibroblade. A space ship crashed through the space station's window and flew toward Justin. Justin backflips out of the way, and slices the wing off with his vibroblade. The space ship crashes in to the wall. Ben, a warrior for the Flame Order, walks out of the space ship! Ben said, "Commander Plasma, I have received your transmission, and I am here to protect you." Commander Plasma said, "Stay back, son, it's too dangerous." Justin swings his vibroblade and strikes the lightning back at Commander Plasma. Commander Plasma smashes in to the wall, and his helmet gets smashed to pieces. Justin walked toward Commander Plasma, and bent down. Justin tore the remains of Commander Plasma's helmet off of Commander Plasma's face, and lifts the vibroblade over Commander Plasma's body. Commander Plasma said, "Ben, I am sorry for letting you watch me die." Justin stabbed his vibroblade in to Commander Plasma's skull. Blood gushed out of Commander Plasma's skull, as he laid on the ground. Ben was terrified in horror by the blood and said, "NOOOOOOOOOOOOOOOOOOOOOOO!!!" Ben wiped the tears from his eyes, as he watched Commander Plasma die in front of him. Justin got up from the ground, and wiped the blood off of his vibroblade, with a piece of cloth, that was laying on the ground. Ben walked up to Justin and said, "You're a monster for killing Commander Plasma! My troopers and I will deal with you, human scum." Ben growled and pressed a button on his wrist. Ben's troopers surrounded Justin. Justin got out his vibroblade, and sped toward Ben's troopers. Justin slashed through the troopers with his vibroblade. The troopers laid on the ground in puddles of blood. More troopers entered the room, as they answered Ben's call for reinforcements. The troopers shot their weapons at Justin. Justin deflected the blaster bolts back at the troopers. The troopers laid on the ground. A group of troopers with blasters and a missile launcher walked in to the room. The troopers bent down, and put the missile launcher on the ground. The trooper set up a missile, and aimed it at Justin. The trooper launched the missile at Justin. The missile smashed Justin in to the wall. Justin laid on the ground, and attached the vibroblade to his belt. The group of troopers took out their blasters and shot Justin with blaster bolts. Justin got hit by the blaster bolts, as blood dripped from his body. Justin screamed in pain, as the troopers shot him with their blasters. Ben smiled and said, "Feel the pain, that my dad felt when you crushed his soul with your vibroblade. Ben walked up to Justin, and grabbed his neck. Ben picked up Justin, and smashed him in to the wall. Ben said, "This is a small taste of my strength and power, human scum. You have been a thorn in our side, since you escaped from The Crimson Wing. " Ben throws Justin on to the ground. Blood dripped on the ground from Justin's body. Ben stepped on Justin's arm. Justin screamed in pain! Ben said, "Let the pain flow through your body, and feel the wrath of the Flame Order." Ben stepped on Justin's chest, and punched him in the face, multiple times. Blood dripped from Justin's body on to the ground. Justin laid on the ground, with blood dripping from his body. Ben gave the signal to the troopers. The group of troopers walked up to Justin, and electrocuted him with their electric batons. The pain flowed through Justin's body, as he got electrocuted. Justin closed his eyes, as he got electrocuted. The troopers picked up Justin, and carried him on their back. Ben and the troopers threw Justin in to a laser cage on the prisoner level of the space station. Justin laid on the floor of the laser cage. Ben walked in to the laser cage, and stabbed a healing pack in to Justin's arm. The healing pack went in to Justin's body, and healed him. Ben wiped the blood off of Justin's body with the towel, that was hanging in the laser cage. Ben walked out of the laser cage, and defended the prisoner level with his troopers. Ben contacted the supreme leader on his wrist. Ben said, "Justin, the scavenger, has been captured, and the Flame Order is under our control!" Supreme Leader Stardust said, "Good job, the next phase of our plan can go in to motion." Ben said, "The galaxy will feel the wrath of the Flame Order." Supreme Leader Stardust said, "The galaxy will be under our control, and the scum will fear us, as we send chills in to their bodies." Ben smiled as he ended the transmission on his wrist. Ben's trooper's saluted Ben, as he patrolled the prison level. Ben said, "The Flame Order will make Commander Plasma proud of what we accomplished in the galaxy." Ben walked to the space station window. Ben looked outside the space station window and smiled, as he looked at the galaxy filled with stars and planets.

2

In a galaxy far far away, Ben and his troopers patrolled the space station! Justin laid in his cell, with his arms chained to the wall. Justin used his leg, and whacked the chain cutter closer to him. Justin lifted the chain cutter in to the air, with his leg, and kicked it in to the air. Justin caught the chain cutter in his mouth, and used it to cut the chains, that were on his arms. The chains were cut, and Justin got his arms unchained. Justin got up , and walked to the door panel. Justin stabbed his vibroblade in to the door panel. The door opened, and Justin walked out of it. The Flame Order Troopers were patrolling the area. Justin sneaked through the hallway, and avoided the troopers. Justin noticed the security camera on the walls, and took his blaster out. Justin shot the security camera with his blaster. The security cameras exploded, as Justin ran through the hallway. The troopers noticed the commotion from the hallway, and spotted Justin. The troopers took out their blasters, and shot them at Justin. Justin dodged the blaster bolts, and shot the troopers with his blaster. The troopers laid on the ground in puddles of blood. Justin walked to the security room. Justin noticed that the door panel was red, and the door was locked with a security key. Justin shot the door panel with his blaster. The door panel exploded, and the door opened. Justin walked in to the security room. The security room had a bookshelf, that was filled with books, and a computer that controlled every security camera on the space station. Justin walked to the computer, and logged in to it. Justin tapped on the computer, and made every security camera malfunction in the hallway. The security cameras in the hallway malfunctioned, and exploded. The explosion killed every Flame Order Trooper on the space station. Ben saw every Flame Order Trooper laying on the ground, and growled. Ben smashed his control panel with his vibroblade. Justin watched Ben's rage on the computer. Justin logged out of the computer, and walked out of the security room. Justin walked through the hallway. Ben walked off the space station's bridge, and looked for Justin. Ben patrolled the area, and tore the security cameras off of the wall, with his powers. Justin ran through the hallway, and took out his blaster. The blaster bolts bounced off of the wall. Ben saw the blaster bolts, and deflected them with his vibroblade. The blaster bolts deflected back to Justin. Justin backflipped out of the way, and landed on the ground. Ben saw Justin and walked toward him. Ben used his powers to pull Justin toward him. Justin was struggling in Ben's grip. Ben said, "You are like a slippery little mouse, that wants to ruin the Flame order's plans for the galaxy." Justin struggled as he said, "I am slippery, and it is fun to make you rage." Ben growled, as he threw Justin in to the wall. Justin got up from the ground! Ben took out his vibroblade, and ran toward Justin. Justin backflipped, and kicked Ben in the face. Ben slid backwards, and growled. Justin landed on the ground, and took out his vibroblade. Justin swung his vibroblade at Ben. Ben dodged, and clashed his vibroblade with Justin's vibroblade. Ben backflipped, and kicked Justin in the chest. Justin slid backwards in to the wall. Ben sped in to Justin, and smashed him in to the wall. Ben swung his vibroblade through Justin's hair, and cut several pieces off of his head. Justin's hair landed on the ground, as Justin growled. Justin grabbed his blaster from his belt, and shot Ben in the chest. Ben slid backwards, as blood dripped on the ground. Ben stabbed a healing pack in to his arm. Justin sped in to Ben, and tackled him in to the ground. Justin punched Ben in the face, multiple times. Ben growled, and used his powers to electrocute Justin. Justin got electrocuted, and smashed in to the wall. Ben got up from the ground, and walked toward Justin. Justin laid next to the wall, and rubbed his head. Justin grabbed his blaster from his belt, and shot it at Ben. Ben deflected the blaster bolts from his vibroblade. The blaster bolts were deflected in to the wall. Ben sped in to Justin, and kicked him in the chest. Justin growled, and swung his vibroblade at Ben's face. The vibroblade scratched Ben's face! Ben growled, and electrocuted Justin. Justin screamed in pain, as he laid on the ground. Ben continued electrocuting Justin. Justin tried to deflect the electric energy with his vibroblade to prevent the pain from his body. Ben ignited an electric blast from his body, that covered the area with electric energy. Justin smashed through the wall, and laid on the ground, with his body being paralyzed. Justin couldn't move off of the ground. Ben laughed, as he walked toward his prey. Ben stepped on Justin's chest! Ben said, "Don't bother fighting back, you are outmatched by the strength and power of The Flame Order!" Ben grabbed Justin's neck, and picked him up! Ben smashed Justin against the wall! Justin growled, as the pain flowed through his body. Ben walked toward the command panel, and strapped Justin to one of the chairs with his powers. Ben said, "Watch the power of The Flame order in motion!" The rebel space fighter ships went out of hyperspace, and flew toward the space station. The Flame Order space fighter ships surrounded the rebel space fighter ships. The Flame order space fighter ships shot their weapons at the rebel space fighter ships. The rebel space fighter ships exploded! The rebel space fighter ships sent reinforcements. The rebel commander ship went out of hyperspace, and started firing at The Flame Order space fighter ships. The Flame Order space fighter ships exploded, and the rebel commander ship started firing at the space station. Ben pressed some buttons on the control panel, and the space station's laser charged up. Ben pressed the button on the control panel, and the space station laser fired at the rebel commander ship. The rebel commander ship exploded, as Ben smiled at the destruction. Justin was terrified in fear! Ben said, "This is why, you don't mess with The Flame Order!" The Flame Order flight ship flew out of hyperspace, and landed on the space station. Ben said, "The supreme leader is here to congratulate me on my performance." Supreme Leader Stardust walked on to the bridge of the space station.

Supreme Leader Stardust walked toward Ben. Ben bowed to Supreme Leader Stardust! Justin grabbed his blaster from his belt, and aimed it at Supreme Leader Stardust. Justin shot Supreme Leader Stardust with his blaster. Supreme Leader Stardust growled and said, "You tried to kill me!" Supreme Leader Stardust electrocuted Justin and Ben with his electric powers. Justin got electrocuted, and Ben deflected the electricity with his vibroblade. Supreme Leader Stardust deflected the electricity with his vibroblade. Ben and Supreme Leader Stardust growled at each other, as they shot their electric powers at each other. Ben threw a electric ball at Supreme Leader Stardust. The electric ball hit Supreme Leader Stardust in the chest. Supreme Leader Stardust slid backwards, and shot another strand of electricity at Ben. Ben deflected the electricity in to the wall strap. The electric powers broke the strap, that was holding Justin to the wall. Justin landed on the ground, and walked behind Supreme Leader Stardust. Supreme Leader Stardust was distracted by Ben, and didn't see Justin behind him. Justin took out his vibroblade, and stabbed Supreme Leader Stardust in the back. Blood poured on to the ground, as Supreme Leader Stardust screamed in pain. Justin took his vibroblade out of Supreme Leader Stardust's back. Supreme Leader Stardust laid on the ground in a puddle of blood. Supreme Leader Stardust's troopers walked in to the room, and pointed their weapons at Justin and Ben. The troopers started firing at Justin and Ben. Ben and Justin deflected the blaster bolts at the troopers. More troopers marched in to the room, and fired their weapons! Justin backflipped behind a trooper, and stabbed his vibroblade in to the trooper's head. Justin pulled the vibroblade out, and the trooper laid on the ground, as blood poured out of his head. Justin wiped the blood off of his vibroblade with a towel, while Ben electrocuted the troopers with his powers. Reinforcements marched in to the room! Ben created a electric ball with his powers, and threw it at the reinforcements! The reinforcement troopers exploded in the blast of electricity. The reinforcement leader, Sir Phantom, walked in to the room, and shot a electric blast at Ben. Ben backflipped over the blast, and stabbed his vibroblade in to Sir Phantom's arm. Sir Phantom smiled, as he lifted Ben in to the air with his other arm. Sir Phantom threw Ben in to the wall. Ben laid against the wall, as Sir Phantom took Ben's vibroblade out of his arm, and threw it on the ground. Justin growled, and sped toward Sir Phantom. Sir Phantom grabbed Justin's arm, and kicked him in the chest. Justin stood in place, and took out his blaster. Justin shot Sir Phantom in the chest. Sir Phantom slid backwards! Justin ran toward Sir Phantom, and stabbed him in the chest with his vibroblade. Blood dripped on the ground. Justin pulled his vibroblade out of Sir Phantom's chest. Ben used his powers to pull his vibroblade in to his hand. Ben got up from the ground. Ben sped toward Sir Phantom, and backflipped over Justin. Ben jumped in to the air, and stabbed Sir Phantom in the head with his vibroblade. Ben pulled his vibroblade out of Sir Phantom's head. Blood poured on the ground. Sir Phantom laughed, as he punched Ben in the chest. Ben smashed in to the wall. Sir Phantom said, "You think that you can defeat me, I am the most powerful trooper in the galaxy." Sir Phantom threw a electric ball at Justin and Ben. Justin blocked the electric ball with his vibroblade, as he slid backwards. The electric ball hit Ben in the chest. Ben smashed through the wall, and laid against it. Blood poured on the ground from Ben's face. Ben got up from the ground, while gripping the vibroblade in his hand. Sir Phantom said, " For being the commander of The Flame Order, you're not putting up much of a fight, you are just as weak as Commander Plasma." Sir Phantom shot his electric powers at Justin and Ben!" Justin and Ben deflected the electricity with their vibroblades. Ben growled and said, "I am not weak, My leadership fuels The Flame Order!!" Sir Phantom said, "Prove it! Prove to me and the rest of The Flame Order that you're not a weakling, that can be easily tossed around like a rag doll." Justin backflipped, and shot Sir Phantom in the head with his blaster. Sir Phantom slid backwards! Ben and Sir Phantom shot their electric powers at each other. Ben and Sir Phantom growled, as their electric powers surged as they expanded in power. The electricity covered the area, as Justin watched in shock. Justin used his electric powers to make the electric surge stronger. Ben and Sir Phantom slid to the wall, as their powers collided. The electric surge exploded, and electricity covered the area. Justin defended himself with the electric shield, that was on his belt. Sir Phantom and Ben laid on the ground, while gripping their vibroblades. Blood was pouring out of their bodies, as they slowly got up from the ground. Sir Phantom coughed, as he walked toward Ben. Sir Phantom shot lightning at Ben. Ben used his vibroblade to deflect the lightning back at Sir Phantom. The lightning hit Sir Phantom in the chest! Sir Phantom smashed through the wall, and laid on the ground. Blood poured out of Sir Phantom's body. Ben walked toward Sir Phantom, and stabbed him in the chest with his vibroblade. Sir Phantom's body laid on the ground, in the puddle of blood as he died. Ben laid against the wall, and sighed in a breath of relief, as he cleaned his vibroblade with a towel. Ben stabbed a health pack in to his arm, as he wiped the blood off of his body. Justin got up from the ground. Justin walked toward Ben. Ben shook Justin's hand. Ben said, "As a thank you for helping me defeat Sir Phantom, you are now a member of The Flame Order! As a combination of our strength, lets show the galaxy that The Flame Order is strong, and can take down anything in our path." Justin salutes Ben! Ben gives Justin his new Flame Order uniform! Justin puts on his Flame Order uniform, and stood next to Ben. Ben pressed the buttons on the control panel, and sent the space station in to hyperspace. The rest of The Flame Order ships went in to hyperspace, and followed the space station. The space station and The Flame Order troopers went out of hyperspace, and stopped at a planet, named Oceanvile. Oceanvile was filled with lush green grass and blue skies. The planet had various species of aliens and humans living peacefully. The Flame Order command ship opened fire on the planet. The aliens and humans were screaming in pain, as they got murdered by the Flame Order ships. Their bodies laid in puddles of blood. The smaller attack ships for The Flame Order flew down to the planet's surface, and opened fire on the planet's surface and the rest of the citizens, that lived on the planet. The blaster bolts from the ships tore everything on the planet's surface to shreds, and murdered all of the citizens, that were terrified in horror from the chaos. The bodies of the citizens laid in puddles of blood. Everything on the planet was destroyed, and burning to a crisp. The trees were lifeless, and didn't have any branches or leaves on them. The Flame Order space station activated its laser, and the planet exploded in to millions of pieces. The Flame Order ships flew back in to space, and landed on the space station. Ben and Justin smiled, as they watched the chaos outside the space station's window. The Flame Order troopers stood in place behind them, and saluted Ben and Justin. Ben said, "The galaxy has felt the wrath of The Flame Order!" Justin said, "The Flame Order will destroy everything in its path." The troopers marched in place, as Justin bowed. Ben put his vibroblade on Justin's shoulder, and knighted him as a commander. Justin stood up, as Ben lifted his vibroblade in the air. Justin held out his hand. Ben gave Justin a red crystal for his vibroblade. The red crystal laid in Justin's hand. Justin took his vibroblade off of his belt, and put the red crystal in to the compartment. The vibroblade set off a red glow, as Justin closed the compartment. Justin put the vibroblade on his belt. The troopers saluted Justin, as he took his vibroblade off of his belt, and lifted it in to the air.

Section Break 2

Crimson Fox:
1. Crimson Fox: Jungle Warrior
2. Crimson Fox: Mouse Hunter
3. Crimson Fox: Wolf Hunter
4. Crimson Fox: Raccoon Hunter
5. Crimson Fox: Chipmunk Hunter
6. Crimson Fox: Squirrel Hunter
7. Crimson Fox: Jackal Hunter

3

In the jungle wilderness of Sunshine Paradise, there lived an family of foxes! Crimson was the son, and he had two parents, that were named Emily and Sam. The foxes were living an wonderful life, until they heard some rustling in the bush. Emily and Sam went to the bush to check it out. An group of raccoons ambushed them! Karson, the raccoon leader grabbed Emily by the neck, as she struggled in his grip. Sam jumped in to action, and bit Karson's tail. Karson screamed in pain, and swats Sam away with his paw. Sam smashed in to an tree! Karson sharpens his claws, and whacked Emily on the head, knocking her out. The raccoon bandits tied up Sam and Emily, and threw them in to Karson's bag. Karson picks up the bag, and carried them to his hideout, with the raccoon bandits following behind him. Crimson was terrified, as he hides in his house, covering himself with his paws and tail. Crimson fell asleep, and used his tail as a pillow. The sun rose on an brand new day in the jungle. Crimson yawned and rubbed his eyes. Crimson got up, and stretched his paws. Crimson walked to the berry bush, and ate some berries for breakfast. He walked to his favorite rock, and did some pushups on the ground. He swung on the vines, and flipped in the air. Crimson walked through the jungle, and the wind blew through his fur. While walking through the jungle, he was admiring the plants and bugs, because they were amazing to look at. There was rustling in the bush! Crimson growled as he walked towards the bush, with his claws sharpened. Crimson walked to the bush, and there was an terrified raccoon named Paul. Paul said while trembling, "Don't hurt me, my fur is chewy!" Crimson put his paw on Paul's chest, as he continued growling! Crimson said, "Where did your leader take my parents!" Paul said, "He took them to the crocodile's lair." Crimson said, "Thanks for the tip!" He stabs his claws through the raccoon's chest, splattering blood everywhere, as Paul's dead body laid on the ground. Crimson continued walking through the jungle. The jungle was nice and calm, with the birds singing and the leaves moving in the wind. Crimson stopped at the pond, and drank some water to rehydrate his body. Crimson continued walking through the jungle! The air started to get mucky, and the trees started to change! Crimson knew that he was getting closer to the crocodile's lair, where his parents were held captive. Crimson swung on an vine to get himself over an fallen log. Crimson flipped in the air, and landed on his paws. Crimson walked through the jungle, admiring the different bugs and plants. Crimson saw an mucky pond, filled with muddy water and crocodiles, while he was walking through the jungle! He walked closer to the pond to check out the crocodile's foot prints. The foot prints were going in an certain direction! Crimson followed the footprints! An crocodile jumped out of the water and pounced on Crimson. Crimson growled, and swatted the crocodile in the face. Crimson sharpened his claws, and grabbed the crocodile by the neck. Crimson stabs his paw through the crocodile's chest, and the crocodile laid on the ground. Crimson brushed the dirt off of his fur with his paw, as he continued following the footprints. Crimson noticed that he was getting close to an huge castle, guarded by crocodiles. He slowly walked to it, thinking that this must be the place where his parents have been kidnapped. An barricade of crocodiles swarmed Crimson, as he got closer to the castle. Crimson growled, as the crocodiles got closer to him. One of the crocodiles swung its tail at Crimson. Crimson dodged, and grabbed the crocodile's tail. Crimson swung the crocodile around the area, hitting his other crocodile buddies in to the pond. Crimson threw the crocodile in to the air, and stabbed his claws through its chest. The crocodile laid on the ground, in an puddle of blood. Crimson was determined to rescue his parents, as he walked closer to the castle. Crimson walked in to the castle, and he got swarmed by crocodiles. The crocodile leader, Matt, walked toward Crimson and said, "Who trespasses in our castle without permission?" Crimson growled and said, "I am here to rescue my parents! The raccoon bandits took them here, and I followed their paw prints to your castle." Matt said, "If you want your parents back, you have to go through us." The crocodile leader raised his flag, and sent his crocodile troopers after Crimson. The crocodiles swarmed Crimson! Crimson growled, and grabbed an crocodile's tail, swinging him around, and knocking the other troopers down. Crimson pounced on each crocodile with his claws sharpened, as he sped towards Matt. Crimson tackled Matt in to the ground. Crimson stabbed his claws through Matt's neck, as blood splatters out of his body. Crimson growled and said, "Give me my parents back, you monster!" Crimson picks up Matt with his paw, and stabs his claws through Matt's chest. Blood splattered, as Crimson dropped Matt on the ground. Matt's body laid on the ground, as Crimson walked further in to the castle. Crimson walked in to the castle's kitchen! Karson, the raccoon leader, was dropping Crimson's parents in to the shark tank! Karson stopped, when he saw Crimson walk in. Crimson growled and said, "Drop my parents, I am here to rescue them." Karson said, "Perfect timing, little fox, you can join my meal, when I am done with you!" Karson dropped Sam and Emily on the ground! Karson tackled Crimson in to the ground! Karson tried to scratch Crimson's face, but Crimson swats him away with his paw. Crimson sharpens his claws and scratches Karson's neck. Karson screams in pain, as he slides backwards. Crimson kicks Karson in the chest. Karson slides backwards in to the shark tank. Crimson sped towards Karson and grabbed him by the neck. Crimson smashed Karson in to the ground. Crimson sharpened his claws, and stabbed them through Karson's neck. Blood splattered on to the ground. Crimson picked up Karson with his paw, and stabbed his claws through Karson's chest! Karson's body laid on the ground. Crimson walked toward Sam and Emily, and untied them. Crimson said, "Mom and Dad, you are safe!" Crimson hugged Sam and Emily! Sam and Emily hugged Crimson back! Sam and Emily said, "You are an brave fox, I am glad that you rescued us." Crimson walks out of the crocodile's castle with Sam and Emily, as the sun sets.

6

4

In Sunshine Paradise, the sun was shining and the birds were chirping. Crimson was sitting on an log, enjoying the breeze flowing through his fur. An butterfly landed on Crimson's head, while he was eating his popsicle. The bush behind Crimson started moving and shaking! Crimson finished his popsicle, and he jumped off the log. Crimson growled, as he moved closer to the bush. The bush continued moving and shaking. Crimson continued growling, as he got to the bush. An little mouse crawled out of the bush, and scurried towards Crimson's paw. The mouse was terrified in fear, while Crimson was growling at it. Crimson whacked the mouse with his paw! The mouse squeaked, as Crimson grabbed it by the tail. Crimson lifted the mouse in the air, and started whacking it with his paw. Crimson played with the mouse by throwing in the air, and catching it with his paws. Crimson spun the mouse, by whacking it with his tail. The mouse spun in an circle, as Crimson smiled. The mouse stopped spinning and regained its balance. Crimson sharpened his claws and whacked the mouse with his paw. The mouse spun super fast in an circle, while Crimson smiled. Crimson threw the mouse in the air, and caught it with his paws. Crimson picked up the mouse and tied him on to the log with its tail. Crimson took two branches and rubbed them together. An spark lit up on the branches and they caught on fire. Crimson picked up an set of logs, and put them on the branches to create a fire. Crimson untied the mouse from the log, and picked him by the tail. Crimson lowered the mouse in to the fire, and started barbecuing it. Smoke rose from the flames, as the fur on the mouse was cooking. Blood squirted on to the ground, as the mouse got barbecued. Crimson licked his lips, as the fire made the mouse smell so good. Crimson knew the mouse would be nice and tasty to eat as a snack. The fire finished cooking the mouse! Crimson lifted the mouse out of the fire by its barbecued tail. Crimson opened up his mouth, and ate the mouse in one big gulp. Crimson licked his lips, since the mouse was nice and crunchy. It was an good snack for a healthy fox like Crimson. The snack gave Crimson a nice energy boost. Another mouse scurried over to Crimson's paw. Crimson growled at the mouse! The mouse was terrified in fear! Crimson picked up the mouse by its tail, and whacked it with his paw. The mouse struggled, while Crimson was playing with it. An shadow appeared over the area! It was the ruler of the mouse kingdom, King Squeaky! King Squeaky picked Crimson up by his tail. The mouse crawled on to King Squeaky's shoulder. Crimson struggled in King Squeaky's grip, while King Squeaky was whacking him with his paw. King Squeaky whacked Crimson's chest with his paw. Crimson spun in an circle, while in King Squeaky's grip. Crimson growled, and slashed King Squeaky's chest with his claws. King Squeaky lost his grip on Crimson. Crimson flipped in the air, and on to the ground. King Squeaky kicked Crimson in the chest with his foot. Crimson rolled in to an tree! King Squeaky laughed, as he picked up the little mouse. King Squeaky put the little mouse on his shoulder, and walked closer to Crimson. Crimson stepped backwards, as King Squeaky got closer to him. Crimson threw an branch at King Squeaky! King Squeaky broke the branch in half, by whacking it with his paw. Crimson growled, as he sharpened his claws! The army of mice crawled toward Crimson! Crimson jumped on an vine and swung toward King Squeaky. Crimson jumped off the vine, and flipped in the air. Crimson jumped on to King Squeaky's head, with his claws out. Crimson's claws sank in to King Squeaky's head, as blood gushed out everywhere! King Squeaky screamed in pain, while Crimson flicked mice off of King Squeaky's shoulder with his tail. The mice crawled on to Crimson's fur! Crimson was whacking mice off of him with his claws. Crimson pounced on the mice with his claws out! Blood splashed everywhere, as mice laid on the ground. King Squeaky fell on the ground, and Crimson jumped on to an tree! Crimson climbed up the tree to pinpoint the perfect area to attack King Squeaky. Crimson smiled, when he saw the perfect area to strike on King Squeaky's body! Crimson jumped out of the tree and on to an vine. Crimson swung on the vines, until he saw King Squeaky's body. Crimson jumped off the vines, and flipped in the air. Crimson landed on King Squeaky's body, and sharpened his claws. Crimson growled as he sank his claws in to King Squeaky's neck. Crimson picked up King Squeaky! King Squeaky struggled in his grip, as blood leaked from his body. Crimson smiled, as he stabbed his claws in to King Squeaky's chest! Blood gushed out of King Squeaky's body! The mice screamed in horror! Crimson threw King Squeaky's body on to the ground! Crimson jumped on to an vine, and swung himself in to the lake. Crimson washed the blood off of his fur and paws. Crimson cleaned his fur with his paws! Crimson swam back to the shore, and shook the water out of his fur. Crimson walked to the tree, while he was sharpening his claws. Crimson was having fun, whacking the mice around. One of the mice jumped in the air toward Crimson! Crimson flipped in the air, and stabbed the mouse in the chest with his claw. Blood landed in a puddle, as the mouse's body fell on to the ground. Crimson smiled, as the mouse's body laid on the ground. One of the mice scurried toward Crimson! Crimson grabbed the mouse with his paw, and whacked it around. The mouse squeaked and said, "Please don't hurt us, mice don't taste very good!" Crimson smiled as he sharpened his claws! Crimson stabbed the mouse in the chest with his claw. Blood poured out of the mouse! Crimson threw the mouse's dead body on to the ground in front of the other mice. Crimson walked in to the lake, and washed the blood off of his fur and paws. Crimson walked out of the lake and shook the water out of his fur. Crimson walked toward King Squeaky's body, and noticed the group of mice around it! The group of mice were sad, that their leader was dead! Crimson watched the mice, as they cried their tears on King Squeaky's body! King

Squeaky's body laid in the puddle of blood, while the mice mourned over him! It was depressing to see the mice crying over their leader, but Crimson didn't feel the depression in the air at all. Crimson felt the mice didn't need a happy ending, because they ruined his relaxation. Crimson wanted to end the despair for the mice. Crimson growled at the mice, while his tail was swaying back and forth. Crimson sharpened his claws and jumped on to the group of mice! Crimson whacked the mice with his paws, as blood flew everywhere and bodies of mice laid on the ground in a circle! Crimson smiled as he walked toward his log. Crimson sat on the log and listened to the tweeting birds. Butterflies were flying over the lake, while the water was shining. It was an wonderful sight for Crimson to watch. Sam and Emily sat on the log with Crimson! Sam and Emily hugged Crimson, while the birds tweeted in the background! The sun was setting, as the wind blew through Crimson's fur. The water in the lake was shining with the moon reflecting on it. The birds flew over the lake. Emily kissed Crimson on the head and said, "I love you, Crimson! I am glad that you are my son." Crimson said, "I love you too, Emily!" Crimson kissed Emily on her head and hugged her with his paws. Emily and Crimson smiled at each other. Sam moved closer to Crimson and Emily, and hugged them with his paws. The family of foxes smiled at the moon, while the wind blew through their fur.

7

5

In Sunshine Paradise, the sun was shining and the birds were chirping. Crimson was exercising and doing push ups, while the breeze was flowing through his fur. An butterfly landed on Crimson's head, while he was doing an roundhouse kick on the tree. The bush behind Crimson started moving and shaking! Crimson walked towards the bush, with his tail swaying back and forth. Crimson growled, as he moved closer to the bush. The bush continued moving and shaking. Crimson continued growling, as he got to the bush. An wolf crawled out of the bush, and walked towards Crimson's paw. The wolf was growling at Crimson, while Crimson was growling at it. Crimson whacked the wolf with his paw! The wolf pounced Crimson, and sharpened its claws. The wolf stabbed its claws in to Crimson's fur! Crimson growled and whacked the wolf on the head. Crimson sharpened his claws, and stabbed his claws in to the wolf's neck. Crimson lifted the wolf in the air, and started whacking it with his paw. Crimson played with the wolf by throwing in the air, and catching it with his paws. Crimson spun the wolf, by whacking it with his tail. The wolf spun in an circle, as Crimson smiled. The wolf stopped spinning and regained its balance. Crimson sharpened his claws and whacked the wolf with his paw. The wolf spun super fast in an circle, while Crimson smiled. Crimson threw the wolf in the air, and caught it with his paws. Crimson bit in to the wolf's tail! The wolf howled in pain, as Crimson's fangs sunk in to the wolf's fur. Crimson was spitting the fur out of his mouth, as he thought to himself. Crimson said, "The wolf tasted a bit plain, let's add some flavor to make it nice and yummy to eat." Crimson licked his lips to get the leftover wolf fur out of his mouth. Crimson picked up the wolf and tied him on to the log with its tail. Crimson took two branches and rubbed them together. An spark lit up on the branches and they caught on fire. Crimson picked up an set of logs, and put them on the branches to create a fire. Crimson untied the wolf from the log, and picked him by the tail. Crimson lowered the wolf in to the fire, and started barbecuing it. Smoke rose from the flames, as the fur on the wolf was cooking. Blood squirted on to the ground, as the wolf got barbecued. Crimson licked his lips, as the fire made the wolf smell so good. Crimson knew the wolf would be nice and tasty to eat as a snack. The fire finished cooking the wolf! Crimson lifted the wolf out of the fire by its barbecued tail. Crimson opened up his mouth, and ate the wolf in one big gulp. Crimson licked his lips, since the wolf was nice and crunchy. It was an good snack for a healthy fox like Crimson. The snack gave Crimson a nice energy boost. An pack of wolves pounced on Crimson and sank their fangs in to Crimson's fur. Crimson screamed in pain, as he rolled on the ground. The wolves jumped on to Crimson's tail, and bit it. Crimson spun in a circle and flung the wolves off of his body. Crimson growled at the wolves, and sharpened his claws. Crimson pounced on the wolves, and killed them with his claws. Blood gushed everywhere, as the wolves laid on the ground. Crimson smiled, as he walked through the jungle. An wolf pounced on Crimson through the bushes! Crimson's tail was swaying back and forth, as he jumped through the air with his claws out. Crimson sunk his claws in to the wolf's chest, as he back flipped and knocked the wolf in to the air. The wolf fell on the ground in an puddle of blood. Crimson landed on the ground! An shadow appeared over the area! It was the ruler of the wolf kingdom, King Wolf! King Wolf picked Crimson up by his tail. An wolf ran out of the bushes, and crawled on to King Wolf's shoulder. Crimson struggled in King Wolf's grip, while King Wolf was whacking him with his paw. King Wolf whacked Crimson's chest with his paw. Crimson spun in an circle, while in King Wolf's grip. Crimson growled, and slashed King Wolf's chest with his claws.

King Wolf lost his grip on Crimson. Crimson flipped in the air, and on to the ground. King Wolf kicked Crimson in the chest with his foot. Crimson rolled in to an tree! King Wolf laughed, as he walked closer to Crimson. Crimson stepped backwards, as King Wolf got closer to him. Crimson threw an branch at King Wolf! King Wolf broke the branch in half, by whacking it with his paw. King Wolf pounced on Crimson, and sharpened his claws. King Wolf stabbed his claws in to Crimson's fur. Crimson screamed in pain, as blood leaked out of his fur. King Wolf kicks Crimson in the chest. Crimson rolled in to a tree, as King Wolf walked closer to him. King Wolf tackled Crimson through the tree. Crimson bit King Wolf's paw with his fangs. King Wolf howled in pain, as he slid backwards. Crimson kicked King Wolf in the chest! King Wolf slid in to a tree. Crimson sharpened his claws, and pounced on King Wolf. King Wolf rolled on to the ground! Crimson scratched King Wolf's chest with his claws. Blood leaked out on the ground! Crimson punched King Wolf in the face! King Wolf grabbed Crimson's paw, and kicked him in the face. Crimson slid backwards! King Wolf got up from the ground. Crimson growled at King Wolf, with his tail swaying back and forth. Crimson sharpened his claws! Crimson pounced on King Wolf and bit his tail. King Wolf howled in pain. Crimson stabbed his claws in to King Wolf's chest. Blood squirted on to the ground. Crimson climbed up the tree! King Wolf grabbed Crimson's tail, and pulled him in to the ground. Crimson fell on the ground, while King Wolf sharpened his claws. King Wolf scratched Crimson's fur with his claws. King Wolf hit Crimson in the face with his tail. Crimson bit King Wolf's tail with his fangs. King Wolf howled in pain. Crimson pulled King Wolf's tail! King Wolf growled, as he punched Crimson in the face with his paws. Crimson grabbed King Wolf's paws, and roundhouse kicked King Wolf in the face. King Wolf slid backwards, and Crimson back flipped in the air. Crimson ran toward the tree, and climbed it. Crimson grabbed on to an vine and swung toward King Wolf. Crimson jumped off the vine, and flipped in the air. Crimson jumped on to King Wolf's head, with his claws out. Crimson's claws sank in to King Wolf's head, as blood gushed out everywhere! King Wolf howled in pain, and grabbed Crimson by the neck. Crimson struggled in King Wolf's grip! King Wolf sharpened his claws, and scratched Crimson's chest. Blood leaked out of Crimson's fur. Crimson growled, and sharpened his claws. Crimson swung himself at King Wolf's neck, and stabbed his claws in to it. Crimson hit King Wolf with his tail. Crimson kicked King Wolf in the chest with his paw. Crimson tackled King Wolf in to a tree, and stabbed his claws in to King Wolf's chest. King Wolf howled in pain! Blood poured out of King Wolf's body on to the ground. Crimson pounced King Wolf and knocked him in to the ground. Crimson flipped in the air, and stabbed his claws in to King Wolf's chest. Blood poured out of King Wolf's body, while the other wolves crowded around Crimson. Crimson whacked wolves out of his path with his paws. The wolves pounced on to Crimson! Crimson growled, while he was whacking wolves off of him with his paws. Crimson pounced on the wolves with his claws out! Blood splashed everywhere, as the wolves laid on the ground. Crimson ran towards the tree, and jumped on to it! King Wolf was climbing up the tree to catch Crimson. Crimson kicked King Wolf off of the tree with his paw. King Wolf jumped up the tree and scratched Crimson's paw with his claws. Crimson screamed in pain, and hung on the tree with one paw. Crimson was swaying back and forth in the tree. He was hanging on with one paw on the branch. King Wolf jumped at Crimson and tackled him out of the tree. King Wolf held Crimson on to the ground by stepping on his paws. King Wolf sharpened his claws, and scratched Crimson in the chest. Crimson growled and kicked King Wolf in the chest. King Wolf slid backwards, and sunk his claws in to Crimson's chest. Blood leaked out of Crimson's fur! Crimson roundhouse kicked King Wolf in the face. King Wolf slid backwards! Crimson got up from the ground! King Wolf grabbed Crimson's tail, and pulled him in to the ground. King Wolf stepped on Crimson's back, and sunk his claws in to Crimson's neck. Blood poured on to the ground, as Crimson screamed in pain. King Wolf sunk his claws further in to Crimson's neck and picked him up from the ground. King Wolf kicked

Crimson in the chest! Blood poured out of his fur on to the ground! Crimson struggled in King Wolf's grip. King Wolf kicked Crimson in the chest. Crimson growled, as he was swinging back and forth, while in King Wolf's grip. King Wolf smashed Crimson in to a tree. Crimson fell on the ground. King Wolf held Crimson on the ground, by stepping on his paws. King Wolf growled, while his tail was swaying back and forth. King Wolf sharpened his claws, and scratched at Crimson's chest. Crimson grabbed King Wolf's paw, and roundhouse kicked King Wolf in the face. Crimson took out his claws, and punched King Wolf in the face. Blood leaked out of King Wolf's fur. Crimson tackled king Wolf in to the tree, and smashed the tree in half. Crimson tore the tree out of the ground, and hit King Wolf in the chest with it. King Wolf rolled on to the ground. Crimson stepped on King Wolf's tail, and scratched King Wolf's chest with his claws. King Wolf kicked Crimson in the face with his paw. Crimson slid backwards! Crimson ran towards the tree. King Wolf ran after Crimson towards the tree. Crimson jumped on to the tree and started climbing it. King Wolf climbed up the tree to chase Crimson. Crimson climbed up to the tree branch. King Wolf grabbed Crimson's tail with his paw, and bit it. Crimson screamed in pain, as his paw lost his grip on the branch. King Wolf sunk his claws in to Crimson's tail, as he climbed up Crimson's back on to the tree branch. King Wolf climbed up to the tree branch. Crimson growled as he climbed further in to the tree. Crimson sunk his claws in to King Wolf's tail, to keep his balance on the tree. Crimson climbed up to the top of the tree. King Wolf climbed to the top of the tree, and pounced Crimson out of the tree! Crimson fell out of the tree! King Wolf jumped on to Crimson's chest, and took out his claws. Crimson grabbed King Wolf by the neck with his claws. Crimson sunk his claws in to King Wolf's neck! Blood squirted everywhere! Crimson kicked King Wolf in the chest, and flipped in the air. King Wolf smashed in to the ground. Crimson landed on the ground and smiled! King Wolf slowly got up and growled at Crimson. Crimson growled back, with his tail swaying back and forth. Crimson sharpened his claws, and was ready to strike at his enemy!

Crimson tackled King Wolf on to the ground. Crimson knelt over King Wolf's body! Crimson sharpened his claws. Crimson sank his claws in to King Wolf's neck. Crimson picked up King Wolf! King Wolf struggled in his grip, as blood leaked from his body. Crimson smiled, as he stabbed his claws in to King Wolf's chest! Blood gushed out of King Wolf's body! The wolves screamed in horror! Crimson threw King Wolf's body on to the ground! Crimson jumped on to an vine, and swung himself in to the lake. Crimson washed the blood off of his fur and paws. Crimson cleaned his fur with his paws! Crimson swam back to the shore, and shook the water out of his fur. Crimson walked to the tree, while he was sharpening his claws. Crimson growled with his tail swaying back and forth. Crimson pounced on the group of wolves. Crimson was having fun, whacking the wolves around. One of the wolves jumped in the air toward Crimson! Crimson flipped in the air, and stabbed the wolf in the chest with his claw. Blood landed in a puddle, as the wolf's body fell on to the ground. Crimson smiled, as the wolf's body laid on the ground. Crimson jumped in to the lake, and washed his fur. Crimson dunked his head in to the water, and washed his face. The water felt nice and cool on his fur. Crimson splashed water on his fur, and washed his paws. Crimson swam back to shore, and shook the water out of his fur. An pack of wolves were waiting in the bushes, with their tails swaying back and forth. Crimson walked towards the bush to investigate it! Crimson knelt near the bush, and put his paws toward the ground. One of the wolves whacked Crimson's paw, while Crimson smiled. Crimson grabbed the wolf out of the bush and dragged it out by the tail. The wolf was scared by Crimson's appearance! The wolf struggled in Crimson's grip, while Crimson was whacking it around. Crimson growled at the wolf and sharpened his claws. The wolf got scared, while Crimson was scratching the wolf's fur with his claws. The wolf growled and said, "Please don't hurt us, wolves don't taste very good!" Crimson smiled as he scratched the wolf's fur. Crimson stabbed the wolf in the chest with his claws. Blood poured out of the wolf! Crimson threw the wolf's dead body on to the ground in front of the other wolves. Crimson walked in to the lake, and washed the blood off of his fur and paws. Crimson walked out of the lake and shook the water out of his fur. Crimson walked toward King Wolf's body, and noticed the group of wolves around it! The group of wolves were sad, that their leader was dead! Crimson watched the wolves, as they cried their tears on King Wolf's body! King Wolf's body laid in the puddle of blood, while the wolves mourned over him! It was depressing to see the wolves crying over their leader, but Crimson didn't feel the depression in the air at all. Crimson felt the wolves didn't need a happy ending, because they ruined his relaxation. Crimson wanted to end the despair for the wolves. The wolves noticed that Crimson was watching them. The wolves gathered in their pack, with their tails swaying back and forth, and they growled at Crimson. Crimson growled at the wolves and sharpened his claws. Crimson's tail was swaying back and forth. Crimson jumped on to the group of wolves! Crimson whacked the wolves with his paws, as blood flew everywhere and bodies of wolves laid on the ground in a circle! An pack of wolves jumped out of the bushes and pounced on Crimson. Crimson rolled on to the ground, as the wolves bit in to Crimson's fur. Crimson growled at the wolves, and whacked them away with his paws. One of the wolves jumped on Crimson's tail, and bit it. Crimson screamed in pain! Crimson spun in a circle, and shook the wolf off of his tail. Crimson growled, with his tail swaying back and forth. Crimson pounced on the wolves, and sharpened his claws. Crimson took his claws out, and whacked the wolves. Blood fell on the ground, as the wolves landed near the lake. Crimson pounced on the wolves, and stabbed his claws in to their chest. The wolves laid on the ground, as blood poured out of their body. Crimson walked in to the lake, and cleaned his fur. Crimson shook the water out of his fur. Crimson smiled as he walked toward his log. Crimson sat on the log and listened to the tweeting birds. Butterflies were flying over the lake, while the water was shining. It was an wonderful sight for Crimson to watch. Sam and Emily sat on the log with Crimson! Sam and Emily hugged Crimson, while the birds tweeted in the background! The sun was setting, as the wind blew through Crimson's fur. The water in the lake was shining with the moon reflecting on it. The birds flew over the lake. Emily kissed Crimson on the head and said, "I love you, Crimson! I am glad that you are my son." Crimson said, "I love you too, Emily!" Crimson kissed Emily on her head and hugged her with his paws. Emily and Crimson smiled at each other. Sam moved closer to Crimson and Emily, and hugged them with his paws. The family of foxes smiled at the moon, while the wind blew through their fur.

In Sunshine Paradise, it was a cloudy day, and the birds were tweeting. Crimson was exercising and doing push ups, while the breeze was flowing through his fur. An butterfly landed on Crimson's head, while he was doing an roundhouse kick on the tree. The bush behind Crimson started moving and shaking! Crimson walked towards the bush, with his tail swaying back and forth. Crimson growled, as he moved closer to the bush. The bush continued moving and shaking. Crimson continued growling, as he got to the bush. An raccoon crawled out of the bush, and walked towards Crimson's paw. The raccoon was growling at Crimson, while Crimson was growling at it. Crimson whacked the raccoon with his paw! The raccoon pounced Crimson, and sharpened its claws. The raccoon stabbed its claws in to Crimson's fur! Crimson growled and whacked the raccoon on the head. Crimson sharpened his claws, and stabbed his claws in to the raccoon's neck. Crimson lifted the raccoon in the air, and started whacking it with his paw. Crimson played with the raccoon by throwing in the air, and catching it with his paws. Crimson spun the raccoon, by whacking it with his tail. The raccoon spun in an circle, as Crimson smiled. The raccoon stopped spinning and regained its balance. Crimson sharpened his claws and whacked the raccoon with his paw. The raccoon spun super fast in an circle, while Crimson smiled. Crimson threw the raccoon in the air, and caught it with his paws. Crimson bit in to the raccoon's tail! The raccoon howled in pain, as Crimson's fangs sunk in to the raccoon's fur. Crimson was spitting the fur out of his mouth, as he thought to himself. Crimson said, "The raccoon tasted a bit plain, let's add some flavor to make it nice and yummy to eat." Crimson licked his lips to get the leftover raccoon fur out of his mouth. Crimson picked up the raccoon and tied him on to the log with its tail. Crimson took two branches and rubbed them together. An spark lit up on the branches and they caught on fire. Crimson picked up an set of logs, and put them on the branches to create a fire. Crimson untied the raccoon from the log, and picked him by the tail. Crimson lowered the raccoon in to the fire, and started barbecuing it. Smoke rose from the flames, as the fur on the raccoon was cooking. Blood squirted on to the ground, as the raccoon got barbecued. Crimson licked his lips, as the fire made the raccoon smell so good. Crimson knew the raccoon would be nice and tasty to eat as a snack. The fire finished cooking the raccoon! Crimson lifted the raccoon out of the fire by its barbecued tail. Crimson opened up his mouth, and ate the raccoon in one big gulp. Crimson licked his lips, since the raccoon was nice and crunchy. It was an good snack for a healthy fox like Crimson. The snack gave Crimson a nice energy boost. An pack of raccoons pounced on Crimson and sank their fangs in to Crimson's fur. Crimson screamed in pain, as he rolled on the ground. The raccoons jumped on to Crimson's tail, and bit it. Crimson spun in a circle and flung the raccoons off of his body. Crimson growled at the raccoons, and sharpened his claws. Crimson pounced on the raccoons, and killed them with his claws. Blood gushed everywhere, as the raccoons laid on the ground. Crimson smiled, as he walked through the jungle. An raccoon pounced on Crimson through the bushes! Crimson's tail was swaying back and forth, as he jumped through the air with his claws out. Crimson sunk his claws in to the raccoon's chest, as he back flipped and knocked the raccoon in to the air. The raccoon fell on the ground in an puddle of blood. Crimson landed on the ground! An shadow appeared over the area! It was the ruler of the raccoon kingdom, King Raccoon! King Raccoon picked Crimson up by his tail. An raccoon ran out of the bushes, and crawled on to King Raccoon's shoulder. Crimson struggled in King Raccoon's grip, while King Raccoon was whacking him with his paw. King Raccoon whacked Crimson's chest with his paw. Crimson spun in an circle, while in King Raccoon's grip. Crimson growled, and slashed King Raccoon's chest with his claws. King Raccoon lost his grip on Crimson. Crimson flipped in the air, and on to the ground. King Raccoon kicked Crimson in the chest with his foot. Crimson rolled in to an tree! King Raccoon laughed, as he walked closer to Crimson. Crimson stepped backwards, as King Raccoon got closer to him. Crimson threw an branch at King Raccoon! King Raccoon broke the branch in half, by whacking it with his paw. King Raccoon pounced on Crimson, and sharpened his claws. King Raccoon stabbed his claws in to Crimson's fur. Crimson screamed in pain, as blood leaked out of his fur. King Raccoon kicks Crimson in the chest. Crimson rolled in to a tree, as King Raccoon walked closer to him. King Raccoon tackled Crimson through the tree. Crimson bit King Raccoon's paw with his fangs. King Raccoon howled in pain, as he slid backwards. Crimson kicked King Raccoon in the chest! King Raccoon slid in to a tree. Crimson sharpened his claws, and pounced on King Raccoon. King Raccoon rolled on to the ground! Crimson scratched King Raccoon's chest with his claws. Blood leaked out on the ground! Crimson punched King Raccoon in the face! King Raccoon grabbed Crimson's paw, and kicked him in the face. Crimson slid backwards! King Raccoon got up from the ground. Crimson growled at King Raccoon, with his tail swaying back and forth. Crimson sharpened his claws! Crimson pounced on King Raccoon and bit his tail. King Raccoon howled in pain. Crimson stabbed his claws in to King Raccoon's chest. Blood squirted on to the ground. Crimson climbed up the tree! King Raccoon grabbed Crimson's tail, and pulled him in to the ground. Crimson fell on the ground, while King Raccoon sharpened his claws. King Raccoon scratched Crimson's fur with his claws. King Raccoon hit Crimson in the face with his tail. Crimson bit King Raccoon's tail with his fangs. King Raccoon howled in pain. Crimson pulled King Raccoon's tail! King Raccoon growled, as he punched Crimson in the face with his paws. Crimson grabbed King Raccoon's paws, and roundhouse kicked

King Raccoon in the face. King Raccoon slid backwards, and Crimson back flipped in the air. Crimson ran toward the tree, and climbed it. Crimson grabbed on to an vine and swung toward King Raccoon. Crimson jumped off the vine, and flipped in the air. Crimson jumped on to King Raccoon's head, with his claws out. Crimson's claws sank in to King Raccoon's head, as blood gushed out everywhere! King Raccoon howled in pain, and grabbed Crimson by the neck. Crimson struggled in King Raccoon's grip! King Raccoon sharpened his claws, and scratched Crimson's chest. Blood leaked out of Crimson's fur. Crimson growled, and sharpened his claws. Crimson swung himself at King Raccoon's neck, and stabbed his claws in to it. Crimson hit King Raccoon with his tail. Crimson kicked King Raccoon in the chest with his paw. Crimson tackled King Raccoon in to a tree, and stabbed his claws in to King Raccoon's chest. King Raccoon howled in pain! Blood poured out of King Raccoon's body on to the ground. Crimson pounced King Raccoon and knocked him in to the ground. Crimson flipped in the air, and stabbed his claws in to King Raccoon's chest. Blood poured out of King Raccoon's body, while the other raccoons crowded around Crimson. Crimson whacked raccoons out of his path with his paws. The raccoons pounced on to Crimson! Crimson growled, while he was whacking raccoons off of him with his paws. Crimson pounced on the raccoons with his claws out! Blood splashed everywhere, as the raccoons laid on the ground. Crimson ran towards the tree, and jumped on to it! King Raccoon was climbing up the tree to catch Crimson. Crimson kicked King Raccoon off of the tree with his paw. King Raccoon jumped up the tree and scratched Crimson's paw with his claws. Crimson screamed in pain, and hung on the tree with one paw. Crimson was swaying back and forth in the tree. He was hanging on with one paw on the branch. King Raccoon jumped at Crimson and tackled him out of the tree. King Raccoon held Crimson on to the ground by stepping on his paws. King Raccoon sharpened his claws, and scratched Crimson in the chest. Crimson growled and kicked King Raccoon in the chest. King Raccoon slid backwards, and sunk his claws in to Crimson's chest. Blood leaked out of Crimson's fur! Crimson roundhouse kicked King Raccoon in the face. King Raccoon slid backwards! Crimson got up from the ground! King Raccoon grabbed Crimson's tail, and pulled him in to the ground. King Raccoon stepped on Crimson's back, and sunk his claws in to Crimson's neck. Blood poured on to the ground, as Crimson screamed in pain. King Raccoon sunk his claws further in to Crimson's neck and picked him up from the ground. King Raccoon kicked Crimson in the chest! Blood poured out of his fur on to the ground! Crimson struggled in King Raccoon's grip. King Raccoon kicked Crimson in the chest. Crimson growled, as he was swinging back and forth, while in King Raccoon's grip. King Raccoon smashed Crimson in to a tree. Crimson fell on the ground. King Raccoon held Crimson on the ground, by stepping on his paws. King Raccoon growled, while his tail was swaying back and forth. King Raccoon sharpened his claws, and scratched at Crimson's chest. Crimson grabbed King Raccoon's paw, and roundhouse kicked King Raccoon in the face. Crimson took out his claws, and punched King Raccoon in the face. Blood leaked out of King Raccoon's fur. Crimson tackled King Raccoon in to the tree, and smashed the tree in half. Crimson tore the tree out of the ground, and hit King Raccoon in the chest with it. King Raccoon rolled on to the ground. Crimson stepped on King Raccoon's tail, and scratched King Raccoon's chest with his claws. King Raccoon kicked Crimson in the face with his paw. Crimson slid backwards! Crimson ran towards the tree. King Raccoon ran after Crimson towards the tree. Crimson jumped on to the tree and started climbing it. King Raccoon climbed up the tree to chase Crimson. Crimson climbed up to the tree branch. King Raccoon grabbed Crimson's tail with his paw, and bit it. Crimson screamed in pain, as his paw lost his grip on the branch. King Raccoon sunk his claws in to Crimson's tail, as he climbed up Crimson's back on to the tree branch. King Raccoon climbed up to the tree branch. Crimson growled as he climbed further in to the tree. Crimson sunk his claws in to King Raccoon's tail, to keep his balance on the tree. Crimson climbed up to the top of the tree. King Raccoon climbed to the top of the tree, and pounced Crimson out of the tree! Crimson fell out of the tree! King Raccoon jumped on to Crimson's chest, and took out his claws. Crimson grabbed King Raccoon by the neck with his claws. Crimson sunk his claws in to King Raccoon's neck! Blood squirted everywhere! Crimson kicked King Raccoon in the chest, and flipped in the air. King Raccoon smashed in to the ground. Crimson landed on the ground and smiled! King Raccoon slowly got up and growled at Crimson. Crimson growled back, with his tail swaying back and forth. Crimson sharpened his claws, and was ready to strike at his enemy! Crimson tackled King Raccoon on to the ground. Crimson knelt over King Raccoon's body. Crimson sharpened his claws. Crimson sank his claws in to King Raccoon's neck. Crimson picked up King Raccoon! King Raccoon struggled in his grip, as blood leaked from his body. Crimson smiled, as he stabbed his claws in to King Raccoon's chest! Blood gushed out of King Raccoon's body! The raccoons screamed in horror! Crimson threw King Raccoon's body on to the ground! Crimson jumped on to an vine, and swung himself in to the lake. Crimson washed the blood off of his fur and paws. Crimson cleaned his fur with his paws! Crimson swam back to the shore, and shook the water out of his fur. Crimson walked to the tree, while he was sharpening his claws. Crimson growled with his tail swaying back and forth. Crimson pounced on the group of raccoons. Crimson was having fun, whacking the raccoons around. One of the raccoons jumped in the air toward Crimson! Crimson flipped in the air, and stabbed the raccoon in the chest with his claw. Blood landed in a puddle, as the raccoon's body fell on to the ground. Crimson smiled, as the raccoon's body laid on the ground. Crimson jumped in to the lake, and washed his fur. Crimson dunked his head in to the water, and washed his face. The water felt nice and cool on his fur. Crimson splashed water on his fur, and washed his paws. Crimson swam back to shore, and shook the water out of his fur. An pack of raccoons were waiting in the bushes, with their tails swaying back and forth. Crimson walked towards the bush to investigate it! Crimson knelt near the bush, and put his paws toward the ground. One of the raccoons whacked Crimson's paw, while Crimson smiled. Crimson grabbed the raccoon out of the bush and dragged it out by the tail. The raccoon was scared by Crimson's appearance! The raccoon struggled in Crimson's grip, while Crimson was whacking it around. Crimson growled at the raccoon and sharpened his claws. The raccoon got scared, while Crimson was scratching the raccoon's fur with his claws. The raccoon growled and said, "Please don't hurt us, raccoons don't taste very good!" Crimson smiled as he scratched the raccoon's fur. Crimson stabbed the raccoon in the chest with his claws. Blood poured out of the raccoon! Crimson threw the raccoon's dead body on to the ground in front of the other raccoons. Crimson walked in to the lake, and washed the blood off of his fur and paws. Crimson walked out of the lake and shook the water out of his fur. Crimson walked toward King Raccoon's body, and noticed the group of raccoons around it! The group of raccoons were sad, that their leader was dead! Crimson watched the raccoons, as they cried their tears on King Raccoon's body! King Raccoon's body laid in the puddle of blood, while the raccoons mourned over him! It was depressing to see the raccoons crying over their leader, but Crimson didn't feel the depression in the air at all. Crimson felt the raccoons didn't need a happy ending, because they ruined his relaxation. Crimson wanted to end the despair for the raccoons. The raccoons noticed that Crimson was watching them. The raccoons gathered in their pack, with their tails swaying back and forth, and they growled at Crimson. Crimson growled at the raccoons and sharpened his claws. Crimson's tail was swaying back and forth. Crimson jumped on to the group of raccoons! Crimson whacked the raccoons with his paws, as blood flew everywhere and bodies of raccoons laid on the ground in a circle! An pack of raccoons jumped out of the bushes and pounced on Crimson. Crimson rolled on to the ground, as the raccoons bit in to Crimson's fur. Crimson growled at the raccoons, and whacked them away with his paws. One of the raccoons jumped on Crimson's tail, and bit it. Crimson screamed in pain! Crimson spun in a circle, and shook the raccoon off of his tail. Crimson growled, with his tail swaying back and forth. Crimson pounced on the raccoons, and sharpened his claws. Crimson took his claws out, and whacked the raccoons. Blood fell on the ground, as the raccoons landed near the lake. Crimson pounced on the raccoons, and stabbed his claws in to their chest. The raccoons laid on the ground, as blood poured out of their body. Crimson walked in to the lake, and cleaned his fur. Crimson shook the water out of his fur. Crimson smiled as he walked toward his log. Crimson sat on the log and listened to the tweeting birds. Butterflies were flying over the lake, while the water was shining. It was an wonderful sight for Crimson to watch. Sam and Emily sat on the log with Crimson! Sam and Emily hugged Crimson, while the birds tweeted in the background! The sun was setting, as the wind blew through Crimson's fur. The water in the lake was shining with the moon reflecting on it. The birds flew over the lake. Emily kissed Crimson on the head and said, "I love you, Crimson! I am glad that you are my son." Crimson said, "I love you too, Emily!" Crimson kissed Emily on her head and hugged her with his paws. Emily and Crimson smiled at each other. Sam moved closer to Crimson and Emily, and hugged them with his paws. The family of foxes smiled at the moon, while the wind blew through their fur.

9

7

In Sunshine Paradise, it was a sunny day, and the birds were tweeting. Crimson was exercising, while the breeze was flowing through his fur. An butterfly landed on Crimson's head, while he was doing an round-house kick on the tree. The tree behind Crimson started moving and shaking! Crimson walked towards the tree, with his tail swaying back and forth. Crimson growled, as he moved closer to the tree. The tree continued moving and shaking. Crimson continued growling, as he got to the tree. An chipmunk climbed out of the tree, and walked towards Crimson's paw. The chipmunk was chattering at Crimson, while Crimson was growling at it. Crimson whacked the chipmunk with his paw! The chipmunk jumped on Crimson's tail. The chipmunk played with Crimson's tail! Crimson growled, and whacked the chipmunk on the head as he spun in a circle. Crimson sharpened his claws, and whacked the chipmunk off of his tail. The chipmunk rolled on the ground. Crimson lifted the chipmunk in the air, and started whacking it with his paw. Crimson played with the chipmunk by throwing in the air, and catching it with his paws. Crimson spun the chipmunk, by whacking it with his tail. The chipmunk spun in an circle, as Crimson smiled. The chipmunk stopped spinning and regained its balance. Crimson sharpened his claws and whacked the chipmunk with his paw. The chipmunk spun super fast in an circle, while Crimson smiled. Crimson threw the chipmunk in the air, and caught it with his paws. Crimson bit in to the chipmunk's tail! The chipmunk howled in pain, as Crimson's fangs sunk in to the chipmunk's fur. Crimson was spitting the fur out of his mouth, as he thought to himself. Crimson said, "The chipmunk tasted a bit plain, let's add some flavor to make it nice and yummy to eat." Crimson licked his lips to get the leftover chipmunk fur out of his mouth. Crimson picked up the chipmunk and tied him on to the log with its tail. Crimson took two branches and rubbed them together. An spark lit up on the branches and they caught on fire. Crimson picked up an set of logs, and put them on the branches to create a fire. Crimson untied the chipmunk from the log, and picked him by the tail. Crimson lowered the chipmunk in to the fire, and started barbecuing it. Smoke rose from the flames, as the fur on the chipmunk was cooking. Blood squirted on to the ground, as the chipmunk got barbecued. Crimson licked his lips, as the fire made the chipmunk smell so good. Crimson knew the chipmunk would be nice and tasty to eat as a snack. The fire finished cooking the chipmunk! Crimson lifted the chipmunk out of the fire by its barbecued tail. Crimson opened up his mouth, and ate the chipmunk in one big gulp. Crimson licked his lips, since the chipmunk was nice and crunchy. It was an good snack for a healthy fox like Crimson. The snack gave Crimson a nice energy boost. An pack of chipmunks pounced on Crimson and tickled him. Crimson laughed, as he rolled on the ground. The chipmunks jumped on to Crimson's tail, and whacked it. Crimson spun in a circle and flung the chipmunks off of his tail. Crimson growled at the chipmunks, and sharpened his claws. Crimson pounced on the chipmunks, and killed them with his claws. Blood gushed everywhere, as the chipmunks laid on the ground. Crimson smiled, as he walked through the jungle. An chipmunk pounced on Crimson through the tree. Crimson's tail was swaying back and forth, as he jumped through the air with his claws out. Crimson sunk his claws in to the chipmunk's chest, as he back flipped and knocked the chipmunk in to the air. The chipmunk fell on the ground in an puddle of blood. Crimson landed on the ground! An shadow appeared over the area! It was the ruler of the chipmunk kingdom, King Chipmunk! King Chipmunk picked Crimson up by his tail. An chipmunk ran out of the tree, and crawled on to King Chipmunk's shoulder. Crimson struggled in King Chipmunk's grip, while King Chipmunk was whacking him with his paw. King Chipmunk whacked Crimson's chest with his paw. Crimson spun in an circle, while in King Chipmunk's grip. Crimson growled, and slashed King Chipmunk's chest with his claws. King Chipmunk lost his grip on Crimson. Crimson flipped in the air, and on to the ground. King Chipmunk kicked Crimson in the chest with his foot. Crimson rolled in to an tree! King Chipmunk laughed, as he walked closer to Crimson. Crimson stepped backwards, as King Chipmunk got closer to him. Crimson threw an branch at King Chipmunk! King Chipmunk broke the branch in half, by whacking it with his paw. King Chipmunk pounced on Crimson, and sharpened his claws. King Chipmunk stabbed his claws in to Crimson's fur. Crimson screamed in pain, as blood leaked out of his fur. King Chipmunk kicks Crimson in the chest. Crimson rolled in to a tree, as King Chipmunk walked closer to him. King Chipmunk tackled Crimson through the tree. Crimson bit King Chipmunk's paw with his fangs. King Chipmunk howled in pain, as he slid backwards. Crimson kicked King Chipmunk in the chest! King Chipmunk slid in to a tree. Crimson sharpened his claws, and pounced on King Chipmunk. King Chipmunk rolled on to the ground! Crimson scratched King Chipmunk's chest with his claws. Blood leaked out on the ground! Crimson punched King Chipmunk in the face! King Chipmunk grabbed Crimson's paw, and kicked him in the face. Crimson slid backwards! King Chipmunk got up from the ground. Crimson growled at King Chipmunk, with his tail swaying back and forth. Crimson sharpened his claws! Crimson pounced on King Chipmunk and bit his tail. King Chipmunk howled in pain. Crimson stabbed his claws in to King Chipmunk's chest. Blood squirted on to the ground. Crimson climbed up the tree! King Chipmunk grabbed Crimson's tail, and pulled him in to the ground. Crimson fell on the ground, while King Chipmunk sharpened his claws. King Chipmunk scratched Crimson's fur with his claws. King Chipmunk hit Crimson in the face with his tail. Crimson bit King Chipmunk's tail with his fangs. King Chipmunk howled in pain. Crimson pulled King Chipmunk's tail! King Chipmunk growled, as he punched Crimson in the face with his paws. Crimson grabbed King Chipmunk's paws, and roundhouse kicked King Chipmunk in the face. King Chipmunk slid backwards, and Crimson back flipped in the air. Crimson ran toward the tree, and climbed it. Crimson grabbed on to an vine and swung toward King Chipmunk. Crimson jumped off the vine, and flipped in the air. Crimson jumped on to King Chipmunk's head, with his claws out. Crimson's claws sank in to King Chipmunk's head, as blood gushed out everywhere! King Chipmunk howled in pain, and grabbed Crimson by the neck. Crimson struggled in King Chipmunk's grip! King Chipmunk sharpened his claws, and scratched Crimson's chest. Blood leaked out of Crimson's fur. Crimson growled, and sharpened his claws. Crimson swung himself at King Chipmunk's neck, and stabbed his claws in to it. Crimson hit King Chipmunk with his tail. Crimson kicked King Chipmunk in the chest with his paw. Crimson tackled King Chipmunk in to a tree, and stabbed his claws in to King Chipmunk's chest. King Chipmunk howled in pain! Blood poured out of King Chipmunk's body on to the ground. Crimson pounced King Chipmunk and knocked him in to the ground. Crimson flipped in the air, and stabbed his claws in to King Chipmunk's chest. Blood poured out of King Chipmunk's body, while the other chipmunks crowded around Crimson. Crimson whacked chipmunks out of his path with his paws. The chipmunks pounced on to Crimson! Crimson growled, while he was whacking chipmunks off of him with his paws. Crimson pounced on the chipmunks with his claws out! Blood splashed everywhere, as the chipmunks laid on the ground. Crimson ran towards the tree, and jumped on to it! King Chipmunk was climbing up the tree to catch Crimson. Crimson kicked King Chipmunk off of the tree with his paw. King Chipmunk jumped up the tree and scratched Crimson's paw with his claws. Crimson screamed in pain, and hung on the tree with one paw. Crimson was swaying back and forth in the tree. He was hanging on with one paw on the branch. King Chipmunk jumped at Crimson and tackled him out of the tree. King Chipmunk held Crimson on to the ground by stepping on his paws. King Chipmunk sharpened his claws, and scratched Crimson in the chest. Crimson growled and kicked King Chipmunk in the chest. King Chipmunk slid backwards, and sunk his claws in to Crimson's chest. Blood leaked out of Crimson's fur! Crimson roundhouse kicked King Chipmunk in the face. King Chipmunk slid backwards! Crimson got up from the ground! King Chipmunk grabbed Crimson's tail, and pulled him in to the ground. King Chipmunk stepped on Crimson's back, and sunk his claws in to Crimson's neck. Blood poured on to the ground, as Crimson screamed in pain. King Chipmunk sunk his claws further in to Crimson's neck and picked him up from the ground. King Chipmunk kicked Crimson in the chest! Blood poured out of his fur on to the ground! Crimson struggled in King Chipmunk's grip. King Chipmunk kicked Crimson in the chest. Crimson growled, as he was swinging back and forth, while in King Chipmunk's grip. King Chipmunk smashed Crimson in to a tree. Crimson fell on the ground. King Chipmunk held Crimson on the ground, by stepping on his paws. King Chipmunk growled, while his tail was swaying back and forth. King Chipmunk sharpened his claws, and scratched at Crimson's chest. Crimson grabbed King Chipmunk's paw, and roundhouse kicked King Chipmunk in the face. Crimson took out his claws, and punched King Chipmunk in the face. Blood leaked out of King Chipmunk's fur. Crimson tackled King Chipmunk in to the tree, and smashed the tree in half. Crimson tore the tree out of the ground, and hit King Chipmunk in the chest with it. King Chipmunk rolled on to the ground. Crimson stepped on King Chipmunk's tail, and scratched King Chipmunk's chest with his claws. King Chipmunk kicked Crimson in the face with his paw. Crimson slid backwards! Crimson ran towards the tree. King Chipmunk ran after Crimson towards the tree. Crimson jumped on to the tree and started climbing it. King Chipmunk climbed up the tree to chase Crimson. Crimson climbed up to the tree branch. King Chipmunk grabbed Crimson's tail with his paw, and bit it. Crimson screamed in pain, as his paw lost his grip on the branch. King Chipmunk sunk his claws in to

Crimson's tail, as he climbed up Crimson's back on to the tree branch. King Chipmunk climbed up to the tree branch. Crimson growled as he climbed further in to the tree. Crimson sunk his claws in to King Chipmunk's tail, to keep his balance on the tree. Crimson climbed up to the top of the tree. King Chipmunk climbed to the top of the tree, and pounced Crimson out of the tree! Crimson fell out of the tree! King Chipmunk jumped on to Crimson's chest, and took out his claws. Crimson grabbed King Chipmunk by the neck with his claws. Crimson sunk his claws in to King Chipmunk's neck! Blood squirted everywhere! Crimson kicked King Chipmunk in the chest, and flipped in the air. King Chipmunk smashed in to the ground. Crimson landed on the ground and smiled! King Chipmunk slowly got up and growled at Crimson. Crimson growled back, with his tail swaying back and forth. Crimson sharpened his claws, and was ready to strike at his enemy! Crimson tackled King Chipmunk on to the ground. Crimson knelt over King Chipmunk's body. Crimson sharpened his claws. Crimson sank his claws in to King Chipmunk's neck. Crimson picked up King Chipmunk! King Chipmunk struggled in his grip, as blood leaked from his body. Crimson smiled, as he stabbed his claws in to King Chipmunk's chest! Blood gushed out of King Chipmunk's body! The chipmunks screamed in horror! Crimson threw King Chipmunk's body on to the ground! Crimson jumped on to an vine, and swung himself in to the lake. Crimson washed the blood off of his fur and paws. Crimson cleaned his fur with his paws! Crimson swam back to the shore, and shook the water out of his fur. Crimson walked to the tree, while he was sharpening his claws. Crimson growled with his tail swaying back and forth. Crimson pounced on the group of chipmunks. Crimson was having fun, whacking the chipmunks around. One of the chipmunks jumped in the air toward Crimson! Crimson flipped in the air, and stabbed the chipmunk in the chest with his claw. Blood landed in a puddle, as the chipmunk's body fell on to the ground. Crimson smiled, as the chipmunk's body laid on the ground. Crimson jumped in to the lake, and washed his fur. Crimson dunked his head in to the water, and washed his face. The water felt nice and cool on his fur. Crimson splashed water on his fur, and washed his paws. Crimson swam back to shore, and shook the water out of his fur. An pack of chipmunks were waiting in the trees, with their tails swaying back and forth. Crimson walked towards the tree to investigate it! Crimson knelt near the tree, and put his paws toward the ground. One of the chipmunks whacked Crimson's paw, while Crimson smiled. Crimson grabbed the chipmunk out of the tree and dragged it out by the tail. The chipmunk was scared by Crimson's appearance! The chipmunk struggled in Crimson's grip, while Crimson was whacking it around. Crimson growled at the chipmunk and sharpened his claws. The chipmunk got scared, while Crimson was scratching the chipmunk's fur with his claws. The chipmunk growled and said, "Please don't hurt us, chipmunks don't taste very good!" Crimson smiled as he scratched the chipmunk's fur. Crimson stabbed the chipmunk in the chest with his claws. Blood poured out of the chipmunk! Crimson threw the chipmunk's dead body on to the ground in front of the other chipmunks. Crimson walked in to the lake, and washed the blood off of his fur and paws. Crimson walked out of the lake and shook the water out of his fur. Crimson walked toward King Chipmunk's body, and noticed the group of chipmunks around it! The group of chipmunks were sad, that their leader was dead! Crimson watched the chipmunks, as they cried their tears on King Chipmunk's body! King Chipmunk's body laid in the puddle of blood, while the chipmunks mourned over him! It was depressing to see the chipmunks crying over their leader, but Crimson didn't feel the depression in the air at all. Crimson felt the chipmunks didn't need a happy ending, because they ruined his relaxation. Crimson wanted to end the despair for the chipmunks. The chipmunks noticed that Crimson was watching them. The chipmunks gathered in their pack, with their tails swaying back and forth, and they growled at Crimson. Crimson growled at the chipmunks and sharpened his claws. Crimson's tail was swaying back and forth. Crimson jumped on to the group of chipmunks! Crimson whacked the chipmunks with his paws, as blood flew everywhere and bodies of chipmunks laid on the ground in a circle! An pack of chipmunks jumped out of the trees and pounced on Crimson. Crimson rolled on to the ground, as the chipmunks bit in to Crimson's fur. Crimson growled at the chipmunks, and whacked them away with his paws. One of the chipmunks jumped on Crimson's tail, and bit it. Crimson screamed in pain! Crimson spun in a circle, and shook the chipmunk off of his tail. Crimson growled, with his tail swaying back and forth. Crimson pounced on the chipmunks, and sharpened his claws. Crimson took his claws out, and whacked the chipmunks. Blood fell on the ground, as the chipmunks landed near the lake. Crimson pounced on the chipmunks, and stabbed his claws in to their chest. The chipmunks laid on the ground, as blood poured out of their body. Crimson walked in to the lake, and cleaned his fur. Crimson shook the water out of his fur. Crimson smiled as he walked toward his log. Crimson sat on the log and listened to the tweeting birds. Butterflies were flying over the lake, while the water was shining. It was an wonderful sight for Crimson to watch. Sam and Emily sat on the log with Crimson! Sam and Emily hugged Crimson, while the birds tweeted in the background! The sun was setting, as the wind blew through Crimson's fur. The water in the lake was shining with the moon reflecting on it. The birds flew over the lake. Emily kissed Crimson on the head and said, "I love you, Crimson! I am glad that you are my son." Crimson said, "I love you too, Emily!" Crimson kissed Emily on her head and hugged her with his paws. Emily and Crimson smiled at each other. Sam moved closer to Crimson and Emily, and hugged them with his paws. The family of foxes smiled at the moon, while the wind blew through their fur.

10

8

In Sunshine Paradise, it was a sunny day, and the squirrels were tweeting. Crimson was exercising, while the breeze was flowing through his fur. An butterfly landed on Crimson's head, while he was doing an roundhouse kick on the tree. The tree behind Crimson started moving and shaking! Crimson walked towards the tree, with his tail swaying back and forth. Crimson growled, as he moved closer to the tree. The tree continued moving and shaking. Crimson continued growling, as he got to the tree. An squirrel climbed out of the tree, and walked towards Crimson's paw. The squirrel was chattering at Crimson, while Crimson was growling at it. Crimson whacked the squirrel with his paw! The squirrel jumped on Crimson's tail. The squirrel played with Crimson's tail! Crimson growled, and whacked the squirrel on the head as he spun in a circle. Crimson sharpened his claws, and whacked the squirrel off of his tail. The squirrel rolled on the ground. Crimson lifted the squirrel in the air, and started whacking it with his paw. Crimson played with the squirrel by throwing in the air, and catching it with his paws. Crimson spun the squirrel, by whacking it with his tail. The squirrel spun in an circle, as Crimson smiled. The squirrel stopped spinning and regained its balance. Crimson sharpened his claws and whacked the squirrel with his paw. The squirrel spun super fast in an circle, while Crimson smiled. Crimson threw the squirrel in the air, and caught it with his paws. Crimson bit in to the squirrel's tail! The squirrel howled in pain, as Crimson's fangs sunk in to the squirrel's fur. Crimson was spitting the fur out of his mouth, as he thought to himself. Crimson said, "The squirrel tasted a bit plain, let's add some flavor to make it nice and yummy to eat." Crimson licked his lips to get the leftover squirrel fur out of his mouth. Crimson picked up the squirrel and tied him on to the log with its tail. Crimson took two branches and rubbed them together. An spark lit up on the branches and they caught on fire. Crimson picked up an set of logs, and put them on the branches to create a fire. Crimson untied the squirrel from the log, and picked him by the tail. Crimson lowered the squirrel in to the fire, and started barbecuing it. Smoke rose from the flames, as the fur on the squirrel was cooking. Blood squirted on to the ground, as the squirrel got barbecued. Crimson licked his lips, as the fire made the squirrel smell so good. Crimson knew the squirrel would be nice and tasty to eat as a snack. The fire finished cooking the squirrel! Crimson lifted the squirrel out of the fire by its barbecued tail. Crimson opened up his mouth, and ate the squirrel in one big gulp. Crimson licked his lips, since the squirrel was nice and crunchy. It was an good snack for a healthy fox like Crimson. The snack gave Crimson a nice energy boost. An pack of squirrels pounced on Crimson and tickled him. Crimson laughed, as he rolled on the ground. The squirrels jumped on to Crimson's tail, and whacked it. Crimson spun in a circle and flung the squirrels off of his tail. Crimson growled at the squirrels, and sharpened his claws. Crimson pounced on the squirrels, and killed them with his claws. Blood gushed everywhere, as the squirrels laid on the ground. Crimson smiled, as he walked through the jungle. An squirrel pounced on Crimson through the tree. Crimson's tail was swaying back and forth, as he jumped through the air with his claws out. Crimson sunk his claws in to the squirrel's chest, as he back flipped and knocked the squirrel in to the air. The squirrel fell on the ground in an puddle of blood. Crimson landed on the ground! An shadow appeared over the area! It was the ruler of the squirrel kingdom, King Squirrel! King Squirrel picked Crimson up by his tail. An squirrel ran out of the tree, and crawled on to King Squirrel's shoulder. Crimson struggled in King Squirrel's grip, while King Squirrel was whacking him with his paw. King Squirrel whacked Crimson's chest with his paw. Crimson spun in an circle, while in King Squirrel's grip. Crimson growled, and slashed King Squirrel's chest with his claws. King Squirrel lost his grip on Crimson. Crimson flipped in the air, and on to the ground. King Squirrel kicked Crimson in the chest with his foot. Crimson rolled in to an tree! King Squirrel laughed, as he walked closer to Crimson. Crimson stepped backwards, as King Squirrel got closer to him. Crimson threw an branch at King Squirrel! King Squirrel broke the branch in half, by whacking it with his paw. King Squirrel pounced on Crimson, and sharpened his claws. King Squirrel stabbed his claws in to Crimson's fur. Crimson screamed in pain, as blood leaked out of his fur. King Squirrel kicks Crimson in the chest. Crimson rolled in to a tree, as King Squirrel walked closer to him. King Squirrel tackled Crimson through the tree. Crimson bit King Squirrel's paw with his fangs. King Squirrel howled in pain, as he slid backwards. Crimson kicked King Squirrel in the chest! King Squirrel slid in to a tree. Crimson sharpened his claws, and pounced on King Squirrel. King Squirrel rolled on to the ground! Crimson scratched King Squirrel's chest with his claws. Blood leaked out on the ground! Crimson punched King Squirrel in the face! King Squirrel grabbed Crimson's paw, and kicked him in the face. Crimson slid backwards! King Squirrel got up from the ground. Crimson growled at King Squirrel, with his tail swaying back and forth. Crimson sharpened his claws! Crimson pounced on King Squirrel and bit his tail. King Squirrel howled in pain. Crimson stabbed his claws in to King Squirrel's chest. Blood squirted on to the ground. Crimson climbed up the tree! King Squirrel grabbed Crimson's tail, and pulled him in to the ground. Crimson fell on the ground, while King Squirrel sharpened his claws. King Squirrel scratched Crimson's fur with his claws. King Squirrel hit Crimson in the face with his tail. Crimson bit King Squirrel's tail with his fangs. King Squirrel howled in pain. Crimson pulled King Squirrel's tail! King Squirrel growled, as he punched Crimson in the face with his paws. Crimson grabbed King Squirrel's paws, and roundhouse kicked King Squirrel in the face. King Squirrel slid backwards, and Crimson back flipped in the air. Crimson ran toward the tree, and climbed it. Crimson grabbed on to an vine and swung toward King Squirrel. Crimson jumped off the vine, and flipped in the air. Crimson jumped on to King Squirrel's head, with his claws out. Crimson's claws sank in to King Squirrel's head, as blood gushed out everywhere! King Squirrel howled in pain, and grabbed Crimson by the neck. Crimson struggled in King Squirrel's grip! King Squirrel sharpened his claws, and scratched Crimson's chest. Blood leaked out of Crimson's fur. Crimson growled, and sharpened his claws. Crimson swung himself at King Squirrel's neck, and stabbed his claws in to it. Crimson hit King Squirrel with his tail. Crimson kicked King Squirrel in the chest with his paw. Crimson tackled King Squirrel in to a tree, and stabbed his claws in to King Squirrel's chest. King Squirrel howled in pain! Blood poured out of King Squirrel's body on to the ground. Crimson pounced King Squirrel and knocked him in to the ground. Crimson flipped in the air, and stabbed his claws in to King Squirrel's chest. Blood poured out of King Squirrel's body, while the other squirrels crowded around Crimson. Crimson whacked squirrels out of his path with his paws. The squirrels pounced on to Crimson! Crimson growled, while he was whacKing Squirrels off of him with his paws. Crimson pounced on the squirrels with his claws out! Blood splashed everywhere, as the squirrels laid on the ground. Crimson ran towards the tree, and jumped on to it! King Squirrel was climbing up the tree to catch Crimson. Crimson kicked King Squirrel off of the tree with his paw. King Squirrel jumped up the tree and scratched Crimson's paw with his claws. Crimson screamed in pain, and hung on the tree with one paw. Crimson was swaying back and forth in the tree. He was hanging on with one paw on the branch. King Squirrel jumped at Crimson and tackled him out of the tree. King Squirrel held Crimson on to the ground by stepping on his paws. King Squirrel sharpened his claws, and scratched Crimson in the chest. Crimson growled and kicked King Squirrel in the chest. King Squirrel slid backwards, and sunk his claws in to Crimson's chest. Blood leaked out of Crimson's fur! Crimson roundhouse kicked King Squirrel in the face. King Squirrel slid backwards!

Crimson got up from the ground! King Squirrel grabbed Crimson's tail, and pulled him in to the ground. King Squirrel stepped on Crimson's back, and sunk his claws in to Crimson's neck. Blood poured on to the ground, as Crimson screamed in pain. King Squirrel sunk his claws further in to Crimson's neck and picked him up from the ground. King Squirrel kicked Crimson in the chest! Blood poured out of his fur on to the ground! Crimson struggled in King Squirrel's grip. King Squirrel kicked Crimson in the chest. Crimson growled, as he was swinging back and forth, while in King Squirrel's grip. King Squirrel smashed Crimson in to a tree. Crimson fell on the ground. King Squirrel held Crimson on the ground, by stepping on his paws. King Squirrel growled, while his tail was swaying back and forth. King Squirrel sharpened his claws, and scratched at Crimson's chest. Crimson grabbed King Squirrel's paw, and roundhouse kicked King Squirrel in the face. Crimson took out his claws, and punched King Squirrel in the face. Blood leaked out of King Squirrel's fur. Crimson tackled King Squirrel in to the tree, and smashed the tree in half. Crimson tore the tree out of the ground, and hit King Squirrel in the chest with it. King Squirrel rolled on to the ground. Crimson stepped on King Squirrel's tail, and scratched King Squirrel's chest with his claws. King Squirrel kicked Crimson in the face with his paw. Crimson slid backwards! Crimson ran towards the tree. King Squirrel ran after Crimson towards the tree. Crimson jumped on to the tree and started climbing it. King Squirrel climbed up the tree to chase Crimson. Crimson climbed up to the tree branch. King Squirrel grabbed Crimson's tail with his paw, and bit it. Crimson screamed in pain, as his paw lost his grip on the branch. King Squirrel sunk his claws in to Crimson's tail, as he climbed up Crimson's back on to the tree branch. King Squirrel climbed up to the tree branch. Crimson growled as he climbed further in to the tree. Crimson sunk his claws in to King Squirrel's tail, to keep his balance on the tree. Crimson climbed up to the top of the tree. King Squirrel climbed to the top of the tree, and pounced Crimson out of the tree! Crimson fell out of the tree! King Squirrel jumped on to Crimson's chest, and took out his claws. Crimson grabbed King Squirrel by the neck with his claws. Crimson sunk his claws in to King Squirrel's neck! Blood squirted everywhere! Crimson kicked King Squirrel in the chest, and flipped in the air. King Squirrel smashed in to the ground. Crimson landed on the ground and smiled! King Squirrel slowly got up and growled at Crimson. Crimson growled back, with his tail swaying back and forth. Crimson sharpened his claws, and was ready to strike at his enemy! Crimson tackled King Squirrel on to the ground. Crimson knelt over King Squirrel's body. Crimson sharpened his claws. Crimson sank his claws in to King Squirrel's neck. Crimson picked up King Squirrel! King Squirrel struggled in his grip, as blood leaked from his body. Crimson smiled, as he stabbed his claws in to King Squirrel's chest! Blood gushed out of King Squirrel's body! The squirrels screamed in horror! Crimson threw King Squirrel's body on to the ground! Crimson jumped on to an vine, and swung himself in to the lake. Crimson washed the blood off of his fur and paws. Crimson cleaned his fur with his paws! Crimson swam back to the shore, and shook the water out of his fur. Crimson walked to the tree, while he was sharpening his claws. Crimson growled with his tail swaying back and forth. Crimson pounced on the group of squirrels. Crimson was having fun, whacking the squirrels around. One of the squirrels jumped in the air toward Crimson! Crimson flipped in the air, and stabbed the squirrel in the chest with his claw. Blood landed in a puddle, as the squirrel's body fell on to the ground. Crimson smiled, as the squirrel's body laid on the ground. Crimson jumped in to the lake, and washed his fur. Crimson dunked his head in to the water, and washed his face. The water felt nice and cool on his fur. Crimson splashed water on his fur, and washed his paws. Crimson swam back to shore, and shook the water out of his fur. An pack of squirrels were waiting in the trees, with their tails swaying back and forth. Crimson walked towards the tree to investigate it! Crimson knelt near the tree, and put his paws toward the ground. One of the squirrels whacked Crimson's paw, while Crimson smiled. Crimson grabbed the squirrel out of the tree and dragged it out by the tail. The squirrel was scared by Crimson's appearance! The squirrel struggled in Crimson's grip, while Crimson was whacking it around. Crimson growled at the squirrel and sharpened his claws. The squirrel got scared, while Crimson was scratching the squirrel's fur with his claws. The squirrel growled and said, "Please don't hurt us, squirrels don't taste very good!" Crimson smiled as he scratched the squirrel's fur. Crimson stabbed the squirrel in the chest with his claws. Blood poured out of the squirrel! Crimson threw the squirrel's dead body on to the ground in front of the other squirrels. Crimson walked in to the lake, and washed the blood off of his fur and paws. Crimson walked out of the lake and shook the water out of his fur. Crimson walked toward King Squirrel's body, and noticed the group of squirrels around it! The group of squirrels were sad, that their leader was dead! Crimson watched the squirrels, as they cried their tears on King Squirrel's body! King Squirrel's body laid in the puddle of blood, while the squirrels mourned over him! It was depressing to see the squirrels crying over their leader, but Crimson didn't feel the depression in the air at all. Crimson felt the squirrels didn't need a happy ending, because they ruined his relaxation. Crimson wanted to end the despair for the squirrels. The squirrels noticed that Crimson was watching them. The squirrels gathered in their pack, with their tails swaying back and forth, and they growled at Crimson. Crimson growled at the squirrels and sharpened his claws. Crimson's tail was swaying back and forth. Crimson jumped on to the group of squirrels! Crimson whacked the squirrels with his paws, as blood flew everywhere and bodies of squirrels laid on the ground in a circle! An pack of squirrels jumped out of the trees and pounced on Crimson. Crimson rolled on to the ground, as the squirrels bit in to Crimson's fur. Crimson growled at the squirrels, and whacked them away with his paws. One of the squirrels jumped on Crimson's tail, and bit it. Crimson screamed in pain! Crimson spun in a circle, and shook the squirrel off of his tail. Crimson growled, with his tail swaying back and forth. Crimson pounced on the squirrels, and sharpened his claws. Crimson took his claws out, and whacked the squirrels. Blood fell on the ground, as the squirrels landed near the lake. Crimson pounced on the squirrels, and stabbed his claws in to their chest. The squirrels laid on the ground, as blood poured out of their body. Crimson walked in to the lake, and cleaned his fur. Crimson shook the water out of his fur. Crimson smiled as he walked toward his log. Crimson sat on the log and listened to the tweeting squirrels. Butterflies were flying over the lake, while the water was shining. It was an wonderful sight for Crimson to watch. Sam and Emily sat on the log with Crimson! Sam and Emily hugged Crimson, while the squirrels tweeted in the background! The sun was setting, as the wind blew through Crimson's fur. The water in the lake was shining with the moon reflecting on it. The squirrels flew over the lake. Emily kissed Crimson on the head and said, "I love you, Crimson! I am glad that you are my son." Crimson said, "I love you too, Emily!" Crimson kissed Emily on her head and hugged her with his paws. Emily and Crimson smiled at each other. Sam moved closer to Crimson and Emily, and hugged them with his paws. The family of foxes smiled at the moon, while the wind blew through their fur.

11

9

In Sunshine Paradise, it was a sunny day, and the birds were tweeting. Crimson was exercising, while the breeze was flowing through his fur. An butterfly landed on Crimson's head, while he was doing an roundhouse kick on the tree. The tree behind Crimson started moving and shaking! Crimson walked towards the tree, with his tail swaying back and forth. Crimson growled, as he moved closer to the tree. The tree continued moving and shaking. Crimson continued growling, as he got to the tree. An jackal climbed out of the tree, and walked towards Crimson's paw. The jackal was chattering at Crimson, while Crimson was growling at it. Crimson whacked the jackal with his paw! The jackal jumped on Crimson's tail. The jackal played with Crimson's tail! Crimson growled, and whacked the jackal on the head as he spun in a circle. Crimson sharpened his claws, and whacked the jackal off of his tail. The jackal rolled on the ground. Crimson lifted the jackal in the air, and started whacking it with his paw. Crimson played with the jackal by throwing in the air, and catching it with his paws. Crimson spun the jackal, by whacking it with his tail. The jackal spun in an circle, as Crimson smiled. The jackal stopped spinning and regained its balance. Crimson sharpened his claws and whacked the jackal with his paw. The jackal spun super fast in an circle, while Crimson smiled. Crimson threw the jackal in the air, and caught it with his paws. Crimson bit in to the jackal's tail! The jackal howled in pain, as Crimson's fangs sunk in to the jackal's fur. Crimson was spitting the fur out of his mouth, as he thought to himself. Crimson said, "The jackal tasted a bit plain, let's add some flavor to make it nice and yummy to eat." Crimson licked his lips to get the leftover jackal fur out of his mouth. Crimson picked up the jackal and tied him on to the log with its tail. Crimson took two branches and rubbed them together. An spark lit up on the branches and they caught on fire. Crimson picked up an set of logs, and put them on the branches to create a fire. Crimson untied the jackal from the log, and picked him by the tail. Crimson lowered the jackal in to the fire, and started barbecuing it. Smoke rose from the flames, as the fur on the jackal was cooking. Blood squirted on to the ground, as the jackal got barbecued. Crimson licked his lips, as the fire made the jackal smell so good. Crimson knew the jackal would be nice and tasty to eat as a snack. The fire finished cooking the jackal! Crimson lifted the jackal out of the fire by its barbecued tail. Crimson opened up his mouth, and ate the jackal in one big gulp. Crimson licked his lips, since the jackal was nice and crunchy. It was an good snack for a healthy fox like Crimson. The snack gave Crimson a nice energy boost. An pack of jackals pounced on Crimson and tickled him. Crimson laughed, as he rolled on the ground. The jackals jumped on to Crimson's tail, and whacked it. Crimson spun in a circle and flung the jackals off of his tail. Crimson growled at the jackals, and sharpened his claws. Crimson pounced on the jackals, and killed them with his claws. Blood gushed everywhere, as the jackals laid on the ground. Crimson smiled, as he walked through the jungle. An jackal pounced on Crimson through the tree. Crimson's tail was swaying back and forth, as he jumped through the air with his claws out. Crimson sunk his claws in to the jackal's chest, as he back flipped and knocked the jackal in to the air. The jackal fell on the ground in an puddle of blood. Crimson landed on the ground! An shadow appeared over the area! It was the ruler of the jackal kingdom, King Jackal! King Jackal picked Crimson up by his tail. An jackal ran out of the tree, and crawled on to King Jackal's shoulder. Crimson struggled in King Jackal's grip, while King Jackal was whacking him with his paw. King Jackal whacked Crimson's chest with his paw. Crimson spun in an circle, while in King Jackal's grip. Crimson growled, and slashed King Jackal's chest with his claws. King Jackal lost his grip on Crimson. Crimson flipped in the air, and on to the ground. King Jackal kicked Crimson in the chest with his foot. Crimson rolled in to an tree! King Jackal laughed, as he walked closer to Crimson. Crimson stepped backwards, as King Jackal got closer to him. Crimson threw an branch at King Jackal! King Jackal broke the branch in half, by whacking it with his paw. King Jackal pounced on Crimson, and sharpened his claws. King Jackal stabbed his claws in to Crimson's fur. Crimson screamed in pain, as blood leaked out of his fur. King Jackal kicks Crimson in the chest. Crimson rolled in to a tree, as King Jackal walked closer to him. King Jackal tackled Crimson through the tree. Crimson bit King Jackal's paw with his fangs. King Jackal howled in pain, as he slid backwards. Crimson kicked King Jackal in the chest! King Jackal slid in to a tree. Crimson sharpened his claws, and pounced on King Jackal. King Jackal rolled on to the ground! Crimson scratched King Jackal's chest with his claws. Blood leaked out on the ground! Crimson punched King Jackal in the face! King Jackal grabbed Crimson's paw, and kicked him in the face. Crimson slid backwards! King Jackal got up from the ground. Crimson growled at King Jackal, with his tail swaying back and forth. Crimson sharpened his claws! Crimson pounced on King Jackal and bit his tail. King Jackal howled in pain. Crimson stabbed his claws in to King Jackal's chest. Blood squirted on to the ground. Crimson climbed up the tree! King Jackal grabbed Crimson's tail, and pulled him in to the ground. Crimson fell on the ground, while King Jackal sharpened his claws. King Jackal scratched Crimson's fur with his claws. King Jackal hit Crimson in the face with his tail. Crimson bit King Jackal's tail with his fangs. King Jackal howled in pain. Crimson pulled King Jackal's tail! King Jackal growled, as he punched Crimson in the face with his paws. Crimson grabbed King Jackal's paws, and roundhouse kicked King Jackal in the face. King Jackal slid backwards, and Crimson back flipped in the air. Crimson ran toward the tree, and climbed it. Crimson grabbed on to an vine and swung toward King Jackal. Crimson jumped off the vine, and flipped in the air. Crimson jumped on to King Jackal's head, with his claws out. Crimson's claws sank in to King Jackal's head, as blood gushed out everywhere! King Jackal howled in pain, and grabbed Crimson by the neck. Crimson struggled in King Jackal's grip! King Jackal sharpened his claws, and scratched Crimson's chest. Blood leaked out of Crimson's fur. Crimson growled, and sharpened his claws. Crimson swung himself at King Jackal's neck, and stabbed his claws in to it. Crimson hit King Jackal with his tail. Crimson kicked King Jackal in the chest with his paw. Crimson tackled King Jackal in to a tree, and stabbed his claws in to King Jackal's chest. King Jackal howled in pain! Blood poured out of King Jackal's body on to the ground. Crimson pounced King Jackal and knocked him in to the ground. Crimson flipped in the air, and stabbed his claws in to King Jackal's chest. Blood poured out of King Jackal's body, while the other jackals crowded around Crimson. Crimson whacked jackals out of his path with his paws. The jackals pounced on to Crimson! Crimson growled, while he was whacKing Jackals off of him with his paws. Crimson pounced on the jackals with his claws out! Blood splashed everywhere, as the jackals laid on the ground. Crimson ran towards the tree, and jumped on to it! King Jackal was climbing up the tree to catch Crimson. Crimson kicked King Jackal off of the tree with his paw. King Jackal jumped up the tree and scratched Crimson's paw with his claws. Crimson screamed in pain, and hung on the tree with one paw. Crimson was swaying back and forth in the tree. He was hanging on with one paw on the branch. King Jackal jumped at Crimson and tackled him out of the tree. King Jackal held Crimson on to the ground by stepping on his paws. King Jackal sharpened his claws, and scratched Crimson in the chest. Crimson growled and kicked King Jackal in the chest. King Jackal slid backwards, and sunk his claws in to Crimson's chest. Blood leaked out of Crimson's fur! Crimson roundhouse kicked King Jackal in the face. King Jackal slid backwards! Crimson got up from the ground! King Jackal grabbed Crimson's tail, and pulled him in to the ground. King Jackal stepped on Crimson's back, and sunk his claws in to Crimson's neck. Blood poured on to the ground, as Crimson screamed in pain.

King Jackal sunk his claws further in to Crimson's neck and picked him up from the ground. King Jackal kicked Crimson in the chest! Blood poured out of his fur on to the ground! Crimson struggled in King Jackal's grip. King Jackal kicked Crimson in the chest. Crimson growled, as he was swinging back and forth, while in King Jackal's grip. King Jackal smashed Crimson in to a tree. Crimson fell on the ground. King Jackal held Crimson on the ground, by stepping on his paws. King Jackal growled, while his tail was swaying back and forth. King Jackal sharpened his claws, and scratched at Crimson's chest. Crimson grabbed King Jackal's paw, and roundhouse kicked King Jackal in the face. Crimson took out his claws, and punched King Jackal in the face. Blood leaked out of King Jackal's fur. Crimson tackled King Jackal in to the tree, and smashed the tree in half. Crimson tore the tree out of the ground, and hit King Jackal in the chest with it. King Jackal rolled on to the ground. Crimson stepped on King Jackal's tail, and scratched King Jackal's chest with his claws. King Jackal kicked Crimson in the face with his paw. Crimson slid backwards! Crimson ran towards the tree. King Jackal ran after Crimson towards the tree. Crimson jumped on to the tree and started climbing it. King Jackal climbed up the tree to chase Crimson. Crimson climbed up to the tree branch. King Jackal grabbed Crimson's tail with his paw, and bit it. Crimson screamed in pain, as his paw lost his grip on the branch. King Jackal sunk his claws in to Crimson's tail, as he climbed up Crimson's back on to the tree branch. King Jackal climbed up to the tree branch. Crimson growled as he climbed further in to the tree. Crimson sunk his claws in to King Jackal's tail, to keep his balance on the tree. Crimson climbed up to the top of the tree. King Jackal climbed to the top of the tree, and pounced Crimson out of the tree! Crimson fell out of the tree! King Jackal jumped on to Crimson's chest, and took out his claws. Crimson grabbed King Jackal by the neck with his claws. Crimson sunk his claws in to King Jackal's neck! Blood squirted everywhere! Crimson kicked King Jackal in the chest, and flipped in the air. King Jackal smashed in to the ground. Crimson landed on the ground and smiled! King Jackal slowly got up and growled at Crimson. Crimson growled back, with his tail swaying back and forth. Crimson sharpened his claws, and was ready to strike at his enemy! Crimson tackled King Jackal on to the ground. Crimson knelt over King Jackal's body. Crimson sharpened his claws. Crimson sank his claws in to King Jackal's neck. Crimson picked up King Jackal! King Jackal struggled in his grip, as blood leaked from his body. Crimson smiled, as he stabbed his claws in to King Jackal's chest! Blood gushed out of King Jackal's body! The jackals screamed in horror! Crimson threw King Jackal's body on to the ground! Crimson jumped on to an vine, and swung himself in to the lake. Crimson washed the blood off of his fur and paws. Crimson cleaned his fur with his paws! Crimson swam back to the shore, and shook the water out of his fur. Crimson walked to the tree, while he was sharpening his claws. Crimson growled with his tail swaying back and forth. Crimson pounced on the group of jackals. Crimson was having fun, whacking the jackals around. One of the jackals jumped in the air toward Crimson! Crimson flipped in the air, and stabbed the jackal in the chest with his claw. Blood landed in a puddle, as the jackal's body fell on to the ground. Crimson smiled, as the jackal's body laid on the ground. Crimson jumped in to the lake, and washed his fur. Crimson dunked his head in to the water, and washed his face. The water felt nice and cool on his fur. Crimson splashed water on his fur, and washed his paws. Crimson swam back to shore, and shook the water out of his fur. An pack of jackals were waiting in the trees, with their tails swaying back and forth. Crimson walked towards the tree to investigate it! Crimson knelt near the tree, and put his paws toward the ground. One of the jackals whacked Crimson's paw, while Crimson smiled. Crimson grabbed the jackal out of the tree and dragged it out by the tail. The jackal was scared by Crimson's appearance! The jackal struggled in Crimson's grip, while Crimson was whacking it around. Crimson growled at the jackal and sharpened his claws. The jackal got scared, while Crimson was scratching the jackal's fur with his claws. The jackal growled and said, "Please don't hurt us, jackals don't taste very good!" Crimson smiled as he scratched the jackal's fur. Crimson stabbed the jackal in the chest with his claws. Blood poured out of the jackal! Crimson threw the jackal's dead body on to the ground in front of the other jackals. Crimson walked in to the lake, and washed the blood off of his fur and paws. Crimson walked out of the lake and shook the water out of his fur. Crimson walked toward King Jackal's body, and noticed the group of jackals around it! The group of jackals were sad, that their leader was dead! Crimson watched the jackals, as they cried their tears on King Jackal's body! King Jackal's body laid in the puddle of blood, while the jackals mourned over him! It was depressing to see the jackals crying over their leader, but Crimson didn't feel the depression in the air at all. Crimson felt the jackals didn't need a happy ending, because they ruined his relaxation. Crimson wanted to end the despair for the jackals. The jackals noticed that Crimson was watching them. The jackals gathered in their pack, with their tails swaying back and forth, and they growled at Crimson. Crimson growled at the jackals and sharpened his claws. Crimson's tail was swaying back and forth. Crimson jumped on to the group of jackals! Crimson whacked the jackals with his paws, as blood flew everywhere and bodies of jackals laid on the ground in a circle! An pack of jackals jumped out of the trees and pounced on Crimson. Crimson rolled on to the ground, as the jackals bit in to Crimson's fur. Crimson growled at the jackals, and whacked them away with his paws. One of the jackals jumped on Crimson's tail, and bit it. Crimson screamed in pain! Crimson spun in a circle, and shook the jackal off of his tail. Crimson growled, with his tail swaying back and forth. Crimson pounced on the jackals, and sharpened his claws. Crimson took his claws out, and whacked the jackals. Blood fell on the ground, as the jackals landed near the lake. Crimson pounced on the jackals, and stabbed his claws in to their chest. The jackals laid on the ground, as blood poured out of their body. Crimson walked in to the lake, and cleaned his fur. Crimson shook the water out of his fur. Crimson smiled as he walked toward his log. Crimson sat on the log and listened to the tweeting birds. Butterflies were flying over the lake, while the water was shining. It was an wonderful sight for Crimson to watch. Sam and Emily sat on the log with Crimson! Sam and Emily hugged Crimson, while the birds tweeted in the background! The sun was setting, as the wind blew through Crimson's fur. The water in the lake was shining with the moon reflecting on it. The birds flew over the lake. Emily kissed Crimson on the head and said, "I love you, Crimson! I am glad that you are my son." Crimson said, "I love you too, Emily!" Crimson kissed Emily on her head and hugged her with his paws. Emily and Crimson smiled at each other. Sam moved closer to Crimson and Emily, and hugged them with his paws. The family of foxes smiled at the moon, while the wind blew through their fur.

Section Break 3

Spider Crusader:
1. Supersonic Warrior vs the Shopping Carts
2. Supersonic Warrior: Becoming An Superhero
3. Supersonic Warrior: Escape From Electric Industries
4. Supersonic Warrior: Fire vs Ice
5. Supersonic Warrior: Finding Love
6. Supersonic Warrior: Shattered Love
7. Supersonic Warrior: Consumed By Darkness
8. Supersonic Warrior: Taking Down The Darkness
9. Fire Slinger: Battling Through Post Depression
10. Fire Slinger: Despair
11. Spider Crusader: Destruction Of Zoomopolis

10

On an stormy night, an car was speeding through the city with rain drops hitting the windows. An small black kitten was in the back seat of the car, with his paws outside the window. The car hit an bump and an lightning bolt hit the car. Echo, the small black kitten, got spooked and fell out of the window into the parking lot of an grocery store called World of Food. The parking lot was filled with scary cars zooming everywhere. Echo got scared and ran towards the vending machine. Echo got to the vending machine, and he started whacking the buttons on it. The machine shook and he got scared, and ran behind the vending machine. Echo was cowering in fear behind the machine and he was crying in meows. He was so scared! He was in an new world and he didn't know what to do. The night got even worse for him though! The shopping carts came alive, and started growling and howling. The shopping carts pounced while growling into the vending machine. The vending machine fell over and spooked Echo! Echo was terrified and he was cowering in fear. The shopping carts were about to tear him apart and Echo was too scared to respond. World of Food was about to close down for the night, and the employees looked out the window. The employees saw the commotion outside. Justin, one of the World of Food employees, tapped Christina on the shoulder and said, "You should probably help the kitten outside, our shopping carts are about to tear him apart." Christina said, "I agree, the kitten will get badly injured." Christina went outside towards the vending machine. Christina stopped at the vending machine, and saw the growling shopping carts with the terrified black kitten. Christina jumped into action! She took out her superhero device and yelled out "Lets Go Supersonic!" An explosion of rainbow energy surrounded Christina and she transformed into Supersonic Warrior. Supersonic Warrior charged into the shopping carts and knocked them into the air. She roundhouse kicked them into the vending machine. The shopping carts got mad and growled in anger. Echo was terrified and hid in the corner. The shopping carts pounced at Supersonic Warrior, and bit her on the arm. Their fangs were attached to her arm, and the shopping carts shook Supersonic Warrior and threw her into the air. One of the shopping carts jumped in the air and kicked Supersonic Warrior in the chest. Supersonic Warrior was sent flying into the side of the grocery store. The shopping carts grinned and walked closer to their prey as the Supersonic Warrior laid next to the wall. The shopping carts pounced at the Supersonic Warrior, but she outsmarted them. Supersonic Warrior punched them backwards with an Lightning Punch from her arm. One of the shopping carts were defeated and disappeared into dust, but his buddy didn't like that. The other shopping cart got super mad and howled. The shopping cart powered up from his howling and an aura of red energy surrounded it. The shopping cart grinned with his fangs out, and he zoomed straight at Supersonic Warrior. Supersonic Warrior responded with an roundhouse kick. The shopping cart dodged and countered with an flying punch. Supersonic Warrior fell back and rolled on to the ground. The shopping cart opened his mouth, and blew super hard to create an huge gust of wind. Supersonic Warrior took out her sword and threw it like an boomerang at the shopping cart. The sword hit the shopping cart on the side of his head, and the shopping cart screamed in pain. The shopping cart regained his thoughts, and he shot out an energy beam from his mouth. Supersonic Warrior summoned an energy shield with her sword to block the energy beam. The shopping cart's aura powered up the energy beam, and the beam grew bigger. Supersonic Warrior said an enchantment by shouting, "Supersonic Enchant!", and the energy shield got enchanted, and deflected the energy beam back into the shopping cart. There was an huge explosion when the energy beam hit the shopping cart. The explosion smashed Supersonic Warrior into the grocery store, that shattered multiple windows, and the shopping cart got pushed back an couple of feet, and he was enraged. The fangs on the shopping carts sharpened as the Supersonic Warrior got up and was catching her breath. The shopping cart zoomed at Supersonic Warrior. Supersonic Warrior rocket kicked the shopping cart into the air. The shopping cart smashed into the ground, and evaporated into dust. The dust cleared and Supersonic Warrior breathed an sigh of relief as she was brushing the dirt and dust off of her suit. Echo was hiding behind the vending machine, trying to hide himself with his paws. Supersonic Warrior walked to the vending machine and bended down to comfort the kitten. Supersonic Warrior said calmly, "It's ok, little buddy, I won't hurt you. I am not with the scary monsters, I am an friendly superhero, it is my job to make sure that you are safe." Echo walked closer to the Supersonic Warrior, and started growling. Echo had an stressful life, and didn't like trusting strangers. Echo pounced and grabbed Supersonic Warrior's arm. Supersonic Warrior screamed in pain as Echo started using his claws on her. Supersonic Warrior calmed down, and thought, "If I calm him down, The pain will go away." Supersonic Warrior started petting Echo and he stopped scratching her arm. Echo leaped off of her arm and started purring. Supersonic Warrior said an spell, "Supersonic Cat Food!", and summoned an can of cat food with her sword. She opened it up for Echo to snack on. Echo munched on the cat food and was purring happily. Supersonic Warrior demorphed in an flash of rainbow energy! Christina comforted Echo and was petting him. Echo was smiling while he was munching his cat food. Christina walked over to her car and opened it up. She got out her cat carrier and walked back to Echo. She set the cat carrier down in front of Echo. Echo was interested, and he started smelling and checking out the cat carrier. Christina said, "I am going to take you home, little buddy. The world is unsafe for you!" Echo was interested, and he started whacking at the cat carrier. Christina opened the cat carrier, and locked Echo inside. She walked to her car with the cat carrier. She opened the car, and put the cat carrier in the back seat. Christina started up the car, and drove out of the parking lot. Echo and Christina drove off into the sunset back to their house.

It was an bright and sunny day in Zoomopolis. Zoomopolis was filled with young and old citizens, living their lives to survive. In Zoomopolis, there was an red house with an shiny roof. This house was owned by Morgan and Matt. Morgan and Matt have an daughter named Christina. In your heads, you might think this is an normal family surviving their lives by arguing about financial problems and craziness every day, while their daughter tries to deal with them. This is not the case, since something crazy was about to happen and the family didn't know about it. Morgan and Matt were making breakfast in the kitchen, while the news station was playing on the television in the background. Morgan was making bacon on the stove, and Matt was making toast in the toaster. In the background, the news station reported, "Crazy Max has been spotted near Oasis Falls High School, please keep all students safe!" Matt said to Morgan, "Isn't that the school that our daughter is attending?" Morgan said, "Yes, but I am trying to cook bacon, don't distract me!" The bacon and the toast catches on fire! The smoke alarm goes off in the house! Morgan said, "AHHHHHHHHHHHHHHH, you idiot, you made me burn the bacon! This is what happens when you distract me." Matt said, "No, it is the television's fault for distracting us, it put that news report in our head." Christina was getting ready for school by styling her hair in her room. She heard the commotion in the background and went toward the kitchen to check on her mom and dad. Christina said, "Is everything ok?" Matt said, "Yes, sweetheart, we were just turning off the smoke alarm." Christina said,

"OK, I am heading off to school, see you later!" Christina walks out the door toward the sidewalk. Christina walked on to the sidewalk toward the school bus. On the side of the sidewalk, there was an group of bushes that can camouflage anyone that is hiding in them. In the bushes, there was an shadowed figure that is ready to cause chaos and despair to the city. The shadowed figure said, "Let's launch the fireworks!" The shadowed figure laughs as he pushes the button on his wrist. Christina's house blows up in an fiery explosion. Matt and Morgan's bodies are lying on the ground in an puddle of blood. The shadowed figure does an maniacal laugh that echoes through the area. The shadowed figure said, "That was fun, It is time to add to the chaos and despair." Christina was on the school bus, heading off to school. She didn't know what chaos that the shadowed figure was about to bring to her life. The school bus arrived at Oasis Falls High School, and there were police cars surrounding the area. At the school flag, in the center of the campus was an muscular man that weighed 300 pounds. He was wearing an leather jacket, red pants, and military boots. His hair was orange, spiky, and stylized like an Japanese character. There were several police officers surrounding him with their guns pointed out. Sam, one of the police officers, took out his megaphone. Sam shouted, "You are under arrest, Crazy Max! Surrender Now, and no one gets hurt!" Crazy Max laughs and says, "Surrender, you are so funny! The fun is about to begin!" Daniel, one of the police officers, decided to jump in on the action, and charged toward Crazy Max with his gun out. Sam shouted, "No, Daniel, It is too risky, we don't know how dangerous that he could be." Sam tried to reach for Daniel's arm. Daniel pushed Sam's arm away, and roundhouse kicked Sam in the chest. Sam fell on to the ground and growled, "You idiot, you will get yourself killed!" Daniel said, "This is for the team's safety!" Daniel charged toward Crazy Max and shot his gun at his chest. The bullet hit Crazy Max's chest with an small blood mark. Crazy Max said, "Nice shot, kid! You made me lose some blood, but it wasn't good enough." Daniel was shocked, that his gun barely made an mark. Crazy Max laughed as he charged toward Daniel. Daniel shot his gun multiple times at Crazy Max. The bullets hit Crazy Max, but he was still charging at Daniel. Crazy Max said, "This is pathetic for an police officer, Police Officers are supposed to be brave and courageous, and you are just disrespecting your team." Crazy Max takes out his whip, and throws it at Daniel. The whip wraps around Daniel, and Crazy Max drags Daniel closer to him. Crazy Max unwraps the whip, and kicks Daniel in the chest with his leg. Daniel falls on the ground in pain. Crazy Max punches Daniel into the ground multiple times. An puddle of blood appears underneath Daniel as he tries to catch his breath. Crazy Max laughs and says, "An pathetic soul in an body, It makes me smile to see it break so easily." Crazy Max picks up Daniel by his neck, and he squeezes his neck as Daniel struggles to breathe. Daniel coughs and says, "Have mercy, monster!" Crazy Max smiled and said, "This is part of the fun!" Crazy Max throws Daniel in the air and he roundhouse kicks Daniel in to the flag pole. Daniel smashes into the flag pole, knocking it over. Daniel tries to catch his breath, as he tries to stand up. Crazy Max towers over him and said, "Surrender Now, or your entire team will die!" Daniel shouted, "NEVER!", and he charged toward Crazy Max, while resisting the pain that he was in. Crazy Max said, "Then, you must die with your team!" Crazy Max charged toward Daniel, and lightning punches him in the chest. Daniel stumbled and fell backwards. Crazy Max grabbed Daniel by the neck, while squeezing to prevent Daniel from breathing. Crazy Max throws Daniel in the air, and body slams him into the ground. Daniel smashes in to the ground, and doesn't move at all. Crazy Max picks up Daniel's body, and punches him in the chest. Daniel lies on the ground with an huge puddle of blood underneath his lifeless body. The rest of the police officers were terrified! Crazy Max takes out his throwing daggers and throws them at the police officers. The throwing daggers hit the police officers in the chest, and their lifeless bodies fall on to the ground in puddles of blood. Crazy Max smiled as he grabs the throwing daggers like an boomerang, and puts them in his pocket. The students saw the entire scene outside the school bus windows, and they were shocked with horror. Peter, the school bus driver, said to the students, "I think it is safe to leave the school bus. The bloodshed from the crazy lunatic, Crazy Max, has calmed down." Christina's body was shaking in fear as she was trying to focus. Justin, one of the students, noticed Christina shaking, and said to the bus driver, "The chaos has calmed down, but there is something wrong with Christina." Peter said, "She'll be fine, her body vitals will be back to normal once she walks to class. That fight was pretty intense to watch." The school bus driver opened the doors and decided to let the students off. Christina stood up from her seat, and started to walk to the doors. There was an loud beeping in the background, and students were covering their ears. Crazy Max was hiding behind the tree, and smiled. Crazy Max said, "The students fell right into my trap!" Crazy Max presses an button on his wrist, and the school bus explodes in an fiery explosion. Christina ran super fast and dived out of the school bus on to the sidewalk covering her ears. School bus parts went flying everywhere, bouncing off of trees and other cars in the area. The school bus drivers and the students were on the ground, lying dead in puddles of blood. Crazy Max leaves for his hideout on his glider. Christina was lying on the ground, with her arms and legs bruised. The principal of the school, Edward, walked over to Christina and said, "Wow, you survived the explosion, That was pretty lucky of you. I was so worried about you, since you were our top student at the school." The principal helped Christina up on her feet and they walked to the school. Edward said, "Let me walk you to our science lab! In our science lab, we are working on the Supersonic Project. The Supersonic Project enhances the abilities of an human being and makes them stronger." Christina said, "Sounds Interesting!" Edward said, "Someone needs to take care of Crazy Max, he is causing chaos in our city, and from that fight, we know that the police can't handle him. With our project, we might have an chance to stop Crazy Max for good." Christina nodded and walked to the science lab with Edward. Edward and Christina were at the science lab, and they opened the door to walk in. Edward introduced Christina to Sam, one of the scientists that worked on the Supersonic Project. Edward said, "Sam is my best friend, and one of our top scientists at the school. He has spent multiple months testing and configuring the machine to make sure that the Supersonic Project was safe to use." Sam said, "Yep, we are going to plug you in to the machine and enhance your abilities. If you don't feel good, or something is wrong, let us know, and we will try to turn off the machine. We don't want any accidents occurring at the school." Christina nodded and grabbed Sam's hand. Sam and Christina walked over to the machine. Sam opened up the pod on the machine! Christina stepped into the machine and laid her arms on her side. Sam strapped Christina into the machine, and closed up the pod. Sam pressed some buttons on the machine panel, and walked behind his barrier for safety. The machine started up and the gears in the pod started turning. Sam, Edward, and the group of scientists were watching behind the barrier. An explosion of rainbow energy happened inside the machine as the gears were turning. The gears slow down and stop, and the panel shows the message, "Process Complete!" Sam walked out from behind the barrier to the machine. He unlocked the pod and unstrapped Christina. Sam held out his hand and helped Christina out of the machine. Sam said, "Keep it nice and slow, your body isn't used to its new abilities. We don't want you injuring yourself, the effects will wear off as your body gets used to its new form." Christina nodded as she held Sam's hand. Sam and Christina walked over to the cooler in the science lab! Sam grabbed an water bottle from the cooler and gave it to Christina. Sam said, "Drink Up, this is to rehydrate after the body enhancements." Christina nods, and she unscrews the bottle cap and chugs down the water bottle. Christina said, "The water tasted so refreshing, and brought relief to my body. I feel refreshed, since my life has been crazy." Sam said, "What Happened?" Christina said, "I witnessed multiple deaths today that Crazy Max caused. He killed my parents when I got on the school bus, he killed an team of police officers, and he killed the school bus driver, and fellow students. My life has been an mess, and I want revenge on Crazy Max." Sam said, "I have an device that my team created that will help you get revenge on Crazy Max"

Sam took out an superhero device from his pocket. Sam said, "This device is called the Supersonic Link! It links you to the superhero morphing network, and transforms you into the Supersonic Warrior! When you say the activation phrase, Lets Go Supersonic!, the superhero morphing network will fuse an spandex suit to your body, and transforms you into the Supersonic Warrior. Supersonic Warrior's suit comes with the ability to heal damage that is caused to it during an fight. When you are the Supersonic Warrior, you get to use your body enhancements to fight and take down super villains with ease like Crazy Max." Christina nodded and said, "That sounds awesome, I am ready for action!" Sam smiled, and handed Christina the device. Sam said, "Good, Lets show Crazy Max that his reign of chaos is over." Sam said, "Before we go after Crazy Max, lets give the device an test run, so it doesn't malfunction while you are out beating up super villains." Christina agreed to the idea and nodded. Sam said, "OK, to activate the device and transform into the Supersonic Warrior, just shout Let's Go Supersonic, and the transformation process will start." Christina nodded and took out the device. She raised her arm out in front of her and shouted, "Let's Go Supersonic!" An explosion of rainbow energy surrounded her, and she transformed into the Supersonic Warrior. Sam smiled and said, "Perfect, how does the suit feel?" Supersonic Warrior said, "The suit feels great, it is like an breathe of fresh air. Crazy Max will be scared, when I come after him." Sam said, "Let's analyze your muscle mass and your punching power." Supersonic Warrior nodded and said, "Sounds Good!" Sam and Supersonic Warrior walk over to the punching bag in the science lab. Sam said, "Punch the punching bag as hard as you can, and I will analyze your muscle mass and punching power on my machine." Supersonic Warrior nodded and punched the punching bag multiple times and finished off with an Lightning Punch. The punching bag spun around its stand multiple times. Sam smiled, "Muscle mass and punching power looks good." Supersonic Warrior said, "What's the next test?" Sam said, "Your next test is your strength! To analyze your strength, lift up the 200 pound cooler right in front of us." Supersonic Warrior nodded and lifted the 200 pound cooler over her head with both of her arms easily without struggling. Sam smiled and said, "Perfect! Your final test is acrobatics. Do multiple flips in the air, and do an spinning roundhouse kick in to the cardboard cutout." Supersonic Warrior set down the cooler back onto the floor, and nodded at Sam. Supersonic Warrior flipped in the air multiple times, and did an spinning roundhouse kick in to the cardboard cutout. Supersonic Warrior lands on her feet and poses. The cardboard cutout explodes and cardboard flied everywhere. Sam smiled and said, "Perfect, you did great!" Sam walks over and hugs Supersonic Warrior and says, "I am glad that our science project worked out great" Supersonic Warrior hugs Sam back, "Me Too, buddy, Lets show Crazy Max that his fun is over." Sam said, "I agree, the world needs an protector, and we don't need chaos ruining our world." Supersonic Warrior and Sam fist bump and high five each other. Supersonic Warrior demorphs in an flash of rainbow energy. Sam gives Christina an water bottle. Lets rehydrate your body from the fun workout. Christina nodded and chugs down the water bottle. Christina smiled as the refreshing water rehydrates her body. Sam said, "Your body should be good and stable to go after Crazy Max." Edward walked over and said, "I have heard reports of Crazy Max being near World of Medicine. Christina might want to check it out." Sam said, "Be safe, Crazy Max is pretty dangerous, we don't want you getting injured." Christina nodded and walked out of the science lab. World of Medicine employees were restocking shelves and taking care of customers, until an glider landed in front of the store. Crazy Max got off the glider and walked in to the store. Crazy Max said, "I am looking for some pills to enhance my body?" Justin said, "I am sorry, but we ran out of them last week, and our delivery truck hasn't come in yet." Crazy Max set up some of his explosives on the store display stands and the foundation. Justin said, "I am sorry, I wish I had those pills for you" Crazy Max stands up and gets angry! Crazy Max grabs Justin by the throat and squeezes super hard. Crazy Max said, "I need those pills to crush my enemies." Justin said wile trying to breathe, "I am sorry, but we don't have them in stock."

Crazy Max smashes Justin into the wall! Justin falls on to the ground, bleeding. Christina was walking outside the store, and noticed the commotion. Christina said, "Looks like Crazy Max is causing some trouble!" Crazy Max said, "Time for some fireworks!" Crazy Max pushes an button on his wrist, and World of Medicine explodes in an fiery explosion. The lifeless bodies of Justin, the other World of Medicine employees, and the customers were on the ground, with an huge puddle of blood flowing from under them. Christina ducks behind an tree. Crazy Max walks through the debris and says, "That was fun, time for chaos!" Christina jumps out from the tree and says, "Stop right there, Crazy Max, your reign of terror is over." Crazy Max laughs and says, "I am your worst nightmare!" Christina said, "I have had crazier nightmares than you!" Christina takes out her superhero device and says, "Let's Go Supersonic!" An flash of rainbow energy transforms Christina into the Supersonic Warrior. Supersonic Warrior said, "Let's have some fun!" Crazy Max said, "Feel the world of pain that I will bring down on you." Supersonic Warrior takes out his gun and fires it at Crazy Max. Crazy Max dodges the bullets and the bullets hit the tree. Crazy Max zooms into Supersonic Warrior and uppercuts her in the neck. Supersonic Warrior slides backwards. Crazy Max roundhouse kicks Supersonic Warrior in the chest! Supersonic Warrior slides into an tree, and hangs on to the tree to keep her footing. Supersonic Warrior picks up an car, and throws it at Crazy Max. Crazy Max gets hit by the car and smashes into the building. Car pieces fly everywhere as Crazy Max catches his breath and stands up. Crazy Max picks up the car doors and zooms into Supersonic Warrior. Crazy Max said, "Nice shot, kid, but it is time for me to cause some pain and suffering." Crazy Max kicks Supersonic Warrior in the chest with his leg. Supersonic Warrior said, "It was just an little bit of pain!" Crazy Max smiles and said, "That's not all!" Crazy Max punches Supersonic Warrior in the chest multiple times with the car doors. Supersonic Warrior screams in pain. Crazy Max roundhouse kicks Supersonic Warrior in the chest. Supersonic Warrior slams into the car and it explodes. The explosion smashes Supersonic Warrior into the building. Supersonic Warrior gets up, while catching her breath. Crazy Max walks over and said, "The pain will be over soon!" Supersonic Warrior lightning punches Crazy Max in the chest. Crazy Max slides backwards. Supersonic Warrior flips in the air and said, "Supersonic Drill!" The Supersonic Drill appears in Supersonic Warrior's arm, and she zooms into Crazy Max. Supersonic Warrior punches Crazy Max's chest with the Supersonic Drill. Crazy Max smashes into the World of Movies display, and glass flies everywhere. Crazy Max's face is bleeding, and there is an puddle of blood forming as he stands up to catch his breath. Supersonic Warrior walks toward her prey! Crazy Max said, "Have mercy, I am injured! If you defeat me here, It will be an unfair fight." Supersonic Warrior said, "You're an monster, you have caused chaos to the city." Crazy Max said, "I am an monster, but it would be unfair for an superhero to finish off their enemies when they are injured." Supersonic Warrior said, "You're right, lets finish this fight later." Crazy Max gets up and summons his glider. Supersonic Warrior walks out of World of Movies and hides behind an tree. Supersonic Warrior demorphs in an flash of rainbow energy. Crazy Max walks on to his glider and flew back to his hideout. Christina walks back to Oasis Falls High School to rehydrate her body at the science lab. Down the road in an huge building owned by Electric Industries is Crazy Max's hideout. Crazy Max's hideout is filled with gadgets and weapons to cause chaos and despair. Crazy Max lands inside the hideout on his glider. He walks off the glider toward his scientist named Adrian. Crazy Max picks Adrian by the neck and said, "Make me stronger! That pest, Supersonic Warrior humiliated me when I was terrorizing the employees at World of Medicine. I want Supersonic Warrior to suffer!" Adrian coughs and tries to breathe. Adrian said, "With this machine, I can increase your strength by 20%!" Crazy Max said, "Good, I want my enemies to suffer with pain!" Crazy Max sets Adrian back on to the ground. Adrian and Crazy Max walk over to the machine. Adrian opens up the machine and starts up the panel. Crazy Max walks into the machine and plugs himself in. Adrian presses some buttons on the panel and starts up the machine. The machine shakes, and the muscles on Crazy Max's body grow in mass. The machine dings and the process is complete. Adrian unlocks the machine and unplugs Crazy Max. Crazy Max walks out, feeling refreshed and ready for chaos. Adrian said, "How do you feel?" Crazy Max said, "I feel great, Supersonic Warrior won't know the pain that I will cause to her." Adrian said, "I have also added enhancements to your glider, and added an missile launcher and an rocket launcher." Crazy Max said, "Perfect enhancements to cause despair and mayhem!" Adrian said, "There is an warehouse filled with valuable resources for Zoomopolis down the road that would be perfect for us to destroy." Crazy Max said, "I will head there right now, and destroy the resources." Crazy Max walks on to his glider and flies out of the hideout. Christina walks into the science lab at Oasis Falls High School. Sam said, "How are you feeling? We saw your fight with Crazy Max, and it was intense." Christina said, "I feel good, and the suit handled pretty well during the fight." Sam said, "That's good, buddy!" Sam hands Christina an water bottle. Sam said, "Here's some water to rehydrate your body." Christina said, "Thanks, you're the best!" Christina chugs down the water bottle, and throws the empty bottle into the trash can. Christina said, "The water tasted nice and refreshing!" Sam said, "It's time for an small workout!" Christina said, "Sounds good, An small workout would be nice to keep my body healthy." Christina takes out her superhero device and says, "Lets Go Supersonic!" An flash of rainbow energy forms and Christina transforms into Supersonic Warrior. Sam said, "Perfect, let's start with some jogging!" Supersonic Warrior jogs in place and Sam keeps track of the stats on his clipboard. Sam said, "Looks good!" Supersonic Warrior stops jogging in place! Sam said, "Good Job, our next activity is 500 jumping jacks." Supersonic Warrior does 500 jumping jacks without breaking an sweat. Sam said, "Perfect, your final activity is punching this dummy figure of Crazy Max!" Supersonic Warrior punches the dummy figure of Crazy Max until the figure's head flew off. Sam said, "Perfect, your physical abilities are in the green zone." Supersonic Warrior said, "Awesome, my body is nice and healthy!" Sam said, "Yep, you did great during the workout!" Sam hugs Supersonic Warrior and said, "You are so warm and soft to cuddle." Supersonic Warrior hugs Sam back and said, "Yep, it is so nice to wear!" Sam said, "I installed heated padding into your suit to keep you warm while you were battling supervillains." Supersonic Warrior said, "That's awesome, you always think of everything." Sam said, "Are you ticklish in any parts of your body?" Supersonic Warrior said, "Yes, I am pretty ticklish!" Sam tickles Supersonic Warrior's chest! Supersonic Warrior starts laughing! Sam said while tickling Supersonic Warrior, "How do you feel?" Supersonic Warrior continues laughing and says, "I feel great, I haven't been tickled in an while." Supersonic Warrior tickles Sam's chest! Sam starts laughing! Supersonic Warrior said, "This is fun!" Sam said, "I agree, tickling each other is so much fun." Supersonic Warrior and Sam continued tickling each other. Edward walks in and says, "Sorry to interrupt your fun, but there's an building on fire down the street and an kid is trapped in the building." Sam stops tickling Supersonic Warrior and said, "Oh No, Supersonic Warrior, you have to check it out and save the kid from danger." Supersonic Warrior stops laughing and tickling Sam! Supersonic Warrior said, "I agree, the fire will spread and endanger the kid, if we don't handle it." Supersonic Warrior demorphs in an flash of rainbow energy. Sam hands Christina an water bottle. Christina chugs it down and throws the empty bottle in to the trash can. Christina walks out of the science lab. Christina walked down the street and saw the building on fire. Anha ran down the street panicking, and ran into Christina. Christina said, "Calm down, what's the problem?" Anha said, "Help me, my son is trapped in the building that's on fire." Christina said, "What's your son's name?" Anha said, "His name is Ian, he got trapped in his room, when the fire started. I couldn't save him, so I decided to save my own life and run out of the house." Christina said, "I will save your son for you, don't worry." Christina hides behind an tree and takes out her superhero device. Christina said "Let's Go Supersonic!", and an flash of rainbow energy transforms her into the Supersonic Warrior. Supersonic Warrior runs into the burning building and smashes down the door with her leg. Supersonic Warrior walks around and said, "Whew, it's pretty toasty in here with all of the flames! I wonder where the kid could be?" Ian yells in the background, "Help!, I am trapped!" Supersonic Warrior said, "I'm coming, hold on!" Supersonic Warrior runs up the stairs and kicks down the wood blocking the path. Supersonic Warrior gets to the top of the stairs, and she gets hit by an explosion from the flames. Supersonic Warrior smashes in to the wall and falls on the ground. Supersonic Warrior said, "I have to be careful, this building is falling part from the inside by the flames." Supersonic Warrior gets up and walks around to look for Ian. Supersonic Warrior walks toward an door with an poster of Ian's favorite video game character, Lightning the Hedgehog. Supersonic Warrior said, "This must be Ian's room, The poster looks pretty cool." Supersonic Warrior kicks down the door to Ian's room and walks in. Ian said, "Who are you?" Supersonic Warrior walks over to Ian and said, "I am your rescuer, your mom is worried about you." Ian said, "Yeah, the fire is scary, I got trapped in my room, and my mom left me to save herself." Supersonic Warrior said, "The fire is spreading, and your room is burnt up." Ian said while depressed, "Yep, the fire made me lose my action figure collection. They are melted and ruined." Supersonic Warrior bends down, and comforts Ian by rubbing his back. Supersonic Warrior said, "Everything will be fine, climb onto my back and I will get you out of the burning building safely." Ian nods in agreement, and climbs onto Supersonic Warrior's back. Ian said, "You are so soft and warm to cuddle, like an stuffed animal." Supersonic Warrior said, "Yep, my suit has heated padding, and hang on tight. I don't want you getting injured." Ian nods, and he hangs onto Supersonic Warrior tightly by wrapping his arms around her. Supersonic Warrior runs down the hallway and dives out of the window. The glass in the windows shatter, as flames blast through them. Supersonic Warrior rolls on to the ground and lands safely without getting injured. Ian gets down on to the ground! Supersonic Warrior said, "We made it out of the building safely." Ian said, "Yep, I wouldn't of survived without your help. Thanks for protecting me, Supersonic Warrior." Supersonic

Warrior bends down and fist bumps Ian. Ian fist bumps Supersonic Warrior back! Anha runs toward Supersonic Warrior and Ian! Anha said, "Ian, you're safe!" Ian said, "Yes, Mom, the nice superhero helped me!" Anha and Ian hug each other! Anha said, "Supersonic Warrior, thanks for saving my son. You're the best." Supersonic Warrior nodded and said, "No Problem, It is part of being an superhero to keep everyone safe." Anha hugs Supersonic Warrior and said, "Stay Safe, you've inspired my son to stay positive! Supersonic Warrior hugs Anha back and said, "I hope your family stays safe too!" Ian and Anha walk down the street and wave goodbye to Supersonic Warrior. Supersonic Warrior wave back to them!Supersonic Warrior walks down the street, when the communicator on his wrist starts blinking. Supersonic Warrior presses the button on his wrist to answer the call. Supersonic Warrior said, "Is everything alright?" Sam said, "Everything is good at the lab, we have detected Crazy Max on our radar. He is flying toward your location on his glider. Keep your eye out for him, and be careful! According to our visuals, his glider has some upgrades and Crazy Max got some new tricks up his sleeve as well." Supersonic Warrior said, "Sounds good, I will keep an eye out for his glider." Sam said, "Stay safe, buddy!" Supersonic Warrior said, "I hope you stay safe as well." Supersonic Warrior presses the button on his wrist to end the call. Supersonic Warrior continues walking down the street, keeping an eye out for Crazy Max's glider. An glider zooms into Supersonic Warrior and smashes him into the building. Supersonic Warrior gets up as Crazy Max walks off of the glider. Crazy Max said, "I hope you are ready for pain and suffering." Supersonic Warrior said, "Your reign of chaos and despair is over, Crazy Max!" Crazy Max runs toward Supersonic Warrior and tackles her into the ground. Crazy Max punches Supersonic Warrior in the face, multiple times. Supersonic Warrior grabs Crazy Max's arm, and kicks him in the face with her leg. Crazy Max slides backwards! Supersonic Warrior gets up and picks up an car! Supersonic Warrior throws the car at Crazy Max! The car smashes into Crazy Max, and it smashes him into the building! Crazy Max laid against the building, catching his breath.

Supersonic Warrior walks toward her prey! Crazy Max gets up and uses his whip on Supersonic Warrior! The whip wraps around Supersonic Warrior's neck, and Crazy Max pulls Supersonic Warrior toward him. Crazy Max punches Supersonic Warrior in the chest! Supersonic Warrior kicks Crazy Max in the leg! Crazy Max grabs Supersonic Warrior by the neck. Crazy Max body slams Supersonic Warrior into an car, and the car explodes. Supersonic Warrior falls on to the ground, and the whip recoils back to Crazy Max. Supersonic Warrior slowly gets up as she catches her breath. Supersonic Warrior flips in the air, kicks Crazy Max in the face and back flips off of him. Crazy Max slides backwards and zooms into Supersonic Warrior! Supersonic Warrior grabs an street sign out of the ground, and hits Crazy Max with it. Crazy Max slides backwards into an pole! The pole smashes on to the ground! Crazy Max throws an car at Supersonic Warrior! Supersonic Warrior flips in the air and dodges the car. Supersonic Warrior lands on an tree and said, "Supersonic Drill!" , and she shoots it at Crazy Max. The Supersonic Drill hits Crazy Max, drilling him into the building. The building explodes and the debris falls on top of Crazy Max. Supersonic Warrior backflips out of the tree, and lands on the ground. Crazy Max gets angry and picks up the building debris and throws it at Supersonic Warrior. Supersonic Warrior catches the debris, and throws it at Crazy Max, knocking him on to the ground. Crazy Max gets up and said, "Time for an little joy ride, Supersonic Warrior!" Crazy Max pushes an button on his wrist to summon his glider. The glider flies toward Crazy Max! Crazy Max walks on to the glider, and he threw his whip at Supersonic Warrior. The whip wraps around Supersonic Warrior, and Crazy Max pulls her on to the glider. Crazy Max recoils the whip and the glider flies in to the air. Supersonic Warrior and Crazy Max are standing on the glider, as the glider flies on its own. Supersonic Warrior roundhouse kicks Crazy Max in the face. Crazy Max slides backwards! Supersonic Warrior grabs Crazy Max by the neck and body slams Crazy Max in to the glider's floor. The glider starts to go out of control and starts flying through the glass window of an building. Crazy Max gets up and sweeps his legs under Supersonic Warrior. Supersonic Warrior trips and falls on to the floor of the glider. Crazy Max punches Supersonic Warrior in the face! Supersonic Warrior grabs Crazy Max's arm, and kicks him in the face. Crazy Max stumbles backwards! Supersonic Warrior kicks Crazy Max in the chest. Crazy Max falls off the glider, and hangs on to the edge with his hand. Crazy Max gets back on to the glider. Crazy Max roundhouse kicks Supersonic Warrior in the chest. Supersonic Warrior falls off the glider, and hangs on the edge with her hand. Supersonic Warrior flips in the air, roundhouse kicks Crazy Max in the face, and lands back on the glider. Crazy Max slides backwards and tackles Supersonic Warrior on to the glider's floor. Crazy Max punches Supersonic Warrior in the chest. Supersonic Warrior kicks him in to the air and body slams Crazy Max in to the glider's floor. Crazy Max gets up and catches his breath. The glider flied to the top of the abandoned warehouse! Crazy Max said, "Here's our stop!" Crazy Max grabs Supersonic Warrior by the neck and throws her off the glider! Crazy Max jumps on top of Supersonic Warrior, smashing her through the abandoned warehouse. Supersonic Warrior gets up as an puddle of blood drips from her arm. Crazy Max pushes an button on his wrist, and the glider flies down towards the bottom of the abandoned warehouse. The glider shoots an rocket at Supersonic Warrior. Supersonic Warrior smashes through the walls of the abandoned warehouse! An wall of warehouse debris fell on top of Supersonic Warrior. An puddle of blood formed under Supersonic Warrior. Supersonic Warrior gets up as Crazy Max walks toward his prey. Crazy Max kicks Supersonic Warrior in the chest! Supersonic Warrior slides backwards. Crazy Max roundhouse kicks Supersonic Warrior in the face. Supersonic Warrior smashes into the wall and stumbles backwards. Crazy Max tackles Supersonic Warrior to the ground and the wall falls on top of them. Crazy Max punches Supersonic Warrior in the face multiple times. Blood leaks out of Supersonic Warrior's suit as an puddle forms. Crazy Max continues punching Supersonic Warrior as the puddle grows. Supersonic Warrior's visor breaks as she holds Crazy Max's arm back with her strength. Supersonic Warrior growls as she kicks Crazy Max in the face with her leg. Crazy Max stumbles backwards as Supersonic Warrior gets up! Blood is leaking out of her helmet as she roundhouse kicks Crazy Max in the chest. Crazy Max smashes into the wall. Supersonic Warrior said, "Supersonic Drill!", and the Supersonic Drill summons in her hands. Supersonic Warrior runs into Crazy Max and punches him with the Supersonic Drill. Crazy Max smashes through multiple walls! Crazy Max falls on to the ground in an puddle of blood, with blood leaking from his chest. Supersonic Warrior walks up to Crazy Max! Supersonic Warrior said, "You must pay for the chaos that you have done to the city." Supersonic Warrior picks up Crazy Max by the neck while squeezing, kicks him in the chest with her leg, and body slams him into the ground. Crazy Max coughs while he laid on the ground, struggling to get up. Supersonic Warrior said, "Suffer the pain, you deserve it for ruining everyone's lives." Supersonic Warrior steps on Crazy Max's chest, holding him down as she punches him in the face multiple times. Blood leaks from Crazy Max's face as Supersonic Warrior punches him. Crazy Max tries to hold back Supersonic Warrior's arm, but she grabs Crazy Max's arm and breaks it in half. Crazy Max screams in pain, as Supersonic Warrior steps harder on Crazy Max's chest, making it hard for Crazy Max to breathe. Crazy Max roundhouse kicks Supersonic Warrior in the face. Supersonic Warrior slides backwards! Crazy Max tackles Supersonic Warrior to the ground. Crazy Max punches Supersonic Warrior in the face multiple times, as blood leaks from her helmet. Supersonic Warrior growls as she grabs Crazy Max's neck with her hand and chokes him. Crazy Max coughs as Supersonic Warrior roundhouse kicks him in the face. Crazy Max slides backwards and smashes into an wall. Crazy Max walks slowly to Supersonic Warrior as blood leaks from his body. Crazy Max kicks Supersonic Warrior in the chest! Supersonic Warrior grabs Crazy Max's leg and breaks it in half. Crazy Max screams in pain, as he stumbles backwards. Supersonic Warrior tears an pillar out of the warehouse foundation and she hits Crazy Max in the chest with it. Crazy Max stumbles as blood splashes on to the ground. Supersonic Warrior smashes Crazy

Max in to the ground with the pillar. Crazy Max falls on the ground laying in an puddle of blood. Supersonic Warrior said, "Die, you monster!" Supersonic Warrior smashes Crazy Max in the face with the pillar multiple times. Crazy Max said while coughing, "Have mercy!" Supersonic Warrior said, "Monsters like you don't deserve to have mercy." Supersonic Warrior sets the pillar down. Supersonic Warrior grabs Crazy Max by the neck, breaks his neck by squeezing super tightly, and throws him in to the air. Supersonic Warrior flips in the air, and does an spinning kick into Crazy Max's chest. Crazy Max smashes through multiple walls and falls on the ground. Supersonic Warrior walks to his prey, and punches Crazy Max in the face multiple times. Blood squirts out of his face as the puddle of blood grows. Supersonic Warrior grabs Crazy Max by his shirt, smashes him into the wall, and kicks him in the chest with her leg. Crazy Max coughs up blood as he screams in pain! Crazy Max slowly gets up and catches his breath as blood drips from him. Supersonic Warrior growls and tackles Crazy Max to the ground. Supersonic Warrior punches Crazy Max in the face and blood squirts out! Supersonic Warrior said, "Time to end your life permanently!" Supersonic Warrior grabs Crazy Max by the neck, and smashes him into the ground. Crazy Max laid on the ground in an puddle of blood. Supersonic Warrior picks up Crazy Max's glider, and smashes Crazy Max multiple times with it. An explosion of energy from the glider smashes Supersonic Warrior through multiple walls. Supersonic Warrior falls on the ground as blood leaks from her body. An puddle of blood formed below Supersonic Warrior, as she slowly got up to catch her breath. The warehouse was shaking, and there wasn't enough walls to support the foundation. The unstable foundation of the warehouse falls apart, and debris falls on top of Crazy Max's glider and Supersonic Warrior. The glider gets smashed to pieces and explosions go off from the stored missiles and rockets in the glider. The warehouse explodes and debris flies everywhere. Supersonic Warrior runs out of the warehouse and dives on the ground to avoid the radius of the explosion. Crazy Max's body lies on the ground, in an huge puddle of blood in the warehouse debris. Supersonic Warrior slowly gets up, and wipes the dust off her suit, while resisting the pain that she was in. Supersonic Warrior said, "Whew, that was an tough battle, and the crazed maniac has been defeated." Supersonic Warrior slowly walks behind the tree, and demorphs in an flash of rainbow energy. Christina walks back to the science lab at Oasis Falls High School. Christina walks back to the science lab, with blood dripping from her as she walks. Sam and Edward run over and help Christina to an chair. Sam said, "Whew, you made it back safely, that was an rough fight. We were worried that you wouldn't make it back alive." Edward wraps up Christina's arm and said, "Atleast you defeated Crazy Max, the city can breathe again without all of his chaos." Christina nods as Sam and Edward wrap up the rest of Christina's body with bandages to stop the bleeding. Sam said, "Your body is all wrapped up, so just rest to let yourself heal." Christina said, "Sounds good, I am exhausted from battling Crazy Max, an good rest would be great." Sam hands Christina an water bottle! Christina chugs it down and hands it back to Sam. Sam throws the empty water bottle in to the trash can. Sam said, "How do you feel?" Christina said, "I feel better now, thanks for wrapping me up!" Sam said, "No problem, buddy! The fight was intense while we were watching it on our monitors." Christina said, "Yeah, Crazy Max and I were battling each other aggressively! There was an ton of blood on the battlefield from both of our bodies." Sam said, "I am glad that you survived the fight!" Sam walks over and grabs some glasses of lemonade from the cooler! Sam sits down next to Christina! Christina and Sam chug down their lemonade, and put the empty cups back on the side table. Sam and Christina relax together in their chairs.

15

12

Christina was in the science lab, sitting on the bed, drinking an bottle of lemonade. Sam was cleaning the equipment, making sure they were shiny and polished. Sam walked over to Christina and said, "Are you ready to check your health stats, to see how your body is functioning?" Christina nodded, as she held Sam's hand. Sam and Christina walked over to the machine. Sam opened the machine's pod, and Christina walked in. Sam strapped Christina in, and closed the pod. Sam started up the machine, and the machine activated! The machine's laser scanned Christina's body! Christina's health stats showed up on Sam's panel! Sam looked over the stats and nodded! The machine slowed down to an stop! Sam opened the pod and unstrapped Christina. Christina held Sam's hand, as she stepped out of the machine. Sam said, "The health stats looked good, The healing process after the fight with Crazy Max helped the functionality of the body stabilize back to normal at 100%." Christina said, "That's great, I am going to step out to get some fresh air." Sam said, "Sounds good, be careful!" Christina walked out of the science lab! Christina walked down the street, admiring the environment around her. Christina was admiring the plants next to the sidewalk, when an squad of police cars blazed past her, with their sirens flashing. Christina got closer to Game World, when she noticed an crowd of panicking citizens were running out of the store. Christina walked through the crowd, as she was getting pushed and shoved by the citizens. Christina checked out the store to see the commotion. Christina saw an guy with an black hoodie, threatening the cashier at the cash register. Steve slammed an copy of Angry Spiders on the counter. Tony said, "Is everything ok, sir?" Steve yelled at Tony and said, "No, I wanted to trade in this game, but you would only give me $2 for it." Tony said, "Yes, it is part of our policy, and the game is an couple of years old." Steve gets angry and said, "I will show you what I think of your policy!" Steve picks up an shelf and throws it at Tony! Tony dodges the shelf, as it smashes against the wall. Tony said, "Sir, I suggest that you calm down, before I call the police." Steve picks up Tony by his neck and smashes him against the wall! Steve said, "You just want to call the police to get rid of me." Steve takes out his knife and stabs it through Tony's chest. Tony's body bleeds out, as Steve throws him on to the ground. Christina saw the scene from the side of the store, and jumped into action. An flash of rainbow energy covered the area, as Supersonic Warrior walked in to the store. Supersonic Warrior walked towards Steve and said, "Stop right there!" Steve sighs and said, "The colorful hero came to save the day, looks like I can't get away with anything in this city anymore." Supersonic Warrior said, "Surrender Now, or you will be sorry!" Steve said, "Surrender, how pathetic, I won't back down that easily!" Supersonic Warrior speeds in to Steve, and punches him in the face. Steve slides backwards and kicks Supersonic Warrior in the chest. Supersonic Warrior slides backwards, as Steve picks up an shelf, full of games! Steve throws the shelf at Supersonic Warrior! Supersonic Warrior flips in the air, and grabs the shelf! Supersonic Warrior throws the shelf back at Steve! Steve gets hit by the shelf, and smashes in to the wall. Steve laid next to the wall! Supersonic Warrior knelt down, and punched Steve in the face. Supersonic Warrior grabbed Steve's neck, and smashes him against the wall. Blood leaked out of his body! Supersonic Warrior picked up Steve, and body slammed him in to the ground. Steve slowly got up, with blood leaking from his arm. Supersonic Warrior kicks Steve in the chest! Supersonic Warrior shouts, Sonic Blast, as she summons an ball of energy! Supersonic Warrior kicks the ball of energy at Steve! The ball of energy hits Steve in the chest, as the wall explodes. Steve slowly gets up, as blood leaks from his body. Supersonic

Warrior tackled Steve in to the ground. Supersonic Warrior growled, as she knelt down next to Steve! Supersonic Warrior punched Steve in the face, as blood leaked out. Steve said, "Have mercy, All I did was threaten an cashier, because he wouldn't accept my trade in request for an game." Supersonic Warrior said, "You are scum, like every other supervillain and thug. You killed the cashier in cold blood, and disturbed the peace of the city." Supersonic Warrior picks up Steve, and roundhouse kicks him in to the wall. Steve laid next to the wall, as Supersonic Warrior walks towards him. Supersonic Warrior grabs Steve's neck, and smashes him in to the wall. Blood leaks on to the floor, as Steve coughs. Supersonic Warrior said, "To restore the peace, you must be eliminated, so you won't cause any more chaos in the city." Supersonic Warrior squeezes Steve's neck and crushes it. Supersonic Warrior does an energy blast with her arm! The energy blast hits Steve, as he smashes through the wall, and laid on the ground in an puddle of blood. Supersonic Warrior wipes the blood off of her gloves. Supersonic Warrior walked out of the store, and noticed an squad of police cars parked outside. A group of police officers stood outside the store, with an high school student right next to them. Supersonic Warrior walked toward the police officers until Sheriff Bucky stopped her. Sheriff Bucky said, "We got reports of some commotion happening at Game World from Justin, an fellow high school student. I don't want to cause any trouble between us, hero! We are here to clean up the mess, since it looks like you dealt with the thief." Justin said, "My life fell apart after my dad died! You don't understand what I have been through since the warehouse explosion." Justin pushes Sheriff Bucky in to his police car. Sheriff Bucky stumbles backwards, as the other police officers point their guns at Justin. Sheriff Bucky said, "Calm down, you were an good student at Oasis Falls High School, you shouldn't throw all of it away just for revenge from your dad's death. Supersonic Warrior puts her hand on Justin's shoulder. Justin pushes her hand away and said, "Don't touch me, you ruined my life!" Supersonic Warrior said, "Take deep breaths and calm down, you don't want anyone to get hurt." Justin picked an tree and said, "Leave me alone!" Justin swings the tree and hits Supersonic Warrior and the squad of police officers. Supersonic Warrior slides backwards, as she growls. The squad of police officers laid on the ground, bleeding! The squad slowly get up from the ground, with their legs shaking from the blood leaking out of their body. Sheriff Bucky said, "Men, point your guns at Justin and shoot him down! He is an threat to the city." The police officers point their guns at Justin, and they started shooting them! Bullets were flying as Supersonic Warrior speeds toward Justin, while dodging the bullets. Supersonic Warrior throws an energy blast from her hand at the police officers! The energy blast hits the police car, and it explodes! The explosion hits the squad of police officers, and they fell on the ground in an puddle of blood. Sheriff Bucky slowly got up, as he noticed that his squad was dead. Supersonic Warrior had Justin in her arms, as she laid next to the wall. Sheriff Bucky called in to the local police department and said, "My squad is dead, send reinforcements!" Sheriff Bucky walks over to Supersonic Warrior! Sheriff Bucky said, "My squad is dead, I have called reinforcements. Protecting Justin was an good call, but attacking my men was reckless for an hero." Supersonic Warrior said, " Justin was an innocent citizen, he let his anger control his actions." Sheriff Bucky said, "I know that you are getting used to your powers, but you need to think before you act. Certain actions can affect everyone around you." Supersonic Warrior said, "Thanks for the advice!" Sheriff Bucky said, "The reinforcements will be here soon, I will let you check on Justin!" Supersonic Warrior nods and walks over to Justin! Sheriff Bucky stands next to his police car! Supersonic Warrior checks on Justin! Supersonic Warrior said, "Are you ok, Justin, did you get injured!" Justin said, "I am good, I wasn't expecting them to fire their guns on me!" Supersonic Warrior said, "You need to control your anger!" Justin said, "Ever since my dad's death, I have been angry, and blaming myself for it!" Supersonic Warrior said, "That is depressing to hear!" An squad of police cars drive up, and they park next to Sheriff Bucky's car. The squad of police officers get out of the car and walk towards Sheriff Bucky! Officer Nick said, "Bucky, is everything ok, we got your call!"

Sheriff Bucky said, "My squad died, I needed reinforcements to handle the threat." Officer Nick walks over to Supersonic Warrior and Justin with his squad of police officers. Officer Nick said, "We are here to do our job, hand over Justin, or there will be blood." Supersonic Warrior growls and said, "I am not handing over Justin, he is an innocent citizen, that had anger issues." Officer Nick said, "Get out of the way, hero, and let us do our job." Supersonic Warrior said, "I won't let you hurt Justin!" Officer Nick commands his squad to point their guns at Supersonic Warrior and Justin! Officer Nick said, "My squad will take you down, surrender now or there will be extreme consequences!" Supersonic Warrior said, "I am an hero, they need to be smart to take me down!" Supersonic Warrior held Justin in her arms and took him to an safe spot to hide. Justin said, "Be careful, their guns are scary!" Supersonic Warrior said, "I will try to be careful, it is part of my job being an hero." Supersonic Warrior speeds into Officer Nick with her super speed! Officer Nick commands his squad to shoot their guns at Supersonic Warrior. Supersonic Warrior dodges the bullets and tackles Officer Nick in to the police car. Officer Nick laid next to the police car, as Supersonic Warrior punches him in the face. One of the police officers threw an chain at Supersonic Warrior! The chain latched on to one of Supersonic Warrior's arms. One of the police officers threw another chain at Supersonic Warrior, while the other officer was pulling on the first chain! Supersonic Warrior was sliding backwards, away from Sheriff Nick! Supersonic Warrior flipped in the air, and grabbed on to the other chain with her arm. Supersonic Warrior landed on the ground, and pulled the chain. The police officer got pulled closer to her. Supersonic Warrior jumped on to the tree, with the chain in her arm! She pulled on the chain, knocking the police officer in to the squad. Supersonic Warrior threw an energy blast at the squad with her arm. The energy blast hit the squad, and they smashed against the wall, and laid on the ground in an puddle of blood. Supersonic Warrior pulled the chain off of her other arm, with her strength. Supersonic Warrior flips in the air out of the tree, jumps off the police car, and punches Officer Nick in the face with an Supersonic Punch. Officer Nick laid on the ground, with blood leaking out of his arm. Officer Nick slowly got up, as his squad got up from the ground! Officer Nick grabs Supersonic Warrior by the neck, and body slams her in to the police car, causing an dent in the hood. Supersonic Warrior slides her leg under Officer Nick, that causes him to trip. Officer Nick falls on the ground! One of the police officers tackle Supersonic Warrior in to the ground! The other police officers jump on top of Supersonic Warrior, holding her down! Supersonic Warrior growls, as she does an Supersonic Blast from her body! The explosion covered the area, as debris flied everywhere! The squad of police officers and Officer Nick smashed in to Sheriff Bucky and his police car! Sheriff Bucky's police car explodes, which smashed Sheriff Bucky, the squad of police officers, and Officer Nick in to Game World! Their bodies laid on the ground in an puddle of blood! Officer Nick slowly gets up, holding his arm, as he walks toward Supersonic Warrior! Supersonic Warrior gets up from the ground, wiping the dust off of her suit. Supersonic Warrior speeds in to Officer Nick, and grabs his neck. Supersonic Warrior body slams Officer Nick in to the ground! Officer Nick kicks Supersonic Warrior in the chest! Supersonic Warrior slides backwards! Supersonic Warrior tackles Officer Nick in to the ground, and punches him in the face. Officer Nick kicks Supersonic Warrior in the face. Officer Nick takes out his shock baton, and hits Supersonic Warrior in the chest, electrocuting her. Supersonic Warrior screams in pain. Officer Nick kicks Supersonic Warrior in the chest, and puts his foot on her back. Officer Nick holds Supersonic Warrior on to the ground, while punching her in the face. Supersonic Warrior growls, and does an energy blast from her body. Officer Nick smashed against the wall. Supersonic Warrior got up, and walked towards Officer Nick. Officer Nick took his tranquilizer gun off of his belt, and aimed it at Supersonic Warrior. Supersonic Warrior grabbed Officer Nick's arm, and flipped in the air. Supersonic Warrior kicked the gun out of Officer Nick's arm, and it laid on the ground. Officer Nick scrambled for the gun, and Supersonic Warrior tackled Officer Nick to keep him away from the gun.

Supersonic Warrior kicks Officer Nick in the face, as her arm touched the gun. Officer Nick kicked Supersonic Warrior in the chest, and the gun falls out of her hand. Officer Nick grabs Supersonic Warrior's leg and throws her in to the wall. Officer Nick grabbed the gun, while Supersonic Warrior got up. Supersonic Warrior flipped in the area, and landed next to Officer Nick. Officer Nick pulls the trigger on the gun, and the dart hits Supersonic Warrior in the chest. Supersonic Warrior laid on the ground! Officer Nick took the dart off of Supersonic Warrior's chest! Officer Nick said, "Don't worry, this gun doesn't hurt, your reckless actions as an hero has caused you to be captured for my friend at Electric Industries." Officer Nick picks up Supersonic Warrior and carried her back to his police car. Officer Nick opens up the back seat of the police car, straps Supersonic Warrior in, and closes the door! Officer Nick gets in the police car and drives off to Electric Industries. Officer Nick called on his radio and said, "The hero has been captured, I am taking her to you right now!" Adrian said, "Good, I need to know how her powers work!" Justin sat in his hiding spot, and noticed how quiet it was. Justin got up, and checked the area. He saw the puddles of blood, and saw the dead police officers laying on the ground. He noticed that Supersonic Warrior was missing, so he laid against the tree, and started crying! Justin cried and said, "This is all my fault, if I controlled my anger and my actions, the police officers wouldn't have captured Supersonic Warrior for protecting me." Justin got up, and walked back to Oasis Falls High School. Officer Nick drove up to Electric Industries, with Adrian waiting at the front of the building. Officer Nick parks the police car at the building and opens the door to get out of the car. Officer Nick opens the back door of the police car, and unstraps Supersonic Warrior. Officer Nick picked up Supersonic Warrior and carried her on his back, as he walked toward Adrian. Adrian said, "Is the hero dead or alive?" Officer Nick said, "She's still alive, just knocked out for now, until the effects wear off." Adrian said, "Good, let's take her to my machine in my lab, so I can analyze her powers." Adrian walks to his science lab, and Officer Nick follows him! Adrian walks through

Electric Industries, while showing Officer Nick various creations, that he experimented on. Adrian stops at a jail cell and said, "This is Bruce, he has super strength, and he likes to smash stuff." Bruce growls as he picks up an desk, and throws it at the cell. Officer Nick is amazed, as he continues walking through the building with Adrian. Adrian unlocks the door to his science lab with his special code on the panel. The door opens as Adrian walks in to the science lab. Officer Nick was amazed by all of the gadgets and gizmos. Adrian walks over to the machine, and unlocks the pod. Adrian said, "The machine will let me analyze Supersonic Warrior's powers, by taking blood samples from her body with electrical energy." Officer Nick put Supersonic Warrior in to the machine, straps her in, and closes the pod. Adrian starts up the machine, as the gears in the pod spin to life. Adrian said, "Lets wake up our hero with some electrical energy." Adrian sends some electrical energy in to the pod with his panel. The pod gets electrocuted, and the energy goes through Supersonic Warrior's body. The electrical energy goes through Supersonic Warrior's body, as she screams in pain. Supersonic Warrior rubs her head, and punches the pod super hard! Supersonic Warrior growled and said, "Where am I, and what have you done to me?" Adrian said, "Calm down, you're in my science lab at Electric Industries, and you're in my machine for science experiments. Be an good hero, and cooperate with my experiments." Adrian pushes an button on the machine! The pod electrocutes Supersonic Warrior! Supersonic Warrior screamed in pain! The machine scans Supersonic Warrior's body in the pod, and downloads data in to Adrian's panel. Adrian looks over the data, as he rubs his chin! Adrian said, "This is some interesting data, this would be great for my future experiments." Adrian pushes some buttons on the machine, and it saves the data to an flash drive! Adrian puts the flash drive in his vault with the rest of his research. Adrian said, "Time for one more test on the hero, before our work is done!" Adrian presses some buttons as an tube connects to the cuff on Supersonic Warrior's arm. The machine beeps and buzzes, as electrical energy fills up the pod, and Supersonic Warrior screams in pain. The cuff on Supersonic Warrior's arm gets electrified, as it takes Supersonic Warrior's blood, and puts it in to the tube. The tube pours Supersonic Warrior's blood into an canister! The canister gets sealed, and drops in to the slot, next to Adrian. Adrian smiles, as the machine finished the process. The tube disconnects from Supersonic Warrior's arm, and it swings back into idle position. Adrian said, "The tests are done!" Officer Nick nodded, as he walked over to the machine. Officer Nick unlocked the pod, and unstrapped Supersonic Warrior. Officer Nick helped Supersonic Warrior out of the pod. Supersonic Warrior rubbed his head, as she regained her composure. Adrian said, "We don't need the hero anymore, take her to the cell with Bruce." Officer Nick walks over to Bruce's cell with Supersonic Warrior. Officer Nick unlocks the cell with the special security code, and pushes Supersonic Warrior in to the cell. Officer Nick locked the cell. Bruce walked over to Supersonic Warrior and said, "Oh boy, an new toy to play with!" Officer Nick said, "Don't play rough with her!" Bruce said, "I won't break her, we will have some fun together." Officer Nick walked back to Adrian in the science lab. Adrian was at his machine, with the canister of Supersonic Warrior's blood on an stand! The stand had wires and tubes, that were connected in to Adrian's machine. Adrian was smiling, while looking at elements on his screen. Adrian said, "Lets see if the fire element works with her blood." Adrian clicks on the fire element, and analyzes its data. Adrian said, "With the fire element, I can add it to her blood, and give someone the ability to use fire powers, and the powers of Supersonic Warrior." Adrian clicks on the button, and the machine spins to life. The fire element pours in to the tubes, connected to the stand. Supersonic Warrior's blood turns orange in the canister. Adrian said, "The element went into her blood, now to process the blood to see if it worked." Adrian pushes an button, and the machine scans the canister. The machine displays data on the screen. Adrian said, "The data looks amazing, the fire element got added to Supersonic Warrior's DNA in the blood. When it gets injected into someone's body, it will give them the ability to use the powers. If it is successful, the powers will make them dangerous, but if the body rejects the formula, they will lay dead on the ground as an empty shell of their former life." Officer Nick was amazed at the work! Adrian said, "Thank you, Officer Nick, for letting me expand my experiments with this discovery." Officer Nick said, "No problem, it was my pleasure to work with you." Adrian takes the canister off of the stand, and puts in his vault. Adrian said, "I just need the right person to showcase their skills to earn the powers."

Bruce walked toward Supersonic Warrior, growling while Supersonic Warrior walked backwards. Supersonic Warrior said, "Let's talk out our differences, like ordinary beings." Bruce said, "I don't want to talk out our differences, The only activity that I like to do is smash stuff." Bruce punches Supersonic Warrior in the face! Supersonic Warrior smashes in to the cell wall! Supersonic Warrior speeds in to Bruce and punches him in the chest. Bruce slides backwards! Bruce kicks Supersonic Warrior in the chest. Supersonic Warrior slides backwards! Supersonic Warrior kicks Bruce in the face. Bruce dodges, and grabs Supersonic Warrior's leg. Bruce smashes Supersonic Warrior in to the wall. Supersonic Warrior laid on the ground! Supersonic Warrior got up from the ground! Bruce speeds in to Supersonic Warrior and picks her up by the neck! Bruce body slams Supersonic Warrior in to the ground! Bruce steps on Supersonic Warrior's chest, while he punches her in the face. Supersonic Warrior growls, and does an Supersonic Blast from her body! Bruce smashes in to the cell wall, while the foundation of Electric Industries shakes! Supersonic Warrior gets up from the ground! Bruce gets up from the ground, and growls at Supersonic Warrior. Supersonic Warrior speeds in to Bruce and kicks him in the chest. Bruce dodges Supersonic Warrior's leg, and grabs it! Bruce throws Supersonic Warrior in to the wall! Supersonic Warrior falls on the ground! Bruce walks up to Supersonic Warrior, and picks her up by the neck. Bruce smashes Supersonic Warrior in to the wall. Supersonic Warrior gets up, and flips in the air. Supersonic Warrior lands on the side of the wall, with her hand on the wall, holding her up. Supersonic Warrior flips in the air, and smashes Bruce in to the ground. Supersonic Warrior lands on Bruce's chest, and punches him in the face with an Sonic Punch. Blood leaks out of Bruce's body, as he slowly gets up. Supersonic Warrior summons an energy beam from her hand, and aims it at Bruce. Bruce gets hit by the beam, as he smashes against the wall. Bruce slowly gets up as blood leaks from arm. Supersonic Warrior speeds in to Bruce and tackles him in to the wall. Supersonic Warrior punches him in the face, multiple times while blood leaks out. Supersonic Warrior growls, while she picks up Bruce and body slams him in to the ground. Blood squirts out of his body. Bruce slowly gets up from the ground! Supersonic Warrior flips in the air, and roundhouse kicks Bruce in the chest. Bruce smashes against the wall. Bruce laid against the wall, while blood is pouring from his body. Supersonic Warrior does an Supersonic Blast from her body! It shakes the area, and smashes Bruce in to the wall. Bruce laid on the ground in an puddle of blood! The cell's security system explodes as the cell door unlocks. Supersonic Warrior wipes the blood from her gloves, as she walks out of the cell. Officer Nick was outside the cell, and noticed all of the blood and despair on the cell's floor. Officer Nick trembled in fear as Supersonic Warrior walked closer to him. Supersonic Warrior grabbed Officer Nick by the neck, and choked him. Officer Nick was gasping for air, while Supersonic Warrior was squeezing his neck. Supersonic Warrior smashed Officer Nick in to the wall, and does an Supersonic Blast from her arm. Officer Nick smashes through the wall, and laid on the ground, bleeding. Supersonic Warrior picks up Officer Nick and body slams him in to the ground. Supersonic Warrior knelt down, and punches Officer Nick in the face, multiple times, while blood leaks out of his body. Officer Nick kicks Supersonic Warrior in the face. Supersonic Warrior slides backwards. Officer Nick tackles Supersonic Warrior in to the ground, and punches her in the face. Supersonic Warrior growls and roundhouse kicks Officer Nick in the face. Officer Nick falls on the ground! Officer Nick gets up from the ground! Supersonic Warrior forms an energy blast with her hand and throws it at Officer Nick. Officer Nick gets hit by the blast, and smashes in to the wall. Officer Nick stood against the wall, as he slowly got up. Blood leaked from Officer Nick's body! Supersonic Warrior spins in an circle, forming an Supersonic Tornado, that spins through the area! Supersonic Warrior stops spinning, as Officer Nick laid on the ground in an puddle of blood. Debris was everywhere! Supersonic Warrior wiped the blood from her gloves, as she walked out of Electric Industries. Adrian walked out of the science lab, and saw all of the chaos. He walked over to Officer Nick's dead body and noticed all of the blood. Adrian sighed as he walked over to the cell. He saw all of the blood in the cell, as he walked over to Bruce's dead body. Adrian said, "My poor science experiment, he had an good life!" Adrian walked out of the cell and said, "Let's start cleaning up this mess!" Supersonic Warrior was walking back to Oasis Falls High School, admiring the environment, and listening to the tweeting birds. The building for Oasis Falls High School was in the distance, so Supersonic Warrior went down the hill, and got to the flag pole. Justin was next to the flag pole, wiping away his tears. Justin saw Supersonic Warrior, and ran towards her. Supersonic Warrior stopped in the grass field. Justin ran over and gave Supersonic Warrior an hug. Supersonic Warrior hugged Justin back! Justin said, "I thought that I lost you forever!" Supersonic Warrior said, "Never underestimate an hero!" Supersonic Warrior ruffled up Justin's hair! Justin fixed his hair, while hugging Supersonic Warrior. The school bell rings in the background! An flash of rainbow energy covers the area, as Supersonic Warrior demorphs in to Christina. Christina walked alongside Justin to their Math class.

16

13

Christina and Justin were walking to their Math class! They were watching the other students go through their lockers as they grab and put stuff in to their bags for their classes. Christina and Justin walked to the door for their Math class. Christina turned the door knob and opened the door. Christina walked to her seat. Justin walked to his seat! Paul, the Math teacher, smiled as the students walked in, while he wrote the daily Math equation on the board next to him. Paul said, "Welcome to today's session of Math class, hope you guys have fun, because learning Math can be fun for everyone." The students sighed as they listened to Paul! Paul points to the daily Math equation and said, "Students, what is 4 x 12?" Christina raised her hand! Paul points to Christina and said, "Do you have the answer for the class?" Christina said, "Yes, the answer for 4 x 12 is 48! Paul said, "Perfect, See students, this is how you listen in class." Justin groans and said, "Show Off! Why does she have to be so perfect all the time?" James said, "She is interested in expanding her knowledge, like the rest of us." The bell rings in the background! Paul said, "Looks like class is over, have an great day!" The students got up from their seats and walked out of the door. Justin gets up from his seat, and walks to the door. While walking to the door, James trips him and Justin falls on the ground. Justin said, "You jerk, what is your problem?" James said, "Just cool down and chill!" Justin said, "You are just an little pest, that wants to be smushed." Justin kicks James in the chest. James coughs as he slides backwards. Justin grabs James by the throat, and walks in to the hallway! James struggles in Justin's grip and said, "Why are you doing this?" Justin smashes James in to the water fountain, while holding his throat, and said "My life has been an mess!" James said while struggling, "I am sorry that life isn't going very well for you." Justin said, "You're not sorry at all" Justin body slams James in to the ground. Justin punches James in the face, as he laid on the ground. James holds Justin's arm back, and kicks him in the face. Justin slides back in to the locker! James growls and tackles Justin in to the ground! James punches Justin in the face! Justin roundhouse kicks James in the face! James slides backwards! Justin tackles James in to the locker, and the locker falls on top of him. James picks up the locker, with blood pouring from his face, and he hits Justin with it. Justin falls on the ground! James sets the locker on the floor as he walks to his prey. James picks up Justin by his throat and squeezes him. Justin coughs, while struggling in his grip. James slams Justin in to the ground. Justin is lying on the ground, and James is towering over him! James kneels down and punches Justin in the face, multiple times as blood leaks on to the ground. Justin grabs James's arm and roundhouse kicks him in the face. James slides backwards! Justin tackles James in to the locker. The locker shakes from James slamming in to it. Justin picks up the locker, and hits James in the chest with it. James fell on the ground! Justin stepped on James's chest, while holding the locker. Justin hits James in the face with the locker, multiple times. James grabs the locker with his hands, and kicks Justin in the chest. Justin slides backward, as the locker fell on to the ground. James slowly gets up, with blood leaking from his arm and face. An flash of rainbow energy covers the area, and Supersonic Warrior walks through the hallway toward them. Supersonic Warrior said, "Break up the fight, let me handle this!" Supersonic Warrior said to James, "James, go clean up in the nurse's office, I will help Justin get up!" James nodded and walked to the nurse's office. Supersonic Warrior walks over to Justin, and gives him an towel. Justin grabs the towel, and wipes the blood and dust off of his body. Supersonic Warrior said to Justin, "How are you feeling?" Justin said, "I feel fine, that kid shouldn't have picked an fight with me." Supersonic Warrior said, "Why shouldn't James have picked an fight with you?" Justin said, "I can't control my anger, it is spiraling out of control! My anger is making me an dangerous threat to anyone around me." Justin grabs Supersonic Warrior by the neck and slams her in to the locker. Justin said, "You ruined my life, by killing my dad." Supersonic Warrior coughs and said, "I was just doing my job by protecting the city. Your dad was killing innocent citizens." Justin said, "Yes, you were just playing the hero! You didn't think about the lives of the people that you were screwing over." Justin kicks Supersonic Warrior in the chest. Supersonic Warrior slides backwards and kicks Justin in the chest. Justin smashes in to the wall and falls on the ground. Justin gets up and catches his breath. Supersonic Warrior tackles Justin to the ground! Supersonic Warrior punches Justin in the face. Justin holds Supersonic Warrior's arm back, and roundhouse kicks her in the face. Supersonic Warrior slides backwards and growls! Supersonic Warrior super speeds into Justin and uppercuts him in the neck! Justin slides backwards in to the locker! Supersonic Warrior back flips in the air, and kicks Justin in the face. Justin slams in to the locker, and the locker shakes! Justin picks up the locker and hits Supersonic Warrior in the chest. Supersonic Warrior smashes in to the wall and makes an dent as she falls on the ground. Supersonic Warrior laid on the ground, as she slowly gets up. Justin steps on Supersonic Warrior's chest! Justin punches Supersonic Warrior in the face! Supersonic Warrior growls and said, "Supersonic Explosion!" An sonic blast explodes from Supersonic Warrior's body, and it smashes Justin in to the wall. Justin laid on the ground and slowly gets up! Supersonic Warrior slowly gets up and walks toward Justin. Supersonic Warrior kicks Justin in the chest. Justin coughs as he slides backwards! Justin roundhouse kicks Supersonic Warrior in the chest. Supersonic Warrior slams in to the wall, and leans against the locker. Justin speeds into Supersonic Warrior and grabs her by the neck. Justin chokes Supersonic Warrior, as he lifts her in the air. Supersonic Warrior said while struggling in Justin's grip, "If you killed me, would your life get better?" Justin sighs and said, "No, it wouldn't, but it feels good seeing you suffer!" Justin smashes Supersonic Warrior in to the wall. Justin kicks Supersonic Warrior in the chest! Supersonic Warrior falls on the ground as she coughs. Justin picks up Supersonic Warrior and body slams her in to the ground. Supersonic Warrior kicks Justin in the face. Supersonic Warrior gets up, as Justin falls on the ground. Supersonic Warrior punches Justin in the face! Justin holds Supersonic Warrior's arm back and roundhouse kicks her in the face. Supersonic Warrior slides backwards, as Justin gets up. Supersonic Warrior picks up an locker and hits Justin in the chest, sending him flying in to the wall. Justin smashes in to the wall, as an puddle of blood forms. Supersonic Warrior picks Justin up by the neck and chokes him! Supersonic Warrior smashes Justin into the wall, as she squeezes his neck. Blood is dripping from Justin, as Supersonic Warrior chokes him. Supersonic Warrior punches him in the face multiple times while she said, "Your life won't get better, give up on the past, and focus on the present!" Supersonic Warrior throws Justin on to the ground. Justin coughs as he gets up, while blood drips from his face. Supersonic Warrior kicks Justin in the chest, sending him flying in to the wall. Supersonic Warrior speeds toward the wall, and picks Justin up by the neck, choking him! Supersonic Warrior slams Justin in to the ground, as blood pours out of his body. Justin slowly gets up, while Supersonic Warrior wipes the blood off of her gloves. Justin brushes the dirt off of him! Supersonic Warrior brushes the dirt off of her suit. Justin walks in to the restroom, and washes the blood off of his face. Justin said, "I will show that colorful hero and the rest of the world that no one should mess with me." Justin washes the rest of the blood and dirt off of him, and walks out of the school. Justin was walking toward the school's flagpole, when an hooded figure ran in to him. Justin said, "Sorry, today has been crazy for me!" The hooded figure took off his hood, and smiled! Adrian said, "Hi Justin, I am Adrian from Electric Industries." Justin said, "Adrian, did you know my dad!" Adrian said, "Yes, I gave your dad the gadgets that he used in his battle against Supersonic Warrior. He was an good man, but his actions were scary for everyone." Justin said, "OK, I want to feel the same power that Supersonic Warrior had." Adrian said, "You're in luck, my boy! With this needle, I can inject you with this serum that can give you fire powers. The serum was created with Supersonic Warrior's blood in my science lab." Justin said, "Awesome, I had an fight with Supersonic Warrior earlier." Adrian said, "I saw the fight! With these powers, you can make Supersonic Warrior and the rest of your enemies suffer." Adrian stabs the needle into Justin's arm. Adrian said, "Give the powers some time to kick in! Once you activate them, the fire powers are pretty strong and powerful." Justin said, "Sounds good, thanks for the help!" Adrian said, "No problem, be careful, the world can be an scary and dangerous place." Justin nods and continues walking off of the school campus. Adrian puts his hood back on, and walks back to Electric Industries. Supersonic Warrior walks in to the nurse's office and checks on James. Nurse Carlos said, "My favorite colorful hero, Supersonic Warrior! I saw your fight with Justin earlier, it was intense to watch." Supersonic Warrior said, "I had to knock some sense into him." Nurse Carlos said, "James is doing pretty good, he cleaned himself up, and is laying on the bed." Supersonic Warrior walks to the bed! James sits up on the bed and said, "Hey Supersonic Warrior, thanks for the save back there, you are awesome." Supersonic Warrior said, "No problem, It is part of being an superhero." James stands up and said, "Your suit is pretty cool!" Supersonic Warrior said, "Thanks, the gadgets in my suit help me defeat my enemies." James hugs Supersonic Warrior and said, "Your suit is nice and warm. Supersonic Warrior hugs James back and said, "My suit has heated padding, it keeps me warm, while I am defeating supervillains. James said, "Awesome, I am glad that you are protecting the city!" James and Supersonic Warrior fist bump each other. James laid back down on the bed! Supersonic Warrior walks out of the nurse's office as she demorphs in an flash of rainbow energy. Justin was walking back to his house, when an pair of police cars stopped right in front of him. The police officers walked out and pointed their guns at Justin. Justin said, "Out of my way, I have to get back to my house. Police Commander Logan said, "We have the neighborhood under patrol for safety precautions." Justin said, "It's time to sling some fire!" Justin's eyes glow red, as he spins in an circle, turning into an fiery tornado. Fire Slinger spins through the police barricade, as he sets everything on fire in front of him. The police barricade explodes in an fiery explosion behind Fire Slinger and the dead police officers laid on the ground in puddles of blood. An scared high school student named Peter saw the mayhem from the side of the road. Peter said, while shaking in terror, "Who are you?" Fire Slinger picked up Peter by the throat and said, "I Am Fire Slinger!" Fire Slinger summoned flames in his hand, and he burns Peter alive. Peter's body crumbles into ash, as it burns. Fire Slinger blows the ashes of Peter's body in to the air. Fire Slinger walks closer to his house!

Another round of police cars drive up to Fire Slinger to block his path. Fire Slinger said, "Perfect, More pests to burn apart!" Fire Slinger flips in the air and throws fire balls at the police cars! The police cars explode in a fiery explosion, as Fire Slinger walks through the explosion. Fire Slinger's eyes turn back to normal as Justin stops at his house. Justin walks to the front door, and looks through the window. Inside the window, Justin noticed that the lights were off inside the house. Justin kicks down the front door and walks inside. Justin slowly walks through the house! An hooded figure sneaks up on Justin and tackles him in to the ground. The hooded figure punches Justin in the face. Justin's eyes glow red, as he shoots an fire ball out of his hand. The hooded figure slides backwards, as Fire Slinger gets up. Fire Slinger spins and speeds into the hooded figure. The hooded figure smashes in to the wall! Fire Slinger picks up the hooded figure by the neck. The hooded figure struggles in Fire Slinger's grip, as they take off their hood. The hooded figure takes off their hood and said, "You probably remember me, Justin, I am Emily, and I am your mother." Fire Slinger said, "You are an pest that needs to be smushed, like the rest of my enemies!" Emily said, "You turned yourself into an monster!" Fire Slinger gets angry and said, "I am not an monster!" Fire Slinger explodes an burst of flames from his body! Emily smashes in to the wall and falls on the ground in an puddle of blood as Fire Slinger walks toward his prey. Fire Slinger said, "Crazy Max would be proud of me for avenging his death. You don't care about me at all!" Fire Slinger steps on Emily's chest, as he summons flames with his hands. Fire Slinger punches Emily in the face, as blood pours on to the ground. Emily holds Fire Slinger's arm back, as she slowly gets up. Emily gets up and grabs an baseball bat. Emily swings the baseball bat at Fire Slinger! Fire Slinger dodges and roundhouse kicks Emily in the chest! Emily slides backwards in to the bookcase. An glass vase falls on top of Emily's head, and she stumbles backwards. Blood falls off of her head, as she regains her footing. Fire Slinger grabs Emily by the throat and smashes her in to the ground. An puddle of blood forms below her! Emily slowly gets up, while blood leaks from her body. Fire Slinger opens his mouth and an blast of flames shoots out at Emily, smashing her through the bookshelf. The bookshelf explodes, as she falls on the ground in an puddle of blood. Fire Slinger walks to Emily, as she slowly gets up. Fire Slinger kicks Emily in the chest! Emily coughs up blood, as she stumbles! Fire Slinger picks up Emily by the neck and chokes her. Fire Slinger said, "You think, that you made this family so special by pretending to love me. Emily struggles and said, "I supported you, but your dad corrupted you!" Fire Slinger smashes Emily in to the wall, as blood leaks out of her. Fire Slinger said, "You never supported me for my education, and you never served me my favorite food when we ate together as an family." Fire Slinger squeezes harder on Emily's neck! Emily said, "I tried asking you what you wanted to eat, but you were always busy with your technology in your room." Fire Slinger kicks Emily in the chest while choking her. Fire Slinger said, "You never knocked on the door, when you wanted my attention." Emily said, "I never wanted to hurt you!" Fire Slinger said, "I hate you, and I want you to die!" Fire Slinger summons flames in his hand, and punches his arm through Emily's chest, setting her body on fire. An puddle of blood falls on the floor, as Emily's body burns to ash. Fire Slinger explodes an burst of flames from his body, causing an huge fiery explosion to destroy the house. Fire Slinger walks through the explosion and walks outside. Miles, an high school student saw the explosion. Fire Slinger grabbed Miles by the neck, as he summons flames in his hand. Miles said while terrified, "Please don't hurt me!" Fire Slinger said, "I won't hurt you, I will just burn your body to ash, and make you suffer!" Fire Slinger chokes Miles and explodes an burst of flames from his body. Miles laid on the ground in an puddle of blood. Fire Slinger's eyes return back to normal, as he smiled. The sun rises at Oasis Falls High School, as students walk through the hallways to get to their classes on time. Justin walks through the hallway, and passes by Christina, while she grabs her homework out of her locker. Christina sees Justin walk by and stops him in the hallway. Christina said, "Hey Justin, did you do your homework for Paul's class?" Justin said while rubbing his head, "It was pretty easy to figure out!" Christina said, "Are you ok, you are rubbing your head!" Justin said, "I am fine, I just had an rough night." Christina closes her locker, and puts her backpack on. Christina walks to Paul's Math class, and Justin walks behind her. Christina and Justin stop at the door to Paul's Math class. Christina opens the door, while Paul writes the daily equation. Christina and Justin walk to their seats. The rest of the students find their seats for Paul's Math class, as the school bell rings. Paul said, "Welcome to another fun session of learning Math, students!" James cheers and said, "Yay, more fun Math knowledge, I love Math!" Paul said, "Thank you for showing your enthusiasm to learn some Math, James!" Paul taps on the daily equation on the board! Paul said, "Students, what is 10 x 5?" Justin raised his hand! Paul pointed at Justin! Justin said, "The answer for 10 x 5 is 50, it is pretty simple to figure out!" Paul said, "Good job Justin!" The school bell rings, and the students get up from their seats and walk out the room. Christina gets up from her seat! James gets up from his seat and walks toward Christina. James said, "Christina, there is an party later tonight at my house, do you want to come?" Christina said, "Sure, I love parties, what is the dress code?" James said, "The dress code is your normal clothes." Christina said, "Cool, I can't wait to party with you!" James winks at Christina and said, "Me too, you are cool to hang out with." Justin walks past James and Christina to the door. Justin walks out the door to the restroom. James said, "Do you think Supersonic Warrior is an cool superhero?" Christina said, "Yeah, she is pretty cool!" James said, "See you later tonight!" Christina said, "You too, stay safe!" James said, "I will try to stay safe!" Christina and James walk out of the door! Justin walks in to the restroom and washes his hair. Justin's eyes glow red as he said, "Time for me to crash an party! Fire Slinger flips in the air and he throws an fire ball at the restroom stall, blowing the door to pieces! Fire Slinger walks out of the restroom, as his eyes return to normal. The sun sets as James sets up the party decorations and the snacks at his house. The chocolate cake was being decorated in the kitchen by the master chef, Steve. Clint was organizing the soda and the snacks on the table in the living room. The students were slowly arriving at the party, as James was letting them in. DJ Shadow was spinning the DJ table in the living room, next to the table, rocking out some fresh beats. Christina knocks on the door, and James lets her in. James sees Christina's outfit, and said, "Wow, you look amazing!" Christina said, "Thanks, you look amazing as well." James said, "Thanks, my parents helped me pick it out." Steve rolls the chocolate cake in to the living room. Steve said, "The chocolate cake came out of the oven, be careful when eating it, so you won't burn your mouth." The door gets kicked down and an ball of flames gets thrown at James. Christina tackles James out of the way and lands on the ground. Fire Slinger walks in with flames in his hands. Fire Slinger said, "You held an party, and you didn't invite me!" James said, "Who are you?" Fire Slinger said, "I am Fire Slinger, and you are about to be destroyed." Fire Slinger opens his mouth and an blast of flames gets shot at James. An blast of rainbow energy covers the area! Supersonic Warrior jumps in front of James and activates an Supersonic barrier. The blast of flames hits the barrier and evaporates, before it hits Supersonic Warrior and James. Fire Slinger said, "Grrrrr, that colorful pest!" Supersonic Warrior said, "James, get the other party attendees to safety." James nods and said, "Sure, what will you do?" Supersonic Warrior said, "I will deal with Fire Slinger!" James said, "Be careful!" Supersonic Warrior said, "I will try to be careful!" James hugs Supersonic Warrior! Supersonic Warrior hugs James back! James gathers the other party attendees, and they hide in the basement. Supersonic Warrior said, "Fire Slinger, it is rude to interrupt someone's party without being invited." Fire Slinger said, "It is fun to interrupt parties though." Fire Slinger shoots an blast of flames out of his mouth at Supersonic Warrior. The blast of flames hits Supersonic Warrior, and she smashes in to the book shelf. Fire Slinger spins in to an fiery tornado, and he spins in to Supersonic Warrior. Furniture flied everywhere as Fire Slinger spins toward his target. Supersonic Warrior tries to dodge the fiery tornado, but she gets caught in the tornado. The fiery tornado throws Supersonic Warrior in to the table, and the bowl of snacks falls on top of her. Supersonic Warrior gets up,as the snacks fall on the ground. Supersonic Warrior speeds toward Fire Slinger. Fire Slinger lights up his leg with flames, and roundhouse kicks Supersonic Warrior in the chest. Supersonic Warrior slides backwards! Supersonic Warrior tackles Fire Slinger in to the ground. Supersonic Warrior punches Fire Slinger in the face. Fire Slinger lights his arm on fire, while he holds Supersonic Warrior's arm back. Fire Slinger kicks Supersonic Warrior in the face. Supersonic Warrior slides back, as she screams in pain. Fire Slinger lights his leg on fire, and he roundhouse kicks Supersonic Warrior in the chest. Supersonic Warrior smashes in to the snack table. The snack table smashes in to the wall! Fire Slinger grabs Supersonic Warrior by the neck, and body slams her in to the chocolate cake. The chocolate cake explodes, covers Supersonic Warrior's suit, and blocks her helmet visor with chocolate frosting. Fire Slinger punches Supersonic Warrior in the face, multiple times, as her visor starts to break. Supersonic Warrior holds Fire Slinger's arm back, and kicks him in the face. Fire Slinger slides backwards. Supersonic Warrior gets up and growls. Fire Slinger speeds in to Supersonic Warrior, and wraps his arms around her. Fire Slinger lights up his arms with flames, while Supersonic Warrior screams in pain. Fire Slinger unleashed an blast of flames out of his body! The explosion smashes Supersonic Warrior in to the wall. Supersonic Warrior laid on the ground, with blood leaking out of her suit. Fire Slinger stepped on Supersonic Warrior's chest, while his leg was lit up with flames. Supersonic Warrior screamed in pain, as blood leaks on to the floor. Supersonic Warrior emits an Supersonic Blast from her arm, and hits Fire Slinger in the chest. Fire Slinger slides backwards, while Supersonic Warrior gets up from the ground. Supersonic Warrior unleashes an sonic blast from her body! The blast smashes Fire Slinger through the dresser. Fire Slinger laid on the ground as shattered glass falls around him. Supersonic Warrior picks up Fire Slinger by the neck and smashes him in to the wall. Blood falls on the ground from Fire Slinger's body. Supersonic Warrior punches Fire Slinger in the face, as blood drips out of his body. Fire Slinger kicks Supersonic Warrior in the chest! Supersonic Warrior smashes in to the TV cabinet. The TV falls off the stand on to Supersonic Warrior's head. Supersonic Warrior slowly gets up from the ground. Fire Slinger throws an fire ball at Supersonic Warrior. Supersonic Warrior dodges the fire ball, and it hits the bookcase. The bookcase explodes and wood pieces fly everywhere. Supersonic Warrior speeds toward Fire Slinger and tackles him in to the ground. Supersonic Warrior picks up the chip bowl from the ground and smashes Fire Slinger's face with it multiple times, as blood leaks from his head. Fire Slinger growls and he ignites an blast of flames from his body. An blast of energy covers the house, as Supersonic Warrior smashes through multiple walls. Fire Slinger smashes through multiple walls as well. The area is covered with blood, and most of the house has been destroyed. Supersonic Warrior's visor is shattered, as she slowly gets up with blood leaking from her body. Fire Slinger slowly gets up with blood leaking from his body. Fire Slinger walks toward Supersonic Warrior and grabs her by the neck. Supersonic Warrior struggles in his grip, as Fire Slinger squeezes her neck. Fire Slinger said, "You fought bravely, but your reign of being an hero is coming to an end." Supersonic Warrior coughs and said, "You are strong as well!" Fire Slinger smashes Supersonic Warrior in to the wood foundation, as blood leaks from her body. Supersonic Warrior kicks Fire Slinger in the chest, and back flips in the air. Fire Slinger slides backwards! Supersonic Warrior speeds toward Fire Slinger and body slams him in to the ground. An puddle of blood leaks on to the ground! Supersonic Warrior growls, as she punches Fire Slinger in the face. James sneaks out of the hiding area with the other students! Supersonic Warrior said, "No, get back in the hiding spot, it is too dangerous!" James goes back in to the hiding spot, and the other students don't listen, as they sneak through the debris. Fire Slinger takes advantage of the distraction by kicking Supersonic Warrior in the chest. Supersonic Warrior slides backward. Fire Slinger flips in the area and throws an fire ball at Supersonic Warrior. The fire ball hits Supersonic Warrior in the chest! Supersonic Warrior slides backward, with blood leaking from her suit. Fire Slinger speeds in to Supersonic Warrior and grabs her by the throat. Fire Slinger lifts Supersonic Warrior in to the air, while she struggles in his grip. Fire Slinger lights his arm up with flames, and he puts his hand on Supersonic Warrior's chest. Supersonic Warrior screams in pain, as her suit heats up from the flames. Fire Slinger punches Supersonic Warrior in the chest! Fire Slinger body slams Supersonic Warrior in to the ground. An puddle of blood forms under Supersonic Warrior's body, as she laid on the ground! Supersonic Warrior slowly gets up from the ground. Fire Slinger ignites an blast of flames from his body that covers the entire area. The bodies of the other students laid on the ground in puddles of blood. Supersonic Warrior laid on the ground in an puddle of blood, with blood leaking from her body. Supersonic Warrior's helmet was destroyed, with her suit soaked in blood. Fire Slinger laughs maniacally, as he walks through the destruction. Fire Slinger said, "My job is done for now!" Fire Slinger's eyes return to normal, as he walks out of the destroyed house. James was shaking in fear as he walked out to Supersonic Warrior's body. James noticed all of the blood from her body, and was terrified. James said as he was trembling, "Please don't be dead!" James walked to the sink, and filled up the nearest bucket with water. James picked up the bucket and walked toward Supersonic Warrior's body. James poured the water on to Supersonic Warrior. The water pours on to Supersonic Warrior's face, and on to the suit. Supersonic Warrior wakes up, and gets up slowly. Supersonic Warrior said, "My body is too weak from the fight with Fire Slinger, can you carry me to the science lab at Oasis Falls High

School? The scientists will help me heal back to normal." James nods, as he picks up Supersonic Warrior, and carries her on his back. James walks to Oasis Falls High School, with Supersonic Warrior laying on his back. James walks to the science lab and knocks on the door. James said, "It is an emergency, Supersonic Warrior is losing blood!" Sam opens the door and shakes in terror! Sam said, "What happened to her?" James said, "An supervillain named Fire Slinger attacked my house during the party that I hosted. Several students died during the chaos and Supersonic Warrior got beat up very badly." Sam said, "That must of been traumatizing for you!" James said, while Supersonic Warrior laid on his back, "It was, there was so much blood and chaos." Sam walks to the machine, and opens up the pod. Sam said, "Put Supersonic Warrior in to the machine and strap her in. I will heal her back to full health and do suit repairs." James nods, and puts Supersonic Warrior in to the machine, and straps her in. James closes the machine, and Sam starts it up on the machine panel. The machines spins and makes an ton of noise, as rainbow energy fills up the machine's pod. The machine's speaker said, "Suit repairs and body healing is complete!" The machine slows down to an stop. Sam said, "James, you can rest in the bed, down here in the science lab, since your body is still shocked from the supervillain attack." James nods, as he laid on the bed, and falls asleep with the covers over his head. Sam opens the machine and unstraps Supersonic Warrior from the machine. Sam holds Supersonic Warrior's hand, as she walks out of the machine. Sam said, "You had an rough day, rest in the other bed, and I will prepare you for your rematch with Fire Slinger." Supersonic Warrior nods and walks to the other bed! An flash of rainbow energy covers the area as Supersonic Warrior demorphs. Christina laid on the bed, and falls asleep with the covers over her head. The sun rises on an brand new day! Christina was sitting on the bed, reading an science book, and Sam was reorganizing the cabinets. Sam walks over to Christina, and gives her an bottle of water. Sam said, "How are you feeling?" Christina drank the bottle of water, and gave it back to Sam. Christina said, "Refreshed, I had an good sleeping session as well." Sam threw the bottle of water away. Sam said, "I worked on the machine last night, It can give you ice powers!" Christina said, "That's great, Fire Slinger is an tough supervillain. The ice powers will help me defeat him." Sam walks to the machine and sets it up. Christina opens up the machine's tube, and straps herself in. The machine's tube closes, as Sam starts up the process. An flash of rainbow energy covers the tube, as the machine spins. The machine's speaker said, "Ice Power Transfer is complete!" The machine slows down to an stop, and Sam opens the tube. Sam unstraps Christina from the tube, and helps her out of the machine. Christina said, "I don't feel any different!" Sam said, "Give it an bit for the ice powers to kick in. With your new powers, you should be able to defeat Fire Slinger." Christina nods, as she walks back to the bed. Christina laid on the bed, and continued reading an science book. Christina walked outside to the flag pole for some fresh air. Fire Slinger walked toward her with red glowing eyes. Fire Slinger said, "Ready for our rematch?" An flash of rainbow energy covers the area! Supersonic Warrior said, "Yes, I am ready to defeat you!" Supersonic Warrior flips in the air and throws an ice ball at Fire Slinger! The ice ball hits Fire Slinger's leg, and it freezes him in place. Supersonic Warrior emits an ice beam from her hand at Fire Slinger. Fire Slinger responds by emitting an fire beam from his hand at Supersonic Warrior. The beams hit each other, and they caused an elemental explosion, that pushes Supersonic Warrior and Fire Slinger backwards. Supersonic Warrior speeds toward Fire Slinger and smashes him in to the flag pole. Supersonic Warrior emits an ice blast from her body! Fire Slinger emits an fire blast from his body as well. The elemental explosion covers the area! Supersonic Warrior tumbles on to the ground, and Fire Slinger smashes through the trees. Fire Slinger slowly gets up, and Supersonic Warrior gets up as well. Supersonic Warrior speeds in to Fire Slinger, and grabs him by the neck. Supersonic Warrior emits her hands with ice, and smashes Fire Slinger in to the ground. Supersonic Warrior puts her foot on Fire Slinger's chest, as she punches him in the face. Blood leaks out on to the ground. Fire Slinger throws an fire ball at Supersonic Warrior! Supersonic Warrior flips out of the way, and grabs the fire ball in her hand, turning it in to an ice ball. Supersonic Warrior throws the ice ball back at Fire Slinger, and it freezes his arm in place. Supersonic Warrior emits an ice blast from her body, and Fire Slinger emits an fire blast from his body! The elemental explosion covers the area! Fire Slinger smashes through the school, as the wall foundation crumbles on top of him. Supersonic Warrior's helmet shatters in the explosion, as Supersonic Warrior smashes through the flag pole. Supersonic Warrior slowly gets up from the ground! An blast of flames covers the area, as the wall foundation flied everywhere! Fire Slinger walks towards Supersonic Warrior with blood leaking from his body! Fire Slinger laughs and said, "I'm still alive, colorful pest!" Fire Slinger kicks Supersonic Warrior in the chest! Supersonic Warrior slides backwards and growls! Fire Slinger tackles Supersonic Warrior in to the ground, and steps on her chest! Fire Slinger emits an beam of flames from his hand and hits Supersonic Warrior in the chest with it. Supersonic Warrior screams in pain, as blood leaks out on to the ground! Supersonic Warrior growled and grabbed Fire Slinger's arm, freezing it in place with ice! Supersonic Warrior kicked Fire Slinger in the face! Supersonic Warrior flips in the area, and kicks Fire Slinger in the chest! Fire Slinger slides backwards! Supersonic Warrior grabs the flag pole and hits Fire Slinger with it! Fire Slinger smashes in to the school building! Fire Slinger slowly got up from the ground! Fire Slinger speeds in to Supersonic Warrior and grabs her by the throat. Fire Slinger chokes Supersonic Warrior, while he squeezes her throat. Supersonic Warrior coughs and grabs Fire Slinger's arm. Fire Slinger's arm freezes in ice! Fire Slinger heats up his body, and melts the ice off of his arm. Supersonic Warrior covers his legs in ice, and kicks Fire Slinger in the face. Fire Slinger slides backwards! Fire Slinger grabs Supersonic Warrior by the neck, and body slams her in to the ground. Blood leaks out on to the ground! Supersonic Warrior sweeps her leg under Fire Slinger! Fire Slinger falls on to the ground! Fire Slinger gets up from the ground! Supersonic Warrior speeds into Fire Slinger, and grabs him by his throat. Supersonic Warrior body slams Fire Slinger in to the ground! Fire Slinger gets up from the ground and growls! Fire Slinger emits an beam of flames from his hand! Supersonic Warrior emits an beam of ice from her hand! The beams collide, and they caused an elemental explosion! The explosion covered the area and smashed Fire Slinger and Supersonic Warrior in to the ground! Blood covered the area with destruction and debris. Fire Slinger's eyes returned to normal as he laid on the ground in an puddle of blood. Supersonic Warrior slowly got up, and wiped the blood from her gloves. Supersonic Warrior walked toward Justin's body, and got terrified. James ran out of the school toward Supersonic Warrior and checked on her. James said, "Is everything ok?" Supersonic Warrior said, "Justin was Fire Slinger!" James said, "Oh god, he injected himself with fire powers to get revenge on his enemies from his dad's death." Supersonic Warrior said, "Yep, I feel bad for him! Grab an bucket of water, and we can wash the blood off of him." James grabbed an bucket of water, and poured it on Justin's body. The water cleared the blood off of Justin's body. Justin wakes up, and slowly gets up from the ground! Justin falls in to Supersonic Warrior's arms, as he gains his footing. Justin rubs his head and said, "There is chaos and destruction everywhere!" Supersonic Warrior said, "Your anger spiraled out of control, and you injected yourself with fire powers! We fought against each other, and you caused chaos and destruction to everything around you!" Justin breaks down and starts crying! Justin said, "I am so sorry for hurting you, Supersonic Warrior, I let my emotions control my actions, and it is all my fault." Justin falls in to Supersonic Warrior's arms. Supersonic Warrior rubs Justin's head, and said, "I forgive you, let's get you some help, so this doesn't happen again." Justin nods, as he wipes the tears from his eyes! An flash of rainbow energy covered the area, as Supersonic Warrior demorphed. Justin grabs Christina's hand, and James walks alongside them back to the school. Justin and Christina walk with James in to the school building and towards the gym. They walked in to the gym toward Gym Teacher Harry. Gym Teacher Harry said, "Hello kiddos, what can I do for you, today?" Christina and James said, "Justin needs to control his anger, and he injected himself with fire powers! He needs to learn how to control his powers, so he doesn't hurt anyone around him." Gym Teacher Harry nodded as he looked over Justin! Gym Teacher Harry said, "This will be an hard task, but I bet that I can shape him up to be an better human being!" Christina and James smiled, as they walked out of the gym! They left Justin with Gym Teacher Harry! Gym Teacher Harry said, "Justin, you have tons of work ahead of you, bud!"Justin nodded, as he smiled! Outside the gym, James and Christina smiled and hugged each other! James laid his head in Christina's lap and said, "I hope Justin improves his life by training with Gym Teacher Harry!" Christina ruffles up James's hair and said, "Me too, I hope Justin can turn his life around!" James fixes up his hair, while he smiles at Christina. Christina and James hug each other, as the moon sets, and it turns dark outside the school!

17

14

The moon was shining over Oasis Falls High School! Christina and James were sitting on the steps, watching the moon shine in the sky. James winked and said, "The moon is beautiful tonight, just like you, Christina." Christina blushes and said, "Thanks James, you're the best!" Christina hugs James! James hugs Christina back! James said, "It's getting late, let me walk you back to the science lab." Christina said, "Sure, that would be great." Christina and James got up from the steps and walked in to the school. The school doors auto locked behind them! Christina and James held hands, as they walked down to the science lab. James and Christina walked to the science lab's door! Christina turned the door knob and opened the door. Christina and James walked in to the science lab, and closed the door behind them. James said, "I will stay with you in the science lab, because it is dangerous to travel outside at night. It would be bad if a supervillain attacked me on the way back to my house." Christina said, "True, I wouldn't have enough energy to beat up a supervillain at night." James said, "Think of it as a midnight hangout session." Christina said, "Yep, I like hanging out with you." James smiled and said, "Me too, you are amazing to hangout with as well." James and Christina walked over to the beds. James sat his bag down on the floor, and sat on the bed. Christina sat her bag down on the floor, and sat on the other bed. James was sitting on the bed, studying his Math textbook for Paul's class. James was rubbing his head, while going through the Math equations. James writes the equations in his notebook, and tries to solve them. James drinks a can of Super Pepper, to hydrate his brain. James closes his Math textbook and puts his pencil in his pencil case. James puts his Math textbook and his pencil case in to his bag. James drank down the can of Super pepper, and crushed the can with his foot. James threw the crushed can in to the recycling bin. James zips up his bag. James laid down on the bed, and he put the bed sheets on her head. James fell asleep and closed his eyes. Christina was sitting on the other bed, studying her Math textbook for Paul's class. Christina was rubbing her head, while going through the Math equations. Christina wrote the Math equations in to her notebook, and tries to solve them. Christina drinks a can of Super Pepper, to hydrate her brain. Christina looks over at the clock! Christina said, "Oh boy, it is getting late! It would be bad if I fell asleep in the middle of class for not having enough energy." Christina drank down the can of Super Pepper, and crushed the can with her foot. Christina threw the crushed can in to the recycling bin. Christina closes her notebook and Math textbook, and puts them in her bag. Christina puts the pencil in her pencil case. Christina puts the pencil case in her bag and zips it up. Christina laid down on the bed, and she put the bed sheets on her head. Christina fell asleep and closed her eyes! The sun rose over Oasis Falls High School! Christina woke up and got up from the bed. Christina put the bag on her back! James woke up and got up from the bed. James put the bag on his back. Christina and James walked out of the science lab. James said, "Hey Christina, hope you had a good rest!" Christina said, "I had a good rest, and I am filled with energy." Christina and James hugged each other. James and Christina held hands and walked down the hallway. Students were in the hallway, getting class supplies and textbooks from their lockers. Christina and James smiled at each other. Christina stopped at her locker, while James was sipping water out of the water fountain. Christina sighed and said, "Studying for the Math exam was insane last night! My head is filled with decimals and fractions!" James said, "Don't worry, you will do great on the exam, you will blast the equations apart!" James and Christina hug each other, while laying against the wall. The bell rings in the background!

Christina and James walked to Paul's Math class! Christina and James stopped at the door. Christina turned the door knob! The door swung open, and Paul was cleaning his desk! Christina and James walked to their seats and sat down. The other students sat down as well. Paul handed out the exam to every student, while the students got their pencils and erasers out of their bags. Paul set up the timer on his desk and said, "Students, the exam is 20% of your final grade. Do well on the equations, and work hard to solve them! Turn in your exams, by putting them on my desk, when the timer rings!" The students nodded! Paul activates the timer on his desk and the students started working on the exam. Paul sat at his desk, checking his email, while eraser dust flew in the air. The timer was counting down, while the students were writing on the exam with their pencils. The timer rang, while the students breathed a sigh of relief. The students got up from their seats, and put the finished exam on Paul's desk. The students went back to their seats, and put the pencils away in their bags. The school bell rang, and Paul opened the classroom door. The students walked out of the classroom, and in to the hallway. Christina and James walked out of the classroom together. Christina said, "The exam was tough, I hope I did good on the equations." James said, "I had trouble on the equations as well." Christina and James held hands, as they walked down the hallway toward the gym. Christina said, "It's time for gym class, let's see what kind of exercise that Gym Teacher Harry has for us, today!" James said, "Let's go in to find out!" Christina and James walked toward the doors for the gym. Christina turned the door knob. James and Christina walked in to the gym, and saw the rack of balls. Justin was leaning against the rack, and smiled at them. Justin said, "Hey guys, are you ready for some dodgeball?" Christina said, "I love dodgeball!" James gets terrified by the ball, and hides behind Christina! Justin said, "Don't be scared, James, the ball won't hurt you at all, it is nice and soft." James breathed a sigh of relief, as he held Christina's hand. Gym Teacher Harry walked out of his office, with his whistle around his neck. Gym Teacher Harry said, "Get into positions, students, it's time for some dodgeball."

The students walked in to their positions on the gym floor. James and Christina stood next to each other. Flash stood next to James and got in to position. Justin walked on to the gym floor with the dodgeball in his hand. Justin smiled at the other students, while throwing the ball in the air and catching it. Gym Teacher Harry picked up his whistle and blew it in his mouth. Justin's eyes glowed red, as he clutched the dodge ball in his hand. Justin lit the ball up with flames and threw it at Flash. The ball flew super fast at Flash, and hit him in the chest. Flash smashed in to the wall and laid on the ground! Gym Teacher Harry blew the whistle, and walked over to Flash. Gym Teacher Harry said, "You're out!" Flash rubbed his head, and walked over to the bleachers. Flash sat down on the bleachers. Justin threw the ball in the air, and caught it with his hand! Gym Teacher Harry blew the whistle and the next round of dodgeball has begun. Justin's eyes glowed red as he lit the ball with flames. Justin threw the ball at James. The ball flew at James! James lowered his hands to his chest, as the ball was flying at him. The ball hit James in the chest, while James wrapped his arms around it. James laid against the wall. Gym Teacher Harry blew his whistle and walked over to James. James had his hands around the ball, as Gym teacher Harry walked toward him. Gym Teacher Harry said, "James has caught the ball, which means Justin is out." Justin walked over to the bleachers. Justin sat on the bleachers! Gym Teacher Harry said, "Welcome to the final round of dodgeball, I will be facing against the other group of students. Hope you guys are ready, because this round will be intense." Gym Teacher Harry gave his whistle to Justin on the bleachers. Justin put the whistle around his neck! Gym Teacher Harry picked up the ball with his hand, and walked to the middle of the gym. Christina and James stood next to each other. Gym Teacher Harry threw the ball in the air and caught it with his hand. Justin blew the whistle in his mouth. Gym Teacher Harry clutched the ball in his hand, and threw it at James. The ball flew at James, and it hit him in the chest. James fell on the ground, and the ball rolled next to him. Justin blew the whistle, and Gym Teacher Harry walked over to James. Gym Teacher Harry held out his hand to James! James grabbed Gym Teacher Harry's hand and got up from the ground. James walked over to the bleachers! James sat on the bleachers! Gym Teacher Harry grabbed the ball and walked to the middle of the gym. Christina got in to battle position, as she stared down Gym Teacher Harry. Gym Teacher Harry clutched the ball in his hand. Gym Teacher Harry threw the ball at Christina! Christina flipped in the air, and shot a ice beam with her hand. Christina caught the ball, and it froze in her hand. Christina landed on the ground, and threw the ice ball at Gym Teacher Harry. The ice ball flew at Gym Teacher Harry's chest. The ice crystals collided with Gym Teacher Harry. Gym Teacher Harry smashed in to the wall, and the ice crystals formed around his body to form a wall of ice. Justin blew the whistle, as he got up from the bleachers. Christina and Justin walked over to Gym Teacher harry in the wall of ice. Justin's eyes glowed red, as he put his hand on the wall of ice. The wall of ice melted, while Justin's flames flowed through it. The wall of ice melted, as Justin's eyes went back to normal. Gym Teacher Harry slowly walked toward Justin and Christina. Gym Teacher Harry walked over to Justin and hugged him. Gym Teacher Harry said, "Thanks for rescuing me from the wall of ice." Justin said, "No problem, it looks like Christina won the round of dodgeball. Gym Teacher Harry said, "She did pretty good!" Justin took the whistle off of his neck, and gave it back to Gym Teacher Harry. James and Flash got up from the bleachers and walked over to the water fountain to rehydrate their bodies. The bell rings in the background. Gym Teacher Harry said, "Looks like class is over, see you guys later." Christina puts her bag on her back, and walks over to the water fountain to rehydrate her body. James walked over to Christina and said, "Your dodgeball skills are amazing!" Christina said, "Thanks, you did pretty good as well." Flash walked over to James and Christina! Flash held out his hand and said, "Hi, I am Flash! I am the star quarterback on the football team for Oasis Falls High School." James shook Flash's hand and said, "Nice to meet you, I am James, and this is Christina!" Christina nodded and waved at Flash! Flash said, "Nice to meet both of you, your dodgeball skills were very good!" Christina said, "Thanks, you did good as well." The bell rings in the background! Flash said,"I have a science class to go to, see you guys later!" Christina and James waved to Flash, as he walks down the hallway. Christina said, "This is our free period, let's hang out at the swimming pool!" James said, "Sounds great!" Christina and James held hands and walked down to the swimming pool. Christina and James walked to the door for the swimming pool and turned the door knob. They walked in to the room with the swimming pool, and a burst of cold air blasted on to them. Christina said, "Whew, it is cold in here!" James said, "Awwwww, don't worry, I will keep you warm, so you won't freeze to death." James wraps himself around Christina to keep her warm. Christina said, "Thanks James, you're the best!" Christina and James held hands as they walked toward the changing room. Christina and James walked in to the changing room, and set their bags next to the bench. Christina and James sat on the bench, and took their swim suits out of their bags. Christina and James took off their shirts and stuffed them in their bags. Christina puts on her swim suit. James takes off his pants, and puts them in his bag. James puts on his swimming shorts. Christina said, "Wow James, you look amazing!" James said, "You look amazing as well!" James and Christina held hands and walked toward the swimming pool. James jumps in to the swimming pool and splashes Christina! Christina jumps in to the swimming pool. James and Christina swam laps around the pool. Christina and James splashed each other. Christina and James sat on the edge of the swimming pool, and splashed their feet in the water. Christina said, "The water was so refreshing!" James said, "I agree, it is so nice to relax!" James and Christina wrapped their arms around each other! James and Christina kissed each other! James said, "That was amazing! You are wonderful, Christina!" Christina blushes and said, "You are amazing as well, James!" James and Christina stood up and walked toward the towels. James and Christina grabbed a towel and dried themselves off. James and Christina held hands and walked back toward the changing room. James and Christina sat on the bench! James took off his swimming shorts, and put his pants back on. James took his shirt out of his bag! James put his shirt on. Christina took off her swimming suit, and put her shirt back on. James and Christina zipped up their bags, and stood up from the bench. James and Christina put their bags on their back, and walked out of the room. James and Christina walked in to the hallway! James said, "There is a football game at the field later today, do you want to the game and support Flash!" Christina said, "Sure, I would love to support Flash!" James and Christina walked down to the gym for the pep rally! James and Christina walk in to the gym and they sit on the bleachers! Justin was lifting weights, while Gym Teacher Harry was watching over him with his clipboard. Gym Teacher Harry writes on his clipboard! Gym Teacher Harry said, "Good Job Justin, your stats are better than this morning. You are improving very well." Justin puts the weights back in to Gym Teacher Harry's office. Justin walks to the bleachers and sits next to James and Christina. The cheerleaders and the mascot walk in to the gym with the rest of the students. The rest of the students fill up the bleachers, while the cheerleaders stand in the corner of the gym with the mascot to warm up. Gym Teacher Harry puts the whistle around his neck. Gym Teacher harry blew the whistle! The cheerleaders and the mascot backflipped in to the middle of the gym. The cheerleaders flipped in the air and the students cheered. The cheerleaders flipped in the air and stood on each other to build a tower. The mascot backflipped on to the top of the tower, and landed on the cheerleader's heads. The students cheered while the cheerleaders shouted, "Let's Go Wildcats!" The mascot flipped in the air and landed on the gym floor. The cheerleaders flipped in the air and landed on the gym floor. Gym Teacher Harry walked to the middle of the gym. Gym Teacher Harry said, "Welcome to the Wildcats Pep Rally! Cheer for our amazing mascot and the wonderful cheerleaders!" The students cheered! The cheerleaders bowed their heads and put their pom poms in the air! The mascot flipped in the air, and landed on the gym floor. Gym Teacher Harry said, "Lets bring out the football teams that will be playing in the football game later today! Let's start off with the Oasis Falls Wildcats!" Flash and the rest of the football team marched in to the gym and stood next to Gym Teacher Harry. The students cheered! The football team waved and bowed their heads in honor. Gym Teacher Harry said, "Now for the other football team, the Sunshine Paradise Dragons! Taylor and the rest of the Sunshine Paradise Dragons marched in to the gym and stood on the other side of Gym Teacher Harry! Gym Teacher Harry said, "Please show the Sunshine Paradise Dragons that Oasis Falls is a good community of students." The mascot for the Sunshine Paradise Dragons back flipped in to the gym and had a dance competition with the mascot for the Oasis Falls Wildcats. The marching band for the Wildcats played a arrangement of music on their instruments and marched around the gym. The cheerleaders flipped in the air and did some routines, while the students cheered. The football teams did their own dance moves while the performance was playing in the background. Gym Teacher Harry pulled out the confetti cannon and activated it. Confetti blasted out of the cannon and floated throughout the gym. The mascots flipped in the air and landed on top of the football players. The cheerleaders flipped in the air and landed on top of the mascots to build a tower. The cheerleaders raised their pom poms and shouted, "Let's Go Wildcats!" The students shouted, "Let's Go Wildcats!" Gym Teacher Harry activated the confetti cannon and confetti flew in the air. The cheerleaders flipped in the air and landed on the gym floor. The mascots flipped in the air and landed on the gym floor. Gym Teacher Harry said, "Good luck to both football teams and you're free to enjoy the rest of the day, students!" The bell rang and the students got up and left the gym. The cheerleaders and the marching band put their equipment away. The football teams were training on the fitness equipment to get ready for the football game. James and Christina got up from the bleachers and walked to the middle of the gym with Justin. Justin said, "Are you guys going to be at the football game?" James and Christina said, "Yes, it will be fun to watch both football teams on the field." Flash and Taylor were lifting weights, while the other football players were watching them. Flash said, "I can lift the weights more than you, Taylor!" Taylor said, "Try to beat me, Flash! Being a star quarterback of the football team doesn't mean that you are good at everything." Gym Teacher Harry was writing their stats on his clipboard. Flash and Taylor continued lifting weights. Gym Teacher Harry blew his whistle and said, "Let's check your stats, guys!" Flash and Taylor set the weights on the ground and walked over to Gym Teacher Harry. Gym Teacher Harry said, "It is a tie, the stats are the same." Taylor said, "I am going to get some fresh air." Flash walked over to the water fountain and re-hydrated his body. Taylor walked out of the gym. Taylor walked outside and on to the football field. Taylor walked to the center of the football field and said, "Wow the football field looks cool." A shadowy figure was standing on the sideline. Taylor walked to the sideline! The shadowy figure tackled Taylor in to the ground. Taylor kicks the shadowy figure in the face. The shadowy figure slid backwards, as Taylor got up from the ground. Taylor said, "Who are you?" The shadowy figure took off his hood and said, "I am Adrian from Electric Industries, and your skills have peaked my interest." Taylor rubs his head and said, "I am listening, what is your proposal?" Adrian said, "There's been a thorn in my side! The thorn is known as Supersonic Warrior, and she has been driving me crazy." Adrian takes a bottle and a needle out of his pocket. Adrian said, "This bottle has a liquid! The liquid is a combination of Supersonic Warrior's blood and zombie dna. It will give you the abilities of a zombie and Supersonic Warrior in one package." Taylor said, "Sounds interesting!" Adrian said, "Trust In Me, the liquid is safe for your body." Taylor said, "Fine, I will try out your liquid experiment." Taylor puts out his arm, while Adrian attaches the liquid container to the needle. Adrian opens up the bottle, and pours the liquid in to the liquid container. Adrian sticks the needle in to Taylor's arm. The liquid injects in to Taylor's body. Adrian said, "The effects of the liquid will take a while to affect your body." Taylor said, "Sounds good!" Adrian put his hood back on, and walked off the football field. Taylor walked off the football field and back in to Oasis Falls High School. Taylor walks back in to the gym, and joins with the rest of the football team. Taylor said, "I am ready for the football game!" Flash said, "Same, it would be nice to play, while everyone is cheering you on!" Gym Teacher Harry said, "The football game is in about a hour!" Taylor said, "Sounds good, it gives me time to get one more exercise in." Taylor tackles Flash and wrestles him in to the ground. The other football team members cheer him on. Taylor holds Flash on to the ground, and wraps his arm around Flash's neck. Taylor said, "Say Uncle!" Flash coughs and said, "NEVER!" Taylor gets angry and punches Flash in the chest. Flash growls and said, "Let Me Go, Taylor!" Taylor said, "Not til you say uncle!" Gym Teacher Harry and Justin saw the football players, and walked over to them. Gym Teacher Harry said, "Break It Up Now! We don't want anyone getting hurt before the football game." Justin's eyes glow red while he said, "You guys are morons for showing your strength by wrestling each other. Prove your own strength on the football field as a team." Justin emits a blast of flames from his hand and hits Taylor in the chest. Taylor smashes in to the wall, and laid on the ground. Flash got up from the ground, while the other football team members helped Taylor get up. Taylor said, "You want to fight, pipsqueak?" Justin said, "I will kill you!" Flames appear in Justin's eyes, as he puts his foot on the ground. Fire covers the gym floor, as it flows toward Taylor! A pillar of flames rise under Taylor's feet and knocks him in to the air. Justin flips in the air, and forms a path of lava and flames under his feet as he skates on the path towards Taylor. Justin flips in the air and covers the area with a explosion of flames from his hands. Taylor smashes against the wall. Justin spins in to a fire tornado, and speeds in to Taylor. The wall explodes as Justin hits Taylor's chest. Taylor laid on the ground, with blood leaking on to the ground. Justin picks up Taylor by his neck, and chokes him. Justin squeezes his neck, while Taylor coughs. Justin said, "You don't deserve to live, weakling!" Justin slams Taylor against the wall. Gym Teacher Harry said to Christina, "You must stop Justin, before he kills Sunshine's Paradise's star quarterback." Christina nodded, as your eyes turn blue. Christina said, "Justin, it is time for you to chill!" Christina puts up her hand and a wall of ice forms and freezes Justin in place. Taylor fell out of Justin's grip, and laid on the ground. The other football players helped Taylor off of the ground. Gym Teacher Harry said, "Taylor, you can use the bathroom next to the gym to wash the blood off." Taylor nods and walks over to the bathroom. Taylor walks in to the bathroom and washed the blood and dirt off of his body. Taylor dried himself off with the towel and walked back in to the gym. Taylor hung out with the other football players. Gym Teacher Harry used his hair dryer on Justin's body to melt the ice. The ice melted and Justin's eyes returned to normal. Justin rubbed his head and said, "Thanks Christina for cooling me down!" Christina nodded and said, "No Problem!" Gym Teacher Harry blew his whistle and said, "It's almost time for the football game." Gym Teacher Harry and the football team members walked over to the football field. Justin walked to the football field with James and Christina. James and Christina held hands, and Justin walked behind them, as they walked on to the football field. James, Christina, and Justin walked to the bleachers. James, Christina, and Justin sat on the bleachers together. Gym Teacher Harry walked to the sideline with the football players for Oasis Falls and Sunshine Paradise. The football players stood next to Gym Teacher Harry, while he set up the water cooler for the football players. The mascots walked on to the sideline with the cheerleaders. The mascots and the cheerleaders stood next to Gym Teacher Harry and the football players. The other students filled up the bleachers, as the sun set over the football field. The lights for the football field lit up, while the moon rose over the school. Gym Teacher Harry walked in to the middle of the football field, and blew his whistle. The cheerleaders rolled the confetti cannon on to the field and stood next to Gym Teacher Harry. The mascots backflipped on to the field, and landed next to Gym Teacher Harry. Gym Teacher Harry walked to the microphone stand and said, "Welcome to the football game, everyone!" Hope all of you have fun watching the game. Let's get the party started!" Gym Teacher Harry activated the confetti cannon, and confetti floated in the air, and covered the football field. The cheerleaders flipped in the air, and waved their pom poms. The students cheered! The mascots flipped in the air and landed on the ground. The mascots grabbed t shirt cannons and ran down the football field, shooting shirts in to the bleachers. The students caught the shirts and cheered. Flash and the other football players were on the sideline, stretching their legs and tossing the football around. Taylor sat on the sideline drinking water. Max walked over to Taylor and said, "Are you ready to have some fun on the football field?" Taylor said, "I am ready!" Taylor's skin turned pale, the muscles in his arms expanded, and his hair turned green. Max said, "Taylor, are you feeling ok?" Taylor said, "I am feeling fine, let's have some fun!" Taylor got up from the sideline and drank some water. Max was stretching his legs, as he ran in place. Taylor and the rest of his team walked to their side of the field. Flash and the rest of his team walked to their side of the field with the football. Sam kicked the football, and the football game started. Max caught the football and ran down the field. Miles tackled Max and Gym Teacher Harry blew the whistle. Taylor and the rest of his team huddled around each other. Taylor said, "I will hike the ball to Max, and he will catch it for the first down." The team nodded their heads, and got in to position. Matt tossed the ball to Taylor! Taylor hiked the ball and waited for Max to get in to position. Tyler, the right tackle for the Oasis Falls Wildcats, ran towards Taylor. Taylor spun in a circle and kicked Tyler in the chest. Tyler fell on to the field, as Taylor threw the football to Max. Max caught the ball, while Duncan chased after Max. Duncan tackled Max to the ground. Taylor stepped on Tyler's hand as he got up from the ground. Tyler got mad and pushed Taylor. Taylor picked up Tyler and body slammed him in to the ground. Gym Teacher Harry blew the whistle and walked over to the field! Gym Teacher Harry said, "Roughing the player, -10 yards!" Taylor growled as he walked back to his team! Taylor hiked the ball, and waited for the other players to get in to position. Duncan sped through the defense and sacked Taylor in to the ground. Duncan kicked Taylor in the chest! Taylor got up from the ground and growled at Duncan! Phil kicked the field goal, as Taylor and his team walked off the field. Phil kicked the football down the field! Flash and his team caught the ball and ran it down the field. Flash hiked the ball and threw it down the field. His team mate caught the ball and ran it for the touchdown. Taylor threw his helmet on the ground. It was half time, as Flash walked off the field with the rest of his team. The marching band marched on to the field and did the performance on their instruments. Fireworks exploded over the football field, as the students cheered. Taylor walked over to Flash and pushed him in to the water cooler, knocking it over. Flash fell on the ground! Flash said, "What is your problem?" Taylor growled and said, "You're my problem, prepare to be eliminated!" Taylor pulls the football helmet off of Flash, and throws it on the ground. Taylor steps on Flash's chest, and punches him in the face. Max walked over to Taylor, and grabbed his arm. Max said, "What is wrong with you?" Taylor kicks Max in the chest! Max falls on the ground, and is terrified in fear! Gym Teacher Harry blows the whistle! Gym Teacher Harry walked over to Taylor. Gym Teacher Harry said, "Get off of Flash Now!" Taylor growled and picked Gym Teacher Harry up by the neck. Flash got terrified and ran toward the bleachers with Max and the other football players. Taylor choked Gym Teacher Harry and smashed him through the sideline table. Gym Teacher Harry laid on the ground in a puddle of blood. Justin growled and his eyes glowed red. Justin jumped off of the bleachers and hit Taylor in the chest with a explosion of flames. Justin said, "You will die for killing Gym Teacher Harry!" Taylor slid backwards. Justin shot Taylor with a beam of flames from his hand. Taylor slid backwards! Taylor sped toward Justin and grabbed his arm. Justin said, "Attacking me when I am distracted was a mistake!" A explosion of flames exploded from Justin's body! Taylor smashed in to the bleachers and fell on the ground. Christina jumped off of the bleachers and morphed in to the Supersonic Warrior with a blast of rainbow energy that covered the area. Supersonic Warrior kicked Taylor in to the air with a roundhouse kick. Supersonic Warrior summoned a pillar of ice that froze Taylor in the air. Justin flipped in the air, and kicked Taylor in to the ground with a firey kick in the chest. Taylor smashed in to the ground. Justin and Supersonic Warrior stood on each side of Taylor. Taylor grabbed the goal post and tore it out of the ground. Taylor swung the goal post at Justin and Supersonic Warrior. Justin and Supersonic Warrior backflipped out of the way, and jumped in to the air. Justin and Supersonic Warrior sent a blast of flames and ice out of their hands at Taylor. The explosion hit Taylor and it sent him flying in to the water cooler. The water cooler exploded, and water fell on to the field. Taylor slowly got up from the ground. Taylor roared, and charged toward Supersonic Warrior. Supersonic Warrior shot ice blasts at Taylor! Taylor charges through them and smashes Supersonic Warrior in to the goal post. Taylor tears the goal post out of the ground, and hits Supersonic Warrior in the chest. Supersonic Warrior smashes in to the bleachers. Taylor jumps on to Supersonic Warrior and punches her in the face. Supersonic Warrior shoots Taylor in the face with a ice blast! Taylor stumbles backwards! Taylor picks up Supersonic Warrior and smashes her in to the ground. Justin growls and shouts, "Get away from her, monster!" Justin speeds in to Taylor and hits him with a explosion blast from his hand. Taylor falls on the ground! Supersonic Warrior gets up from the ground! Taylor gets up from the ground! Supersonic Warrior stepped on the ground, and a ice wall froze Taylor in place. Justin walked up to Taylor and smiled! Justin's hand lit up with flames as he said, "Prepare to die, Your life is about to end!" Justin put his hand on Taylor's neck! Taylor's body burned alive, and his ashes fell on the ground. Justin and Supersonic Warrior high fived each other as they walked back to the bleachers. James ran over and hugged Supersonic Warrior. A group of security officers walked over to Supersonic Warrior and Justin, with a hooded figure handcuffed. Eddie said, "We spotted this guy on the football field. He was disturbing the peace mixing liquids together for science experiments." The security officers took the hood off of the figure. Adrian said, "Let me go, I am from Electric Industries, and my work is very important." Justin walked over to the security officers and said, "I saw Adrian on the school's security cameras. He was talking to Taylor, while he was getting fresh air. He poked him with a needle and injected him with a liquid. This scientist is putting citizen's lives in danger with his experiments." The security officers nodded and said, "What should we do with him?" Justin said, "He deserves to be in a jail cell!" The security officers opened up their car and threw Adrian in to the backseat. Supersonic Warrior said, "I have a bad feeling about this. Adrian is going to jail, but I have a feeling that this isn't the last time that we will see him and his experiments." Justin said, "Knowing how our lives have been going, another super villain might break him out of jail, and everything will go downhill from here." Justin walked in to the school with James and Christina. Police cars drove away from Oasis Falls High School. Adrian was in the back seat of the car with his arms handcuffed. The police cars drove past Electric Industries. The police cars stopped at the Oasis Falls Jail, and turned off the police car. An hooded figure stood on the rooftop of the jail. The hooded figure stabbed a needle in to his arm, that was filled with a liquid combination of spider dna and Supersonic Warrior's blood. The hooded figure bent down, as the liquid flowed through his body. The police officers walked out of the car. The hooded figure jumped down and tackled the police officer. The police officer walked behind the hooded figure and said, "Put your hands up!" The hooded figure laughed and took off his hood. The hooded figure kicked the police officer in the chest, and wrapped him in a web cocoon. The hooded figure said, "I am the Spider Crusader. Give me Adrian, and no one gets hurt!" The other police officer said, "No way, you crazy villain." Spider Crusader said, "Then you must die!" Spider Crusader grabs the police officer by the neck and chokes him. Spider Crusader stabs the police officer in the chest with his web sword. Blood poured on to the ground! Spider Crusader throws the body on to the ground, as he walked toward Adrian. Spider Crusader said, "Adrian, I will take you to your new science lab. Spider Crusader presses a button on his wrist, as the glider lands. Spider Crusader and Adrian walk on to the glider. The glider flew in to the air! The glider flied to the new science lab. Spider Crusader taps a button on his wrist and the glider parked it self in the corner of the science lab. Spider Crusader taps a button on his wrist, and his mask flipped open. Peter said, "Adrian, this lab will help you continue your science experiments. Every container has your previous work from Electric Industries before you got caught by the police." Adrian said, "Sounds good, thanks for the help!" Peter said, "I will recharge in the science lab, before I pay a small visit to the colorful pest, Supersonic Warrior." Peter walked over to his tube, and walked in to it. Peter connected himself to the tube and started it up. The tube recharged his body, as the energy flows around him. Justin laid against the school wall as James and Christina held hands. Justin said, "Both of you are so cute as love birds." James said, "Thanks for supporting our relationship!" Justin drank out of the water fountain as James and Christina wrapped their arms around each other and kissed. Christina said, "I love you James, I hope the world doesn't take you away." James said, "I love you too, Christina, you are the smartest girl that I have met in my entire life." Justin said, "It is so nice seeing love come together, it is so magical." Christina ruffles up James's hair, and Justin laughs. James fixes his hair and laughs! Justin said, "You guys are perfect for each other!" Christina said, "James, do you want to be my boyfriend?" James said, "I would love to!" James kissed Christina on the lips, and wrapped his arms around her. Christina kissed James and wrapped her arms around him. James said, "Yep, this is the ending to a perfect day." The moon rose over Oasis Falls High School while James, Christina, and Justin hung out with each other.

18

15

The sun rose over Electric Industries! Peter was in the recharge tube, replenishing his energy to get ready for destruction. Adrian walked in to the science lab. Adrian said, "Good morning, sleepy head!" Peter rubbed his head, as he woke up. Adrian said, "How are you feeling?" Peter said, "I am energized, and ready for battle." Adrian unlocked the tube, as Peter walked out. The robots in the science lab turned on automatically and surrounded Peter. Peter growled at the robots. The robots said, "Threat detected, exterminate the intruder." Peter said, "I am not a threat, robotic scum." Peter backflipped in the air and wrapped the robots in a web cocoon with his web shooters. Peter stabbed his web sword in to the robots, as they fell on to the ground. Peter puts the web sword on his back, as he walked toward his glider. Peter walked on to the glider, and flew out of the science lab. Peter put his hood over his head, as he flew in to the air. James and Christina sat on the steps outside Oasis Falls High School. The birds were tweeting in the background! Christina said, "It is so nice to hear the birds tweeting in the background." James wrapped his arm around Christina and said, "Yep, it is a beautiful day outside!" James kissed Christina on the cheek! Christina smiled at James! Web bombs flew past James and Christina, as the glider flew towards them. The web bombs hit the front door of Oasis Falls High School, and exploded behind them. The foundation of the school shook as it fell on the front steps. Christina grabbed James and dived in to the bush, so they wouldn't get injured. Spider Crusader parked the glider, next to the tree. Spider Crusader walked off of his glider with his web sword and cut down the bushes. Christina and James hid behind the bush, as Spider Crusader patrolled the area. Spider Crusader patrolled around the area and said, "Come out, come out, little pests, so I can squish you like bugs on the cement." Christina morphed in to Supersonic Warrior, in a flash of rainbow energy. Supersonic Warrior shot a ice beam at Spider Crusader. Spider Crusader deflected the ice beam back at Supersonic Warrior, with his web sword. Spider Crusader tackled Supersonic Warrior in to the flag pole. The flag pole got dented, as Supersonic Warrior laid on the ground. Supersonic Warrior got up from the ground. Supersonic Warrior picked up the flag pole! Supersonic Warrior swung the flag pole like a golf club, and hit Spider Crusader in to the building. Spider Crusader smashed in to the wall, as Supersonic Warrior sped toward Spider Crusader. Spider Crusader punched Supersonic Warrior in the face. Supersonic Warrior slid backwards. Spider Crusader picked Supersonic Warrior up by the neck, and threw her through the building. The building foundation crumbled, and fell on top of Supersonic Warrior. Supersonic Warrior laid on the ground! Supersonic Warrior got up from the ground, while pieces of building foundation fell off of her suit, and on to the ground. Spider Crusader flipped in the air, and roundhouse kicked Supersonic Warrior in the chest. Supersonic Warrior laid against the wall. Spider Crusader growled, and threw the web bomb at Supersonic Warrior. Supersonic Warrior smashed through the wall, as her visor shattered and blood fell on the ground. The visor reconfigured itself over Supersonic Warrior's eyes, as she got up from the ground. Supersonic Warrior backflipped on to the tree. Supersonic Warrior swung on the tree branch, and flipped out of the tree. Supersonic Warrior tackled Spider Crusader in to the ground. Supersonic Warrior punched Spider Crusader in the face. Spider Crusader growled, and kicked Supersonic Warrior in the chest. Supersonic Warrior slid backwards! Spider Crusader backflipped off of the ground. Spider Crusader tackled Supersonic Warrior, and body slammed her in to the ground. Spider Crusader held Supersonic Warrior on the ground, and punched her in the face, multiple times. Blood leaked out of her suit, on to the ground. Supersonic Warrior growled and grabbed Spider Crusader's arm. Supersonic Warrior threw Spider Crusader off of her, and got up from the ground. Supersonic Warrior backflipped in to the air, and kicked Spider Crusader in the chest. Spider Crusader slid backwards! Supersonic Warrior shot a ice beam from her hand at Spider Crusader. Spider Crusader took out his web sword and reflected it back at Supersonic Warrior. Supersonic Warrior smashed in to the wall, as the ice beam froze her in place. Spider Crusader flipped in the air and roundhouse kicked Supersonic Warrior in the chest. Supersonic Warrior smashed through the wall, as the building's foundation crumbled on to the ground. Supersonic Warrior got up from the ground, as blood dripped on to the ground. Spider Crusader backflipped, and shot webs at Supersonic Warrior with his web shooters. The webs attached to Supersonic Warrior's arms. Spider Crusader pulled on the webs, and threw Supersonic Warrior in to the building. Supersonic Warrior smashed in to the building, and laid on the ground. Supersonic Warrior got up from the ground. Justin saw the chaos from the classroom window. Justin jumped out of the classroom window in a fiery tornado! The window shattered from the explosion, as Justin landed in front of Spider Crusader and Supersonic Warrior. Justin growled, as he ignited a explosion of flames from his hand. Justin said, "Get away from her, villain!" The explosion shook the building's foundation and knocked Spider Crusader, Justin, and Supersonic Warrior backwards. The building foundation fell on the ground! Spider Crusader got up from the ground! Spider Crusader summoned his glider from his wrist. Spider Crusader walked on to his glider, and flew through the area to check on Justin and Supersonic Warrior. Supersonic Warrior laid on the ground, while blood soaked through her suit. Justin got up from the ground, and held out his hand. Supersonic Warrior grabbed Justin's hand, as she got up from the ground. Spider Crusader flew toward Justin and Supersonic Warrior. Justin and Supersonic Warrior shot beams of fire and ice from their hands at Spider Crusader. Spider Crusader spun in a circle on his glider and avoided the beams.

Spider Crusader flew at Justin and Supersonic Warrior. Justin and Supersonic Warrior backflipped in the air, and avoided Spider Crusader's glider. Spider Crusader threw web bombs at Justin and Supersonic Warrior. Justin and Supersonic Warrior dodged the web bombs, by sliding out of the way. The web bombs exploded the wall behind them. Building debris flew everywhere, and landed on the ground! Justin and Supersonic Warrior held their hands out, and ignited a explosion of fire and ice energy in front of Spider Crusader. The explosion smashed Spider Crusader through the wall, as the ground shook around them. Supersonic Warrior and Justin walked toward Spider Crusader, as he got up from the ground. Spider Crusader growled and said, "You win this round, heroes!" Spider Crusader walked on to his glider and flew in to the air. Justin and Supersonic Warrior walked through the debris. Supersonic Warrior demorphed in a flash of energy. Christina and Justin sat on the bench. James sat next to them, and wrapped his arm around them. A couple of blocks down the road, Spider Crusader landed his glider at a hot dog stand. Spider Crusader stood in line for his hot dog. Matt said, "What would you like on your hot dog, sir?" Spider Crusader said, "Mustard and mayonnaise would be good to squirt on the hot dog!" Matt squirts mustard and mayonnaise on the hot dog, and gives it to Spider Crusader. Spider Crusader grabbed the hot dog with his hand, as he walked back on to his glider. Spider Crusader took his hood off, while he ate his hot dog. Peter finished his hot dog, and wiped off his gloves. Peter grabbed a water bottle from the hot dog stand, and drank it. Peter recycled the water bottle. Peter put his hood back on, and flew in to the air on his glider. James, Christina, and Justin got up from the bench, and walked toward the bridge, that was in the distance. James kissed Christina on the cheek. Christina blushed, while Justin was walking next to them. James, Christina, and Justin got to the bridge, and looked over it. James, Christina, and Justin were shocked by the view from the bridge. The water was shining, and the birds were tweeting around them. A gust of wind blew on them, and James fell off the bridge. Christina morphed in a flash of rainbow energy in to Supersonic

Warrior. Supersonic Warrior ran and did a backflip off the bridge. James was falling super fast in to the water. Supersonic Warrior shot a ice beam from her hand at the bridge, and at James to form a rope. The ice beam attached on to James and the bridge. Supersonic Warrior was hanging on to the ice beam with her hand, as she was hanging back and forth. Supersonic Warrior said, "Everything will be fine, I won't let you fall." James said, "I hope so, it looks like a long fall from up here." Supersonic Warrior said, "Don't look down!" James said, "I won't, I don't want my life to end!" James slowly climbed up the ice beam, as he got closer to Supersonic Warrior. Supersonic Warrior held out her hand to James. James grabbed Supersonic Warrior's hand! Supersonic Warrior helped James up the ice beam. James wrapped his arms around Supersonic Warrior, while Supersonic Warrior backflipped in the air. Supersonic Warrior summoned a path of ice under her feet, as she skated back to the top of the bridge. James hung on to Supersonic Warrior, while she skated on the path of ice. Supersonic Warrior backflipped on to the top of the bridge. James got on to the ground and hugged Justin. Justin hugged James back, and ruffled up his hair. James fixed his hair, while Supersonic Warrior demorphed in to Christina. Christina and James leaned against the tree, while Justin was next to the bridge. James and Christina hugged each other! A gust of wind blew through the area, and a glider flew toward Justin. Justin backflipped out of the way, and shot a fire beam at the glider. The glider spun in a circle, and landed in front of James and Christina. Spider Crusader walked off of his glider and toward Justin. Justin nodded at James and Christina! James and Christina hid out of Spider Crusader's view, while Justin raised his hand and summoned a flaming sword. Spider Crusader took his web sword off of his back. Justin and Spider Crusader ran at each other. Spider Crusader swung his sword at Justin! Justin swung his sword at Spider Crusader. Spider Crusader threw a web bomb in to the air, and hit it with his sword. Justin flipped in the air, and hit the web bomb back at Spider Crusader. The web bomb hit Spider Crusader in the chest, as he slid backwards. Justin flipped in the air, and hit Spider Crusader in the arm with his sword. The explosion knocked Spider Crusader on the ground. Spider Crusader rolled on the ground, and flipped back on his feet. Spider Crusader backflipped on to the tree, and swung on the tree branch. Spider Crusader jumped out of the tree, and hit Justin in the arm with his web sword. Justin slid backwards, as a drop of blood fell on the ground. Justin growled, and hit Spider Crusader in the chest, with his sword. Spider Crusader slid backwards! Spider Crusader and Justin ran toward each other and clashed their swords together. Justin slid backwards, as he kicked Spider Crusader in the chest. Spider Crusader slid backwards, and shot webs out of his web shooters. Justin flipped in the air, and sliced the webs with his sword. Justin swung on a tree branch and slashed Spider Crusader in the chest with his sword. Spider Crusader slid backwards in to a wall. Justin sped toward Spider Crusader. Spider Crusader roundhouse kicked Justin in the face. Justin smashed in to the wall, and dropped his sword on the ground. Spider Crusader walked toward Justin with his web sword. Justin got up, and reached for his sword with his hand. Spider Crusader stepped on Justin's hand with his foot. Justin screamed in pain! Spider Crusader kicked Justin in the face. Justin laid on the ground! Spider Crusader laughed and said, " What a pathetic attempt to protect your friends." Spider Crusader grabbed Justin by the neck, and smashed him in to the wall. Blood poured on to the ground from Justin's body. Spider Crusader rubbed his hand through Justin's hair! Spider Crusader said, "I knew your little plan was to distract me, so your friends could stay out of my view." Justin said, "You don't scare me, you're just another ordinary villain that wants to ruin everyone's fun." Spider Crusader punched Justin in the face and said, "I am no ordinary villain, I am smart enough to defeat you and your friends with ease." Spider Crusader body slammed Justin on to the ground! Justin laid on the ground! Justin raised his arm, and shot a fire grenade from his gauntlet at Spider Crusader. The explosion smashed Spider Crusader in to the tree. Justin got up from the ground, and sped in to Spider Crusader. Justin grabbed Spider Crusader by the neck, and threw him through the wall. Spider Crusader laid on the ground. Justin punched Spider Crusader in the face with a fire blast. Blood poured on the ground from Spider Crusader's body. Spider Crusader got up from the ground, and shot Justin with his web shooters. Justin backflipped, and exploded the webs out of the air with his fire gauntlet. Spider Crusader tore a tree out of the ground. Spider Crusader hit Justin in the chest, with the tree. Justin smashed in to the wall. Spider Crusader threw a web bomb at Justin. The web bomb exploded, and Justin smashed through the wall. Justin laid on the ground. Justin got up from the ground! Spider Crusader web crawled on the side of the building. Spider Crusader jumped off of the building, and tackled Justin in to the ground. Spider Crusader stabbed his web knife in to Justin's arm. Justin growled in pain, and put his hand on Spider Crusader's face. Justin ignited his hand with a fire blast. The fire blast smashed Spider Crusader through the wall. Justin backflipped off of the ground, and took the web knife out of his arm. Blood leaked on to the ground! Spider Crusader got up from the ground, and shot a web at his web knife. The web knife was pulled back to Spider Crusader. Spider Crusader put the web knife, back on his belt. Spider Crusader took out his web sword, and walked toward Justin! Christina and James saw the chaos from Spider Crusader and Justin. Justin growled and said, "Guys, stay back!" Spider Crusader said, "How noble for human scum to protect his friends!" Justin shot a fire beam at Spider Crusader! Spider Crusader deflected the beam back at Justin with his web sword. Justin smashed in to the wall, as he laid on the ground. Spider Crusader picked up Justin by the neck, and webbed him to the wall, with his web shooters. Spider Crusader said, "Stay here, while I play with your friends!" James was behind Christina, as she held her hands out! Christina said, "Stay behind me, James, I can handle this!" James nodded and hid behind the tree. Christina morphed in a flash of rainbow energy in to Supersonic Warrior. Spider Crusader sped in to Supersonic Warrior. Supersonic Warrior activated her ice shield! Spider Crusader growled, as he tried punching through it. Supersonic Warrior kicks Spider Crusader in the chest. Spider Crusader slid backwards. Supersonic Warrior stepped on the ground, and summoned a ice wall. The ice wall smashed Spider Crusader through the wall. Spider Crusader got up from the ground. Supersonic Warrior backflipped and kicked Spider Crusader in the face. Spider Crusader stumbled backwards, and stabbed Supersonic Warrior in the chest with his web sword. Supersonic Warrior stumbled backwards, as blood poured on to the ground. Spider Crusader grabbed Supersonic Warrior by the neck and smashed her through the wall. Blood poured on to the ground, while Supersonic Warrior coughed. Spider Crusader smiled and said, "I have you at your peak, battered and bruised!" Spider Crusader punched Supersonic Warrior in the face, multiple times, while her visor gets cracked. Spider Crusader grabs Supersonic Warrior by the neck and blasts her through the wall with a web beam from his hand. Supersonic Warrior's visor shatters, as she smashes through the wall. Blood poured on to the ground, as her visor repairs from the suit's nano technology. Spider Crusader stepped on Supersonic Warrior's chest, as he manically laughs. Spider Crusader said, "You're the city's hero, how pathetic!" Supersonic Warrior growled, as she shot a ice blast with her hand at Spider Crusader. Spider Crusader backflipped, and deflected the blast back at Supersonic Warrior with his web sword. Supersonic Warrior smashed through the wall, and laid next to the ground, with blood leaking from her suit. Spider Crusader picked up Supersonic Warrior by the neck, and webbed her to the wall with his web shooters. Spider Crusader grabbed his web rope, and tossed it at James. The web rope wrapped around James! Spider Crusader pulled on the web rope and dragged James toward him. Spider Crusader grabbed James by the neck. Spider Crusader took out his web sword and stabbed James in the chest with it. Blood poured out on to the ground, as James laid on the ground. Supersonic Warrior and Justin growled as they shouted, "NOOOOOOOOOOOOOOOOOO!" Spider Crusader said, "Your spirit is shattered to pieces!" Supersonic Warrior growled while she said, "I hate you, you're a monster!" Spider Crusader said, "I am not a monster, I am a dangerous threat to anyone, who fights against me." Spider Crusader flew away in the air on his glider.

Justin and Supersonic Warrior tore the webs off of their arms, as they walked towards the dead body. Justin was terrified in fear, when he saw the dead body. Supersonic Warrior bent down and retracted the helmet from her face. Supersonic Warrior cried on top of the dead body. Justin comforted Supersonic Warrior by rubbing her back. Justin sad, "It is tough being a superhero! James wanted you to stay strong and continue fighting." Supersonic Warrior wiped away the tears with her glove. Supersonic Warrior said, "You're right, Justin!" Justin and Supersonic Warrior hugged each other! Supersonic Warrior's helmet covered her face, as she got up from the ground. Supersonic Warrior demorphed in a flash of rainbow energy. Justin and Christina walked down the street. Christina said, "I am going to walk to the local grocery store to control my emotions." Justin said, "Sounds good, be careful!" Christina nodded! Christina and Justin hugged each other. Christina walked to the local grocery store. Christina walked through the parking lot, and entered World of Food. World of Food was filled with multiple types of food and drinks to enjoy. Christina walked to the ice cream aisle, and picked out a container of strawberry ice cream. Christina bought the container of strawberry ice cream with some money, and sat down at the table to eat it. Christina ate the strawberry ice cream with a spoon. Christina cried tears in to the container of strawberry ice cream. Christina cried and said, "The world is so cruel!" A employee for World Of Food saw Christina crying, and sat next to her. The employee for World of Food said, "Hi, I am Miles, and everything will be fine!" Miles rubbed his hand on Christina's back, while she cried in to the container of strawberry ice cream. Christina wiped the tears from her face and said, "Thanks Miles, I feel a little bit better!" Miles smiled at her and said, "No problem!" Miles got up, and walked around the World of Food. Christina walked in to the bathroom, and washed her face. Christina looked at her reflection in the mirror. Spider Crusader appeared in the mirror and covered up her reflection. Spider Crusader said, "You're weak for believing in your friends!" Christina growled and grabbed the mirror off of the wall. Christina smashed the mirror on the floor and said, "I am not weak!" Christina washed her hands, with soap and water. Christina dried off her hands, and walked out of the bathroom! Christina walked out of World of Food and in to the parking lot. A squad of police cars were sitting in the parking lot, with their sirens on. A group of police officers walked out of the police car, and surrounded Christina! Matt, the police officer, pointed his gun at Christina. Matt signaled his squad to point their guns at Christina! Matt signaled his squad to shoot their guns! The squad of police officers shot their guns at Christina. Bullets were flying everywhere, as Christina morphed in a flash of rainbow energy. A small orange cat was running through the parking lot, while the bullets were flying. Supersonic Warrior summoned a ice shield to protect herself from the bullets. Supersonic Warrior ran after the orange cat, while the police officers were chasing her. The orange cat ran behind the vending machine. Supersonic Warrior picked up the vending machine and moved it. The police officers tackled Supersonic Warrior in to the ground. The police officers put their electric batons on Supersonic Warrior's chest, and electrocuted her. The orange cat was scared in the corner. Supersonic Warrior growled and shot a ice blast at the police officers. The police officers smashed in to the building, and froze on to the wall. Supersonic Warrior picked up the orange cat, and ran in to the woods. Bullets were flying in the parking lot, from the other police officers. Supersonic Warrior set the orange cat down in the woods. Supersonic Warrior walked back in to the parking lot. Supersonic Warrior put her foot down on the parking lot, and a blast of ice covered the police officers in a iceberg, stopping them in their tracks. The police officers were frozen in the iceberg, while Supersonic Warrior walked past them. A squad of police cars drove right next to Supersonic Warrior, while she was walking down the sidewalk. The police officer stopped the police car, next to the sidewalk. The police officer and the rest of the squad walked out of the police car, and surrounded Supersonic Warrior. The squad of police officers shot their guns at Supersonic Warrior. Supersonic Warrior backflipped, and dodged the bullets. Supersonic Warrior shot a blast of ice at the police officers, and froze them on the side of the building. Supersonic Warrior picked up the police car, and threw it in the air. Supersonic Warrior shot a ice blast at the police car! The police car got frozen in a giant ice block. The police car fell on the ground, and smashed in a billion of pieces. Supersonic Warrior walked further down the sidewalk. Supersonic Warrior stopped at the water fountain, and retracted her helmet. Supersonic Warrior drank out of the water fountain to rehydrate herself. Supersonic Warrior's helmet covered her face, as she walked further down the sidewalk. Spider Crusader flew at Supersonic Warrior on his glider. Supersonic Warrior backflipped out of the way, and shot a ice blast at the glider! The glider spun in to a tree. the tree fell on the ground. Spider Crusader rubbed the tree branches off of him, with his gloves. Spider Crusader walked off of his glider, and threw web boomerangs at several civilians. The civilians laid on the ground in puddles of blood. Spider Crusader kicked Supersonic Warrior in the chest. Supersonic Warrior slid backwards! Supersonic Warrior shot a ice beam at Spider Crusader! Spider Crusader deflected it with his web sword. Spider Crusader sped toward Supersonic Warrior with his web sword. Spider Crusader swung his web sword at Supersonic Warrior's arm. Supersonic Warrior backflipped, and kicked the web sword out of Spider Crusader's hand. The web sword landed on the ground! Spider Crusader sprinted toward the web sword. Supersonic Warrior shot a ice blast at Spider Crusader's feet. Spider Crusader froze in place! Supersonic Warrior sprinted toward Spider Crusader, and punched him in the face. Spider Crusader landed on the ground! Spider Crusader got up from the ground, and shot webs at Supersonic Warrior from his web shooters. Supersonic Warrior flipped out of the way, and landed on a tree. Supersonic Warrior swung on a tree branch, and roundhouse kicked Spider Crusader in to a wall. Spider Crusader smashed in to the wall, and landed on his glider. Spider Crusader got up from the ground, and activated his glider. Spider Crusader hovered on the ground, and threw a web bomb at Supersonic Warrior. Supersonic Warrior smashed against the pole, and knocked it over. Spider Crusader shot web missiles at Supersonic Warrior. Supersonic Warrior rolled on the ground, and dodged them. Supersonic Warrior backflipped, and got up from the ground. Spider Crusader flew toward Supersonic Warrior on his glider. Supersonic Warrior dodged the glider, by sliding out of the way. Supersonic Warrior tackled Spider Crusader off of the glider. The glider stopped right next to the wall. Supersonic Warrior held Spider Crusader on the ground! Supersonic Warrior punched Spider Crusader in the face. Spider Crusader growled, and kicked Supersonic Warrior in the chest. Supersonic Warrior slid backwards! Spider Crusader got up from the ground, and jumped on to his glider. Spider Crusader flew toward Supersonic Warrior on his glider. Spider Crusader smashed Supersonic Warrior in to the wall. Supersonic Warrior laid against the wall, and shot Spider Crusader with a ice blast. Spider Crusader flew backwards in to a wall. Supersonic Warrior shot a ice beam with her hand at the wall. The wall exploded and fell on top of Spider Crusader! Spider Crusader got up from the ground, as wall pieces fell off of him. Spider Crusader shot a web at a tree, and pulled it out of the ground. Spider Crusader swung the tree at Supersonic Warrior. Supersonic Warrior smashed in to a car, and fell on the ground. Supersonic Warrior got up from the ground, and picked up the car. Supersonic Warrior lifted the car over her head, and threw it at Spider Crusader. The car smashed Spider Crusader in to the building. Blood leaked on to the ground from his suit. Spider Crusader got up from the ground, and walked toward Supersonic Warrior. Supersonic Warrior shot a ice blast at Spider Crusader! Spider Crusader deflected it with his web sword. Supersonic Warrior swung her arm at Spider Crusader! Spider Crusader grabbed Supersonic Warrior's arm, and kicked her in the chest. Supersonic Warrior slid backwards. Spider Crusader backflipped, and wrapped Supersonic Warrior in to a web cocoon with his web shooters. Spider Crusader roundhouse kicked the webbed up Supersonic warrior in to the wall. The web cocoon exploded, and Supersonic Warrior laid on the ground. Spider Crusader picked up Supersonic Warrior and body slammed her on to the ground. Blood leaked on to the ground from her suit. Spider Crusader jumped on to his glider, and flew toward Supersonic Warrior. Supersonic Warrior got up from the ground. Spider Crusader smashed Supersonic Warrior in to the wall with his glider. Supersonic Warrior laid against the wall, and shot Spider Crusader with a ice blast. Spider Crusader flew backwards! Supersonic Warrior backflipped off of a car and roundhouse kicked Spider Crusader in the face. Spider Crusader smashed against the wall! Spider Crusader's glider spun in to a tree. Supersonic Warrior picked up Spider Crusader and threw him in to a car. Spider Crusader laid against the car. Supersonic Warrior put her hand on the ground, and caused a iceberg to form on the ground. The iceberg smashed Spider Crusader in to the air. Supersonic Warrior backflipped in to the tree! Supersonic Warrior swung off of the tree branch, and summoned a ice path with her feet. Supersonic Warrior ice skated on the ice path toward Spider Crusader. Supersonic Warrior backflipped on to Spider Crusader's chest, and smashed him in to the ground. Spider Crusader laid on the ground, in a puddle of blood. Supersonic Warrior held Spider Crusader on the ground, and punched him in the face. Blood poured on the ground! Spider Crusader growled, and kicked Supersonic warrior in the chest. Supersonic Warrior slid backwards! Spider Crusader backflipped off of the ground! Spider Crusader shot tranquilizer webs at Supersonic Warrior. The tranquilizer webs hit Supersonic Warrior in the chest, and they electrocuted her. The suit's AI system said, "AI system is malfunctioning!" Supersonic Warrior laid against the wall! Spider Crusader grabbed a car, and swung it at Supersonic Warrior. Supersonic Warrior's visor shattered, as she smashed through the wall. Supersonic Warrior laid on the ground, with blood leaking from her suit. Spider Crusader laughed and said, "Your spirit has been shattered!" Spider Crusader picked up Supersonic Warrior, and threw her in the air. Spider Crusader kicked Supersonic Warrior in the chest. Supersonic Warrior smashed in to the wall, and laid on the ground. Supersonic Warrior got up from the ground. Spider Crusader tackled Supersonic Warrior, and body slammed her in to the ground. Spider Crusader held Supersonic Warrior on to the ground, and stabbed his web knife in to her arm. Spider Crusader punched Supersonic Warrior in the face, multiple times.

Blood leaked on to the ground! Supersonic Warrior growled, and held Spider Crusader's arm back. Supersonic Warrior kicked Spider Crusader in the chest. Spider Crusader slid backwards, while Supersonic Warrior pulled the web knife out of her arm. Blood leaked on to the ground, while Supersonic Warrior got up from the ground. Spider Crusader shot a web at his web knife, and pulled it back in to his hand. Spider Crusader put the web knife, back on his belt. A explosive fire tornado smashed Spider Crusader in to the building. Spider Crusader laid on the ground! Spider Crusader got up from the ground! Justin landed on the ground, and backflipped on to the tree! Justin swung on the tree branch, and roundhouse kicked Spider Crusader in the face. Spider Crusader smashed through the building. Spider Crusader laid on the ground! Justin held Spider Crusader on the ground! Justin growled and punched Spider Crusader in the face with a fire blast. Blood leaked from Spider Crusader's face. Supersonic Warrior sat on the bench, and wiped blood off of her suit with a towel. Justin picked up Spider Crusader, and threw him in to the car. Justin shot the car with a explosive fire blast from his hand. Spider Crusader laid next to the wall. Justin shot a fire grenade from his gauntlet at the wall. The wall exploded, and fell on top of Spider Crusader. Spider Crusader got up from the ground, while blood leaked from his suit. Justin sped in to Spider Crusader, and tackled him in to the wall. Justin punched Spider Crusader in the chest, with a explosive fire blast. Justin slid backwards, while the explosion smashed Spider Crusader through the wall. Spider Crusader rolled on the ground! Spider Crusader got up from the ground, and jumped on to his glider. Spider Crusader shot a web missile at Justin. Justin smashed in to the wall, and laid on the ground. Justin backflipped off of the ground! Spider Crusader flew toward Justin on his glider. Justin backflipped out of the way, and shot a fire grenade from his gauntlet. The glider spun in to a tree! Spider Crusader caught his balance, by putting his hand on the tree. Spider Crusader flew toward Justin on his glider, and grabbed him by the neck. Spider Crusader threw Justin in to the building. Justin rolled on the ground! Spider Crusader threw a web bomb at the building. The building exploded and fell on top of Justin. Justin laid on the ground! Justin got up from the ground, and picked up the building fragment over his head. Justin threw the building fragment at Spider Crusader. Spider Crusader threw web boomerangs at the building fragment, and sliced it in half. Justin backflipped on to Spider Crusader's glider, and kicked him in the chest. Spider Crusader smashed in to the car. Justin backflipped off of the glider, and shot a fire grenade at the car. The car exploded, and Spider Crusader rolled on to the ground. Spider Crusader backflipped off of the ground! Spider Crusader flipped on to his glider, and flew in to the air. Justin walked toward Supersonic Warrior, and sat on the bench with her. Supersonic Warrior wiped the blood off of her suit with a towel. Supersonic Warrior gave the towel to Justin. Justin wiped the blood off of him with a towel. Justin drank a bottle of water to rehydrate himself. Supersonic Warrior drank a bottle of water to rehydrate herself. Supersonic Warrior demorphed in a flash of rainbow energy. Christina and Justin got up from the bench, and walked to the hot dog stand. Christina and Justin bought a hot dog from the hot dog stand. Justin and Christina walked to the grass field! Justin and Christina sat down on the grass field, and ate their hot dogs. Justin said, "The sky is clear and blue!" Christina said, "Yep, I am glad that we are friends!" Justin wrapped his arm around Christina and said, "Me too, I am glad to have you as a friend."Further down the road, Spider Crusader flew on his glider in to Electric Industries. Spider Crusader parked his glider in to the recharge station, and backflipped off of the glider. Adrian walked toward Spider Crusader and said, "Was your mission successful?" Spider Crusader growled, and threw a container at the wall. The container shattered on the ground! Spider Crusader said, "My mission wasn't successful! Supersonic Warrior and her sidekick got in the way." Adrian said, "For a supervillain, you should of tried harder to defeat them!" Spider Crusader growled and grabbed Adrian by his neck. Spider Crusader smashed Adrian in to the wall. Spider Crusader laughed and said, "Try harder, you think this is a game to you." Supersonic Warrior and her sidekick had explosive powers, that were hard to avoid." Spider Crusader punched Adrian in the chest! Adrian coughed up blood, and the blood splattered on the ground. Spider Crusader tackled Adrian and body slammed him in to the ground. Spider Crusader held Adrian on the ground! Spider Crusader took out his web knife, and pointed it at Adrian's head. Spider Crusader said, "Do you think that I am weak, like the other super villains that have failed to take down Supersonic Warrior?" Adrian trembled in fear and said, "No!" Spider Crusader growled and said, "LIAR!" Spider Crusader stabbed his web knife in to Adrian's head! Blood poured on to the ground! Spider Crusader pulled his web knife out of Adrian's head! Adrian laid on the ground, while coughing. Spider Crusader got up from the ground! Adrian got up from the ground! Spider Crusader kicked Adrian in the chest. Adrian slammed in to the wall. Spider Crusader took out his web sword, and stabbed Adrian in the chest. Blood poured out of Adrian's body, while Spider Crusader took his web sword out of Adrian's chest. Adrian laid on the ground, in a puddle of blood. The cleaning robots for Electric Industries cleaned up the blood, and threw the dead body in to the dumpster. Spider Crusader walked toward his recharge tube. Spider Crusader opened the recharge tube, and walked in to it. Spider Crusader attached himself to the recharge tube, and started it. The recharge tube healed Spider Crusader. Spider Crusader felt recharged from the healing energy, absorbed in to his body. Spider Crusader unlinked himself, and walked out of the recharge tube. A group of robots and Electric Industries employees surrounded Spider Crusader. The group of robots and Electric Industries employees shot their guns at Spider Crusader. Bullets were flying everywhere. Spider Crusader crawled on the walls, and on to the ceiling. Spider Crusader hung upside down on the ceiling, and wrapped a robot up with his webs from his web shooters. Spider Crusader attached the robot to the ceiling. Spider Crusader hung upside down, and tapped a Electric Industries employee on the shoulder. Spider Crusader shot a web on to the Electric Industries employee's mouth, and backflipped on to the ground. Spider Crusader kicked the Electric Industries employee in to the wall, and webbed him up with his web shooters. Spider Crusader backflipped in to the air. and shot webs out of his web shooters. The rest of the robots and Electric Industries employees were wrapped up in web cocoons. Spider Crusader threw a web bomb at the cocoons, and they exploded. The rest of the robots and Electric Industries employees laid on the ground in a pile of robot parts and blood. Spider Crusader took off his hood, and retracted his helmet. Spider Crusader drank a bottle of water and rehydrated himself. Spider Crusader threw the bottle in the recycling bin, while his helmet covered his face. Christina and Justin were walking outside Electric Industries, listening to the birds tweeting in the background. Construction vehicles drove past them on the road. Christina and Justin followed the construction vehicles on the sidewalk. Christina and Justin stopped outside the construction site. Construction vehicles were on the field for Oasis Falls High School. Justin said, "They are probably repairing the school, from all of the damage that Spider Crusader did." Christina said, "Makes sense, I would be bored waiting for supervillains to pop up." Justin said, "True, we need knowledge to expand our brains." Christina and Justin walked to the ice cream stand, and bought two ice cream cones. Justin and Christina sat on the bench together, and ate their ice cream cones. Justin wrapped his arm around Christina, while licking his ice cream cone. Justin said, "Ice cream cones are tasty and refreshing." Christina licked her ice cream cone and said, "I agree!" The sun set appeared over the city, and covered the sky with its beautiful colors. Justin and Christina looked at the sun set. Justin said, "The sun set is colorful tonight!" Christina said, "Yep, it is amazing to watch!"

The sun was shining on Oasis Falls High School. The construction vehicles repaired the building foundation, and students can learn and expand their knowledge. Justin and Christina walked in to the hallways of Oasis Falls High School, and reorganized their lockers. The other students were walking through the hallways! The other students were at their lockers. The intercom went off in the hallway speakers! The intercom said, "Welcome to today's edition of Oasis Falls Wildcats News! Don't forget to buy your Wildcats merchandise at the Wildcats booth in the cafeteria. That is it for today's edition of Oasis Falls Wildcats News, have a good day!" The students sighed, as they put their supplies in their bags. Flash walked through the hallway, and pushed Justin in to his locker. Justin said, "Owwww, what was that for?" Flash said, "You were in my way, punk!" A group of students gathered around them, and shouted, "FIGHT FIGHT FIGHT FIGHT!" Flash grabbed Justin by his neck, and smashed him in to the locker. Justin growled, and shot Flash in the face with a fire blast. Flash slid backwards, and tackled Justin. Flash slammed Justin in to the ground. Flash held Justin on the ground! Flash punched Justin in the face, multiple times. Justin growled, and held Flash's arm back! Justin kicked Flash in the chest. Flash slid backwards! Justin got up from the ground, and shot a fire grenade at Flash. Flash smashed in to the locker. Flash laid on the ground! Justin jumped on to Flash, and punched him in the face, with a fire blast. Flash growled, as Justin held him on the ground. Justin punched Flash in the face, multiple times. Blood poured on the ground!

Flash kicked Justin in the chest! Justin rolled on the ground, as Flash got up. Justin got up from the ground, and tackled Flash in to the locker. Flash laid against the locker! Justin grabbed Flash by the neck, and lit up his hand with a fire blast. Flash's neck was getting barbecued, as his skin burned and blood poured on the ground. Justin threw Flash in to the wall. Flash laid on the ground, as the skin on his neck burned to a crisp. Justin ignited his shoes with flames, and his eyes glowed red! Justin stepped on Flash's chest! Flash's body burned to a crisp, as a blood puddle formed under him. Flash got up from the ground! Justin sped in to Flash, and tackled him in to the wall. Justin picked up Flash by the neck, and threw him in to the locker. Justin shot a fire grenade at Flash. Flash smashed in to the locker, as blood splashed on to the ground. Flash laid on the ground! Justin's eyes went back to normal. Justin drank out of the water fountain, and rehydrated himself. Flash got up from the ground! Flash's body was burnt to a crisp, as Christina saw the chaos from her locker. Christina closed the locker, and walked toward Flash. Christina nodded to Justin and said, "You did good weakening him, I will finish the job." Justin smiled and said, "Sounds good!" Justin walked to his locker, and opened it. Justin reorganized his locker! Justin closed his locker, and laid against the wall. Flash swung his arm at Christina. Christina grabbed Flash's arm, and kicked him in the chest! Flash smashed in to the locker! Flash backflipped off of the ground, and sped in to Christina. Christina backflipped out of the way, and shot a ice beam at Flash. Flash froze in place, in the middle of the hallway. Christina sped in to Flash, and grabbed him by his neck. Christina smashed him in to the ground! Christina held Flash on the ground, and stepped on his chest. Christina punched Flash in the face, multiple times! Flash growled, and held Christina's arm back. Christina kicked Flash in the chest. Christina shot Flash in the face with a ice blast. Christina got off of Flash, and got up from the ground. Flash got up from the ground. Christina summoned a ice wall, and smashed Flash in to the wall. Flash smashed through the wall, and laid on the ground. Flash laid in a puddle of blood. Blood leaked out of Flash's body, and his clothes were soaked with blood. One of the teachers walked out of the teacher's lounge, and saw the fight. Abby shouted and said, "Stop the Fight Now!" Flash didn't move, as blood poured out of his body, and his skin was burnt to a crisp. Flash's clothes were burnt, and torn up! Abby saw Flash's body, and told Harry, one of the students, to take him to the nurse's office. Harry picked up Flash, and laid him on his back! Harry took Flash to the nurse's office. Harry walked to the nurse's office. Harry walked to the door for the nurse's office. Harry knocked on the door! Roman, the nurse, opened the door! Roman said, "Hey Harry, is everything ok?" Harry said, "Flash got injured during a fight in the hallway, and he is unconscious." Roman walked to the healing tube in the middle of the nurse's office. Harry followed Roman to the healing tube. Roman unlatched the tube, and opened the healing tube. Harry laid Flash's body in the healing tube. Roman attached wires to Flash's body. Roman closed the healing tube, and latched it. Roman walked to the computer, and started up the healing tube. Roman walked to the computer, and tapped on some buttons. Roman injected some healing medicines in to the tubes. The healing medicine went in to Flash's body. Roman hoped that the medicine would improve Flash's body, since his body was in critical condition. Roman tapped some buttons, and improved the healing effect of the medicine. Harry walked out of the nurse's office. Harry walked down the hallway. Harry walked to the water fountain, and rehydrated himself. Harry walked to his locker. Harry opened his locker, and unzipped his bag. Harry put some supplies in his bag, and zipped it up. Harry closed his locker, and locked it. Harry walked down the hallway. Harry walked to his Algebra class! Harry stopped at the door for his Algebra class! Harry turned the door knob, and opened the door. Harry walked in to the classroom for Algebra, and sat down at one of the desks. Abby directed the other students to their classes. Abby gave Christina a detention slip, and a warning slip to Justin! Abby walked Christina and Justin to History class! Christina and Justin walked in to History class with Abby! Abraham, the history teacher, said, "Christina and Justin, nice to see you guys, I was about to mark you guys absent on my list." Abby said, "There was a fight in the hallway. Keep a eye on Christina and Justin, they are troublemakers!" Abraham nods, while Christina and Justin sit at their desks. Abby walked out of the classroom. Christina and Justin took their textbooks out of their bags, and opened them on the desks. Justin put his warning slip in to his bag. Abraham wrote on the whiteboard, while the students were sleeping in their textbooks. Abraham said, "Who wrote the Bill of Rights?" Justin raised his hand! Justin said, "James Madison wrote the Bill of Rights!" Abraham nodded and said, "That is correct, Justin!" Abraham erased, and cleaned the whiteboard. The bell rings in the background! Abraham said, "Looks like class is over!" The other students woke up, and put their supplies in their bags. The other students walked out of the classroom, while Justin and Christina put their textbooks in their bags. Justin and Christina zipped up their bags, and walked out of the classroom. Justin and Christina walked together to the detention room. Christina and Justin hugged each other! Christina walked in to the detention room! Justin walked in to the study hall room! Christina walked to the detention teacher's desk. Christina signed her name on the detention form, and sat down in one of the desks. The detention teacher walked out of the detention room. The detention teacher walked toward the teacher's lounge. Christina took a book out of her bag, and read it on the desk. Christina sighed to herself, as she rubbed her hand through her hair. Christina said, "Detention is so boring, I wish time would go by faster!" The other detention room students were sleeping on their desks. A glider flew past the window for the detention room. Spider Crusader landed the glider in the bush. Spider Crusader backflipped off of the glider, and landed on the ground. Spider Crusader crawled on the wall of Oasis Falls High School. Spider Crusader crawled to the roof of Oasis Falls High School. Spider Crusader landed on the roof, and walked toward the air duct. Spider Crusader attached one of his web bombs to the air duct. The web bombs exploded, and the air duct was opened. Spider Crusader crawled in to the air duct. The air duct landed Spider Crusader in to the vents of

Oasis Falls High School. Spider Crusader crawled in the vents. Spider Crusader was ready to pounce on his prey. Spider Crusader crawled to a vent door, that was above the detention room. Spider Crusader knocked down the vent door with his foot, and jumped through the opening. Spider Crusader landed on the ground, and threw web knifes at the students. The students laid on the ground in puddles of blood. Christina hid in the supplies closet. The detention teacher walked back in to the detention room. Spider Crusader took out his web knife, and sped in to the detention teacher. Spider Crusader grabbed the detention teacher by the neck, and smashed him in to the ground. Spider Crusader held the detention teacher on the ground. Spider Crusader took his web knife off of his belt, and stabbed it in to the detention teacher's skull. The detention teacher laid on the ground in a puddle of blood. Christina morphed in a flash of rainbow energy! Spider Crusader walked to the supplies closet, and kicked the door down! Supersonic Warrior shot Spider Crusader with a ice blast from her hand. Spider Crusader slid backwards! Supersonic Warrior picked up the teacher's desk, and threw it at Spider Crusader. The teacher's desk smashed Spider Crusader in to the book shelf. The teacher's desk shattered in to pieces! The book shelf shook, and fell on top of Spider Crusader. Spider Crusader ignited a web explosion from his body! The book shelf shattered in to pieces, while Spider Crusader got up from the ground. Spider Crusader growled, and threw a web bomb at Supersonic Warrior. The web bomb exploded, and smashed Supersonic Warrior in to the wall. Supersonic Warrior laid on the ground! Supersonic Warrior got up from the ground! Spider Crusader sped in to Supersonic Warrior, and grabbed her by the neck. Spider Crusader threw Supersonic Warrior in to the door. Supersonic Warrior smashed in to the door, and laid on the ground. Spider Crusader walked toward Supersonic Warrior, and stepped on her chest. Spider Crusader punched Supersonic Warrior in the face, multiple times. Supersonic Warrior's visor was getting cracked! Supersonic Warrior growled, and held Spider Crusader's arm back. Supersonic Warrior ignited a ice explosion from her body! Supersonic Warrior rolled on the ground, as her visor repaired itself. Spider Crusader rolled on the ground. Spider Crusader and Supersonic Warrior got up from the ground. Spider Crusader backflipped, and shot webs at Supersonic Warrior. The webs attached to Supersonic Warrior's body. Spider Crusader pulled on the webs, and dragged Supersonic Warrior toward him. Spider Crusader kicked Supersonic Warrior in the chest. Supersonic Warrior smashed in to the wall. Supersonic Warrior got up from the ground! Supersonic Warrior shot a ice beam at Spider Crusader! Spider Crusader froze in place, as Supersonic Warrior sped in to him. Supersonic Warrior grabbed Spider Crusader by his neck, and threw him in to the wall. Spider Crusader laid on the ground! Spider Crusader got up from the ground! Spider Crusader sped in to Supersonic Warrior. Supersonic Warrior flipped over Spider Crusader, and kicked him in the back. Spider Crusader stumbled, and smashed in to the wall. Spider Crusader laid against the wall. Spider Crusader shot webs at Supersonic Warrior. Supersonic Warrior flipped in the air, and froze the webs with her ice blast. Supersonic Warrior landed on the ground. Supersonic Warrior backflipped and roundhouse kicked Spider Crusader in the face. Spider Crusader laid on the ground! Spider Crusader got up from the ground! Spider Crusader growled and shot a web at the desk with his web gauntlet. The web attached to the desk. Spider Crusader grabbed the web, and swung the desk at Supersonic Warrior. Supersonic Warrior smashed in to the wall, and the desk smashed in to pieces. Spider Crusader threw web knives at Supersonic Warrior. The web knives sliced through Supersonic Warrior's arm! Blood leaked on to the ground! Spider Crusader flipped in the air, and shot webs at Supersonic Warrior. The webs wrapped around Supersonic Warrior! Supersonic Warrior was webbed in to a web cocoon. Spider Crusader sped in to the webbed up Supersonic Warrior and kicked the web cocoon in to the whiteboard. The web cocoon bounced off of the whiteboard, and back at Spider Crusader. Spider Crusader kicked the web cocoon in to the air. The web cocoon smashed on the ground. Supersonic Warrior laid on the ground! Supersonic Warrior got up from the ground. Supersonic Warrior tackled Spider Crusader in to the wall. Spider Crusader laid against the wall. Supersonic Warrior punched Spider Crusader in the face! Spider Crusader growled, and kicked Supersonic Warrior in the chest. Supersonic Warrior slid backwards. Spider Crusader got up, and sped in to Supersonic Warrior. Spider Crusader grabbed Supersonic Warrior by the neck, and smashed her through the desk. Supersonic Warrior laid on the ground! Spider Crusader held Supersonic Warrior on the ground, and stabbed his web knife in to her neck. Blood leaked on to the ground! Supersonic Warrior growled, and shot a ice blast at Spider Crusader. Spider Crusader slid backwards! Supersonic Warrior got up from the ground, and took the web knife out of her neck. Spider Crusader webbed the web knife, back to his hand! Spider Crusader put the web knife on his belt. Spider Crusader backflipped in the air, and shot electric webs at Supersonic Warrior. Supersonic Warrior got hit by the electric webs, and got electrocuted. Supersonic Warrior's suit malfunctioned, and the repair function has temporally stopped responding! Spider Crusader tackled Supersonic Warrior, and body slammed her in to the ground. Spider Crusader webbed a book shelf with his webs, and pulled it in to his hand. Spider Crusader smashed Supersonic Warrior in to the ground, multiple times with the book shelf. Supersonic Warrior's visor shattered, as she laid on the ground, in a puddle of blood. Supersonic Warrior growled, and kicked Spider Crusader in the chest! Supersonic Warrior slid backwards, and the book shelf fell on the ground. Supersonic Warrior's suit was soaked in blood! Spider Crusader slid backwards, and threw a web bomb at Supersonic Warrior. Supersonic Warrior smashed through the wall, and laid on the ground. Supersonic Warrior got up from the ground. Spider Crusader shot Supersonic Warrior with tranquilizer webs! Supersonic Warrior got hit by the tranquilizer webs, and laid on the ground! Spider Crusader picked up Supersonic Warrior, and laid her on his back. Spider Crusader walked out of the school! Spider Crusader walked on to his glider, and latched Supersonic Warrior to the glider's storage unit. Spider Crusader flew in to the air on his glider. The bell rang in the background! The students were walking out of study hall. Justin put his supplies in to his bag, and walked out of study hall. Justin walked across the hall to the detention room. Justin walked in to the detention room. Justin was terrified in fear, from the chaos on the ground. There was puddles of blood everywhere. Justin tried to call Supersonic Warrior on his communication device. The communication device didn't respond, and disconnected the call. Justin walked out of the detention room! Justin walked down the hallway! The other students were reorganizing their lockers. Justin walked to the water fountain! Justin drank some water out of the water fountain, and rehydrated himself. Justin walked to the exit for Oasis Falls High School. Justin walked out of Oasis Falls High School! Justin walked past the flag pole, and stepped on to the sidewalk. Justin walked down the sidewalk! Police cars were zooming through the area, with their sirens on. Birds were tweeting, and the bugs were buzzing in the background. Justin walked down the sidewalk, and stopped at a small retail store. The small retail store had some vending machines inside it. Justin walked in to the small retail store. Justin walked to the vending machine. Justin paid for his drink. The drink rolled out of the vending machine. Justin grabbed the drink, and opened it. Justin drank it, and recycled the drink in the recycling bin. Justin walked out of the small retail store. Justin walked down the sidewalk. There was smoke in the air, and flames were burning on the side of a building. Justin looked in to the sky, and noticed that one of the buildings were on fire! Justin sped toward the burning building, and kicked the door down. Justin walked through the burning building. Flames were hot, and smoke covered the area. Justin was walking through the burning area. Justin shot fire grenades at the burning debris in the building. The fire grenades exploded, and the burning foundation fell in to the flames. The flames rose, as Justin slid backwards! The foundation was blocking the entrance for the kitchen. The flames were surrounding it. Justin kicked the foundation down, and he took out his fire gauntlet. Justin threw a fire grenade at the kitchen. The burning debris in the kitchen exploded, and the flames consumed the burning debris. Justin walked to the stairs, and threw a fire grenade at the foundation. The foundation exploded, and the pieces flew in to the flames. The flames grew behind Justin, as they consumed the house's foundation! Justin went up the stairs, and saw the bedroom blocked off with the foundation, and flames surrounding it. Justin heard someone crying in the background. In the background, Matt cried for help in his bedroom. Justin threw a fire grenade at the foundation. The foundation exploded, and Justin ran toward the bedroom. Justin kicked the door down! The bedroom was filled with smoke, and surrounded by flames. Justin backflipped over the burning flames. Matt was crying on his bed! The furniture in the bedroom was burnt to a crisp, as flames took over the bedroom. Matt's bed was surrounded by flames. Matt cried and said, "Help me, I am trapped!" Justin said, "Don't worry, I am here to help you!" Justin backflipped on to the bed. Justin wrapped his arms around Matt, and picked him up! Justin carried Matt on his back, and walked to the other side of the bedroom. Justin shot a fire grenade with his gauntlet at the window. The window shattered, and glass pieces landed on the ground. The flames were growing bigger in the bedroom. Justin ran toward the window! Justin jumped out of the window, and landed on the ground. Justin set Matt down on the ground! Justin and Matt hugged each other. Matt said, "You're my hero, thanks for saving me!" Justin smiled and said, "You're welcome, stay safe!" Matt walked down the street to the ice cream stand. Justin walked to the parking lot of World of Food. Birds were tweeting and the bugs were buzzing, while Justin was walking to the parking lot. Cars were zooming through the parking lot for World of Food, when Justin walked toward it. Police cars were speeding through the area, with their sirens on. Daniel and his parents were walking through the parking lot of World of Food. A car was speeding toward them. Justin sped toward Daniel and his parents, and shot the speeding car, with a grenade from his fire gauntlet. The speeding car exploded, and car parts were falling on to the ground. Justin wrapped his arms around Daniel and his parents, and took them to the vending machines of World of Food. Daniel said, "Thanks for saving us!" Justin said, "No problem, parking lots are dangerous to walk through." Daniel and his parents smiled at Justin, while they walked in to World of Food. Justin walked in to World of Food! Justin walked to the ice cream aisle, and grabbed a container of strawberry ice cream. Justin walked to the check out section, and paid for the strawberry ice cream. Justin sat at the table, and ate the strawberry ice cream. Justin tried to call Supersonic Warrior on his communication device. Justin said, "Supersonic Warrior, I hope everything is ok, you never ignore the communication device." Justin finished the container of strawberry ice cream. Justin got up from the table, and walked to the recycling bin.

Justin threw away the container of strawberry ice cream, and walked out of World of Food. Justin walked to the vending machine in the parking lot. Justin put some money in to the vending machine, and bought a soda. The soda rolled out of the vending machine. Justin picked up the soda, and sat down on the sidewalk. Justin opened the soda, and drank it. The soda rehydrated Justin's body! Justin got up from the sidewalk, and recycled the soda can. A truck zoomed through the parking lot, and dropped off a black and white cat on the sidewalk. The truck zoomed away! The black and white cat was scared, and hid behind the shopping carts. Justin walked to the shopping carts! Justin bent down, next to the shopping carts, and held out his hand to the scared black and white cat. The black and white cat whacked his hand away with their paw. Justin said, "Don't be scared, I won't hurt you!" The black and white cat meowed, as they slowly walked toward Justin. Justin picked up the black and white cat, and walked in to the woods. Justin set the black and white cat down in the woods. Justin smiled, as he walked back through the parking lot. Cars were zooming out of the parking lot, while Justin walked on the sidewalk. Justin walked out of the parking lot, and down the street. Cars were zooming past him, blasting their loud music. Justin stopped at a hot dog stand, and bought a hot dog. Justin sat on the bench, and ate the hot dog. Justin got up from the bench, and walked further down the street. Bees were buzzing, and the birds were tweeting. Cars and trucks were zooming by, blasting their music. Police cars were zooming through the streets, with their sirens on. The wind was blowing through Justin's hair, as he enjoyed the environment. Justin walked by a record store, and looked through the window. There was a robber, dressed up in black clothing. The robber had his gun pointed at the cashier. Justin took out his fire gauntlet, and exploded the window with a fire blast. Justin backflipped in to the record store, and landed in front of the robber. Justin tackled the robber in to the wall, and ignited his arm with flames. Justin put his hand on the robber's neck. The robber's neck burnt to a crisp. Justin picked the robber up by their neck, and smashed them in to the ground. Justin stepped on the robber's chest, and ignited his shoes with flames. The robber's body was set on fire, and burnt to a crisp. Blood soaked through the robber's body on to the ground. The robber's body laid in a puddle of blood. Justin picked up the robber's gun, and snapped it in half. Justin smiled, as the cashier hugged him for saving their store. Justin walked out of the record store! Justin walked further down the street, and saw a huge building in the distance. Justin walked closer to the building. The building sign was for Electric Industries. Justin walked to the entrance for Electric Industries. There was a security guard, standing right next to the door, and robots around the area. Justin backflipped, and shot fire grenades at the robots. The robots exploded, and robot parts fell on to the ground. Justin tackled the security guard, and body slammed him in to the ground. Justin held the security guard on the ground. Justin wrapped his arm around the security guard's neck in to a choke hold. The security guard was coughing, and struggling in Justin's grip. Justin sharpened the spikes on his shoes, and stabbed them in to the security guard's legs. Blood poured on to the ground! Justin released his grip on the security guard's neck. The security guard laid on the ground, in a puddle of blood. Justin took the security key off of the security guard's neck. Justin slid the security key in to the door, and walked in to Electric Industries. Electric Industries had security cameras on each side of the hallway. Justin hid in the supplies closet in Electric industries. The glider flew through the air, and landed in front of the security door for

Electric Industries. Spider Crusader unlatched Supersonic Warrior, and carried her on his back. Spider Crusader walked off of the glider! Spider Crusader walked in to Electric Industries. Spider Crusader walked through the hallway, and inserted his security key in to the door for the science lab. Spider Crusader walked in to the science lab! Spider Crusader walked to the machine, and unlatched the experiment tube. Spider Crusader opened the experiment tube, and laid Supersonic Warrior inside the tube. Spider Crusader connected the wires to Supersonic Warrior's body. Spider Crusader closed the tube, and latched it. Spider Crusader started up the machine, and the tube started up. The tube's energy went through Supersonic Warrior's body. Supersonic Warrior woke up, and was dazed. Spider Crusader said, "Perfect timing to wake up, I am doing a couple of experiments on you." Supersonic Warrior got comfortable in the tube. Several robots were patrolling the hallways of Electric Industries. One of the robots walked toward the supplies closet. The robot said, "Beep Beep Beep, scanning for intruders!" The robot scanned the door for the supplies closet. The robot's scanner flashed red! The robot pulled the door off of its hinges, and walked in to the supplies closet. The robot said, "Threat detected, intruder must be exterminated!" The robot saw Justin, and walked toward him. Justin backed up in to the wall, and put a fire grenade in to his fire gauntlet. Justin shot the fire grenade at the robot. The fire grenade pushed the robot backwards. The robot hovered toward Justin, and grabbed him with its arm. The robot threw Justin across the hallway. Justin slammed in to the wall! Justin got up, and spun in to a fire tornado. The fire tornado spun in to the robot, and smashed it in to the wall. The robot got up, and shot a missile at the fire tornado. The fire tornado fizzled, and Justin landed on the ground. The robot hovered toward Justin. Justin punched the robot in the chest. The robot barely moved a inch. The robot wrapped its arms around Justin, and smashed him in to the ground. The robot punched Justin in the face. Justin growled, and shot the robot with a fire blast with his arm. The robot smashed in to the wall. Justin shot a fire grenade from his gauntlet, at the robot. The robot exploded, and robot parts flew everywhere. Justin walked further down the hallway. The hallway floor was sparkling, while Justin walked on it. Justin destroyed the security cameras, with a fire blast from his gauntlet. Justin walked to the science lab. Justin shot a fire grenade at the security door panel, and destroyed it. Justin walked in to the science lab, and hid in the closet. Spider Crusader pressed some buttons, and attached some wires to the container. Spider Crusader electrocuted Supersonic Warrior with some energy. Supersonic Warrior's blood went through the wires, and poured in to the container. The process finished, and the container sealed itself. Spider Crusader disconnected the wires from the container. Spider Crusader took out a needle, and unsealed the container. Spider Crusader connected the container to the needle's special compartment. Spider Crusader stabbed the needle in to his arm. Supersonic Warrior's blood flowed from the needle in to Spider Crusader's arm. Spider Crusader's body grew in muscle mass, as it absorbed Supersonic Warrior's blood. Spider Crusader said, "The blood was refreshing!" Spider Crusader plugged the flash drive in to the computer. He went in to the flash drive's storage, and uploaded the Extreme virus in to the operating system for Supersonic Warrior's suit. The Extreme virus shut down the suit's AI, and restarted the operating system. Supersonic Warrior's visor glowed red, and her suit turned black. Supersonic Warrior's suit AI said, "Extreme Virus is online!" Spider Crusader smiled at the results on the screen. Justin walked out of the closet, and pointed his fire gauntlet at Spider Crusader! Justin said, "Stop right there, Spider Crusader, I am here to save my friend!" Spider Crusader laughed and said, "You're the one that needs saving, hero!" Spider Crusader sped in to Justin, and grabbed him by the neck. Spider Crusader threw him in to the wall. Justin rolled on the ground, and shot a fire blast at Spider Crusader. Spider Crusader slid backwards, and backflipped in the air. Spider Crusader shot webs at Justin's arm. The webs attached to Justin's arm! Spider Crusader pulled on the web, and threw Justin in to the wall. Justin laid on the ground! Spider Crusader wrapped Justin up in a web cocoon. Spider crusader kicked the web cocoon in to the closet.

The web cocoon bounced off of the walls, and smashed in to pieces. Justin laid on the ground! Spider Crusader threw a web bomb at Justin. The web bomb exploded, and Justin rolled on the ground. Justin got up from the ground, and spun in to a fire tornado. The fire tornado flew toward Spider Crusader. Spider Crusader slid backwards. Justin landed on the ground. Spider Crusader tackled Justin, and slammed him in to the ground. Spider Crusader punched Justin in the face, multiple times. Justin growled and shot Spider Crusader in the face, with a fire blast. Spider Crusader slid backwards, while Justin got up from the ground. Justin shot a fire grenade at Spider Crusader. Spider Crusader smashed in to the wall, and laid on the ground. Justin sped toward Spider Crusader, and held him on the ground. Justin punched Spider Crusader in the face, multiple times! Justin put his hand on Spider Crusader's neck. The flames from Justin's hand slowly burned through Spider Crusader's armor. Justin picked up Spider Crusader by his neck, and smashed him in to the wall. Spider Crusader's body was heating up from the flames in Justin's hand. Spider Crusader growled, and shot a web in Justin's face. Spider Crusader flipped over Justin, and kicked him in the back. Justin smashed in to the wall! Justin laid against the wall. Spider Crusader threw a web bomb at Justin. The web bomb exploded, and Justin laid on the ground. Justin got up from the ground. Spider Crusader sped in to Justin, and tackled him in to the book shelf. Justin laid against the book shelf. Spider Crusader roundhouse kicked Justin in the face. Justin smashed through the book shelf. The book shelf shattered in to pieces. Justin laid on the ground, as book shelf pieces fell around him. Justin got up from the ground. Spider Crusader sped in to Justin, and punched him in the face. Justin smashed through the wall, and laid on the ground. Spider Crusader picked up Justin by his neck, and smashed him in to the ground. Justin backflipped off of the ground, and ignited his leg with flames. Justin roundhouse kicked Spider Crusader in the face. Spider Crusader's helmet burned, as he slid backwards. Spider Crusader sped in to Justin, and slammed him in to the ground. Spider Crusader stepped on Justin's chest, and held him on the ground. Spider Crusader punched Justin in the face, multiple times. Justin growled, and held Spider Crusader's arm back. Justin ignited his arm with flames. Spider Crusader's arm lit on fire, and Spider Crusader pulled his arm back. Spider Crusader's arm burnt to a crisp. Justin got up from the ground, and shot Spider Crusader with a fire blast, from his arm. Spider Crusader smashed in to the wall, as his arm healed itself. Spider Crusader got up from the ground, and threw a web bomb at Justin. Justin backflipped, and avoided the web bomb. The web bomb exploded behind him. Spider Crusader pressed a button on his wrist! The spider bots entered the room, and surrounded Justin. Spider Crusader shot webs at the book shelf, and swung it at Justin. The book shelf smashed Justin in to the wall. Spider Bots jumped on Justin, and held him on the ground. Justin ignited a fire explosion from his body. The spider bots exploded, and their parts fell on the ground. Justin got up from the ground, and shot a fire blast at Spider Crusader. Spider Crusader slid backwards, as his chest got burnt. Spider Crusader's chest armor repaired itself. Spider Crusader shot a web at Justin. The web attached to Justin's chest. Spider Crusader pulled the web, and dragged Justin, closer to him. Spider Crusader kicked Justin in the chest. Justin smashed through the wall, and laid on the ground. Spider Crusader walked toward Justin! Spider Crusader said, "The little hero is battered and bruised! I have a little surprise for you!" Spider Crusader walked toward the panel, and pressed some buttons on his computer. The wires in the tube lit up, as energy flowed through it. Supersonic Warrior woke up in the tube, and disconnected the wires from her body. The tube unlatched, and swung open. Supersonic Warrior walked out of the tube, and menacingly walked toward Spider Crusader. Supersonic Warrior stood next to Spider Crusader. Spider Crusader said, "Hope you liked the surprise, your best friend has turned to the dark side." Justin was terrified in fear, as Supersonic Warrior's red visor glowed in his eyes. Supersonic Warrior shot a dark energy blast at Justin. Justin rolled on the ground! Spider Crusader threw a web bomb at Justin. Justin smashed in to the wall, and laid on the ground. Justin got up from the ground.

Supersonic Warrior sped in to Justin, and smashed him through the wall. Justin laid on the ground! Supersonic Warrior stepped on Justin's chest, and held him on the ground. Supersonic Warrior said, "Prepare to be exterminated, scum!" Justin was terrified and said, "Snap out of it, we are friends!" Supersonic Warrior said, "I have no friends, I am superior on my own." Supersonic Warrior punched Justin in the face, multiple times. Blood poured on the ground! Justin growled, and shot Supersonic Warrior with a fire blast. Supersonic warrior slid backwards! Justin got up from the ground! Supersonic Warrior grabbed Justin with shadow tendrils from her suit. The shadow tendrils wrapped around Justin's body. Supersonic Warrior threw Justin in to the experiment table. Justin smashed through the experiment table, and laid on the ground. Experiment tubes shattered, and the glass shards fell on the ground. Justin got up from the ground, and shot a fire blast at Supersonic Warrior. Supersonic warrior froze the fire blast with her ice blast. The ice blast smashed Justin in to the wall! Justin was frozen on the wall. Justin ignited a fiery explosion from his body. Supersonic Warrior slid backwards! Justin shot a fire grenade at Supersonic Warrior. Supersonic Warrior smashed in to the wall, and laid on the ground. Justin lit his arm up with flames, as he grabbed Supersonic Warrior by her neck. Supersonic warrior's suit was slowly heating up. Supersonic Warrior growled and said, "My weakness, it is weakening our power and strength. Supersonic Warrior shot shadow tendrils out of her suit at Justin. Justin backflipped and dodged the shadow tendrils. Justin ignited his leg with flames, and kicked Supersonic Warrior in the chest. Supersonic Warrior smashed through the wall, and laid on the ground. Supersonic Warrior got up from the ground, and growled. Supersonic Warrior backflipped, and shot Justin with a shadow blast. Justin slid backwards! Supersonic Warrior sped in to Justin, and tackled him in to the wall. Justin laid against the wall. Supersonic Warrior grabbed Justin by the neck with shadow tendrils, and threw him in to the cabinet. Justin smashed in to the cabinet, and laid on the ground. The cabinet fell on top of Justin and shattered in to pieces. Justin got up from the ground, and sped in to Supersonic Warrior. Supersonic Warrior hit Justin in the chest with her shadow tendrils. Justin smashed in to the wall. Justin laid next to the wall. Supersonic Warrior grabbed Justin by the neck, with shadow tendrils. The shadow tendrils wrapped around Justin's neck. Supersonic Warrior said, "Surrender to the darkness!" Justin growled and said, "Never, I will continue fighting!" Supersonic Warrior said, "Your spirit will be crushed, hero scum." Supersonic Warrior smashed Justin in to the wall! Blood poured on to the ground!" Supersonic Warrior's shadow tendrils pulled Justin in to the air, and smashed him in to the ground, multiple times. Supersonic Warrior's shadow tendrils threw Justin in to the glass shelf, filled with experiment tubes. The glass shelf shattered in to pieces, as Justin smashed through it. The experiment tubes fell on to the ground, and shattered in to glass shards. Justin laid on the ground, in a puddle of blood. Supersonic Warrior wrapped her shadow tendrils around Justin's body, and lifted him in to the air. Spider Crusader walked toward Justin and said, "Your spirit is shattered and crushed by the power of darkness." Spider Crusader retracted his helmet and licked the blood, that was leaking from Justin's arm. Spider Crusader smiled and said, "Your blood is tasty, it is nice seeing the blood of my enemies poured on the ground." Spider Crusader's helmet covered his face. Justin growled and said, "Heroes always find a way to win, even when it seems hopeless." Spider Crusader said, "Darkness will take over the world!" Justin said, "I will find a way to defeat you, even if it takes all of my strength." Justin ignited a fire blast from his body. Supersonic Warrior and Spider Crusader slid backwards. Justin landed on the ground, and shot a fire grenade at Supersonic Warrior and Spider Crusader. Spider Crusader and Supersonic Warrior smashed in to the wall. Spider Crusader got up from the ground. Supersonic Warrior growled, as she backflipped off of the ground. Supersonic Warrior shot shadow tendrils at Justin. Justin backflipped and dodged them. Supersonic Warrior shot a shadow blast at Justin. Justin slid backwards. Supersonic Warrior sped in to Justin, and grabbed him by his neck. Supersonic Warrior slammed Justin in to the ground. Supersonic Warrior held Justin on the ground. Supersonic Warrior punched Justin in the face, multiple times. Blood poured on the ground! Justin's arm ignited with flames, as he held Supersonic Warrior's arm back. Supersonic Warrior's arm was being burnt to a crisp. Supersonic Warrior growled, as she got off of Justin. Supersonic Warrior's arm healed, as she shot her shadow tendrils at Justin. The shadow tendrils wrapped around Justin. Supersonic Warrior's shadow tendrils smashed Justin in to the ground, multiple times. Blood poured on the ground. Supersonic Warrior's shadow tendrils threw Justin in to the wall. Justin smashed through the wall, and laid on the ground in a puddle of blood. Spider Crusader stepped on Justin's chest. Spider Crusader said, "Don't bother getting up, hero!" Spider Crusader shot electric webs at Justin. The electric webs electrocuted Justin, as he screamed in pain. Supersonic Warrior walked next to Spider Crusader. Supersonic Warrior's shadow tendrils opened up the experiment tube. Spider Crusader shot tranquilizer webs at Justin. Supersonic Warrior's shadow tendrils picked up Justin's body, and put him in to the experiment tube. Supersonic Warrior connected the wires to Justin's body, and closed the tube. Supersonic Warrior latched the tube, and walked to Spider Crusader. Spider Crusader pressed a button on his wrist. The ceiling opened, and the glider landed in to the room. Supersonic Warrior walked on to the glider. Supersonic Warrior flew in to the air. The ceiling closed, as the glider flew out of Electric Industries. Spider Crusader pressed another button on his wrist, and the secret door opened in the science lab. Spider Crusader walked through the secret door!

17

Justin laid in the experiment tube, with the wires connected to his body. His body was weak, from the energy that was drained during the battle with Spider Crusader and Supersonic Warrior. Justin ignited his body with flames, and heated himself up. The experiment tube shattered, as the wires disconnected from Justin's body. Justin walked out of the experiment tube, as the glass shards landed on the ground. Justin stretched his arms and legs! Justin jogged in place to energize himself. Justin walked to the cabinet, and grabbed a water bottle. Justin grabbed a towel from the table. Justin opened up the water bottle, and poured the water on to his arm. Justin wiped the blood off of his arm with the towel. Justin threw the water bottle in to the recycling bin. Justin opened up another water bottle and poured the water all over his face and body. The water washed the blood off of Justin's face and body. Justin poured some water on to his hair. Justin dried himself with the towel, and threw the water bottle in to the recycling bin. Justin put the towel on the table, and walked toward the debris on the floor. Justin walked through the debris, from the chaos that happened during the battle. Justin rubbed his head and said, "That was a rough battle." Justin looked around the room for a window, that he can jump through, since Supersonic Warrior is probably causing chaos in the city. Justin walked to the other side of the room, and saw a window. Justin smashed the window open with a fire blast. Justin climbed out of the window, and ignited his body with flames to protect himself. Justin landed on the ground, while the birds tweeted in the background. Justin saw the glider in the air, and noticed that he isn't far from Supersonic Warrior's location. Justin walked down the sidewalk, and cars were zooming down the street. Police cars zoomed past Justin, with their sirens on. Justin walked further down the sidewalk, and noticed the gasoline station in front of him. Justin noticed that the glider was parked at the gasoline station. Justin hid behind the pole, and looked inside the window. The gasoline store was filled with drinks and snacks that can be bought at the register. Supersonic Warrior was in the gasoline station, threatening the cashier. Supersonic Warrior growled and said, "Give me all of your money, human scum, or you will die." Daniel trembled in fear and said, "I don't have much money in the cash register, and the gas station will collapse without it." Supersonic Warrior's shadow tendrils grabbed Daniel by the neck, and smashed him through the counter. Daniel laid on the ground! Supersonic Warrior said, "Don't make me angry, or you will regret it." Supersonic Warrior stepped on Daniel's chest, and her shadow tendrils wrapped around Daniel's neck. Supersonic Warrior summoned a ice shard in to her hand, with her ice blast. Supersonic Warrior's shadow tendrils lifted Daniel in to the air. Supersonic Warrior stabbed the ice shard in to Daniel's chest. Supersonic Warrior's shadow tendrils threw Daniel in to the wall. Daniel laid on the ground, in a puddle of blood. Supersonic Warrior ignited a dark blast from her body. Everything in the gas station exploded! Glass shards and wood pieces landed on the ground. Supersonic Warrior walked through the debris. Justin jumped through the broken window, and pointed his fire gauntlet at Supersonic Warrior. Justin shot a fire blast at Supersonic Warrior. Supersonic Warrior dodged the fire blast, and shot her shadow tendrils at Justin. Justin shot fire blasts at the shadow tendrils. The shadow tendrils burnt to a crisp. Supersonic Warrior growled, and regenerated her shadow tendrils. Supersonic Warrior shot the shadow tendrils at Justin. The shadow tendrils wrapped around Justin. Supersonic Warrior said, "The little pest tried to pounce on the predator." Supersonic Warrior rubbed her hand in Justin's hair. Justin whacked Supersonic Warrior's hand away. Justin said, "I will stop you, because I am a hero!" Supersonic

Warrior said, "Heroes are worthless scum, despair will take over the world!" Supersonic Warrior's shadow tendrils smashed Justin in to the wall. Justin growled and lit up his arm with flames. Justin touched one of the shadow tendrils, and lit it on fire. Supersonic Warrior screamed in pain, as the shadow goop landed on the ground. Justin smiled and said, "Here's my chance to strike back!" Justin shot a fire grenade at Supersonic Warrior. Supersonic Warrior smashed in to the wall. Justin ignited a fire blast from his body. Supersonic Warrior smashed through the wall, and laid on the ground. Supersonic Warrior growled, as she got up from the ground. Justin backflipped in the air, and shot a fire missile from his gauntlet at Supersonic Warrior. Supersonic Warrior smashed through the wall, as shadow goop fell on the ground. Supersonic Warrior laid on the ground! Justin ignited a fire blast from his body. Everything exploded around Justin, as it fell on the ground. Supersonic Warrior got up from the ground, and growled at Justin. Supersonic Warrior said, "You caused me pain and suffering." Supersonic Warrior's shadow tendrils grabbed Justin, and smashed him in to the ground, multiple times. Justin growled, as he lit his body on fire. The shadow tendrils lit on fire, and lost their grip on Justin. Justin roundhouse kicked Supersonic Warrior in the chest. Supersonic Warrior smashed through the counter, and laid next to the wall. Justin walked toward Supersonic Warrior! Justin smiled, as his eyes glowed red. Justin stood in front of Supersonic Warrior and said, "I have figured out your weakness, how does it feel to be another ordinary villain, consumed by darkness?" Supersonic Warrior said, "You can't stop me, I will fill your mind with despair." Justin lit his arm with flames, and picked up Supersonic Warrior by the neck. Justin said, "Despair will not win!" Supersonic Warrior's suit lit on fire, as she growled in pain. The shadow tendrils are weakening, as the flames burnt them. Supersonic Warrior's suit is burnt to a crisp. Justin smashed Supersonic Warrior in to the ground. Supersonic Warrior laid on the ground! Justin punched Supersonic Warrior in the face with a fire blast. Supersonic Warrior's visor shattered, as she laid on the ground. Supersonic Warrior's suit repaired itself, as the shadow goop reconnected to her suit. The visor repaired itself, and Supersonic Warrior got up from the ground. Supersonic Warrior growled, and ignited a shadow explosion from her body. Justin rolled on the ground, and smashed in to the wall. Justin laid against the wall! Justin backflipped off of the ground. Justin loaded a grenade in to his gauntlet, and shot it at Supersonic Warrior. The grenade hit Supersonic Warrior in the chest. Supersonic Warrior slid backwards, as shadow goop fell on to the ground. Supersonic Warrior growled, and sped toward Justin. Supersonic Warrior shot her shadow tendrils at Justin. The shadow tendrils wrapped around Justin's body. Supersonic Warrior smashed Justin in to the ground. Supersonic Warrior pulled Justin in to the air, and threw him in to the wall. Justin laid against the wall. Supersonic Warrior said, "Thanks for the little distraction, human scum." Supersonic Warrior walked to the glider. Supersonic Warrior walked on to the glider, and flew in to the air. Justin got up from the ground, and rubbed his head. Justin walked further down the street. Justin saw the glider hovering over the area, as Supersonic Warrior's shadow tendrils stabbed the citizens in the chest, and killed them. The dead bodies of the citizens laid on the ground, as Justin followed the glider. Supersonic Warrior's shadow tendrils tore the fire hydrants out of the ground, and threw them in to the wall. The water from the fire hydrants poured in to the city. The fire hydrants were spraying water everywhere. Justin walked further down the sidewalk, and got soaked by the fire hydrants. The water dripped off of Justin's body, as he ran after the glider. Citizens were panicking and running away from Supersonic Warrior, as the glider hovered down the sidewalk. Supersonic Warrior shot web bombs from the glider at the buildings. The buildings crumbled, and smashed the panicking citizens on to the ground. Dead bodies laid on the sidewalk in puddles of blood. Justin was jumping over the dead bodies, as he chased the glider down the sidewalk. Justin flipped in to the air, and shot a fire blast from his gauntlet at the glider. The glider spun in to the building, and smashed through one of the citizens. The citizen laid on the sidewalk in a puddle of blood. Justin jumped over the dead body, as Supersonic Warrior regained her balance on the glider. The glider hovered further down the sidewalk. Justin ran after the glider! Panicking citizens were running away from Supersonic Warrior's glider. Supersonic Warrior's shadow tendrils were stabbing various citizens in the chest, as their bodies laid on the ground. Supersonic Warrior's shadow tendrils picked up several cars, and threw them at Justin. Justin backflipped over the cars, and dodged them. Justin swung on a tree branch, and backflipped in to the tree. Justin shot a fire grenade from his gauntlet at the glider. The glider spun in to a building and crashed. Supersonic warrior laid on the glider. Justin backflipped out of the tree, and on to the glider. Justin punched Supersonic Warrior in the chest with a fire blast. Supersonic Warrior growled in pain! Supersonic Warrior shot a shadow tendril at Justin's neck. The shadow tendril wrapped around Justin's neck. Supersonic Warrior smashed Justin in to the wall, multiple times, and threw him in to the pole. Justin smashed in to the pole, and laid on the ground. The pole fell over, and landed on the ground. Supersonic Warrior got up, and reattached herself to the glider. The glider hovered down the sidewalk. Justin got up from the ground. Justin ran further down the sidewalk, and chased the glider. Supersonic Warrior's shadow tendrils threw shadow bombs at Justin. Justin flipped in the air, and shot the shadow bombs out of the air with fire blasts. Justin shot a fire grenade at Supersonic Warrior's glider. The fire grenade exploded one of the shadow tendrils in to shadow goop. Supersonic Warrior growled, as the shadow tendril regenerated. Supersonic Warrior hovered the glider toward Oasis Falls High School. Justin followed behind Supersonic Warrior. Oasis Falls High School was in Supersonic Warrior's view. Supersonic Warrior parked the glider next to the flag pole. Supersonic Warrior detached from the glider, and walked off of the glider. Justin backflipped over the glider, and roundhouse kicked Supersonic Warrior in the chest. Supersonic Warrior slid backwards! Supersonic Warrior tore the flag pole out of the ground, and hit Justin in the chest. Justin rolled on the ground! Justin backflipped off of the ground. Supersonic Warrior shot her shadow tendrils at Justin. Justin backflipped over them, and shot a fire grenade at Supersonic Warrior. Supersonic Warrior smashed in to a tree and growled. Supersonic Warrior laid against the tree. Justin sped toward Supersonic Warrior! Justin lit his arm with flames, and grabbed Supersonic Warrior by the neck. Justin smashed Supersonic Warrior in to the ground, as the shadow goop on her suit burnt in to a crisp. The shadow goop fell off of Supersonic Warrior's suit, and landed on the ground. Supersonic Warrior growled, and ignited a shadow explosion from her body. Justin smashed in to the tree, and got stuck to the tree by a shadow goop web. Justin ignited his body in flames, and burned the shadow goop web off of him. Justin backflipped and roundhouse kicked Supersonic Warrior in the face. Supersonic Warrior slid backwards, and shot shadow tendrils at Justin. Justin backflipped and dodged the shadow tendrils. Justin shot a fire blast at Supersonic Warrior. Supersonic Warrior smashed in to the tree, and laid on the ground. Supersonic Warrior got up from the ground. Justin ran toward Supersonic Warrior, and flipped in to a tree. Justin swung on the tree branch, and flipped in to the air. Justin summoned a fire aura around his body, and spun in to a tornado. Justin spun in to Supersonic Warrior! The shadow goop burnt off of Supersonic Warrior's suit, and fell on the ground. Supersonic Warrior smashed in to the wall, and laid on the ground. Justin landed on the ground, as the fire aura disappeared around his body. Justin backflipped on to Supersonic Warrior, and held her on the ground. Justin ignited his arm with flames, and put his hand on Supersonic Warrior's chest. The shadow goop started to burn, as Supersonic Warrior growled. Supersonic Warrior shot a shadow tendril at Justin, Justin grabbed the shadow tendril, and burnt it to a crisp. The shadow goop fell on to the ground. Supersonic Warrior growled, and tossed Justin off of her. Justin rolled on the ground. Supersonic Warrior got up from the ground. Justin got up from the ground. Justin shot a fire blast at Supersonic Warrior. Supersonic Warrior smashed in to a tree, and laid on the ground. Supersonic Warrior growled, as she backflipped off of the ground! Justin said, "Hey shadow demon, come chase me through the school!" Justin shot a fire grenade at Supersonic

Warrior. The fire grenade hit Supersonic Warrior's chest, and exploded. The shadow goop fell off of her suit, and on to the ground. Supersonic Warrior growled, as the shadow goop regenerated. Justin kicked open the doors for Oasis Falls High School. Justin ran in to Oasis Falls High School. Supersonic Warrior chased after Justin. Supersonic Warrior picked up lockers with her shadow tendrils, and threw them at Justin. Justin backflipped in to the air, and dodged them. The lockers fell on to the ground, as Justin ran further down the hallway. Supersonic Warrior chased after Justin! Justin shot a fire blast at Supersonic Warrior. The fire blast hit Supersonic Warrior in the chest! Supersonic Warrior slid backwards and growled, as the shadow goop fell off of her suit. Justin ran to the water fountain, while Supersonic Warrior was chasing him. Justin stopped at the water fountain, and picked it up. Justin threw the water fountain at Supersonic Warrior. The water fountain splashed water all over Supersonic Warrior. Supersonic Warrior slid backwards! Supersonic Warrior growled, and shot a shadow tendril at Justin. The shadow tendril wrapped around Justin, and smashed him in to the lockers. Justin laid against the lockers. Supersonic Warrior walked toward Justin, and growled at him. Justin shot a fire grenade at Supersonic Warrior. Supersonic Warrior slid backwards, and Justin got up from the ground. Justin ran in to the science lab. Supersonic Warrior chased after Justin! Justin ran toward the science cabinet, and threw containers of chemicals at Supersonic Warrior. The chemicals splashed on to the shadow goop, and dissolved it. The shadow goop fell off of Supersonic Warrior's suit, as she growled in pain. Supersonic Warrior tackled Justin in to the chemical table. The chemicals splashed on top of Supersonic Warrior's suit. Supersonic Warrior growled, as she held Justin on the ground. Supersonic Warrior's visor glowed red, as she stared in to Justin's eyes. Justin growled and punched Supersonic Warrior in the chest, with a fire blast. Supersonic Warrior rolled on to the ground. Justin got up from the ground. Supersonic Warrior got up from the ground! Supersonic Warrior sped toward Justin! Supersonic Warrior ignited a shadow blast from her body. The furniture and the chemical tubes exploded, and fell on the ground. Justin smashed in to the desk, and laid next to it. Supersonic Warrior walked toward Justin, with her red visor glowing. Supersonic Warrior grabbed Justin by his neck, and threw him in to the teacher's desk. Justin smashed through the teacher's desk. Justin got up from the ground, and threw the left over pieces of the teacher's desk at Supersonic Warrior. Supersonic Warrior slid backwards, and growled. Justin tackled Supersonic Warrior through the science lab door, and in to the hallway lockers. Supersonic Warrior laid against the lockers. Justin punched Supersonic Warrior in the chest, with a fire blast. Supersonic Warrior laid on the ground. Justin held Supersonic Warrior on the ground! Justin punched Supersonic Warrior in the face, multiple times. Supersonic Warrior's visor started to crack. Supersonic Warrior growled, and shot a shadow laser from her visor at Justin. Justin rolled on the ground! Supersonic Warrior's visor repaired itself, while she got up from the ground. Justin got up from the ground. Justin shot a fire blast at Supersonic Warrior. The fire blast hit Supersonic Warrior's chest. Supersonic Warrior slid backwards, as shadow goop fell off of her suit. Supersonic Warrior growled, as she grabbed a book shelf with her shadow tendrils. Supersonic Warrior threw the book shelf at Justin. Justin caught the book shelf, as he slid backwards. Justin threw the book shelf at Supersonic Warrior. Supersonic Warrior smashed in to the wall. Supersonic Warrior got up from the ground. Supersonic Warrior growled, and chased after Justin. Justin ran in to the library, and flipped on to the book shelf. Justin balanced himself on the book shelf. Supersonic Warrior growled, as Justin kicked the books off of the book shelf at her. Supersonic Warrior exploded the books to pieces with her shadow blast. Justin kicked the book shelf down on top of Supersonic Warrior, as he flipped on to the next book shelf. Supersonic Warrior smashed the book shelf to pieces with her shadow blast. Justin backflipped off of the book shelf. Justin ignited a fire blast from his body! Everything in the library exploded, and fell on top of Supersonic Warrior. Supersonic Warrior growled, as she got up from the ground. Justin tackled Supersonic Warrior, and body slammed her in to the ground. Justin ignited his arm with flames, as he put his arm on Supersonic warrior's neck. Supersonic Warrior growled in pain, as the flames burnt her suit. Supersonic Warrior shot a shadow laser from her visor at Justin. Justin rolled on the ground. Supersonic warrior got up from the ground. Justin got up from the ground. Justin ran out of the library, and Supersonic Warrior chased after him. Justin ran in to the biology lab. Supersonic warrior growled at Justin. Justin saw the piranha tank, and smiled. Justin ran to the closet in the biology lab, and put on a piranha resistant armor suit. Justin said,"Time for a little swim for you, monster!" Justin stood in front of the piranha tank. Supersonic Warrior ran toward Justin! Justin ignited his arm with flames, and punched Supersonic Warrior in to the air." Justin flipped in the air, and kicked Supersonic Warrior in to the piranha tank. Supersonic Warrior grabbed on to Justin's leg, and pulled him in to the piranha tank with her. Supersonic Warrior and Justin landed in the piranha tank. The piranha fish swam around Justin and Supersonic Warrior, as they floated in the tank. The piranha fish attached to Supersonic Warrior, as she growled in pain. Justin ignited a fire blast from his body. The water heated up, and spun in to a tornado. The shadow goop was boiled off of Supersonic Warrior's suit. Supersonic Warrior was floating in the water, as the piranha fish tore her suit to pieces. Justin swam to the top of the piranha tank. Justin got to the top of the piranha tank, and climbed out of it. Justin landed on the ground! The piranha tank closed, as the piranha fish tore up its prey. The piranha fish summoned a tornado in the tank, as the bubbles in the water started forming together. Supersonic Warrior's suit was torn apart, with her helmet destroyed, and her visor has been shattered. The water turned red, as the blood from Supersonic Warrior's suit soaked through it. The piranha tank opened, and the piranha fish swam in their group. Supersonic Warrior's body laid at the bottom of the tank. Justin grabbed a fishing net, and fished Supersonic Warrior out of the tank. Justin laid Supersonic Warrior on the ground! A glider smashed through the window, and landed in front of Justin. Spider Crusader walked off of the glider, and growled at Justin. Justin pointed his fire gauntlet at Spider Crusader, and loaded a fire grenade in to it. Justin shot the fire grenade at Spider Crusader! The fire grenade hit Spider Crusader in the chest. Spider Crusader slid backwards!Spider Crusader said, "Human scum, prepare to die!" Justin said, "I will defend this city from you, monster!" Spider Crusader said, "I will smash you like a bug, hero." Spider Crusader smiled, as he took out his web sword. Justin said, "You will fail, like every other villain." Justin backflipped in the air, and kicked Spider Crusader in the chest. Spider Crusader smashed in to the wall! Spider Crusader laid against the wall, and growled. Spider Crusader shot a web in Justin's face, and grabbed him by the neck. Spider crusader smashed Justin in to the ground. Justin shot a fire blast at Spider Crusader. Spider Crusader smashed through the wall, and laid on the ground. Spider Crusader backflipped off of the ground. Justin backflipped off of the ground. Justin summoned a flaming sword in to his hand, and sped toward Spider Crusader. Spider Crusader sped toward Justin! Justin and Spider Crusader clashed their swords together, and growled at each other. Justin flipped in the air, and slashed Spider Crusader's arm with his sword. Spider Crusader slid backwards! Spider Crusader shot a web at Justin. The web attached to Justin's body. Spider Crusader pulled on the web, and dragged Justin toward him. Justin backflipped in the air, and stabbed his sword in to Spider Crusader's chest. Spider Crusader slid backwards, and growled. Spider Crusader sped in to Justin, and grabbed him by the neck. Spider Crusader smashed Justin in to the wall. Justin's sword fell on to the ground, and fizzled away. Justin laid against the wall. Justin kicked Spider Crusader in the chest. Spider Crusader slid backwards, and his web sword landed on the ground. Spider Crusader webbed his web sword back to his belt. Justin tackled Spider Crusader, and smashed him in to the ground. Justin lit up his arm with flames, and grabbed Spider Crusader by the neck. Justin lifted Spider Crusader in to the air, and threw him in to the wall. Spider Crusader laid against the wall. Justin punched Spider Crusader in the face, with a fire blast. Spider Crusader laid on the ground! Justin growled and punched Spider Crusader in the face, multiple times. Spider Crusader held Justin's arm back, and kicked him in the chest. Justin slid backwards, and Spider Crusader backflipped off of the ground. Spider Crusader threw a web bomb at Justin. The web bomb exploded, and Justin smashed in to the wall. Justin laid on the ground. Spider Crusader walked toward Justin, and growled at him. Spider Crusader stepped on Justin's chest, and held him on the ground. Spider Crusader shot electric webs at Justin. The electric webs electrocuted Justin, as blood leaked on to the ground. Spider Crusader punched Justin in the face, multiple times. Justin growled, as he lit his arm with flames. Justin held Spider Crusader's arm back. Spider Crusader's arm lit on fire. Justin backflipped off of the ground, and kicked Spider Crusader in the chest. Spider Crusader slid backwards! Spider Crusader's arm healed, as he shot webs at Justin. The webs attached to Justin's body. Spider Crusader pulled Justin toward him! Spider Crusader kicked Justin in the chest. Justin slid backwards! Spider Crusader sped in to Justin, and grabbed him by his neck. Spider Crusader smashed Justin in to the wall. Justin laid against the wall, and ignited a fire blast from his body. Spider Crusader slid backwards. Justin threw a fire grenade at Spider Crusader. Spider Crusader smashed in to the wall. Spider Crusader laid against the wall. Justin walked toward Spider Crusader, with his eyes glowing red. Justin lit his arms with flames, and picked up Spider Crusader's body. Justin smashed Spider Crusader in to the ground. Justin said, "You're a monster for the damage that you have caused to the city." Justin held Spider Crusader on the ground. Justin put his hand on Spider Crusader's chest. Spider Crusader's suit started to heat up. Spider Crusader growled, and shot a web in Justin's face. Justin slid backwards! Spider Crusader backflipped off of the ground. Spider Crusader threw some sticky web bombs on to the walls. The sticky web bombs attached to the walls, and lit up. Spider Crusader backflipped in the air, and shot webs at Justin. The webs wrapped Justin in to a cocoon. Spider Crusader sped in to the web cocoon, and kicked it in to the wall. The cocoon bounced off of the walls! The cocoon smashed on the ground, and exploded. Justin laid on the ground. Justin got up from the ground. Spider Crusader crawled on the walls. Spider Crusader crawled to the light post, above Justin. Spider Crusader shot a web from his web shooter on to the light post, and hung upside down on it. Justin stepped backwards, and pointed his fire gauntlet at Spider Crusader. Justin shot a fire grenade at Spider Crusader. Spider Crusader swung himself on the light post, and flipped in to the air. Spider Crusader shot a web at the fire grenade, and swung it toward Justin. The fire grenade hit Justin in the chest. Justin smashed in to the wall, and laid next to it. Spider Crusader landed on the ground, and pressed a button on his wrist. The glider flew in to the building. Spider crusader backflipped on to the glider, and flew around the room. Spider Crusader attached web bombs to the wall foundation. Justin got up from the ground. Spider Crusader shot a web missile from his glider at the light post. The light post exploded, and fell on to the ground. Justin flipped out of the way, as the light post smashed on to the ground in pieces. Justin loaded a fire grenade in to his fire gauntlet. Justin shot the fire grenade at Spider Crusader's glider. The fire grenade hit the glider! The glider spun in a circle, while Spider Crusader kept his balance. Spider Crusader pressed the button on his wrist, and the web bombs beeped! The web bombs exploded and the wall foundation crumbled to pieces. The wall foundation fell on top of Justin, as he got smashed on to the ground. Spider Crusader flew out of the building. Justin laid under the crumbled wall foundation, in a puddle of blood. Justin used his strength to lift the crumbled wall foundation off of him. Justin threw the crumbled wall foundation to the other side of the room. Justin sat on the ground to catch his breath. Justin wiped the blood off of his body, with a towel. Justin drank a bottle of water to rehydrate himself. Justin got up from the ground, and walked through the crumbled wall foundation. Justin walked to the window, and shattered it open with a fire blast. Justin climbed out of the window. Justin landed on the ground. Justin walked down the sidewalk, and the birds were buzzing in the background. The clouds turned gray, and it started to rain. The rain poured from the clouds, on top of Justin's body. Justin's hair was soaked, while he was walking. The glider flew in the air, while Justin was walking in the rain. Justin walked past Electric Industries. Electric Industries was empty, with no guards patrolling the area. Justin sighed, as he walked further down the sidewalk. The glider flew in to one of the windows of Electric Industries and smashed through it. Spider Crusader backflipped off of the glider, and walked through the science lab. Spider Crusader pressed a button on his wrist, and walked through the secret door. Spider Crusader walked through the secret hallway, in to a giant science lab. The giant science lab was filled with experiment tubes, and other gadgets. Spider Crusader walked to the computer, and plugged in his flash drive. Spider Crusader tapped some buttons, and loaded up the storage for the flash drive. Spider Crusader tapped on the Extreme virus, and loaded it on to the screen. Spider Crusader browsed through the data, and growled at himself. Spider Crusader said, "I thought my calculations were right when creating the virus, but the hero scum, Justin, found a weakness in my data." Spider Crusader scrolled through the data! Spider Crusader said, "The Extreme virus enhances the abilities of the host. If I change some values in the data, maybe the virus can defeat anything in its path." Spider Crusader edited the data for the Extreme virus, and made some enhancements to make it stronger. Spider Crusader smiled and said, "We just need another host for the virus to control." Spider Crusader pressed the save button on the computer, and saved the data to the flash drive. Spider Crusader spun in his chair and said, "This is why I am the smartest villain in the world, I can reconfigure any plan to outsmart my enemies." Justin walked further down the sidewalk! The rain poured harder on top of Justin, as he walked down the sidewalk. The rain was dripping off of Justin's body, as he walked down the sidewalk. Justin saw the gym in the distance, and smiled. Justin said, "The gym looks like a good place to dry for a while." Justin walked to the gym. Justin walked in to the gym, and shook the water off of his body. Justin dried his hair with a towel. Justin walked to the treadmill, and turned it on. Justin ran on the treadmill! Justin turned off the treadmill, and walked off of it. Justin walked to the workout machine, and worked out for 30 minutes. Justin walked away from the workout machine. Justin walked to the punching bag, and punched the bag for 30 minutes. Justin walked away from the punching bag, and drank a bottle of water to rehydrate himself. Justin recycled the bottle of water in the recycling bin. Justin stretched his arms and smiled. Justin said, "That was a good workout session." Justin walked to the snack vending machine in the gym. Justin paid for a ice cream bar. Justin grabbed the ice cream bar out of the snack vending machine. Justin grabbed a napkin from the counter! Justin walked to the bench! Justin sat on the bench, and ate the ice cream bar. Justin wiped his mouth with the napkin. Justin got up from the bench! Justin walked to the trash can! Justin threw the ice cream bar wrapper, and the napkin in to the trash can. Justin walked out of the gym. Justin walked down the sidewalk. Justin walked to a dark alley, and noticed a robber and a girl. The robber was dressed in black, and had a knife in his hand. The girl's name was Ash! Justin walked in to the dark alley. The robber threatened Ash with the knife. The robber said, "Hello little girl, your hair is so soft. Do you mind if I cut it off?" The robber rubbed his knife through Ash's hair. Ash was terrified in fear, and shoved the robber away from her. The robber said, "The little girl is fighting back! Time to crush your soul to pieces!" The robber smiled, as he flipped his knife in to the air. The robber backflipped and caught the knife. The robber landed on the ground. The robber kicked Ash in the back. Ash smashed in to the wall, and laid next to it. The robber slashed his knife through Ash's hair and cut it to pieces. Hair pieces landed on the ground, as Ash screamed and stumbled backwards in to the wall! The robber grabbed Ash by the neck, and stabbed his knife in to Ash's skull. Blood splashed on to the ground, as the robber threw Ash's body on to the ground. Justin walked toward the robber, as he loaded a grenade in to his gauntlet. Justin pointed the gauntlet at the robber, and pulled the trigger. The grenade hit the robber in the chest, and exploded. The robber smashed in to the wall, and laid next to it. Justin sped in to the robber, and grabbed him by the neck. Justin smashed the robber in to the ground. Justin held the robber on the ground, and punched him in the face, multiple times. Blood leaked from the robber's face, on to the ground. Justin lit his arm on fire, and put his hand on the robber's neck. The robber's body lit on fire, as blood poured out of it. The blood soaked through the robber's body, and formed a puddle. Justin got up from the ground, and wiped the blood off of his arm with a towel. Justin walked out of the alley! Justin walked down the sidewalk, and listened to the birds in the background. Justin walked to his house. Justin stopped at the front door of his house, and sighed to himself. Justin's house was blue, and has a descent sized yard for plants and playing outside. Justin took his key out of his pocket, and put it in to the door knob. Justin turned the key, and the door unlocked. Justin opened the door and walked in to the house. Justin put his bag on the rack, next to the door. Justin took his shoes off, and put them next to the rack. Justin walked to the couch, and sat on it. Justin watched football on the television. Justin's parents, Aaron and Sunshine, walked in to the room, and sat on the couch. Aaron and Sunshine sat next to Justin. Justin's eyes were watering, as he thought of Christina in his head. Aaron said, "Just let the tears out, everything will be ok." Justin broke in to tears, and cried in Sunshine's arms. Aaron rubbed Justin's back, as he cried. Sunshine said, "I know it is hard to lose one of your friends, but life will get better." Aaron and Sunshine hugged Justin, as he cried his tears out. Justin lifted his head out of Sunshine's arms, and wiped his tears away with his hands. Justin hugged Aaron and Sunshine. Justin said, "Thanks for making me feel better!" Aaron and Sunshine smiled at Justin and said, "You're welcome!" Justin turned off the television, and got up from the couch. Aaron and Sunshine got up from the couch, and walked out of the room. Justin walked out of the room, and in to the hallway. Justin walked down the hallway to his room. Justin stopped at the door, and turned the door knob. Justin opened the door, and walked in to his room. Justin laid on the bed, and went under the bed sheets. Justin closed his eyes, and fell asleep! Justin had a nightmare! In the nightmare sequence, Justin was in the woods, admiring the water fall. A pack of wolves pounced on Justin. Justin fell in to the water, as the wolves held him down. Justin ignited a fire blast from his body. The wolves got blasted further in to the woods. Justin got up from the water, and bent down. Justin looked in the water, and saw a reflection of Spider Crusader. Spider Crusader's reflection said, "You are worthless and weak, you don't deserve to be a hero." Justin whacked the water with his hand, and the reflection disappeared. Justin said, "I am a hero, and you can't tear me down!" Justin woke up from the nightmare sequence, and took the bed sheets off of his head. Justin laid on his bed, and drank a bottle of water. Justin threw the bottle in to the recycling bin, that was in his room. Justin made his bed, and straighten out the bed sheets. Sunshine knocked on the door of Justin's bed room. Justin said, "Come in!" Sunshine opened the door, and walked in to Justin's bed room. Sunshine said, "Do you want a snack from the kitchen?" Justin said, "Sure!" Justin got up from his bed, and walked to the door. Sunshine walked behind Justin, and closed the door. Justin and Sunshine walked to the kitchen. Justin and Sunshine walked in to the kitchen. Justin went to the cabinet and grabbed a bag of potato chips, and a bowl. Justin poured the bag of potato chips in to the bowl. Justin put the bag of potato chips in to the cabinet, and closed it. Justin sat at the table, and slowly ate the potato chips in the bowl. Aaron was at the table, across from Justin, eating a salad. Aaron said, "I had a friend in the past. His name was Matt!" Justin said, "What happened to Matt?" Aaron said, "Matt and I were at the aquarium, and there was a display with a huge piranha tank. Matt wanted to be confident, and swim with the piranha fish, without the security guards noticing him." Justin said, "Did he get to swim with the piranha fish?" Aaron said, "Nope, the piranha fish got mad at him and tore his body to shreds in front of me." Justin broke in to tears, and cried in his bowl of potato chips. Sunshine hit Aaron in the back, with her hand. Sunshine said, "That story was uncalled for! It wouldn't make Justin feel better!" Aaron said, "I was trying to cheer him up!" Sunshine said, "You should of tried harder!" Justin wiped his tears away with his hand and said, "Stop fighting, family members aren't allowed to fight!" Sunshine said, "Justin is right, we shouldn't fight over silly things!" Aaron and Sunshine apologize to each other, while Justin finished his bowl of potato chips. Justin got up from the table, and pushed his chair in. Justin put the empty bowl in to the dish washer. Justin closed the dishwasher! Justin walked out of the kitchen, and in to the hallway. Justin walked to the workout room. Justin walked to the door, and turned the door knob. Justin opened the door, and walked in to the workout room. Justin did push ups on the ground for 30 minutes. Justin got up from the ground, and climbed on the rock wall for 30 minutes. Justin got off of the rock wall, and took a small break. Justin drank a bottle of water to rehydrate himself. Justin threw the bottle of water in to the recycling bin. Justin walked to the workout machine. Justin worked out on the workout machine for 30 minutes. Justin walked off the workout machine, and walked to the punching bag. Justin punched the punching bag for 30 minutes. Justin walked away from the punching bag. Justin drank another bottle of water to rehydrate himself! Justin threw the water bottle in to the recycling bin. Justin stretched his arms, as he walked out of the workout room. Justin walked down the hallway! Justin walked toward the bathroom. Justin walked to the bathroom door. Justin turned the door knob, and opened the door. Justin walked in to the bathroom, and locked the door behind him. Justin turned on the water in the shower, and took off his clothes. The water warmed up in the shower. Justin walked in to the shower, and closed the shower door. Justin squirted soap out of the bottle on to his hair. Justin rubbed the soap in to his hair, with his hands. Justin washed the soap out of his hair. Justin squirted soap on to his arms. Justin washed the soap off of his arms. Justin stood under the shower head, and let the water pour on to his body. The water washed the dirt off of Justin's body. Justin turned off the water, and opened the shower door. Justin put the towel on his head, and dried off his hair. Justin wrapped the towel around his body, and dried himself. Justin put his clothes back on! Justin walked in to the hallway. Justin walked to his bed room. Justin opened the door, and walked in to his bed room. Justin walked to the bed. Justin laid on the bed. Justin sighed to himself! It was a crazy day for Justin. Justin was glad, that he can lay in bed in the comfort of his house. The sun was setting outside his bed room. The sky turned black, and the moon rose in to the sky. Justin laid under the bed sheets, and fell asleep. Justin slept for multiple hours. The sun rose in the sky, and shined through Justin's bed room window. Justin woke up, and removed the bed sheets off of his head. Justin laid on his bed, and stretched his arms. Justin got up from his bed, and jogged in place to energize himself. Justin drank a bottle of water to hydrate himself. Justin threw the bottle of water in to the recycling bin. Justin walked toward the door. Justin turned the door knob, and opened the door. Justin walked out of his room, and in to the hallway. Justin walked toward the workout room. Justin walked in to the workout room. Justin walked on to the treadmill, and ran on it for 30 minutes. Justin walked to the workout machine, and worked out on it for 30 minutes. Justin walked to the punching bag, and punched it for 30 minutes. Justin drank a bottle of water to hydrate himself. Justin threw the bottle of water in to the recycling bin. Justin walked out of the workout room, and in to the hallway. Justin walked to the bathroom. Justin walked in to the bathroom, and locked the door. Justin turned on the water in the shower, and took off his clothes. The water warmed up in the shower. Justin walked in to the shower, and closed the shower door. Justin squirted soap out of the bottle on to his hair. Justin rubbed the soap in to his hair, with his hands. Justin washed the soap out of his hair. Justin squirted soap on to his arms. Justin washed the soap off of his arms. Justin stood under the shower head, and let the water pour on to his body. The water washed the dirt off of Justin's body. Justin turned off the water, and opened the shower door. Justin put the towel on his head, and dried off his hair. Justin wrapped the towel around his body, and dried himself. Justin put his clothes back on! Justin walked in to the hallway. Justin walked to the front door! Justin stood in front of the front door, and turned the door knob. Justin walked out of the front door. Justin walked to the swing on the front porch, and sat on it. Justin swung on the swing, and listened to the birds tweeting in the background. Butterflies were flying around the flowers, while Justin was swinging. The sky was clear, and the sun was shining. It was a peaceful day, with no chaos happening in the city. Aaron and Sunshine walked out of the front door, and sat next to Justin on the swing. Aaron and Sunshine hugged Justin on the swing. Justin, Aaron, and Sunshine smiled at each other. Justin was swinging with Aaron and Sunshine, enjoying the peaceful nature. Birds were tweeting, and the bugs were buzzing! Aaron tickled Justin on the swing! Justin was laughing super hard on the swing. Justin regained his composure, as Sunshine smiled at him. Sunshine said, "This is what being a family is about, having fun and enjoying each other." Justin and Aaron smiled at each other, as they hugged Sunshine.

In Zoomopolis, It has been 1 month, since the death of Supersonic Warrior. Without a superhero defending the city, crime rates have gone up! The criminals have been breaking in to gas stations, and looting them. The traffic has been crazy, with cars speeding through the streets, and car crashes clogging up the traffic. The students of Oasis Falls High School progressed through their classes and school activities, filled with depression and sadness. The teachers were giving the students their usual lectures. The police officers were busy, making sure the city didn't fall apart. Outside of the house, the birds were tweeting, and the bugs were buzzing. The house of Justin, Aaron, and Sunshine is still alive and functioning. Justin stayed healthy, and did his usual daily showers and workouts. Aaron and Sunshine kept the house clean and polished. Justin laid in his bed, with the bed sheets over his head. One of the pillows were on the floor. The windows were closed, with the curtains covering them. Sunshine walked in to Justin's bed room, and looked at the clock, next to his bed. The clock said that it was 1:00 pm. Sunshine picked up the pillow, and put it on the bed. Sunshine pulled the bed sheets off of Justin's body, and whacked him in the head with a pillow. Justin rubbed his head and said, "Owwww, what was that for?" Sunshine said, "It's a beautiful day, use your time wisely." Justin grumbled, as he got up from the bed. Sunshine walked out of the room. Justin got up from the bed, and straightened out the bed sheets. Justin took some clean clothes out of his drawers. Justin walked in to the bathroom, and turned the shower on. Justin took off his clothes! Justin walked in to the shower, and closed the shower door. Justin took a shower, and cleaned his body. Justin washed his hair and his face. Justin turned off the shower, and wore the clean clothes. Justin brushed his hair, and brushed his teeth. Justin put his tooth brush in to the holder. Justin put his hairbrush in to the drawer. Justin walked out of the bathroom. Justin walked in to his bedroom, and put the dirty clothes in to his laundry basket. Justin grabbed his bag, and put it on his back. Justin walked out of his bedroom, and walked in to the hallway. Justin walked in to the kitchen, and opened the refrigerator. Justin grabbed the orange juice carton. Justin put the orange juice carton on the counter, and opened the cabinet. Justin grabbed a cup from the cabinet, and closed it. Justin put the cup on the counter, and opened the orange juice carton. Justin poured the orange juice in to the cup. Justin closed the orange juice carton, and opened the refrigerator door. Justin put the orange juice carton in to the refrigerator, and closed the door for the refrigerator. Justin drank the orange juice, out of the cup. Justin walked to the dish washer, and opened it. Justin put the cup in to the dish washer. Justin closed the dish washer. Justin walked out of the kitchen. Justin walked to the front door, and opened it. Justin walked out of the front door, and in to the front yard. Justin walked down the driveway, and took a walk down the street. Justin walked down the street, and noticed the robber running away from the bank, with a bag of money in his hand. Justin slowly walked down the street. Cars were speeding down the street in the background. The robber ran in to Justin, and fell on the ground. Justin's eyes glowed red, as he looked at the terrified robber. The robber was terrified in fear, as Justin stepped on the robber's leg. Justin crushed the robber's leg with his foot, and lit his hands up with flames. Justin did a fire blast with his hands! The robber's body caught on fire, and burned in to a crisp. The bag of money burned up, and the smoke evaporated in to the air. Pieces of burnt money floated in the air, and landed in front of the bank. Justin's eyes went back to normal. Justin continued walking down the street. The birds were tweeting, and the bugs were buzzing in the background. Police cars and cars were speeding through the streets. Justin walked to the courtyard of Oasis Falls High School. Justin walked through the courtyard of Oasis Falls High School. Justin walked in to Oasis Falls High School, and the hallways were filled with students, going through their lockers. Justin walked in to the history classroom, and walked to his desk. Justin put his bag, next to his desk. Justin sat at his desk. The teacher was Mr. Glider, and he was teaching the students about the history of cardboard. Justin laid his head down on his desk, and listened to the lecture. Mr. Glider finished his lecture, and the bell rang in the background. The other students got up from their desks. Justin got up from his desk, and put his bag on his back. Justin walked down the hallway. Justin walked in to the cafeteria, and walked toward the vending machine. Justin got a can of Dr. Explosion from the vending machine, and sat at the table. Justin opened the can of Dr. Explosion, and drank it. Justin got up from the table, and threw the can in to the recycling bin. Justin walked in to the hallway. Justin walked in to the gym, and sat on the bleachers. The football team were practicing in the gym to improve their skills. Chase, the quarterback, was huddled behind the offense, while the defense were in position. Chase hiked the ball, and threw it to Adam. Adam caught the ball, and touched the wall with his hand. The coach blew the whistle, and the football team hugged each other. Chase said, "Good work team, our skills have improved, since the last football game." Chase and the rest of the football team sat on the bleachers, while the mascot and the marching band walked in to the gym. The rest of the students walked in to the gym, and sat on the bleachers. The marching band played their instruments, while the mascot did acrobatics, and flips in the gym. The students chanted, "Let's Go Wildcats!", while the marching band played their instruments. The marching band finished playing their instruments, and they marched out of the gym. Justin got up from the bleachers, and hugged the mascot. The mascot hugged Justin, and smiled at him. The rest of the students got up from the bleachers, and hugged the mascot. The mascot hugged the other students, and smiled at them. The rest of the students walked out of the gym. Justin walked out of the gym, and walked in to the hallway. The other students were hanging out in the hallway, and drinking out of the water fountain. The other students finished drinking out of the water fountain, and walked to their classes. The hallway was empty, and it was so quiet. Justin walked in to the exercise room, and lifted the weights. Justin put down the weights, and punched the punching bag for an hour. Justin finished punching the punching bag, and got a bottle of water from the vending machine. Justin drank the bottle of water. Justin walked to the recycling bin, and threw the bottle of water away. Justin walked out of the exercise room. Justin walked in to the hallway, and walked to the science room. Justin walked in to the science room, and leaned next to the wall. Sam, the science teacher, was taking care of the lizards in their containers. Sam gave the lizards some food in their container. Sam had some serums next to the container. One of the lizards climbed out of the container, and grabbed the growth serum with its tail. The container for the growth serum smashed to pieces, as the liquid for the serum splashed all over the lizard's body. The lizard licked up the liquid. The lizard grew and growled at Sam. Sam panicked, as he laid next to his desk. The lizard wrapped Sam up with its tail, and lifted him in to the air. The lizard opened his mouth, and lowered Sam in to his fangs. The lizard was about to chomp Sam's head off with his fangs, when Justin threw a book at the lizard. The lizard growled, and dropped Sam on the ground. The lizard crawled toward Justin. Justin shot fire balls at the lizard with his hands. The lizard dodged the fire balls, and pounced on Justin. The lizard held Justin on the ground, as his claws stabbed through Justin's clothes. Justin growled, as he consumed his body in flames. Justin's eyes glowed red, as he did a fire blast from his body. The fire blast smashed the lizard in to the wall. The lizard got up, and sped toward Justin. Justin got up from the ground, and backflipped on to the lizard's back. Justin rode on the lizard's back, as the lizard raged, and smashed through the hallway. Justin hung on to the lizard's back, as the lizard smashed the lockers. The other students hid in the bathroom and the teacher's lounge.

Justin put his hand on the lizard's head, as the flames covered his arm. The lizard growled, as its body lit on fire. The lizard was consumed in a fiery tornado, as Justin rode on its back. Justin rode the lizard in to the courtyard of Oasis Falls High School, and backflipped off of the lizard's back. Justin's eyes glowed red! Justin said, "Time to barbecue the lizard with my flames." Justin summoned a blast of flames from his body, and covered the area with fire. The lizard's body caught on fire, and burnt to a crisp. Justin landed on the ground! The other students walked out of the bathroom, and the teacher's lounge. The other students walked in to the courtyard of Oasis Falls High School, and cheered for Justin. Justin smiled at the other students, and saluted them. Justin walked out of the courtyard! Justin walked down the sidewalk, and walked to Electric Industries. Justin walked in to Electric Industries, and saw Spider Crusader! Justin went undercover, and hid behind the wall. Otto was standing next to Spider Crusader. Otto said, "I heard that the darkness monster was a failure." Spider Crusader said, "The darkness monster wasn't a failure, it worked perfectly by consuming the host. There were complications though!" Otto growled and said, "What kind of complications?" Spider Crusader said, "There was a major complication with a hero named Fire Slinger. He killed the host, that the darkness monster consumed. I can revive the darkness monster, it just needs a new host." Otto said, "That isn't good enough!" Otto growled and pushed Spider Crusader in to the wall. Otto put his hand on Spider Crusader's neck. Otto said, "Letting heroes destroy your work makes you weak! Showing your weakness makes you unstable!" Spider Crusader growled and said, "I am not weak!" Otto hid behind the wall. Spider Crusader saw Justin behind the wall, and shot a web at Justin's chest with his web shooters. The web attached to Justin's chest. Spider Crusader pulled on the web, and dragged Justin closer to him. Spider Crusader growled at Justin. Justin said, "You don't scare me, Spider Crusader." Spider Crusader said, "The little pest has been spying on me! You have been a thorn in my side." Justin growled and said, "You're a monster for using innocent people for your experiments. My friend died, because of you."

Spider Crusader said, "Awwww, the little hero is upset! The world is a cruel place, deal with it" Spider Crusader kicked Justin in the chest! Justin smashed in to the wall! Justin laid next to the wall! Spider Crusader shot some webs out of his web shooter. The webs attached Justin's arms and legs to the wall. Spider Crusader walked over to Justin! Spider Crusader said, "If you make a wrong move, I can make your life miserable and painful." Spider Crusader rubs his hand through Justin's hair. Justin growled and said, "Don't mess up my hair!" Spider Crusader said, "The little hero doesn't like getting his hair messed up." Justin growled and ignited a blast of flames from his body. Spider Crusader smashed in to the wall, as Justin landed on the ground, with his eyes glowing red. Spider Crusader got up from the ground. Justin threw fire balls at Spider Crusader. Spider Crusader dodged the fire balls, and flipped in to the air. Spider Crusader shot webs at Justin. The webs attached to Justin's chest. Justin lit his body up with flames! The webs evaporated off of Justin's body, and burnt to a crisp. Justin turned in to a fire tornado, and launched himself in to Spider Crusader. Spider Crusader smashed through the wall, and laid on the ground. Justin landed on the ground, and walked toward Spider Crusader. Justin lit his arm up with flames, and put his foot on Spider Crusader's chest. Justin punched Spider Crusader in the face. The flames from Justin's arm heated up Spider Crusader's helmet, and shattered it to pieces. Blood poured on the ground from Spider Crusader's face. Justin picked up Spider Crusader, and threw him in to the wall. Spider Crusader smashed through the wall, and laid on the ground, with blood leaking from his body. Spider Crusader lifted his arm and shot a electric web at Justin's chest. The electric web electrocuted Justin, as he slid backwards. Spider Crusader backflipped off of the ground, and kicked Justin in the chest. Justin smashed in to the wall, and laid next to it. Spider Crusader tackled Justin in to the ground, and wrapped his arm around Justin's neck. Justin lit his body on fire, and did a fire blast. Spider Crusader rolled on the ground. Justin threw a fire ball at Spider Crusader! The fire ball hit Spider Crusader in the leg. Spider Crusader slid backwards! Spider Crusader sped toward Justin. Justin backflipped out of the way, and kicked Spider Crusader in the back. Spider Crusader smashed in to the wall. Spider Crusader laid next to the wall, as Justin landed on the ground. Justin growled and sped toward Spider Crusader. Justin grabbed Spider Crusader's neck, and smashed him in to the wall. Justin lit his body on fire, and did a fire blast. The fire blast covered the area, as everything exploded. The rubble laid on the ground, and Spider Crusader's armor shattered to pieces. Spider Crusader laid on the ground, as Justin stood over him. Otto saw the destruction from the wall, that he was hiding behind. Otto walked away from the wall, and clapped his hands! Justin stepped on Spider Crusader's arm with his foot. Spider Crusader lifted up his other arm, and shot a web in Justin's face. Justin burned the web off of his face with flames, as he growled. Justin punched Spider Crusader in the face. Blood poured on the ground from Spider Crusader's body. Justin summoned a flaming rope with his hand, and threw it at a tranquilizer dart, that was laying on the shelf. Justin pulled on the flaming rope, and put the tranquilizer dart in his hand. Justin lifted up Spider Crusader's arm. Justin stabbed the tranquilizer dart in to Spider Crusader's arm. The tranquilizer dart knocked out Spider Crusader. Justin picked up Spider Crusader's body, and walked in to the science lab. Otto walked behind Justin, and was amazed by all of the gadgets and inventions! Justin walked to the experiment machine, and opened it up. Justin attached Spider Crusader's body to the experiment machine, and strapped him in with the wires. Justin closed the experiment machine. Justin walked to the control panel, and logged in to it. Otto stood next to him, and watched Justin pressed the buttons on the control panel! Justin loaded up the files for the darkness monster on the experiment machine. Justin pressed the button on the control panel, and the darkness monster went in to the experiment machine. The darkness monster consumed and took over Spider Crusader's body, by wrapping its tendrils around Spider Crusader. The darkness monster gave Spider Crusader, new armor that was black, and is stronger than his previous armor. Otto saw the darkness monster, and was amazed at how powerful that it was. Justin walked away from the control panel. Justin walked to the machine, and opened it up. Justin disconnected the wires from Spider Crusader's body. Spider Crusader woke up, and rubbed his head! Spider Crusader growled, as he walked out of the machine. An dark aura surrounded Spider Crusader's body, as he got used to his new form. Spider Crusader said, "I am more powerful, than you could ever imagine." Spider Crusader sped toward Justin, and kicked him in the chest. Justin smashed in to the shelf, and laid next to it. Spider Crusader walked toward Justin, and grabbed him by the neck. Justin struggled in Spider Crusader's grip. Spider Crusader smashed Justin in to the wall, and threw him on to the ground. Justin rolled on the ground! Spider Crusader webbed Justin to the ground, with his web shooters. Justin heated up his body, and burned the web cocoon off of him. Justin got up from the ground! Justin shot fire balls at Spider Crusader. The fire balls bounce off of Spider Crusader's body. Spider Crusader tackled Justin in to the wall. Spider Crusader shot darkness tendrils at Justin. The darkness tendrils wrapped around Justin, and squeezed his body. Justin struggled in the darkness tendrill's grip. Justin lit his body on fire. The darkness tendrils burnt off of Justin's body. Justin shot a fire blast at Spider Crusader. Spider Crusader slid backwards, and punched Justin in the chest. Justin slid backwards in to the control panel. Spider Crusader shot a web at Justin's neck. The web wrapped around Justin's neck. Spider Crusader swung the web in a circle, and threw Justin in to the wall. Justin smashed in to the wall, and laid on the ground. Spider Crusader jumped on to Justin, and held him on to the ground. Spider Crusader punched Justin in the face, multiple times. Justin growled, and lit his body on fire. The darkness tendrils screamed in pain, as Spider Crusader slid backwards. Justin backflipped off of the ground, and kicked Spider Crusader in the face. Justin tackled Spider Crusader in to the control panel. Spider Crusader laid next to the control panel, and growled at Justin. Justin picked up Spider Crusader, and threw him in to the air. Justin ignited a fire blast with his arm at Spider Crusader. The fire blast smashes Spider Crusader on to the ground. Spider Crusader growled, and shot a web at Justin's face. Spider Crusader backflipped, and kicked Justin in the face. Justin slid backwards! Spider Crusader sped in to Justin, and punched him in the chest. Justin stumbled backwards, as he tried to regain his balance. Spider Crusader grabbed Justin's neck, and smashed him in to the ground. Justin growled, as he ignited a fire blast from his body. Spider Crusader smashed in to the chemical shelf. The chemicals fell on the ground, and shattered to pieces. Justin got up from the ground, and stabbed a health pack in to his arm. Spider Crusader got up from the ground, and shot a web at Justin's chest. The web attached to Justin's chest. Spider Crusader pulled on the web, and pulled Justin toward him! Justin ignited his body, and smashed Spider Crusader through the wall like a tornado. Spider Crusader laid on the ground. Justin grabbed a electric baton from the table, and put it on Spider Crusader's chest. The darkness monster screamed in pain, as Spider Crusader's body got electrocuted. The darkness monster detached from Spider Crusader's body, and crawled on to Justin's arm. Justin lit his body on fire. The darkness monster caught on fire, and burned in to a crisp. Spider Crusader laid unconscious on the ground. Justin picked up Spider Crusader's body, and walked to the healing tube. Justin opened up the healing tube, and attached Spider Crusader to it. Justin closed the healing tube, and started it up. Justin stabbed a healing pack in to his arm. Otto finished writing the notes on his notepad. Otto walked over to the control panel, and plugged in his flash drive. Otto transferred the files from the database to his flash drive, and walked out of Electric Industries. The healing tube finished healing Spider Crusader. Justin opened the healing machine, and disconnected Spider Crusader from it. Justin picked up Spider Crusader, and laid him on his back. Justin walked over to one of the gliders, and stepped on it. The glider activated, and Justin shot a fire ball at the window. Justin flew the glider out of the window. Justin flew the glider to his house. Justin landed the glider in the garage. Justin walked off of the glider. Justin walked to the front door, and opened it. Justin walked through the front door. Justin walked in to his bedroom, and laid Spider Crusader on his bed. Justin covered Spider Crusader with his bed sheets. Justin took some clean clothes out of his drawer. Justin closed the drawer, and walked out of his bedroom. Justin walked in to the bathroom, and turned the shower on. Justin took off his clothes, and walked in to the shower. Justin took a shower, and washed his hair and his body. Justin turned off the shower, and walked out of the shower. Justin put on the clean clothes, and brushed his hair. Justin walked out of the bathroom, and walked in to his bedroom. Justin put his dirty clothes in to the laundry basket. Justin laid on the floor, and looked at the ceiling. The floor was soft, and the carpet was red with green stripes on it. Justin got up from the floor, and walked out of his bedroom. Justin walked in to the exercise room, and walked on the treadmill for an hour. Justin walked off of the treadmill, and walked to the punching bag. Justin punched the punching bag for an hour. Justin stopped punching the punching bag, and walked over to the drink cooler. Justin grabbed a bottle of water from the drink cooler, and drank it. Justin wiped the sweat off of his hair and body with an towel. Justin walked over to the weights, and lifted them for a hour. Justin finished lifting the weights, and did some push ups on the ground. Justin walked out of the exercise room, and walked in to his bedroom to check on Spider Crusader. Spider Crusader was sitting on the bed, contemplating about his life. Justin sat next to Spider Crusader. Spider Crusader said, "Justin, can you forgive me for my actions in the past?" Justin said, "I forgive you, you aren't a bad guy to hang out with." Spider Crusader smiled, and hugged Justin. Justin hugged Spider Crusader. Justin and Spider Crusader laid on the bed together. Justin turned on the TV, and switched it to the sports channel. Two football teams were playing against each other. The football teams were the Phoenix Dragons, and the Crimson Bears. Justin and Spider Crusader watched the football game together, and had fun hanging out. The moon shined through the window, and it got dark outside. The Phoenix Dragons won the football game, and Justin turned off the TV. Justin and Spider Crusader went under the bed sheets, and fell asleep together. Spider Crusader and Justin snuggled and slept together for multiple hours. The sun shined on the bed in Justin's bedroom. Justin and Spider Crusader took the bed sheets off of their head, and got out of bed. Justin and Spider Crusader hugged each other, as they stretched their arms and legs. Justin and Spider Crusader straightened out the bed sheets, and made the bed. Justin and Spider Crusader opened up the drink cooler in the bed room, and took out a soda. Justin and Spider Crusader drank the soda, and threw the empty soda cans in to the recycling bin. Justin turned on the TV! Justin and Spider Crusader sat on the bed together, and played video games for an hour. Justin turned off the TV, and Spider Crusader walked out of the bed room. Spider Crusader walked in to the exercise room. Spider Crusader punched the punching bag for an hour. Spider Crusader finished punching the punching bag, and walked on the treadmill for an hour. Spider Crusader walked off the treadmill, and lifted the weights for an hour. Spider Crusader finished lifting the weighs, and walked to the towel rack. Spider Crusader wiped the sweat off of his body and face. Spider Crusader walked out of the exercise room, and walked in to the bathroom. Spider Crusader turned on the shower! Spider Crusader took off his clothes, and walked in to the shower. Spider Crusader washed his body and face. Spider Crusader turned off the shower! Spider Crusader walked out of the shower, and put his clothes on. Spider Crusader walked out of the bathroom! Spider Crusader walked in to Justin's bedroom, and laid on the bed with Justin. Justin and Spider Crusader laid on the bed together. An couple of blocks down the street, there was a tower called Science Incorporated! In Science Incorporated, there was a super villain hideout. The super villain hideout was run by the leader! The leader's name was Norman. Otto walked in to the super villain hideout, and gave the flash drive to Norman. Norman plugged the flash drive in to his computer, that was in front of him. Norman was pleased with the data on the flash drive. The flash drive contained all of the data from Electric Industries, which contained all of Spider Crusader's experiments and blood dna from various subjects and species. Norman looked through the files, and had a big grin on his face, when he clicked on the file for Supersonic Warrior. Otto said, "What are you smiling about, boss?" Norman said, "This file contains the blood dna and the data for Supersonic Warrior." Otto said, "Awesome!" Norman said, "Zoomopolis won't know, what hit them! With this data, we can make our soldiers stronger and more powerful than your average human being." The sun fell asleep, and the moon rose in to the sky. The moon shined over Justin's house. Spider Crusader webbed up the trash with his web shooters, and threw it in to the trash can. Spider Crusader enjoyed the breath of fresh air. Spider Crusader walked back in to the house, and grabbed a dust pan and broom from the closet. Spider Crusader shot a web at the ceiling, and hung upside down. Spider Crusader used the dust pan and broom to clean the dust off of the ceiling. Spider Crusader backflipped off of the web, and on to the ground. Spider Crusader walked in to Justin's bedroom, and turned on the TV. Spider Crusader watched the sports channel. Justin was in the living room, getting ready to walk to Oasis Falls High School. Justin was putting his supplies in to the bag. Justin put the bag on to his back, and walked out the front door. Justin walked to Oasis Falls High School. Justin walked in to the courtyard for Oasis Falls High School. Justin walked in to Oasis Falls High School. The other students were in the hallway, getting ready for their classes. Justin walked in to his science class with Sam. Justin sat at his desk, and listened to the science lecture. The other students were writing down notes in their notebooks. Sam was writing science experiments on the whiteboard, and the students were writing the experiments down in their notebooks. The bell rang in the background. The other students put their supplies in their bags, and walked out of the classroom. Justin put his notebook in to his bag, and got up from his desk. Justin put his bag on to his back, and walked out of the classroom. Justin walked to the water fountain, and drank out of it. Justin walked away from the water fountain. Justin walked in to the exercise room. Ben was laying next to the wall, and saw Justin. Justin opened the locker, and put his bag in to it. Justin closed the locker! Ben walked to Justin and said, "Hey Justin, how is it going?" Justin said, "Pretty good, what's up?" Ben said, "Lets have some fun, and wrestle each other." Justin smirked and said, "I always love an challenge." Ben said, "I love an challenge as well, and I will beat you." Justin laughed and said, "Nope, I will beat you!" Ben and Justin walked to the battling area for the exercise room. Ben sped toward Justin. Justin grabbed Ben, and threw him in to the air. Justin jumped in to the air, and kicked Ben in the chest. Ben rolled on the ground! Justin's eyes glowed red, as he threw fire balls at Ben. Ben dodged the fire balls by rolling on the ground. Ben got up from the ground. Ben backflipped, and swung his arm at Justin. Justin slid backwards, and punched Ben in the chest. Justin did a fire blast from his arm at Ben. The fire blast knocked Ben in to the air. Justin jumped in to the air, and smashed Ben in to the ground. Ben laid on the ground. Justin held out his hand, and helped Ben off of the ground. Ben got up from the ground and said, "That was a good challenge! You have gotten stronger since our last match." Justin smiled and said, "Yep, it was fun!" Justin walked to the drink cooler, and grabbed a bottle of water. Justin drank the bottle of water, and threw it in to the recycling bin. Justin sat on the bench, and wiped the sweat off of his body, with a towel. Justin got up from the bench, and lifted the weights for an hour. Justin walked away from the weights, and punched the punching bag for an hour. Justin finished punching the punching bag, and walked to the locker. Justin opened the locker, and put his bag on to his bag. Justin closed the locker, and walked out of the exercise room. Justin walked in to the hallway. Justin walked in to his health safety class, and sat at his desk. Justin put his bag next to his desk, and listened to the lecture from Andrew. Andrew wrote on the whiteboard, and talked about the history of medicine. The students wrote in their notebooks, and listened to the teacher. The bell rang in the background, and the students put their notebooks in to their bags. Justin put his notebook in to his bag, and got up from his desk. Justin put his bag on to his back, and walked out of the classroom. Justin walked in to the hallway. The hallway was quiet, with the other students in study hall, and the teachers having fun in the teacher's lounge. Justin walked in to study hall, and sat at his desk. Outside the school, Norman flew in to the court-yard on his glider. Norman walked off of the glider, and pressed the button on his wrist. The glider flew back to the villain hideout. Norman grabbed his grappling hook off of his belt, and shot it at the roof of Oasis Falls High School. Norman climbed on the grappling hook. Norman climbed up to the window for the study hall. Norman put his hand on the window, and the glass shattered to pieces. Norman jumped in to the study hall classroom. Bob, the study hall teacher, was reading at his desk. Norman threw a knife at Bob and the other students. The knife stabbed Bob and the other students in the chest. Bob and the other students laid on the ground in puddles of blood. Justin backflipped out of his desk, and shot a fire grenade at Norman. Norman dodged the fire grenade, and kicked Justin in the chest. Justin slid next to the shelf. Norman shot his electric powers out of his hands at Justin. Justin got electrocuted, and screamed in pain. Justin laid next to the shelf. Norman threw an electric ball at Justin. The electric ball hit Justin in the chest, and electrocuted him. Justin smashed through the shelf, and laid on the ground. Norman grabbed a tranquilizer dart from his belt. Norman stabbed the tranquilizer dart in to Justin's arm. Norman walked out of the study hall classroom. The other students ran out of the hallway, and hid in the teacher's lounge. Norman walked through the hallway, and in to the gym. In the gym, there were students watching the basketball players practice. The marching band was playing their instruments, while the basketball players were practicing. The mascot and the cheerleaders were standing on the sideline, and doing acrobatics. Norman walked on to the basketball court. The mascot picked up his megaphone, and turned it on. The basketball players heard the megaphone, and ran in to the supply closet with the basketball. The cheerleaders followed the basketball players. The mascot ran out of the gym, and hid in the teacher's lounge. Norman used his powers, and electrocuted the basketball net. The basketball net fell off its post, and shattered on to the ground. Norman walked out of the gym, and in to the hallway. Norman walked through the hallway, and walked in to the exercise room.

The exercise room was quiet. Ben was hiding in the supplies closet for the exercise room. Norman walked to the supplies closet, and pulled the door off of its hinges with his hand. Ben was terrified in fear! Norman grabbed Ben's arm, and pulled him out of the supplies closet. Ben rolled on the ground! Norman stepped on Ben's leg, and punched him in the face. Blood dripped from Ben's mouth. Norman grabbed Ben by the neck, and threw him in to the wall. Ben laid next to the wall. Norman used his electric powers, and electrocuted Ben. Ben screamed in pain, as blood leaked on to the ground. Norman threw an electric ball at Ben. Ben got electrocuted by the electric ball, and laid on the ground, in a puddle of blood. Ben coughs, as blood leaked from his body. Norman threw a tranquilizer dart at Ben's neck. The tranquilizer dart went in to Ben's neck! Ben closed his eyes, and laid on the ground. Norman picked up Ben, and laid him on his back. Norman pressed a button on his wrist! Norman's glider smashed through the window. Norman walked on to the glider, and flew back to the villain hideout. The glider flew to the villain hideout. Norman walked off of the glider, and opened up the experiment machine. Norman connected Ben to the experiment machine, by connecting all of the wires. Norman closed the experiment machine. Norman walked to the control panel, and logged in to it. Norman tapped the buttons on the control panel, and loaded up the DNA files. Norman loaded up the DNA file for Supersonic Warrior, and the DNA file for Spider Crusader. Norman merged the DNA together, and sent it in to the experiment machine. The DNA went in to the experiment machine, and flowed through the wires. The DNA went in to Ben's body through the wires. Norman tapped on the control panel, and loaded the elemental powers on the screen. Norman loaded the ice powers, and sent them in to the experiment machine. The ice powers flowed through the wires, and went in to Ben's body. Norman logged off of the control panel. Ben opened his eyes, as they glowed blue. Ben ignited a ice blast from his body, that exploded the machine open. Glass shards and wood pieces landed on the floor, as Ben walked out of the machine. Back at Oasis Falls High School, Justin woke up, and took the tranquilizer dart out of his arm. He saw the mess, that was around him. Justin picked up the books from the floor, and put them on the book shelf. Justin picked up the dropped paper, and put them in the recycling bin.

19

In the villain hideout, Ben shot an ice blast at the book shelf, and froze it in a sheet of ice. Norman and Otto were amazed by their creation. Ben summoned an wall of ice, and froze Otto and Norman on to the wall. Ben backflipped on to the desk, as Norman ignited an blast of energy from his body. The ice wall shattered, as Otto and Norman landed on the ground. Ben backflipped off of the desk, and smashed the window open with a ice beam. Ben jumped out of the window, and skated on a sheet of ice toward Justin's house. Justin was at Oasis Falls High School, cleaning up the mess from Norman's rampage. Justin straightened the desks in their rows, and reorganized the teacher's desk in the study hall. Down the street, Ben was skating on the sheet of ice, causing chaos in Zoompolis. Ben walked in to the gas station, and walked toward the cash register. The cashier's name was Daniel. Daniel said, "How can I help you?" Ben's eyes glowed blue, as he summoned a icicle in to his hand. Ben walked toward Daniel, and kicked him in the chest. Daniel bent down, and grabbed his chest. Daniel growled, and threw an punch at Ben. Ben grabbed Daniel's arm, and broke it. Daniel screamed in pain, as he slid backwards. Ben sped in to Daniel! Ben grabbed Daniel by the neck, and threw him in to the wall. Daniel laid next to the wall. Ben wrapped his arm around Daniel's neck, and stabbed the icicle in to Daniel's head. Blood poured on to the ground, as Daniel laid on the ground. Ben ignited a ice blast from his body. The ice blast covered the area, as the gas station exploded. Glass shards and broken items covered the area, as Ben walked through the debris. Police cars sped toward the debris, and stopped next to it. The police officers walked out of their cars, and cleaned up the debris from the area. Ben summoned a sheet of ice, and skated further down the street. Cars were speeding past Ben on the street, as he was skating on the sheet of ice. Ben skated to Justin's house, as the birds tweeted in the background. Ben saw Justin's house, and backflipped off of the sheet of ice. Ben landed on the ground and walked through the grass toward Justin's house. As Ben walked through the grass, the ground turned in to ice. Spider Crusader walked out of the house, and saw Ben. Spider Crusader growled, as he walked toward Ben. Spider Crusader swung through the air, and shot a web at Ben's chest. The web attached to Ben's chest, as Spider Crusader slingshot himself toward Ben. Ben summoned an ice shield, and hit Spider Crusader in the chest. Spider Crusader smashed in to the house. The house shook, as Spider Crusader regained his balance. Ben's eyes glowed blue, as he threw an ice ball at Spider Crusader. Spider Crusader dodged the ice ball. Spider Crusader backflipped, and shot webs at Ben. Ben threw ice balls at the webs, and turned them in to ice. Ben used his powers to throw the ice webs at Spider Crusader. Spider Crusader backflipped out of the way. The ice webs hit the tree. The tree froze in a sheet of ice. Spider Crusader landed on the ground. Spider Crusader backflipped, and kicked Ben in the face. Ben froze his head in a sheet of ice. Spider Crusader's leg froze up in a sheet of ice. Ben ignited an ice blast from his body. Spider Crusader smashed in to the tree. Spider Crusader laid against the tree, as he rubbed his head. Ben sped in to the tree! Spider Crusader's senses tingled, and he backflipped over Ben. Spider Crusader kicked Ben in the back. Ben slid backwards, and threw a ice ball at Spider Crusader. Spider Crusader made a baseball bat with his webs, and hit the ice ball back at Ben. Ben summoned a icicle, and sliced the ice ball in half. Ben shot multiple ice blasts at Spider Crusader. Spider Crusader backflipped, and dodged the ice blasts. Spider Crusader flipped in the air, and landed behind Ben. Ben spun in a circle, and kicked Spider Crusader in the chest. Spider Crusader slid backwards! Spider Crusader threw a punch at Ben's face. Ben caught Spider Crusader's arm, and kicked him in the face. Spider Crusader rolled on the ground. Spider Crusader got up from the ground. Ben sped in to Spider Crusader, and punched him in the face. Spider Crusader fell on to the ground! Ben held Spider Crusader on the ground! Ben punched Spider Crusader in the face, multiple times. Blood dripped from Spider Crusader's armor. Spider Crusader shot a web at Ben's face. Ben froze his face with a sheet of ice, and the web froze in to a ice cube, and smashed on the ground. Ben picked up Spider Crusader by his neck, and threw him in to the tree. Spider Crusader smashed through the tree, and rolled on the ground. Spider Crusader backflipped off of the ground. Ben shot ice blasts at Spider Crusader. Spider Crusader dodged the ice blasts. Spider Crusader shot a web at Ben's chest. Spider Crusader pulled on the web, and dragged Ben closer to him. Spider Crusader kicked Ben in the chest. Ben smashed in to the wall, and laid next to it. Spider Crusader sped toward Ben. Ben backflipped out of the way, and threw a ice blast at Spider Crusader. The ice blast hit Spider Crusader in the chest. Spider Crusader slid in to a tree. Ben tackled Spider Crusader through the tree, and smashed him in to the ground. Ben froze his arm in to a sheet of ice, as he punched Spider Crusader in the face, multiple times. Spider Crusader's helmet started to crack, as he growled. Ben continued punching Spider Crusader in the face. Spider Crusader's helmet shattered, as blood poured on to the ground. Ben grabbed Spider Crusader by the neck, and picked him up from the ground. Spider Crusader struggled in Ben's grip. Ben smashed Spider Crusader against the wall, multiple times. Spider Crusader's armor started to crack. Ben held Spider Crusader on the wall, as he punched him in the face, multiple times. Spider Crusader growled, as blood dripped on to the ground, from his face. Spider Crusader held his arm up, and pressed a button on his wrist. Spider Crusader's communicator activated, as Spider Crusader started talking in to it. Spider Crusader said, "Justin, come in! I need help!" Further down the street, Justin was in the middle of cleaning up the debris at Oasis Falls High School. Justin lifted his arm up, and pressed the button on his wrist. Justin's communicator activated, as Justin started talking in to it. Justin said, "Hey Spider Crusader, what's up!" Spider Crusader spoke in to the communicator and said, "There's a supervillain, and I am having trouble defending myself!" Justin spoke in to the communicator and said, "I am on my way!" Spider Crusader spoke in to the communicator and said, 'Please hurry!" Justin climbed out of the window, and summoned a sheet of flames. Justin skated on the sheet of flames toward his house. Ben grabbed Spider Crusader's arm, and destroyed Spider Crusader's communicator, with a ice blast. Spider Crusader screamed in pain. Ben tightened his grip on Spider Crusader's neck, as he smashed Spider Crusader in to the ground, multiple times. Spider Crusader's armor shattered, as he screamed in pain. Blood poured on to the ground, from Spider Crusader's body. Ben lifted Spider Crusader in to the air, and threw him in to the tree. Spider Crusader smashed in to the tree, and rolled on the ground. Spider Crusader laid on the ground. Ben jumped on to Spider Crusader, and punched him in the face. Blood poured from Spider Crusader's face, as he laid on the ground. Ben grabbed Spider Crusader by the neck, and lifted him in to the air. Ben squeezed Spider Crusader's neck, and choked him. Spider Crusader coughed, as he struggled in Ben's grip. Ben smashed Spider Crusader in to the wall. The wall crumbled, as Spider Crusader laid on the ground. Ben held Spider Crusader on the ground, and punched him in the face. Blood poured on the ground! Ben shot a ice blast at Spider Crusader. The ice blast smashed Spider Crusader through the ground, leaving a hollowed dent. Spider Crusader laid on the ground, with a puddle of blood under him. Justin reached his house, and back-flipped off of the sheet of flames. Justin landed in front of Ben. Ben growled, while his eyes glowed blue. Spider Crusader slowly got up from the ground, and smiled at the sight of Justin. Spider Crusader stabbed a health pack in to his arm. Spider Crusader crawled behind the bush, and cleaned the blood off of him with a towel. Justin's eyes glowed red, as he walked toward Ben. Justin shot a fire blast at Ben. The fire blast smashed Ben in to the tree. Ben laid next to the tree. Justin backflipped, and hit Ben in the face with a roundhouse kick. Ben slid backwards, and smashed through the tree. Ben punched Justin in the face. Justin dodged Ben's arm, and punched Ben in the chest. Ben slid backwards, and shot a ice blast at Justin. Justin dodged the ice blast, and threw a fire ball at Ben. Ben got hit by the fire ball, and smashed in to the house. The house shook, as Ben laid next to it. Ben regained his balance, and flipped on to the tree. Ben swung on the tree branch. Ben swung off of the tree branch, and landed on the ground. Justin threw an fire ball at Ben. Ben dodged the fire ball. The fire ball bounced off of the pole, and hit the wall. Ben threw an ice ball at Justin! Justin dodged the ice ball, and the ice ball hit an car speeding through the street. The car froze in a block of ice, and smashed in to the pole. Ben growled, and sped toward Justin. Ben swung his leg at Justin's face. Justin dodged Ben's leg, and grabbed it with his hand. Justin lit Ben's leg on fire. Ben screamed in pain, as he rolled on the ground. Ben froze his leg in ice to cool himself down. Ben backflipped off of the ground. Justin sped in to Ben! Justin grabbed Ben by the neck, and smashed him in to the ground. Justin punched Ben in the face, multiple times. Blood poured on the ground from Ben's face. Ben growled, as he grabbed Justin's arm. Justin lit his arm on fire. Ben screamed in pain, as his arm got barbecued. Justin growled, as he picked up Ben's body, and threw him in to the wall. Ben smashed through the wall, as blood dripped on the ground from his body. Ben got up from the ground, and growled. Ben ignited an ice blast from his body. The ice blast covered the area, and made the house explode. Aaron and Sunshine laid on the ground, as they coughed. Ben threw an ice whip at Aaron and Sunshine. The ice whip wrapped around Aaron and Sunshine's body. Ben pulled on the ice whip, and dragged Aaron and Sunshine closer to him. Ben summoned an ice sword in to his hand! Ben swung the ice sword at Aaron and Sunshine! The ice sword sliced the bodies of Aaron and Sunshine in half, and killed them. Aaron and Sunshine's bodies laid on the ground, in puddles of blood. Ben laughed maniacally, as he threw an ice blast at Justin. Justin threw an fire blast at Ben. The fire blast and the ice blast collided with each other, and caused a huge blast in the area. The huge blast destroyed all of the trees in the area. Justin's eyes turned flaming red, as he growled in anger. Justin summoned an aura of flames around his body, and shot a flaming blast at Ben from his arm. The flaming blast hit Ben in the chest, and smashed him through the ground. Ben laid on the ground, with blood pouring from his body. Justin growled, as he walked closer to Ben. Justin jumped on to Ben, and punched him in the face, multiple times. Blood dripped from Ben's face! Ben's eyes glowed blue, as he ignited a ice blast from his body. Justin slid backwards, and rolled on the ground! Justin backflipped off of the ground. Ben backflipped off of the ground! Ben threw ice balls at Justin. Justin dodged the ice balls. Ben ignited an icy aura around his body, and sped in to Justin. Ben tackled Justin in to the wall. Justin laid next to the wall, as he growled. Ben growled, as he punched Justin in the face, multiple times. The flames from Justin's body protected Justin from the punches. Ben growled, as he continued trying to punch Justin in the face. The flames from Justin's body absorbed the punches, and burnt Ben's arm. Justin growled, and kicked Ben in the chest. Ben slid backwards! Justin ignited an fire blast from his body. Ben rolled on the ground. Ben backflipped off of the ground. Justin sped in to Ben, and smashed him in to the tree. The tree fell on to the ground. Justin grabbed Ben by his neck, and lifted him in to the air. Justin crushed Ben's neck, and smashed him in to the ground. Ben coughed, as he laid on the ground. Justin punched Ben in the face, multiple times. Blood dripped from Ben's face, as Justin continued punching him. The puddle of blood grew, as blood poured from Ben's face. Justin growled, as he lit up his arm with flames. Justin put his hand on Ben's chest, and burnt his body in to a crisp. Ben's body turned in to ash on the ground. The ash blew away in a gust of wind. Justin's eyes turned back to normal, as the aura of flames disappeared around him. Justin wiped the blood off of his body with a towel. Justin walked to the bush, and sat next to Spider Crusader. Spider Crusader and Justin hugged each other. The clean up crew drove up the street, and parked next to the debris. The clean up crew cleared the debris from the area. Spider Crusader repaired the web shooters on his arm. Justin laid next to the bush, and looked at the clouds. Down the street, the villains were frustrated at the villain hideout. Norman growled, and pushed Otto in to the wall. Norman said, "Heroes are pests, they like to ruin our fun. Otto said, "I wish there was a way to stop the heroes from destroying our experiments." Norman smiled, as he thought of a perfect plan to deal with the heroes. Norman said, "We need to slow the heroes down, which means that we need to work harder to make our experiments better, and stronger." Otto smiled and said, "You always think of the best plans!" Back at the bush, Justin got up from the ground. Justin summoned a sheet of flames, and skated to Oasis Falls High School. Spider Crusader flipped in to the air, and web sung in the air. Spider Crusader followed Justin to Oasis Falls High School. Justin and Spider Crusader got to Oasis Falls High School, and walked in to the courtyard. Justin and Spider Crusader walked through the courtyard, and walked to the doors. Justin and Spider Crusader walked through the doors of Oasis Falls High School. The other students were walking toward the gym. Spider Crusader and Justin followed the other students in to the gym. Justin and Spider Crusader walked toward the bleachers. Justin and Spider Crusader walked up the bleachers. Justin and Spider Crusader sat on the bleachers. The other students sat on the bleachers. The mascot for Oasis Falls High School backflipped in to the gym, and did some flips in the air. The cheerleaders cheered, while the marching band marched in to the gym. The basketball players walked in to the middle of the gym. The basketball players got in to position, as the coach played some music through the school speakers. Drew dribbled the basketball and sung, "We are the Oasis Falls Wildcats!" Drew passed the basketball to Sam! Sam sung while dribbling the basketball, "We are the best team in the world!" Sam passed the basketball to David. David threw the basketball in to the net and sung "We Can crush our opponents, because we are the Amazing Wildcats!" The basketball went in to the net, and bounced on the ground. The students cheered, as the mascot flipped in the air. The cheerleaders flipped in to the air and said, "Lets Go Wildcats!" The basketball players went in to the middle of the gym, and dribbled the ball to each other. Drew spun the basketball on his finger, as the the students cheered. The cheerleaders shook their pom poms, and the mascot flipped in the air. The music stopped playing on the school speakers. The marching band played their instruments for an hour, while the mascot did some flips in the air. The school bell rang in the background. The marching band walked out of the gym, and in to the teacher's lounge. The mascot and the cheerleaders walked out of the gym, and in to the teacher's lounge. The other students walked out of the gym. Justin and Spider Crusader walked out of the gym. Justin and Spider Crusader walked in to the hallway. Justin and Spider Crusader walked out of the hallway, and in to the courtyard for Oasis Falls High School. Justin and Spider Crusader sat on the stairs for Oasis Falls High School. The wind was blowing through Justin's hair, and the birds were tweeting in the background. The bugs were buzzing and the dogs were chasing the squirrels down the street. The sun was setting, and the sun set was amazing. An pack of wolves walked in to the courtyard, and were antagonizing a group of squirrels. The wolves walked closer to the squirrels. The squirrels backed up in to the tree, and they were terrified in fear. The wolves growled, and charged at the squirrels. The wolves pounced on the squirrels! The wolves picked up the squirrels with their fangs, and bit down on the squirrel's fur. Blood poured on the ground from the body of the squirrels. The wolves spit out the squirrels, and they laid on the ground, in puddles of blood. The wolves growled, and walked closer to Spider Crusader. Spider Crusader shot a web at the wolves. The web attached the wolves to the tree. The wolves clawed through the web, and sped toward Spider Crusader. Spider Crusader backflipped, and shot some webs at the wolves. The webs attached to the wolves. Spider Crusader pulled on the web, and threw the wolves in to the building. Spider Crusader sped in to the wolves, and picked them up in to the air. Spider Crusader smashed the wolves in to the ground, and stabbed his web knife in to their necks. The wolves laid on the ground in puddles of blood. Spider Crusader and Justin walked out of the courtyard of Oasis Falls High School. Spider Crusader and

Justin walked down the street. Police cars were speeding through the street, and the citizens were walking through the sidewalks. An crane malfunctioned, and swung its wrecking ball through a building. The building debris were falling on top of the citizens. Justin sprung in to action, and tackled the citizens in to the back alley. Spider Crusader shot webs at the falling debris. The webs attached to the sides of the building, and wrapped around the falling debris. Spider Crusader back-flipped in to the air, and ran on the side of the building. Spider Crusader used his webs as a slingshot, and slingshot himself on to the wrecking ball. Spider Crusader crawled on the wrecking ball, and hung on to the crane. Spider Crusader hung on to the crane, and crawled toward the control panel. Spider Crusader pulled open the control panel with his arms. Spider Crusader disabled the crane by pulling out the electrical wires, that were in the control panel. The crane lost its balance, and starting falling on to the ground. Spider Crusader wrapped up the crane with his webs, to slow down the speed of the crane. The crane fell on to the ground. Spider Crusader hung upside down from his web, and landed on the ground. The citizens cheered for Spider Crusader, as Justin walked out of the back alley. Spider Crusader refilled his web shooters, as he walked toward Justin. Justin and Spider Crusader walked further down the street. Justin and Spider Crusader walked to a hot dog stand, and bought some hot dogs. Justin and Spider Crusader sat on the bench, that was next to the hog dog stand. Justin ate his hot dog. Spider Crusader detracted his helmet, and ate his hot dog. Spider Crusader retracted his helmet, and relaxed on the bench. The birds were tweeting in the background. Justin relaxed on the bench, and listened to the birds. Justin and Spider Crusader wrapped their arms around each other. Justin and Spider Crusader hugged each other. The wind blew through Justin's hair. The tree blew in the wind. Police cars sped through the area, and they were patrolling the streets. The sun disappeared in the sky, and the moon rise. The sky was clear, and the stars were shining. An group of squirrels crawled up to the bench, where Justin and Spider Crusader were sitting. The squirrels crawled up the bench, and jumped on to Justin's hair. The squirrels chewed on Justin's hair. Justin whacked the squirrels out of his hair. The squirrels fell on to the ground, and rubbed their heads. The squirrels crawled up Justin's leg. Justin lit his leg on fire with his flames, and the squirrels burnt to a crisp. Police cars were speeding through the area, with their sirens on. Thieves were speeding away from the police cars, and shooting at the police cars with their weapons. Spider Crusader's spider sense was tingling, and he sprung in to action. Spider Crusader backflipped off of the bench, and detracted his helmet. Spider Crusader's helmet covered his face, as he swung in to the air with his webs. Spider Crusader shot a web at the car of the thieves. The web attached to the car's hood. Spider Crusader grabbed the web, and slingshot himself on to the car. Spider Crusader landed on the car, and punched the windshield with his arm. The windshield shattered to pieces, as the thieves lost control of the car. The car spun out of control, and smashed through the streets. Spider Crusader hung on to the car, and crawled on to the side door. Spider Crusader shot a web at the window, and pulled it off of the car. Spider Crusader crawled in to the car, and stabbed his web knife in to the thieves. The thieves laid on the floor of the car in puddles of blood. Spider Crusader kicked the door open with his leg, and climbed out of it. Spider Crusader crawled on to the hood of the car, and shot webs at the tires. The webs attached to the tires. Spider Crusader backflipped off of the car, and wrapped the car with some webs. The webs wrapped around the car. Spider Crusader pulled on the webs, and lifted the car in to the air. Spider Crusader shot a web at the car, while it was in the air. The web attached the car, to the side of the building. Spider Crusader shot a web, and hung backwards. Spider Crusader landed on the ground, as the citizens saw the chaos from the car. Spider Crusader swung through the air, and landed next to the bench. Spider Crusader sat next to Justin, as he retracted his helmet. Spider Crusader relaxed on the bench. At the villain hideout, Otto was cleaning the hideout with a dust pan. He noticed an folder on the shelf. Otto picked up the folder, and read through it. The folder was filled with experiment research about various species, such as vultures and other animals. Otto found the research fascinating and was amazed at all of the information that he found. Otto smiled, as he put the dust pan away. Otto walked to the computer, and logged in to it. Otto tapped on some keys, and loaded up the data for the research. Otto clicked on the research, and loaded it on to the computer. Otto was amazed by all of the data. Otto scrolled through the data, and wrote some stuff down on his notepad. Otto drew concept art of vulture wings on his notepad. Otto tapped some buttons on the computer, and put his notepad in to the scanner. The drawing of the concept art got scanned in to the computer, and the machines started manufacturing the vulture wings, in front of Otto. The machines finished manufacturing the vulture wings. In the background, there was a sound of the hideout doors opening. Drew walked through the villain hideout! Drew walked in to the laboratory. Otto got up from the computer, and walked toward Drew. Otto walked to Drew, and guided him to the machine. Otto opened up the machine. Drew walked in to the machine. Drew laid in the machine. Otto connected the wires to Drew's body, and closed the machine. Otto walked to the computer, and sat in the chair. Otto tapped some buttons on the computer, and loaded the vulture DNA in to Drew's body. Otto tapped the buttons, and dragged some files on the screen. Otto combined the vulture DNA with Supersonic Warrior's DNA. Otto loaded the merged DNA in to Drew's body. The computer beeped, as it finished the process. Otto logged off the computer, and got up from his chair. Otto walked to the machine, and opened it up. Otto disconnected the wires from Drew's body. Drew opened his eyes, and walked out of the machine. Drew and Otto walked to the vulture wings. Drew attached the vulture wings to his body. The vulture wings activated, and attached themselves to Drew's back. Drew jumped in the air, and flew around the area. The training bots shot their weapons at Drew. Drew dodged the blaster bolts, and flew toward the training bots. Drew swung his wings at the training bots, and smashed them to pieces. Otto was amazed at Drew's strength. Drew jumped on the walls, and landed on the ground. Otto summoned more training bots. The training bots shot their weapons at Drew. Drew flew towards the training bots, and grabbed one of them with his legs. Drew threw the training bot at the table. The training bot smashed through the glass containers, and exploded. Otto cleaned up the glass shards, while Drew flew toward the other training bot. Drew smashed the other training bot in to the wall. The other training bot exploded, as Drew landed on the ground. Otto was amazed by Drew's skills. Drew sat on the bench, and drank a bottle of water. Drew threw the bottle of water in to the recycling bin. Drew got up from the bench, and smashed the window with his wing. Drew jumped out of the window, and flew in to the air. Drew was flying through the air, and heard the cars speeding through the streets. The city was bustling in action, as the citizens of Zoomopolis were living their lives. There were a group of citizens, buying ice cream from the ice cream truck. Drew flew toward the ice cream stand, and landed on top of it. The citizens were terrified in fear! Drew swung his wings at the citizens, and killed them. The citizens laid on the ground, in puddles of blood. The ice cream stand manager grabbed some ice cream bars from his stand, and threw them at Drew. Drew flew in to the air, and dodged the ice cream bars. Drew flew toward the ice cream stand manager, and grabbed him with his legs. Drew flew in to the air, as the ice cream stand manager struggled in his grip. Drew flew toward one of the buildings, and smashed through the glass windows. The glass shards from the glass windows hit the ice cream stand manager, as Drew flew in the air. Drew flew toward the sky, and spun in the air. Drew flew toward the skyscraper! Drew flew over the skyscraper, and dropped the ice cream stand manager. The ice cream stand manager fell from Drew's grip, and smashed through the skyscraper. The skyscraper crumbled to pieces on top of the ice cream stand manager, as he smashed in to the ground. The ice cream stand manager laid on the ground, in a puddle of blood. The citizens were horrified at the destruction of the skyscraper. The police officers saw the destruction, and cleaned up the debris. Drew flew back to the villain hideout. Drew flew through the window of the villain hideout, and landed next to Otto. Otto was watching the security footage on the computer, and was amazed by all of the destruction. An security alert from Otto's hero tracker went off on Otto's computer. Otto opened up the security alert! An map of Zoomopolis showed up on Otto's screen. The map showed the location of Spider Crusader's secret hideout. Otto and Drew smiled at the discovery. Otto said, "It's time to pay our favorite little spider and his buddy a small visit!" Drew smiled and said, "Sounds good, boss, I will cause them pain and misery!" Drew jumped in to the air, and flew out of the window with his vulture wings. Drew flew towards Spider Crusader's secret hideout. Down the street, Justin and Spider Crusader were in Spider Crusader's secret hideout. Spider Crusader's secret hideout was filled with gadgets, and other essential items to stay alive. Spider Crusader and Justin walked in to Spider Crusader's laboratory. The laboratory was filled with books, machines, and gadgets. Justin was amazed by all of the gadgets, that he can use to defeat super villains. Spider Crusader walked toward the desk, and upgraded his webshooters. Justin laid on the bed in the laboratory. Spider Crusader shot a web at the ceiling, and hung upside down on it. Spider Crusader cleaned the dust off of the shelves in the laboratory. Spider Crusader backflipped on to the ground. Justin got up from the bed in the laboratory, and walked in to the bathroom. Justin took off his clothes, and walked in to the shower. Justin turned on the water, and washed the dirt out of his hair. Justin washed the dirt off of his body. Justin turned off the shower, and walked out of it. Justin dried himself off, and put his clothes back on. Justin walked out of the bathroom. Spider Crusader was sitting in the chair, and reading the news on the computer. In the background, cars were speeding down the street, next to the hideout. Justin laid on the bed. Justin closed his eyes! The moon shined through the windows of Spider Crusader's secret hideout. Spider Crusader activated the cleaning robot. The cleaning robot went around the laboratory, and vacuumed the dust from the floors. The cleaning robot washed the floors, and reorganized the shelves. The cleaning robot finished cleaning the secret hideout. The walls of the secret hideout shook, as Drew landed on the side of the window. Drew punched the window with his fist, and shattered it to pieces. Drew flew through the smashed window, and grabbed the cleaning robot with his feet. Drew threw the cleaning robot in to the wall. The cleaning robot smashed in to the wall, and exploded. Spider Crusader grabbed his web shooters off of the laboratory desk, and attached them to his wrist. Drew walked through the laboratory toward Spider Crusader. Spider Crusader shot a web at Drew. Drew sliced the web to shreds with his vulture wings. Drew sped toward Spider Crusader, and tackled him in to the wall. Spider Crusader growled, and backflipped over Drew. Spider Crusader kicked Drew in the back. Drew smashed in to the wall, and growled. Drew flew in to the air, and flew towards Spider Crusader. Drew hovered over Spider Crusader, and wrapped his legs around Spider Crusader's body. Justin woke up, and got up from the bed. Justin saw Drew and said, "Let Him Go!" Drew laughed and said, "Over my dead body, little shrimp!" Justin threw a fire ball at Drew. Drew dodged the fire ball, and flew out of the window. Justin ran after Drew, and backflipped out of the window. Justin summoned a sheet of flames, and followed Drew. Drew flew in to the sky, and smashed through several buildings. The glass shattered around Drew and Spider Crusader, as the buildings fell on to the streets, and killed multiple citizens of Zoomopolis. Drew flew towards the villain hideout. Drew flew in to the villain hideout, and landed next to the experiment machine. Drew opened the experiment machine, and threw Spider Crusader in to it. Drew attached the wires to Spider Crusader's body, and closed the machine. Otto walked in to the room, and was pleased at Drew's success. Drew logged on to the computer, and started up the machine. The machine spun its gears and the wires electrocuted Spider Crusader. Spider Crusader screamed in pain, as his blood flowed through the wires, that are attached to his body. Spider Crusader's blood poured in to a tube, that the machine was attached to. The tube was filled to the top with Spider crusader's blood. Otto walked to the tube, and detached it from the machine. Otto sealed the tube, and put it on to the analyze pad. The analyze pad was connected to the computer. The machine went idle, and the electricity stopped flowing through the wires. Spider Crusader laid in the machine, and was catching his breath. Otto and Drew analyzed Spider Crusader's blood, and was amazed by his DNA. Otto and Drew saved the data to their database. A fireball flew through the window, and hit Otto in the face! Otto smashed in to the wall, and laid on the ground. Justin back-flipped through the window, and tackled Drew in to the ground. Justin growled, as his eyes glowed red. Justin shot a fire laser from his eyes at Drew. Drew blocked the fire laser with his vulture wings, and hit Justin in the chest. Justin slid backwards. Drew roundhouse kicked Justin in the face. Justin rolled on the ground. Justin got up from the ground. Drew flew in to Justin, and hit him in the chest with his vulture wings. Justin slid backwards! Drew used his voice modulation and used his vocal blast on Justin. Justin smashed in to the wall, and laid on the ground. Drew walked toward Justin, and smiled! Drew said, "The slippery hero has fallen!" Justin growled and said, "Don't count me out yet!" Norman walked in to the room and smiled at the success of his team mates. Drew stepped on Justin's chest and said, "You might want to change your tone, hero!" Norman clapped and said, "I am proud of both of you for capturing the heroes!" Norman said, "Drew, put the little pest in to the other machine! Let's have some fun, and torture them!" Drew grabbed Justin by his neck, and picked him up from the ground. Drew lifted Justin in to the air, and opened the other machine ! Drew put Justin in to the other machine, and connected the wires to his body!. Drew closed up the other machine, and walked to the computer. Drew activated the other machine. The machine spun to life, as the electricity flowed through the wires. Drew set the electricity values on the machines, and sent the electrical energy through the wires. The electricity in the wires electrocuted Justin and Spider Crusader, as they screamed in pain. The villains laughed manically, as the heroes were getting tortured by the machines. Spider Crusader and Justin's blood mixed together, as it poured in to the tube on the desk. The tube filled to the top with the blood! Norman disconnected the tube from the computer, and attached the tube to the needle. Norman injected the needle to his arm. Norman's body grew in muscle mass and strength, as the blood flowed through his body. Norman's eyes glowed green, as he smiled. Justin growled, as his eyes glowed red. Justin's body ignited an blast of flames. Everything in the lab exploded, as Justin landed on the ground. Spider Crusader hid behind the shelf! Justin sped in to Otto, and grabbed him by his neck. Justin lifted Otto in to the air, and set Otto's body on fire with his flames. Otto's body burnt in to ashes! Drew growled, and hit Justin in the chest with his vulture wings. Justin summoned an aura of flames! The aura of flames burnt Drew's vulture wings to a crisp. Drew was terrified in fear! Justin punched Drew in the face with a fire blast. Drew smashed in to the wall, and laid next to it. Justin sped in to Drew, and grabbed him by the neck. Justin lifted Drew in to the air, and smashed him in to the ground. Justin held Drew on to the ground, and punched him in the face, multiple times. Justin set his hand on Drew's chest, and set his body on fire. Drew's body turned to ash! Justin got up from the ground, and wiped the dust off of his body. Norman growled, as his eyes glowed green. Norman sped in to Justin, and punched him in the face. Justin slid backwards! Norman walked closer to Justin, as he smiled! Justin shot fire blasts at Norman. The fire blasts fizzled, as they bounced off of Norman's body! Norman said, "That tickled, time for me to smash some sense in to you!" Norman grabbed Justin by his neck, and smashed him through the table. Justin laid on the ground! Norman held Justin on the ground, and grabbed a glass container off of the desk! Norman smashed the glass container on top of Justin's head! The glass container broke, as blood leaked from Justin's head! Norman punched Justin in the face, multiple times, as he laid on the ground. Justin ignited a fire blast from his body. Norman slid backwards, as Justin got up from the ground. Norman grabbed a couple of fire bombs from the desk, and threw them at Justin. The fire bombs exploded, and the explosion smashed Justin in to the wall. Justin laid against the wall, and rubbed his head. Norman sped in to Justin, and grabbed his neck. Norman smashed Justin in to the ground. Justin laid on the ground! Norman ignited a blast from his body. The blast covered the area, and exploded everything in the villain hideout, and set everything on fire. Norman jumped on to the glider, that was sitting in the villain hideout. Norman flew out of the villain hideout, and patrolled the city. The debris from the explosion fell on top of Justin, and buried him. Spider Crusader got up from his hiding spot, and web slinged himself to the debris. The villain hideout was falling apart around him, with the flames growing bigger. Spider Crusader lifted the debris off of Justin. Spider Crusader picked up Justin's body! Spider Crusader laid Justin on his back, and web swung around the villain hideout. The villain hideout was collapsing on itself. Spider Crusader shot a web at the window, and pulled on the web. The web shattered the window. Spider Crusader web swung through the window, and landed on the ground. Spider Crusader walked to the bench! Spider Crusader laid Justin on the bench. Spider Crusader laid his hand on Justin's chest. The health indicator on Spider Crusader's wrist showed that Justin had a pulse, but he is barely breathing. Spider Crusader picked up Justin's body, and laid him on his back. Spider Crusader web swung in to the air, and swung through the city. Spider Crusader saw the courtyard for Oasis Falls High School. Spider Crusader landed in front of Oasis Falls High School, and opened up the doors with his webs. Spider Crusader walked through the hallway, and analyzed everything around him. Spider Crusader found the science lab, and walked toward it. Spider Crusader walked in to the science lab, and opened up the healing tube. Spider Crusader laid Justin in to the healing tube, and connected the wires to his body. Spider Crusader closed the healing tube. Spider Crusader walked to the chair, and sat in it. Spider Crusader logged in to the computer, that was sitting on the desk. Spider Crusader pressed some buttons on the computer, and the healing machine activated. The healing energy flowed through the wires in to Justin's body.

Spider Crusader was standing in Oasis Falls High School, and put his hand on Justin's healing tube. Spider Crusader said, "Don't worry, buddy, you will be healed soon, and will be back to full health." Police cars were zooming through the streets in the background with their sirens on. Spider Crusader said, "That's my queue to jump in to action!" Spider Crusader web swung out of the window, and web swung towards the police cars. Spider Crusader shot a web at the police cars and slingshot himself toward them. Spider Crusader landed on top of the police car, and kept his balance. The other car was speeding through the street, and bashed in to the police car. Spider Crusader said, "Hey bud, your driving skills are as bad as an pigeon on an bicycle." Spider Crusader shot an web at the other car's trunk, and pulled it open. Spider Crusader threw an web grenade at the trunk. The web grenade went in to the trunk, and exploded. The engine exploded in the other car, and caught on fire. The other car lost its control, and smashed in to the light post. The light post fell on top of the other car, and made the other car explode. The leader of the gang drove up next to the police car, and bashed the police car in to the wall. The police car smashed in to the building, and spun out of control. The building's foundation crumbled, and fell on top of the car. Spider Crusader's spider sense went off, and he jumped on to the gang leader's car. Spider Crusader landed on the hood of the gang leader's car. The gang leader got spooked, and started to drive recklessly. The car was speeding through the streets, and smashing in to everything. The citizens of Zoomopolis were running away, as the car was smashing through trash cans, buildings, and hot dog stands. Glass shards and trash were flying everywhere, as Spider Crusader was hanging on to the hood of the car. Spider Crusader punched the windshield with his fist, until it shattered. Glass shards from the windshield fell on to the road, as the car was driving crazily through the neighborhood. The gang leader grabbed his gun from the car seat, and started shooting it at Spider Crusader. Spider Crusader dodged the bullets, with his fast reflexes. Spider Crusader shot an web at the gun, and smashed it in to the car's window. The window shattered as the gun exploded. Spider Crusader shot an web at the gang leader's head, and pulled the gang leader toward him. Spider Crusader grabbed the gang leader's head, and bashed it against the steering wheel. Blood poured from the gang leader's head. Spider Crusader grabbed his web knife from his belt, and stabbed it in to the gang leader's neck. The gang leader laid dead on the steering wheel. The car horn went off, as the car drove in to the gas station, and exploded. Spider Crusader jumped off of the car's hood, and landed on the ground. The gas station was burning to the ground, as the fire trucks drove up to the scene. The fire trucks stopped at the fire, and the fire fighters washed the fire away with the water hose. Spider Crusader sat on the bench, and drank an bottle of water to rehydrate himself. Spider Crusader threw away the water bottle, and web swung through the city. Spider Crusader backflipped through the air, and landed at an middle school called Revolution Middle School. There was an group of kids in the middle of the courtyard. Spider Crusader walked toward the group of kids, and leaned next to the tree. Several students were in an circle around Daniel and Adam. Adam pushed Daniel on to the ground, and bent down over his body. Adam punched Daniel in the face, multiple times. Daniel's face was bleeding, as Adam growled and picked up Daniel's body. Adam threw Daniel in to the flag pole. Daniel smashed in to the flag pole, and rolled on the ground. Adam stepped on Daniel's chest, as Daniel coughed. Daniel coughed, while Adam was crushing him in to the ground. Spider Crusader shot an web at Adam's arm, and pulled him off of Daniel.

Adam stumbled backwards, as Spider Crusader back flipped and kicked Adam in the face. Spider Crusader punched Adam in the chest! Adam smashed against the tree. Spider Crusader web swung himself in to the tree, and kicked Adam in the chest. Adam smashed through the tree, and fell on to the ground. Spider Crusader picked up Adam's body, and smashed him on to the ground. The ground made an dent, as Adam laid on the ground. Daniel got up from the ground, and walked toward Spider Crusader. Daniel said, "Thanks for saving me!" Spider Crusader nodded and said, "No problem, I am here to protect the city and its citizens." Adam got up, and rubbed his head. Adam sat on the school steps, and lowered his head. Spider Crusader and Daniel walked down the street toward Daniel's house. Daniel's house was an blue house with a nice garden. Daniel and Spider Crusader walked toward the front door, and rang the door bell. Daniel's dad, Zach, let Daniel and Spider Crusader in to the house. Daniel and Spider Crusader sat on the couch together. The doorbell rang, and Zach opened the door. Norman was at the front door, on his glider. Norman hovered in to the house on his glider. Zach closed the door and said, "What a beautiful day outside!" Norman said, "It is an beautiful day!" Spider Crusader's spider sense went off, and he got up from the couch with Daniel. Daniel and Spider Crusader walked down the hallway. Spider Crusader and Daniel stopped at the bathroom! Daniel opened the bathroom door, and walked in to it. Spider Crusader locked the door for the bathroom. Daniel said, "Why did you lock the bathroom door?" Spider Crusader said, "It is for your safety!" Spider Crusader walked down the hallway, and spied on Zach and Norman. Norman said, "I am an simple man, that likes to do business!" Zach said, "What does this have to do with me?" Norman said, "There is an colorful pest swinging around the city! He is known as Spider Crusader, and he has been destroying my creations for an while." Zach said, "I am not going to endanger my family, by helping you hunt down superheroes." Norman growled and said, "I don't care about your family, my business is being destroyed by this pest." Zach said, "If you don't care about my family, then get out of my house." Zach swung his arm at Norman. Norman grabbed Zach's arm, and kicked him in the chest. Zach slid backwards! Norman laughed and said, "Attempting to punch me is your first mistake!" Norman grabbed Zach's arm! Norman twisted Zach's arm, and pulled it behind Zach's back. Zach screamed in pain! Norman laughed, as he smashed Zach in to the ground. Zach laid on the ground! Norman took a container off of his belt, and a needle. Norman loaded the liquid from the container in to the needle. Norman stabbed the needle in to Zach's arm. Zach struggled on the ground, as the liquid turned his body in to an monster made out of molten lava. Spider Crusader's spider sense went off! Norman said, "I can sense the spider in the area! Molten Monster, deal with the pest, while I capture the kid." Norman walked on to his glider, and hovered past Spider Crusader to find Daniel. Norman hovered down the hallway, and stopped at the bathroom. Norman grabbed an pumpkin bomb from his belt, and attached it to the door. The pumpkin bomb exploded, and the door opened. Daniel was terrified in fear, and sitting in the corner. Norman electrocuted Daniel with his electric taser! Daniel was electrocuted with electric energy. Daniel passed out on the ground. Norman picked up Daniel's body, and laid him on his shoulder. Norman walked on to the glider, and hovered out of the bathroom. Norman flew down the hallway on his glider. Norman flew in to the living room. Norman said, "I have captured the kid, meet me back at the secret hideout, after you deal with the spider." Molten Monster said, "Yes Master!" Norman flew out of the front door, and toward his secret hideout. Spider Crusader shot a web at Molten Monster. Molten Monster grabbed the web, and pulled Spider Crusader toward him. Molten Monster punched Spider Crusader in the chest. Spider Crusader smashed in to the wall, and laid next to it. Molten Monster charged toward the wall, and tackled Spider Crusader. Molten Monster body slammed Spider Crusader in to the ground, and punched him in the face. Spider Crusader's armor absorbed most of the heat from Molten Monster's arms. Molten Monster growled, as he tried to punch through Spider Crusader's armor. Spider Crusader said, "You need an breath mint, your breath is too hot!" Spider Crusader shot an web at Molten Monster's face. Molten Monster growled in anger, as he melted the web off of his face. Spider Crusader back flipped off of the ground. Spider Crusader shot his web at an book shelf, and threw it at Molten Monster. Molten Monster punched the book shelf, and smashed it to pieces. Molten Monster sped toward Spider Crusader, and grabbed him. Molten Monster wrapped his arms around Spider Crusader, and heated up his body. Spider Crusader said, "Awwwww, you must be an softie, since you like to give out bear hugs." Molten Monster's body ignited an explosion of molten energy. The explosion covered the area, and the house exploded. The house's foundation collapsed on top of Spider Crusader, as he laid on the ground. Spider Crusader got up from the ground, and rubbed his head. The foundation pieces of the house, fell on to the ground, as Spider Crusader got up. Molten Monster smiled, and kicked Spider Crusader in the chest. Spider Crusader slid backwards, and laid next to the car, that was in the middle of the road. Police cars stopped in front of the Molten Monster. Police officers climbed out of the police cars, and started shooting at the Molten Monster. Spider Crusader said, "No, stay back! He is too dangerous for you to handle!" Molten Monster growled, and ignited an explosion from his body. The explosion made the police cars explode, and the police officers laid on the ground in puddles of blood. Spider Crusader laid on the ground, catching his breath. Spider Crusader said, "Police officers are idiots, they never listen to superheroes." Molten Monster walked closer to Spider Crusader, and kicked him in the chest. Spider Crusader rolled on the ground. Molten Monster grabbed Spider Crusader's leg, and threw him in to the pole. The pole fell on to the ground, as Spider Crusader rolled on the ground. Molten Monster walked closer to Spider Crusader. Spider Crusader laid on the ground, and thought of the best strategy to defeat Molten Monster. Spider Crusader shot an web at the ice cream stand. The web attached to the ice cream, and froze the webs in the web shooters in to an shard of ice. Spider Crusader grabbed the fire hydrant next to him, and pulled it out of the ground. The water from the fire hydrant splashed on to the road, and continued splashing water out in to the air. Spider Crusader shot a web at Molten Monster, and a web at the water. The webs froze the water and Molten Monster in to an huge pillar of ice. Spider Crusader got up from the ground, and picked up an car. Spider Crusader threw the car at the frozen Molten Monster. The Molten Monster exploded in to shards of ice. Spider Crusader sat on the bench to catch his breath. Down the street, Norman flew in to his secret hideout, with Daniel on his glider. Norman landed his glider in the secret hideout, and opened up his experiment machine. Norman laid Daniel in to his experiment machine, and attached the wires to Daniel's body. Norman closed the machine! Norman logged on to his computer, and turned on the machine. The machine spun its gears, and sent electric energy in to Daniel's body. The electric energy tortured Daniel by electrocuting his body. Norman laughed manically, at the computer, as the machine tortured Daniel. An woman walked in to the secret hideout with an black latex suit. The woman was Fiona, and she was an high ranked burglar, that can outsmart anyone in her league. Fiona walked toward Norman, and leaned on his chair. Fiona said, "Working on your usual experiments, Norman?" Norman said, "Yep, I am having fun, by torturing him." Fiona said, "Good, I like it when my victims scream in pain and terror." Fiona rubbed some chap stick on her lips, as she played with Norman's hair. Fiona said, "I heard that we have an problem with an colorful spider." Norman said, "Yep, he has defeated our recent henchman, Molten Monster." Fiona said, "I am going to play with the little spider." Norman said, "Be careful, he is an slippery little pest." Fiona back flipped out of the window for the secret hideout, and landed on the ground. Fiona jumped on to the speeding police car, and rode it to the bank. The speeding police car sped down the street, and zoomed past Spider Crusader. Spider Crusader got up from the bench, and shot an web at the police car. Fiona crawled from the trunk of the police car, and jumped through the window. Fiona landed in the car, and stabbed the police officer in the neck with her knife. The police officer laid on the floor of the police car, while Fiona took over the steering wheel. Spider Crusader pulled on the web, and launched himself on to the hood of the police car. The police car sped through the streets, and crashed through various items. Fiona steered the police car, and tried to shake Spider Crusader off of the hood of the police car. Spider Crusader hung on to the hood of the police car. Fiona recklessly drove the police car. The police car was running over trash cans, and food stands, while running over panicking citizens. The bodies of the citizens laid on the road in puddles of blood. The piles of trash, and flying food was bouncing off of Spider Crusader, as he hung on to the police car. Spider Crusader crawled on to the windshield, and smashed his fist through it. The windshield shattered, as Fiona panicked. Fiona steered the police car in to an light pole. The light pole fell on to the road, as Spider Crusader crawled in to the car. Spider Crusader roundhouse kicked Fiona in the face. Fiona tumbled out of the car, and rolled in to the road. Spider Crusader jumped out of the car. Fiona grabbed her taser off of her belt, and electrocuted Spider Crusader. Spider Crusader fell backwards, as Fiona got up from the ground. Fiona kicked Spider Crusader in the chest. Spider Crusader slid backwards in to the wall. Fiona walked to Spider Crusader, and rubbed her hand on his body. Fiona said, "Hello, hot shot, would you retract your helmet for an wonderful woman like me?" Spider Crusader nervously laid next to the wall. Fiona rubbed her hand on Spider Crusader's chest. Fiona said, "Don't be nervous, you're the hottest superhero in Zoomopolis." Spider Crusader retracted his helmet. Fiona said, "You're an good boy!" Fiona kissed Spider Crusader on the cheek. Spider Crusader blushed, as Fiona rubbed his arm. Fiona licked her lips and said, "You are so strong and brave. I like superheroes, who are strong and brave." Fiona kissed Spider Crusader on the lips. Fiona said, "I have an favor to ask?" Spider Crusader said, "What is the favor?" Fiona said, "There is an community gym, with a swimming pool down the street." Spider Crusader said, "Your favor is that you want to go swimming with me?" Fiona smiled and said, "Yes, you are an smart boy!" Fiona ruffled up Spider Crusader's hair, and kissed him on the cheek. Fiona hung on to Spider Crusader's back, as he web swung down the street. Spider Crusader and Fiona landed at the community gym, and walked in to it. Spider Crusader and Fiona walked toward the swimming pool. Spider Crusader and Fiona stood in front of the swimming pool. Fiona pressed an button on her wrist, and her uniform transformed in to an bathing suit. Spider Crusader pressed an button on his belt, and his suit retracted. The suit transformed in to an bathing suit. Fiona saw Spider Crusader's body, and was amazed. Fiona said, "You are so hot, Peter!" Peter blushed, as he nervously smiled. Peter said, "Thanks!" Fiona said, "Don't be nervous, we are here to have fun." Peter and Fiona ran toward the swimming pool, and jumped in to it. Peter and Fiona splashed each other in the swimming pool. Fiona and Peter swam laps around the swimming pool. Peter and Fiona got out of the swimming pool, and sat on the edge of the swimming pool together. Fiona and Peter hugged and kissed each other. Fiona said, "You are fun to hang out with, little spider!" Peter smiled and said, "You are fun to hang out with as well." Fiona ruffled Peter's hair. Fiona's wrist communicator started to go off. Fiona said, "I need to take this call." Peter brushed his hair and said, "Don't worry, I will sit here, and wait for you." Fiona got up, and tapped the button on her wrist communicator. Fiona laid next to the wall. Norman said, "Are you having fun playing with the little spider?" Fiona said, "Yes, what's up?" Norman said, "I need more blood from Spider Crusader for my experiments, can you get me some more?" Fiona said, "That shouldn't be an problem, I have him tangled up in my web" Norman said, "Good, don't fail me!" Fiona said, "I won't!" Fiona pressed an button on her wrist communicator, and ended the conversation. Peter was sitting on the edge of the pool. Fiona walked over to Peter, and sat next to him. Fiona said, "Do you mind, if I take some of your blood? My boss needs it for his experiments." Peter said, "I don't mind at all, I would do anything for you." Fiona smiled, as she took a needle and an canister out of her pocket. Fiona attached the canister to the needle. Peter laid his arm in Fiona's lap. Fiona stabbed the needle in to Peter's arm. Peter's blood poured in to the canister. The canister filled to the top, and Fiona took the needle out of Peter's arm. Fiona sealed the canister with a lid, and put it in her pocket. Fiona took an towel out of her pocket, and wiped the left over blood from Peter's arm. Fiona put an band aid on Peter's arm to stop the bleeding. Fiona said, "Thanks hot shot, you're the best." Fiona kissed Peter's cheek, as Peter blushed. Fiona and Peter got up from the edge of the swimming pool. Fiona pressed an button on her wrist, and her suit covered up her body. Peter pressed an button on his wrist, and his armor covered his body. Peter gave Fiona an spider drone. Peter said, "This will keep track of your location." Fiona grabbed the spider drone, and attached it to her belt. The spider drone activated, and the GPS signal showed up on Peter's wrist communicator. Fiona smiled and walked out of the gym. Fiona said, "Keep being awesome, hot shot." Peter smiled back at Fiona. Fiona stood outside the gym, and pressed an button on her wrist. Fiona's glider flew toward her, and landed in front of the gym. Fiona walked on to her glider, and flew toward Norman's secret hideout. Peter walked out of the gym, and web swung around the city. Spider Crusader followed Fiona's GPS signal, and landed outside the secret hideout. Spider Crusader slowly walked toward the security gate, and hid next to the wall. Fiona landed in front of the secret hideout, and pressed an button on her wrist. Fiona's glider flew in to the secret hideout, and landed in the recharge station. Fiona walked through the security gate, and scanned her security card on the panel. Spider Crusader web crawled on the wall, and followed Fiona. Fiona walked through the hallway of the secret hideout. Spider Crusader web crawled on the ceiling, and avoided the security cameras. Spider Crusader webbed the security cameras with his web shooters, and destroyed them. Fiona walked in to Norman's office! Spider Crusader web crawled in to Norman's office. Spider Crusader jumped off of the wall, and hid behind the book shelf in Norman's office. Fiona walked toward Norman. Norman was at his computer, logging data in to the computer's database. Fiona took the canister of Spider Crusader's blood off of her belt, and laid it next to Norman. Norman smiled, and picked up the canister of Spider Crusader's blood. Norman attached the canister of Spider Crusader's blood to his DNA machine, and pressed the button on the machine. The machine scanned the canister of Spider Crusader's blood, and uploaded the DNA to Norman's computer. Norman saved the DNA results in to the computer's database. Norman noticed that the environment felt off. Norman waved his hand in the air. Norman's security guards saw the signal, and patrolled the area. Fiona walked out of Norman's office, and laid next to the wall. Spider Crusader laid his hand on the wall, and quietly walked around the area. Norman's security guards saw Spider Crusader, and walked behind him. Spider Crusader's spider sense went off, as Norman's security guards stopped behind Spider Crusader. Norman's security guards tackled Spider Crusader, and held him on the ground. Spider Crusader growled, as the security guards electrocuted Spider Crusader with their tasers. Spider Crusader screamed in pain, as he laid on the ground. One of Norman's security guards picked up Spider Crusader, and wrapped their arms around him. Spider Crusader struggled in the security guard's grip, as they walked toward Norman. One of Norman's security guards said, "We found an intruder in your office." Norman smiled and said, "It's the little spider, that likes to ruin my operations." Spider Crusader said, "Your ego is as big as an inflated balloon." Norman growled, and walked over to Spider Crusader. Norman punched Spider Crusader in the face! Norman said, "You better watch your tongue, little spider. You don't want to piss me off!" Spider Crusader said, "Awwwwww, the villain's ego is going to explode" Norman growled, and grabbed Spider Crusader by his neck. Norman lifted Spider Crusader in to the air, and smashed him through the table. Spider Crusader laid on the ground. Norman stepped on Spider crusader's chest, and held him on the ground. Norman said, "This is your last chance, spider, watch your mouth, or you will regret messing with me!" Spider Crusader said, "I can handle anything that you throw at me!" Spider Crusader shot an web in Norman's face. The web attached to Norman's face! Spider Crusader slid backwards, and backflipped off of the ground. Norman growled, as he ripped the web off of his face. Spider Crusader shot a web at Norman's chest. Spider Crusader slingshot himself in to Norman, and kicked him in to the wall. Norman smashed in to the wall, and stumbled backwards. Spider Crusader back flipped, and kicked Norman in the face. Norman growled, and grabbed Spider Crusader's leg. Norman smashed Spider Crusader in to the ground multiple times, and threw him in to the table, that was filled with multiple containers. Spider Crusader smashed through multiple glass containers, and rolled on the ground. Glass shards from the containers fell on to the ground. Spider Crusader backflipped off of the ground, and shot some webs at Norman. The webs bounced off of Norman's chest, as Norman walked toward Spider Crusader. Spider Crusader was terrified in fear, as he slowly walked backwards. Norman walked closer to Spider Crusader! Norman said, "What's wrong, little spider, are you scared that your webs don't work on me?" Spider Crusader said, "I am not scared of you!" Norman grabbed a explosive bomb from his belt, and threw it at Spider Crusader. Spider Crusader shot a web at the bomb, and threw it back at Norman. The bomb exploded, and Norman barely moved an inch. Norman said, "Silly spider, my own weapons don't hurt me!" Norman grabbed Spider Crusader by his neck, and smashed him in to the wall. Spider Crusader's body left an dent on the wall, as Spider Crusader was trying to get out of Norman's grip. Norman smashed Spider Crusader in to the wall multiple times. The wall cracked, as Spider Crusader growled. Norman lifted Spider Crusader in to the air, and smashed him in to the ground. Spider Crusader laid on the ground, as Norman smiled. Norman held Spider Crusader on the ground, as Spider Crusader tried to catch his breath. Norman said, "The spider is battered and bruised, you should surrender, while you have the chance." Spider Crusader growled and said, "Heroes never give up, when their enemy has the upper hand." Norman said, "Those are lame words for an worthless spirit." Spider Crusader lifted his arm, and tried to shoot a web at Norman's face. Norman grabbed Spider Crusader's arm, and lifted him in the air. Norman said, "Your little webs can't save you this time, spider!" Norman punched Spider Crusader in the face. Spider Crusader smashed in to the wall, and laid on the ground, as his helmet shattered to pieces. Spider Crusader got up from the ground, and crawled on the walls! Spider Crusader's spider senses were going crazy, since the stakes have gotten pretty high for the situation. Norman said, "The spider is running away like a little scared cat, how pathetic." Spider Crusader grabbed a web bomb from his belt, and threw it at Norman. The web bomb exploded, and Norman slid backwards! Spider Crusader crawled on the wall, and shot a web at the door panel. The door panel exploded, as the door opened. Spider Crusader crawled to the door, and back flipped through it. Norman pressed the emergency button on the wall, and put the hideout in Red Alert. Security robots rolled in to the hallway, and surrounded Spider Crusader, as the door to Norman's office automatically closed behind him. The security robots were shooting at Spider Crusader. Spider Crusader grabbed web bombs from his belt, and threw them at the security robots. The web bombs exploded, and robot parts flew everywhere. Spider Crusader ran through the hallway, as more security robots chased after him. The security robots shot rockets at Spider Crusader. The rockets hit Spider Crusader in the back, and Spider Crusader smashed in to the wall. The security robots rolled toward Spider Crusader, as he got up from the ground. The security robots shot wires at Spider Crusader. The wires wrapped around Spider Crusader's body, and electrocuted him. Spider Crusader growled in pain, as he laid on the ground. The security robots punched Spider Crusader in the chest, as he laid on the ground. One of the security robots picked up Spider Crusader by his neck, and lifted him in to the air. Spider Crusader growled, as the security robot punched Spider Crusader in the chest multiple times. Spider Crusader growled, as his armor absorbed the damage. The security robot smashed Spider Crusader in to the wall, multiple times. Spider Crusader growled, and attached a web bomb from his belt to the security robot's chest. The web bomb exploded, and the security robot lost their grip on Spider Crusader. Spider Crusader landed on the ground, as the security robot exploded. The security camera was pointing at Spider Crusader. Spider Crusader disabled the camera with his webs, and ran through the hallway. Spider Crusader made it in to the next section of the hallway, as he stopped to catch his breath. The security guard walked toward Spider Crusader. Spider Crusader shot his webs at the security guard. The security guard swung his electric sword at the webs, and sliced them in half. The security guard sped toward Spider Crusader, and kicked him in the chest. Spider Crusader slid backwards. Spider Crusader grabbed the security guard's arm, and shot an web in the security guard's face. The security guard growled and swung his electric sword. Spider Crusader tried to dodge the electric sword. The security guard stabbed Spider Crusader in the chest, with the electric sword. Spider Crusader got electrocuted, as he growled in pain. The security guard kicked Spider Crusader in the chest. Spider Crusader rolled on the ground. Spider Crusader grabbed an web bomb from his belt, and threw it at the security guard. The web bomb exploded, and the security guard smashed in to the wall. The security guard dropped his electric sword. Spider Crusader back flipped off of the ground. Spider Crusader tacked the security guard, and held them on the wall. Spider Crusader stabbed his web knife in to the security guard's neck. The security guard laid on the ground in an puddle of blood. Spider Crusader web swung further in to the hallway. Spider Crusader saw the entrance to the villain hideout, and was relived that he was almost out of the madness. Security turrets guarded the entrance. Spider Crusader's spider senses went off, as the turrets shot at him. Spider Crusader flipped in to the air, and shot webs at the turrets. Spider Crusader ran through the entrance, and made it outside, as the doors closed behind him. Spider Crusader was catching his breath, as Fiona walked toward him. Fiona said, "Hey hot shot, looks like you just made it out of an tough maze!" Spider Crusader was relived to see Fiona, as he walked over to her. Spider Crusader said, "It was crazy in there. There was an psychopath named Norman, and he tried to kill me." Fiona hugged Spider Crusader and said, "Oh my, that is awful!" Spider Crusader hugged Fiona back and said, "I know, it is awful." Fiona said, "To make you feel better, let me take you to my place for some relaxation." Spider Crusader said, "Sounds great, I need some relaxation!" Fiona climbed on to Spider Crusader's back, and hung on to him. Spider Crusader web swung in to the air. Spider Crusader web swung to Fiona's house. Spider Crusader landed on the ground. Fiona got off of Spider Crusader's back, and stepped on to the ground. Fiona and Spider Crusader walked in to Fiona's house. Fiona's house was huge, and it was filled with technology, and various gadgets. Fiona and Spider Crusader sat on the couch together. Fiona wrapped her arm around Spider Crusader's back, as they relaxed together. Spider Crusader retracted his helmet. The helmet uncovered Spider Crusader's face! Fiona and Spider Crusader kissed each other on the couch. Spider Crusader pressed the button on his helmet. The helmet covered Spider Crusader's face. Spider Crusader got up from the couch. Fiona said, "Is everything ok?" Spider Crusader said, "I sense an threat is on the horizon at Oasis Falls High School. Fiona said, "Be safe!" Spider Crusader said, "I will try to be safe!" Spider Crusader shot an web at the window, and pulled it open. Spider Crusader climbed out of the window, and jumped out of it. Spider Crusader landed on the ground. Spider Crusader shot an web at the window, and pulled on the web to close it. Spider Crusader web swung in to the air to Oasis Falls High School. Down the street at the villain hideout, Norman was cleaning the debris from his laboratory. Norman said, "I wish the pest would just go away! He likes to ruin all of my gadgets and fun." Daniel was in the experiment tube, and overheard Norman talking to himself. Daniel said, "Spider Crusader keeps breaking your toys, because you like to mess up Zoomopolis." Norman said, "Shut up, no one asked you, you're my captive!" Norman electrocuted Daniel with his remote. Daniel screamed in pain, as the wires electrocuted him. Norman said, "You are my new toy, and you will obey me!" Norman pressed an button on his computer, and Spider Crusader's blood poured in to the wires from the container, that was attached to the computer. Spider Crusader's blood was injected in to Daniel through the wires. Norman injected some ghost powers in to the wires. The ghost powers flowed in to Daniel's body through the wires. Daniel's eyes glowed green, as he laid in the machine. Daniel's body ignited an explosion! The explosion made the experiment machine explode, and Daniel walked through the debris, as his eyes glowed green. Norman said, "I control you, follow my commands!" Norman pressed the button on his remote, as the signal does nothing to Daniel. Daniel walked toward Norman, with his eyes glowing green. Daniel shoots an energy beam from his hand! The energy beam destroys the remote in Norman's hand. Daniel said, "No one controls me, I am my own being." Norman threw an glass container at Daniel. Daniel went invisible, as he walked closer to Norman. The glass container went through Daniel, and smashed against the wall. Daniel's body went back to normal. Daniel said, "Nothing can hurt me, I am part ghost." Daniel went in to his ghost form, and flew in to Norman. Daniel smashed Norman in to the wall. Daniel's eyes glowed green, as he did an ghostly wail from his mouth. Norman smashed through the wall. Daniel towered over him. Daniel said, "None of your gadgets work on me!" Norman said, "I am your master, you can't beat me with your powers." Norman grabbed an electric baton from his belt, and electrocuted Daniel. Daniel's ghost powers malfunctioned, as he screamed in pain. Norman kicked Daniel in the chest. Daniel slid backwards! Norman got up from the ground, and punched Daniel in the face. Daniel smashed in to the table, and laid on the ground. Norman walked closer to Daniel. Daniel slowly got up from the ground. Norman said, "Don't bother fighting back, I have plenty of electric bombs to keep you down." Norman threw an electric bomb at Daniel. The electric bomb hit Daniel in the chest! The electric bomb exploded, and hit Daniel with electric energy. The electric energy electrocuted Daniel, as he screamed in pain. Daniel laid on the ground, as he tried to catch his breath. Norman walked closer to Daniel. Daniel got up from the ground, and shot an energy blast from his arms at Norman. Norman got hit by the energy blast, and smashed in to the wall. Daniel went in to his ghost form, and flew toward Norman. Daniel went invisible, and smashed Norman through multiple walls. Daniel phased through the walls, and smashed Norman out of the villain hideout. Norman laid on the ground, as Daniel's body went back to normal. Daniel stood over Norman, as his eyes glowed green. Daniel said, "Surrender, Norman, I am stronger than you." Norman said, "I can't be beaten by my own pawn." Daniel growled, as he grabbed Norman by his throat. Daniel lifted Norman in to the air and said, "I am not your pawn!" Daniel threw Norman in to the air. Daniel back flipped, and kicked Norman in the chest. Norman smashed in to the wall. Daniel shot an energy blast from his arm at Norman. The energy blast smashed Norman through the wall. Norman laid on the ground, as the building crumbled on top of him. Daniel said, "Be an good little dog, and stay down. If you don't stay down, I will kill you." Daniel went in to his ghost form, and flew toward Oasis Falls High School. Norman slowly got up from the ground, and caught his breath. He wiped the building debris off of his body. Norman said, "Daniel thinks that, I am down for the count, but what he doesn't know that I have multiple tricks up my sleeve." Norman was disappointed that his hideout was destroyed. Norman said, "All of my wonderful experiments are gone, but villains can easily climb back up from the bottom." Norman pressed an button on his wrist, and his glider flew toward him. Norman's glider landed in front of him. Norman walked on to his glider, and flew in to the air. Norman checked the tracker on his glider. Norman said, "Daniel is heading toward Oasis Falls High School. I will follow him, since the spider will probably be in the area as well." Norman flew toward Oasis Falls High School. Daniel used his ghost powers to control the street lights in Zoomopolis, while he flew toward Oasis Falls High School. The street lights went crazy, as the ghost powers controlled them. The street lights were flashing, as the cars sped through the streets, and crashed in to various buildings and the other objects in the city. Daniel laughed, as the chaos brewed through Zoomopolis. Daniel saw Oasis Falls High School in the distance, as he flew toward the courtyard. Daniel landed in the courtyard, and walked toward the doors of Oasis Falls High School. The security guard was standing in front of the doors. Daniel walked toward the security guard, and lifted him in to the air with his ghost powers from his hands. Daniel threw the security guard in to the flag pole. Daniel used his ghost wail on the security guard. The flag pole and the security guard flew across the street, and smashed through the building. The building crumbled on top of the security guard. Daniel smiled, as he blasted the doors open with his ghost powers. Daniel walked through the doors, and walked through the hallways. Oasis Falls High School looked empty, but Daniel's ghost sense has detected that there were students in the building. Daniel walked toward the teacher's lounge. Daniel saw the door for the teacher's lounge, and looked through the little window on the door. Daniel saw the teachers hiding in the room. Daniel kicked open the door, and broke the lock on the door. Daniel walked in to the teacher's lounge, and scanned the area for the teachers with his ghost vision. The teachers were hiding under the table. Daniel picked up the table and threw it at the wall. The table smashed to pieces, when it hit the wall. Daniel did an ghost wail! The teacher's lounge shook from the ghost wail, and the teachers smashed in to the wall. The teachers laid on the ground in puddles of blood. Daniel smiled, as he walked out of the teacher's lounge. Daniel walked down the hallway, and noticed that the students were terrified in fear, as they hid in the bathroom. Daniel shot an blast of ghost energy from his hand at the students in the bathroom. The students laid on the bathroom floor in puddles of blood. Daniel said, "It is fun to cause chaos!" Daniel walked toward the gym, and noticed that the gym was full of students. Daniel walked in to the gym, and leaned against the wall, as he saw the football team sitting on the stands, watching the cheerleaders practice their routine. The cheerleaders flipped in the air, and landed on the gym floor, as the football team cheered and clapped their hands. The cheerleaders bowed, and walked in to the coach's office to change in to their student clothes. Outside the school, Spider Crusader web swung on to the rooftop of Oasis Falls High School. Spider Crusader landed on the rooftop, and walked toward the vents. Spider Crusader pulled open the vents, and crawled in to them. Spider Crusader crawled in to the vents, and crawled to the vent, that was attached to the gym. Spider Crusader pulled open the vent, and crawled out of it. Spider Crusader hung backwards, and lowered himself in to the gym with one of his webs. Daniel saw Spider Crusader, and shot a ghost blast at the web. The web snapped, and Spider Crusader landed on to the gym floor. Daniel said, "You little pest, are you trying to ruin my fun?" Daniel shot ghost blasts at Spider Crusader. Spider Crusader back flipped over the blasts and said, "That's part of my job description." Spider Crusader shot webs at Daniel! Daniel made his body invisible, as the webs went through him. Daniel smirked and said, "You missed, hot shot!" Daniel did an ghost wail at Spider Crusader! Spider Crusader slid backwards in to the wall. Daniel went in to his ghost form, and flew in to Spider Crusader. Spider Crusader smashed in to the wall. Spider Crusader swung his arm at Daniel. Daniel's body went invisible. Daniel grabbed Spider Crusader's neck, and flew in to the air. Daniel threw Spider Crusader in to the ground, and blasted him in the chest with an ghost blast. Spider Crusader smashed in to the ground, and made an dent in the gym. Daniel flew toward Spider Crusader. Spider Crusader pulled himself backwards with an web! Daniel landed on the ground! Spider Crusader shot electric webs at Daniel. The electric webs electrocuted Daniel, as he slid backwards. Daniel said, "That tickled, do you have any more toys to annoy me with?" Spider Crusader said, "I have plenty of toys to show you!" Daniel said, "Prove it, hero!" Daniel waved his hands, and his ghost powers possessed the football team, that were in the gym. Daniel snapped his fingers, and the football team walked toward Daniel. Daniel used his ghost powers to control the football team. The football team growled, and charged at Spider Crusader. The football team tackled Spider Crusader in to the ground, and held him on the gym's floor. The football team punched Spider Crusader in the chest. Spider Crusader ignited an web explosion from his body. The football team got webbed on to the wall, as the ghost powers disconnected from their bodies. Spider Crusader growled, as he got up from the ground. Spider Crusader said, "You need an better strategy, ghost boy!" Daniel growled, as he flew towards Spider Crusader. Spider Crusader back flipped, and shot an web at Daniel's back. Spider Crusader pulled on the web, and threw Daniel in to the wall. Daniel smashed in to the wall, and laid next to it. Spider Crusader ran toward Daniel. Daniel used his ghost wail on Spider Crusader. Spider Crusader smashed in to the wall. Daniel flew toward Spider Crusader, and grabbed him by the neck. Daniel flew in to the air, and smashed Spider Crusader in to the basketball net. Spider Crusader laid in the basketball net. Daniel shot an ghost blast at the basketball net. The basketball net smashed in to the ground, and laid on top of Spider Crusader. Spider Crusader got up from the ground, as Daniel landed. The walls of Oasis Falls High School shook, as an missile smashed through the windows, and hit the gym walls. The missile exploded, as debris flew everywhere. Daniel and Spider Crusader laid on the ground, as debris fell on top of them. Norman laughed, as his glider landed in the middle of the debris. Norman said, "Two little bugs laying on the ground, in front of my feet." Norman walked off of his glider, and looked at the debris. Norman said, "The ghost boy and the spider in the same room, laying on the ground defeated. It must be my lucky day!" Daniel and Spider Crusader got up from the ground, and rubbed their heads. Norman said, "You guys must have had an good nap, because it is time for round 2 of pain." Norman laughed, as Daniel and Spider Crusader walked backwards. Norman said, "Showing fear makes you weak and worthless." Norman walked closer to Spider Crusader and Daniel, as he pressed an button on his wrists. The gloves on his hands started to glow, as they activated anti gravity mode. Norman lifted his hands in the air, and the anti gravity activated in the room. Daniel and Spider Crusader lifted in to the air. Norman waved his arms around, and smashed Daniel and Spider Crusader in to his other. Norman pressed an button on his gloves, and the anti gravity pulled Daniel and Spider Crusader toward him. Norman punched Spider Crusader and Daniel in the chest with an anti gravity explosion from his gloves. Spider Crusader and Daniel smashed in to the wall, and laid next to the wall, as they regained their balance. Norman laughed and said, "The bugs are trembling in fear, how pathetic."

Norman pressed an button on his wrist, and he teleported behind Spider Crusader and Daniel. Norman grabbed Daniel and Spider Crusader by their neck, and smashed both of them in to the ground. Norman stood on top of Daniel and Spider Crusader, as he crushed them in to the ground. Daniel and Spider Crusader growled, as Norman held them on the ground. Norman said, "Zoomopolis must be so pathetic, if they believed in you to protect them." Daniel and Spider Crusader ignited explosions of energy from their body. The room shook from the explosion, as Norman fell on the ground, and laid next to the wall. Daniel and Spider Crusader got up from the ground. Norman threw an electric bomb at Daniel and Spider Crusader. Spider Crusader and Daniel got electrocuted, as they slid back to the wall. Norman pressed an button on his wrist and summoned his glider. Norman jumped on to his glider, and flew through Oasis Falls High School, toward the recovery room. The recovery room is where Justin is stored in his healing tube. Daniel went in to his ghost form, and flew after Norman. Spider Crusader web swung, and followed Daniel. Norman flew in to the recovery room, and looked for Justin's healing tube. Norman found Justin's healing tube, and flew closer to it. Daniel flew in to the recovery room. Spider Crusader web swung in to the recovery room. Spider Crusader said, "Keep the healing tube away from Norman." Daniel nodded and flew toward the healing tube. Norman grabbed electric bombs from his belt, and threw them at Daniel. Daniel dodged the electric bombs, by flying around them. Daniel grabbed the healing tube, and turned invisible. Daniel flew in to the basement of Oasis Falls High School, and hid the healing tube in the basement closet. Daniel flew out of the basement, and flew back in to the recovery room. Norman got angry, and threw an electric bomb at Spider Crusader. Daniel landed in front of the electric bomb, and pushed it back at Norman with his ghost wail. Norman got electrocuted, and slid backwards. Spider Crusader shot an web at Norman, and launched himself in to Norman with the web. Spider Crusader punched Norman in the face. Norman slid backwards. Daniel flew towards Norman, and swung his arm at Norman.

Norman grabbed Daniel's arm, and lifted him in to the air. Norman punched Daniel in the face. Daniel flew through the air, and smashed in to Spider Crusader. Spider Crusader and Daniel toppled on to the ground. Norman lifted an shelf, and smashed it on top of Daniel and Spider Crusader, multiple times. The shelf shattered, as Daniel and Spider Crusader laid on the ground. Norman pressed an button on his wrist, and all of the electronics exploded in the recovery room, and electrocuted Daniel and Spider Crusader with the electric energy. Daniel and Spider Crusader screamed in pain, as Norman maniacally laughed. Norman pressed an button on his wrist, and summoned his glider. Norman jumped on to his glider, as it flew toward him. Norman grabbed an couple of electric bombs from his belt, and rolled them toward Spider Crusader and Daniel. The bombs exploded in front of Spider Crusader and Daniel. The explosion smashed Spider Crusader and Daniel in to the wall, as they got electrocuted. Spider Crusader's armor shattered to pieces. Daniel growled, as he got up from the ground. Spider Crusader tried to get up, but stumbled on to the ground. Spider Crusader said, "Leave me behind, I am too weak to continue fighting." Daniel said, "I can't leave you behind!" Spider Crusader said, "I will slow you down, the city needs an hero." Norman threw an grenade at Daniel and Spider Crusader. Daniel went in to his ghost form, and turned invisible. The grenade bounced through Daniel, and exploded in front of Spider Crusader. The explosion shattered the foundation of Oasis Falls High School, and the foundation collapsed on top of Spider Crusader, as he laid next to the shattered healing tube in an puddle of blood. Daniel walked over, and saw Spider Crusader's body, soaked in blood. Daniel growled in anger, as his body turned visible. Daniel flew in his ghost form toward Norman. Daniel grabbed Norman by his neck, and flew through the debris of Oasis Falls High School in to the sky. Daniel's eyes glowed green, as he ghost wailed Norman in to the ground. Norman smashed through the sky in to Zoomopolis. Norman laid on the ground, in an puddle of blood. Daniel landed in front of Norman's body, as his eyes returned to normal. Daniel analyzed Norman's body, and noticed there was an device on his wrist. The device exploded and the explosion pushed Daniel in to the car. The car and Daniel flew out of Zoomopolis, and landed in the forest. The explosion from Norman's body covered Zoomopolis, and destroyed the entire city. Zoomopolis was left in ruins, as the remains of the city laid on the ground. Daniel rubbed his hand, as he got up from the ground. Daniel went in to his ghost form, and flew toward the ruins of the city. Daniel landed on the ground, as he walked through the destruction. Various bodies laid on the ground in puddles of blood, while Daniel walked through the shattered glass and building rubble on the ground. Daniel went in to his ghost form, and flew out of Zoomopolis. Daniel flew in to the woods, and found an cabin. Daniel landed in front of the cabin. Daniel walked in to the cabin, and decided to make the cabin his new home. The cabin had an supply of food and water, since there was an huge lake in front of it. Daniel walked out of the cabin, and sat on the stairs. The squirrels ran toward Daniel, and hugged his legs. Daniel petted the squirrels, and smiled at them.

Section Break 4

Acorn High School:
1. Acorn High School: Acorn Dragons vs Shallow Falls Bears

21

Welcome to Fantasyville! In Fantasyville, there are two sections of the city! In one section, humans live in their houses, attend school, hang out with friends and family, and have fun. In the other section, zombies and other fantasy creatures live together, and hang out with each other. The government of Fantasyville doesn't like fantasy creatures hanging out with humans, but the city has changed their ways recently. The government has passed a law that fantasy creatures can attend school with the humans. In Fantasyville, high school students attend Acorn High School to expand their knowledge, and hang out with other students. Justin is a werewolf, and he lived in a blue house all by himself in Fantasyville. A couple of years ago, Justin's parents died in a fiery explosion, when a mad scientist experimented on them for the government. Justin lived a healthy life all by himself. Justin works out on a daily basis, and he is very athletic. Justin's dream was to join the high school football team. Justin laid in his room, under his bed sheets on the bed. The sun shined in Justin's window. Justin threw the bed sheets off of his head, and yawned! Justin climbed out of bed, and walked out of his room. Justin walked in to the bathroom, and locked the door. Justin turned on the shower, and took off his clothes. Justin walked in to the shower, and closed the shower door. Justin washed his hair, and cleaned his body. Justin washed his arms, and legs. Justin rehydrated his body! Justin turned off the shower, and opened the shower door. Justin dried himself with the towel! Justin put on his clothes, and brushed his hair. Justin brushed his teeth! Justin walked out of the bathroom. Justin walked in to the living room, and put his backpack on. Justin walked out the front door. Justin walked down the sidewalk. Justin walked on to the school bus. Justin walked to his seat on the bus. The humans on the school bus were terrified in fear, next to the window. Justin walked to the back of the school bus, and sat next to the window. Justin put his headphones in to his ears, as he listened to music on his phone. The school bus started up, and drove to Acorn High School. The school bus stopped at Acorn High School, and opened the bus doors. The students got up from their seats, and walked out of the bus doors. Justin got up from his seat, and took the head phones out of his ears. Justin put his phone in to his pocket. Justin walked out of the bus doors, and walked on to the sidewalk. Justin walked past the flag pole! Justin walked toward the doors for Acorn High School, and blended in to the crowd of students. Justin walked through the doors for Acorn High School. Justin walked through the hallway. The hallway was filled with students and teachers. The students were organizing their lockers, and hanging out with each other. The teachers were energizing themselves for the day, by reviewing their lesson plans and waking their brains up. Justin walked toward his locker. Justin stood at his locker, and turned the knob on the locker. Justin opened his locker, and organized it. Peter walked toward Justin, and pulled his tail. Justin yelped, and turned around. Peter said, "I am sorry that I have startled you, but I wanted to say hello!" Justin growled and said, "You could of tapped me on the shoulder. Pulling my tail was rude for a human." Peter said, "I am sorry, I am not used to interacting with a werewolf." Justin said, "It is fine, It is just a little reminder for next time." Peter smiled and said, "Cool, hope I see you around the area." Justin said, "Me too, you're a cool human to hang out with." Peter walked down the hallway toward his class. Justin continued organizing his locker. Justin closed his locker, and walked toward the water fountain. Justin drank out of the water fountain, and rehydrated himself. The bell rang in the background. The other students walked to their classes. The teachers walked out of the teachers lounge, and walked to their classrooms. Justin walked to his class. Justin stood in front of the door for his Algebra class. Justin turned the door knob, and walked in to the classroom. The other students stared at him. Justin walked to the back of the classroom, and sat at the empty desk. The algebra teacher's name was Matt. Matt was standing in front of the whiteboard. Matt wrote a Algebra equation on the whiteboard. Justin took his textbook out of his bag, and put it on his desk. Justin opened the textbook, and listened to Matt, while he was solving the equation on the whiteboard. The other students were writing notes in their notebooks, while Justin spun his pencil in his paws. The bell rang in the background. The other students put their supplies back in to their bags, and got up from their seats. Justin put his textbook and pencil in to his bag, and zipped it up. Justin got up from his seat, and put his bag on his back. Justin walked out of the classroom, and in to the hallway. Justin walked toward the water fountain. Justin drank out of the water fountain, and rehydrated himself. Flash walked toward Justin, and pushed him in to the locker. Justin laid against the locker, while Flash towered over him. Justin growled at Flash and said, "What is your problem?" Flash said, "Awww the little wolf wants to pick a fight with a human." Flash sped in to Justin, and smashed him in to the wall. Justin growled, and sharpened his claws. Justin punched Flash in the chest. Justin's claws ripped through Flash's shirt. Flash slid backwards! Justin sped in to Flash, and grabbed him by the neck. Justin stabbed his claws in to Flash's neck. Blood poured on the ground, as Justin lifted Flash in to the air. Justin threw Flash in to the wall! Flash laid on the ground, in a puddle of blood. Justin walked in to the men's bathroom. Harry, one of the other students helped Flash get up from the ground. Harry walked Flash to the nurse's office. Justin walked to the sink in the men's bathroom, and washed his fur. Justin walked out of the men's bathroom, and walked to the announcement board in the hallway. Justin read the announcement board! The announcement board said, "Football Tryouts are open! Come to the gym, if you're interested!" Justin said, "Football is the perfect sport to show the school that werewolves can be trusted." Justin walked toward the nurse's office. Justin walked in to the nurse's office. Ash, the nurse said, "Hey Justin, what's up! Is everything ok?" Justin said, "I am here to check up on Flash!" Ash said, "Flash is fine, I cleaned the blood from his wounds, he is able to play football with the other team members." Flash was sitting on the chair, drinking a bottle of water. Justin said, "I was thinking of joining the football team." Ash said, "Cool, I heard that they opened tryouts in the gym." Justin said, "Yep, I was going to participate in the tryouts." Flash said, "Good luck in the tryouts, wolf! Football is a dangerous sport for a fluffball like you." Justin said, "I am willing to take the challenge, and prove you wrong." Flash said, "It would be entertaining to watch!" Justin walked out of the nurse's office. Justin walked down the hallway. Justin walked to the gym. Justin pushed the door open open, and walked in to the gym. Dodgeballs flew in the air, and hit Justin in the chest. Justin smashed in to the wall. Justin laid against the wall. The dodgeballs bounced on to the ground. Miles blew his whistle, and the other students walked to the side of the room, and put their bags on. The other students walked out of the gym. Justin walked to Miles. Justin said, "I am here to sign up for football tryouts." Miles said, "It isn't normal for a werewolf to tryout for the football team." Justin said, "Yeah, I want to shake things up for the football team." The football team walks in to the gym. James, the quarterback, walks up to Justin. James said, "I heard that you want to try out for the football team." Justin said, "Yep!" James said, "Prove your worth to the football team, fluffball." James waves the rest of the football team over. The rest of the football team walks to the middle of the gym, and get in to tackling position. Justin walks in to the passing position. James grabs a football, and passes it to Justin. Justin catches the football, and runs to the other side of the gym. The rest of the football players chase after Justin. Justin stiff arms one of the football players. The football player rolled on the ground. James was amazed by Justin's performance. The football player got up from the ground. The other football players got out of position, and stood next to James. Justin walked to James. James said, "Good work Justin, you look like a good fit for our team. James and Justin shook hands, as the gym teacher smiled in the background. The bell rang in the background. James said, "the football game is later today, lets get you suited up in your football uniform." Justin nodded, as the football players walked to the locker room. James walked to the locker room with the other football players. Justin followed James and the rest of the football team to the locker room. Justin and the football team walked in to the locker room. Justin was amazed at how big the locker room was. James walked to the closet, where the football uniforms hung. James gave a football uniform to Justin. Justin sat on the bench, and put the football uniform on. James said, "The football uniform looks great on you." Justin nodded, as he high fived James. James high fived Justin. James said, "Let's practice your tackling abilities. James got in to position! Justin sped toward James and tackled him in to the ground. Justin got up from the ground. James got up from the ground. James said, "That was perfect!" The coach for the football team walked in to the locker room, and blew his whistle. Coach Andrew said, "It's time for the football game, lets put on our football uniforms, and walk on to the field." The football team put their uniforms on. The football team got up from the bench. Coach Andrew and the football team walked to the football field. Coach Andrew and the football team walked on to the football field. Shallow Falls Bears were on the football field, waiting for Coach Andrew and the football team. Shallow Falls Bears represent Shallow Falls High School, that is located down the road from Acorn High School. Coach Andrew's football team were the Acorn Dragons. The Acorn Dragons and the Shallow Falls Bears were growling at each other, while the referee stood next to them. Peter, the quarterback for the Shallow Falls Bears, and Justin were growling at each other. Peter said, "Awwww, the football team is trying to be tough. They recruited a little wolf to help them." Justin growled and said, "Who are you calling, little wolf?" Justin walked toward Peter and pushed him in to the water cooler. Peter slid backwards, as the water cooler shook. Peter said, "You want me to beat you up, fluff. I can knock some sense in to you." Peter tackled Justin in to the football field. Justin laid on the football field, as Peter punched Justin's football helmet. Justin growled, and bit Peter's arm with his fangs. The rest of the football team growled, and pounced on Justin, to hold him down. The rest of the Acorn Dragons team helped Justin, by throwing Shallow Falls Bears players off of him. Justin growled, and stabbed his claws in to the Shallow Falls Bears players. Justin threw the players off of him. The football players for the Shallow Falls Bears rolled on the football field. Justin got up from the ground, and picked up Peter by his gloved paw. Justin smashed Peter through the table. Peter laid on the ground, as the water cooler fell and poured water on top of him. Peter got up from the ground, and grabbed Justin by the neck. Peter threw Justin at the bench on the sideline for the Acorn Dragons. Justin smashed through the cooler, and the cooler poured water on top of Justin's uniform. Peter held Justin on the ground, and pulled his helmet off. Peter threw Justin's helmet on to the ground. Justin growled, and sharpened his claws. Justin scratched Peter's arm with his claws. Peter slid backwards! Justin got up from the ground. The referee blew his whistle, and directed Justin and Peter back to their sideline. Justin and Peter stood next to their teams. Coach Andrew said, "Save your strength for the football field." The football team nodded, as they sat on the sideline bench. The football team for the Shallow Falls Bears sat on their sideline bench. The referee blew his whistle, and put the football on the field. The Acorn Dragons football team and the Shallow Falls football team walked on to the football field, and got in to their positions. James and the Acorn Dragons offense hiked the ball, while the Shallow Falls defense growled at them. James stepped backwards and threw the football to Justin. The Shallow Falls defense ran after Justin. Justin stiff armed the defense player on to the field as he ran for the first down. Justin dived on to the football field for the first down. The Acorn Dragons got further down the football field in to the red zone. James hiked the football, and threw it to Justin. Justin caught the football, and scored the touchdown. The students cheered in the bleachers, and the mascot backflipped in the air on the football field. The offense for the Acorn Dragons and the defense for the Shallow Falls Bears walked to their sidelines, and sat on the bench. Peter and the offense for the Shallow Falls Bears walked on to the football field. The defense for the Acorn Dragons walked on to the football field. The offense and the defense got in to their positions. Peter hiked the ball, and analyzed the football field. The defense ran after Peter. The defense player was about to tackle Peter in to the field, but Peter side stepped out of the way. Peter kicked the defense player in the chest with his leg. The defense player rolled on the football field. Peter threw the football player to Miles. Miles ran down the football field, and scored the touchdown. The defense player got up from the football field, and walked to the sideline. The defense player was disappointed in himself, as the offense and the defense walked off the field. The football game continued for 3 more quarters on the football field. The football game was tied 21 - 21 on the scoreboard, with 2 minutes left on the clock. The offense for the Acorn Dragons were on the field, and the defense for the Shallow Falls Bears were growling at them. James hiked the ball, and he got in to position. The offense players ran their routes on the field. The defense players growled, and ran after James. Matt ran to James, and tackled him in to the football field for a sack. The referee blew the whistle, and stopped the clock. James got up from the football field. There was 1 minute left on the clock! The offense and the defense got in to their positions on the football field. James hiked the ball, and the offense players ran their routes. The defense players growled at the offense players. James threw the football to Justin. Justin caught the ball, and ran down the football field. The clock was ticking down, as Justin ran toward the red zone. The defense players ran after Justin. Justin stiff armed the defense players. The defense players rolled on to the football field. Justin scored the touchdown, and the clock ran out. The Acorn Dragons won the football game. Peter, and the rest of the Shallow Falls Bears walked on to the football field. James and the rest of the Acorn Dragons walked toward the Shallow Falls bears and shook their hands. James said, "That was a good game!" Peter said, "I agree, thanks for the fun." The Acorn Dragons and the Shallow Falls Bears walked off of the football field. The Acorn Dragons walked in to the locker room, and sat on the bench. The football players took off their helmets. The Acorn Dragons wiped the sweat from their bodies with their towels. The football players for the Acorn Dragons walked in to the shower area, and took off their football uniforms. They put their football uniforms in to the basket, and took the rest of their clothes off. The football players took a shower and washed the dirt off of their bodies. Justin took off his football uniform, and threw it in to the basket. Justin took the rest of his clothes off, and took a shower. Justin washed the dirt off of his body. Justin and the rest of the football players walked out of the shower, and put their clothes back on. Justin, and the rest of the football team walked out of the locker room, and sat on the football field. The sun was setting, and the moon shined bright on the football field. James and Justin sat next to each other, and watched the stars in the sky. It got cold outside, so the football team walked back in to the locker room. The football team hugged each other, as they went to their assigned beds in the sleeping section of the locker room. Justin sat on his bed, and went under the bed sheets. Justin fell asleep, and closed his eyes. The sun rose over Acorn High School. The football team woke up from their beds, and stretched their legs. The football team walked out of the locker room. The football team walked in to the gym! The football team walked in to the hallway. The students of Acorn High School cheered them on for support. Justin shook hands with the other students, as he smiled at them. The students supported the football team's success on the football field. Justin was glad, that he was part of the football team. Justin walked toward his locker, and opened it. Justin reorganized his locker! Justin hydrated himself at the water fountain. Flash walked up to Justin, and tapped him on the shoulder. Justin said, "Hey, Flash, what's up?" Flash said, "I would like to congratulate you on winning the football game with the rest of the football team." Justin said, "Thanks Flash, you're the best!" Flash said, "No problem, fluff ball. Thanks to your help, the school and the city supports werewolves and humans hanging out together." Justin and Flash high fived each other. Flash walked to his locker. Justin walked down the hallway.

Justin walked out of the school, and sat on the steps. James walked out of the school, and sat next to Justin. James wrapped his arm around Justin. James said, "I am glad that you joined the football team." Justin said, "Me too, we are a good team!" James and Justin smiled at each other. The sun was shining on the school, while they sat on the steps.

26

Section Break 5

Pine Cone Academy:
1. Pine Cone Academy: Hope vs Despair

Welcome to Pine Cone Academy! Pine Cone Academy educates students of various talents to expand their knowledge of the world around them, and use their talents to solve various situations. A group of students walked on to the campus of Pine Cone Academy, with their heads held high for the future of their lives. The students walked in to the doors of Pine Cone Academy! The teachers prepared their classrooms for the new year of students, that were ready to expand their knowledge. The students were in the hallway, decorating their brand new lockers. Sally and Fiona walked through the hallway to the cafeteria. Pine Cone Academy hired them to serve lunch to all of the students. Even though their main goal was to serve lunch, Sally and Fiona had bigger plans for the school. Sally and Fiona's plans involved filling the school's hopeful environment with despair. The students filled their bags with their supplies, and walked to homeroom. The students walked in to the classroom, and sat down in their seats. The teacher was writing her name on the whiteboard. The teacher's name was Ash, and she is very cheerful and hopeful. One of the students put their feet on their desk. The student was Matt! Ash slammed her hands on the desk and yelled at him. Ash said, "No feet on the desk, the staff cleaned the desks earlier this morning." Matt growled and said, "Oh come on, I should be allowed to do whatever I want!" Ash threw a pair of scissors and said, "Don't argue with me, this isn't my first time dealing with troublemakers." Daniel smirked and said, "That's right hot shot, don't make the teacher angry!" Ash said, "No words from you either, Daniel!" Anha said, "Listen to the teacher, pipsqueak!" Matt said, "Shut Up Anha!" Anha and Matt got up from their desks. Tony got up from his desk and said, "Anha calm down, it's the first day of school." Anha said, "Making drama is my specialty." Tony sat down at his desk. Steve said, "Tony, it will be fine, Anha needs to handle this on her own." Tony nods and watches the chaos between Matt and Anha. Matt tackles Anha in to the wall! Anha backflipped and kicked Matt in the face. Matt punched Anha in the face. Anha punched Matt in the face. Matt slid backwards and took out his knife. Anha took out her knife and sped towards Matt. Matt swung his knife at Anha. Anha swung her knife at Matt. Matt kicked Anha in the chest. Anha flinched and slid backwards. Matt grabbed Anha by the neck and choked her. Anha put her hand on Matt's neck and choked him. Anha body slammed Matt in to the ground. Matt got up and sweeped his leg under Anha. Anha fell on the ground! Anha got up from the ground, and roundhouse kicked Matt in the chest! Matt smashed in to the wall! Matt growled, as he got up from the ground. Anha growled at Matt! Ash threw her coffee mug at Matt. The coffee mug hit Matt in the chest, splashing coffee all over his clothes and the floor. Ash said, "That is enough, all of your talents would go to waste if you guys killed each other in my classroom. Matt and Anha, as your punishment, you will be cleaning my classroom." Anha said, "I hate cleaning so much!" Ash said, "No arguments allowed, I am strict, and when you interrupt the flow of my classroom, you will be punished! Both of you sit down, or I will chain you to your desks!" Matt and Anha got terrified in fear and sat down at their desks! The bell rings in the background! Ash said, "Have fun in your classes, students!" Steve put his science notebook, and the rest of his supplies in to his bag. Steve got up from his seat and walked out of the classroom! The rest of the students got up from their seats and walked out of the classroom. Steve and Daniel walked through the hallway together. Steve said, "I wish Anha would cool down, getting in fights with the other students would affect her future." Daniel said, "I agree, but she probably had a bad experience during her life." Steve said, "Her lifestyle is different than us, she probably got her behavior from her parents." Daniel said, "Makes sense, I feel bad for the homeroom teacher." Steve said, "The homeroom teacher was very nice and hopeful!" Steve and Daniel walked by Peter's locker! Peter was at his locker, putting supplies in to his bag. Daniel said, "Hey Peter, how is it going?" Peter said, "I am doing good so far, I am ready for the Algebra class." Daniel said, "That's good, positivity and optimism are needed to succeed in life." Peter, Steve, and Daniel walked in the hallway together to Algebra class. Anha and Tony were walking in the hallway together. Tony said, "Why do you have to make drama, everywhere you go? It frustrates the other students around you." Anha said, "It is part of my talent!" Anha and Tony walked to Algebra class! Anha and Tony walked in to the classroom for Algebra. Anha sat down at her desk. The other students walked in to the classroom and sat down at their desks. Peter and Steve were at their desk, getting their supplies out of their bags. Daniel was at his desk, getting supplies out of his bag. Tony's desk was next to Daniel's desk. Tony sat down at his desk! Tony got his supplies out of his bag, ready to take down any Math equations that were thrown at him. James walked to the whiteboard, and wrote on it. James said, "Welcome to Algebra, students! Some of you know me as the student council president, and I am also your Algebra teacher for the current school year at Pine Cone Academy! Today is the first day of school for everyone, and I have a special surprise." James took out a stack of exam papers and put them on his desk. James said, "This is a surprise exam, do your best everyone! The staff of Pine Cone Academy are counting on all of you to do well." Peter said, "Surprise Exam, with my luck, I can take down every Math equation and pass!" Steve said, "Math exams are a piece of cake, I bet that I will do well." Daniel panics and flips through his notebook. Daniel rubs his hand through his hair and said, "Surprise Exam, but I didn't study! What if I fail, and my entire academic career falls apart? My family members will kill me, if I don't get passing grades in all of my classes." Tony put his hand on Daniel's arm and said, "Daniel, everything will be ok, you are the smartest person that I know. Your opti-

mism has helped me and everyone else survive the world around them."
Daniel smiled at Tony and said, "Thanks buddy for the support!" Tony
said, "No problem, lets take down the Math equations together." Chris
said, "Daniel, you're the smartest person that I know, and you will destroy the Math equations on the exam." Daniel said, "Thanks for the
support, Chris!" Chris said, "I am a good motivator for everyone." Tony
said, "Chris, I hope you do well on the Math exam as well." Chris said,
"Thanks Tony, you're the best!" Anha said, "Shut up, plants are boring to look at, and their pollen messes up my hair, by landing on my
head." Tony said, "Plants are awesome to look at, you can admire the
beauty of them, by examining the details of the flowers on them." Anha
said, "Seems boring, I don't like nature, it annoys me so much." Tony
said, "Just because you don't like nature doesn't mean that you can in-
sult plants." James said, "Both of you quiet down! Save the energy and
motivation for the Math equations on the exam." James walked around
the classroom and put the exam on everyone's desk. James said, "The
exam starts now, and you have until the bell rings to finish the exam
and put it on my desk. Good luck everyone!" The students knocked out
the Math equations on their exams. Daniel moved his hand through his
hair, as he finished the Math equations on his exam. Daniel set his pencil down, and got up from his desk. Daniel walked up to the teacher's
desk and turned in his exam. Tony followed behind Daniel and turned
in his exam. Steve and Peter turned in their exam! Tony and Daniel put
the pencils in their bags, as the other students turned in their exams. The
bell rings in the background. Steve and Peter put their supplies back in
to their bags and zipped them up! Daniel said, "Oh boy, time went by so
fast!" Tony winks and said, "Yep, time goes by fast, when you have fun
taking down Math equations." Steve and Peter got up from their seats
and walked in to the hallway! The other students got up from their seats
and walked in to the hallway. Daniel and Tony walked in to the hallway together. Daniel and Tony walked in to the library and sat down
at the table. Steve and Bob were sitting next to them, laughing while
reading science jokes out of a joke book. Matt was sitting at the table

next to them, reading a history book about technology. In the corner of the library, Noah and Monica were hanging out together, eating popcorn. Noah and Monica smiled at each other! Noah said, "Monica, you have been a wonderful friend, since we have met each other." Monica said, "Noah, you have been a wonderful friend as well. I hope nothing breaks our friendship." Noah and Monica hug each other. Noah and Monica rehydrated themselves, by drinking out of their water bottles. Noah and Monica took out their notebooks and studied for their classes. In the computer lab, Joey and Abby were playing a action role playing game called Dragon Slayers on the computer. Joey said, "Abby, distract the dragon by shooting your fire spell at his head, and I will jump on his head and stab him with my sword." Abby said, "Sounds good, be careful, we don't have alot of health potions left." The dragon roared and walked towards Abby's character. Abby shot her fire spell at the dragon's chest. The dragon growled and chased after Abby, as her character ran in to the forest. Joey jumped through the trees, and chased after the dragon. Joey took out his sword, and flipped out of the tree. Joey jumped on to the dragon's back, and used his sword to help him climb. The dragon swished his tail at Abby! Joey kept his balance on the dragon's back, as he climbed towards the head. Abby ran in to a rock wall, as the dragon got closer to her. The dragon sharpened his fangs and growled at Abby. Joey climbed on to the dragon's head! Joey flipped in the air, and stabbed his sword in to the dragon's head. The dragon roared in pain, as Joey flipped in the air and landed in front of Abby. Abby and Joey high fived and hugged each other, as they celebrated their victory in the computer lab. Joey and Abby saved their game progress on the computer. In the game room, Quentin, Sam, and Peter were playing Monopoly at the table. Quentin was in control of the dark blue properties, and Peter was in control of the red properties. The dark blue properties and the red properties had hotels on them. Sam rolled the dice and moved his game piece. Sam landed on one of the dark blue properties. Quentin smiled and said, "The property rent is $1000!" Sam gave the Monopoly money to Quentin. Sam said, "My Monopoly money is low, I need to be careful." Quentin rolled the dice and moved his game piece. Peter rolled the dice and moved his game piece. Sam rolled the dice and moved his game piece. Sam's game piece landed on one of the red properties. Peter said, "The property rent is $2000! Sam gave the Monopoly money to Peter. Quentin smiled and said, "One more property rent, until Sam goes bankrupt, and we get all of his Monopoly money." Quentin rolled the dice, and moved his game piece. Peter rolled the dice, and moved his game piece. Sam rolled the dice, and moved his game piece. The game piece landed on the dark blue property. Quentin said, "The property rent is $3000!" Sam looked down at his small pile of Monopoly money, and noticed that he doesn't have enough Monopoly money to pay Quentin. Sam sighed and gave the rest of his money to Quentin. Quentin smiled and high fived Peter! Sam broke down in tears, and put his head down in his hands. Sam said, "My luck has failed me, I went bankrupt during a game of Monopoly." Sam sat in the corner, while Quentin and Peter cleaned up and put the Monopoly game away. Jay walked over and sat next to Sam. Jay said, "What's wrong, Sam?" Sam dried up his tears and said, "Peter and Quentin made me go bankrupt in Monopoly." Jay said, "It's just a board game, going bankrupt isn't the end of the world. They were just following the rules and playing fairly." Sam smiled and said, "Thanks for comforting me, Jay, you're an wonderful friend." Sam and Jay hug each other! Jay said, "It's getting close to lunch time, want to walk to the cafeteria with me?" Sam said, "I would love to!" Sam and Jay walked to the cafeteria! The bell rings in the background! Daniel and Tony walked out of the library, and toward the cafeteria. The other students walked out of the library, toward the cafeteria. Sam and Jay were walking toward the cafeteria, when multiple students ran past them. Jay yelled at them and said, "No running in the hallways!" The students ignored Jay and continued running toward the cafeteria. Jay sighed and said, "Students these days don't know the rules of walking in the hallways." Sam said, "It's fine, they probably wanted to get to the food before it got cold." Jay and Sam walked by Ash's classroom! Sam said, "I wonder how Anha and Matt are handling their punishment with Ash." Jay said, "I bet that they are having fun handling their punishment." Jay and Sam walked in to the cafeteria. Ash tied a chain to Matt and Anha's neck. Anha said, "Why did you tie a chain to our neck?" Ash said, "The chain is to help me torture you guys during your punishment. It wouldn't be fun, if you guys tried to escape." Matt said, "Tying a chain to our neck is insane, we are just students." Ash laughed and said, "You guys interrupted the atmosphere of my classroom. As your homeroom teacher, you need to learn respect and teamwork." Anha said, "This is unfair, students shouldn't be tortured for the teacher's entertainment." Ash pulled on the chain and dragged Anha to her. Ash said, "Life isn't fair, deal with it!" Ash gave a mop and a bucket of water to Anha and Matt. Ash said, "Clean the classroom, and exterminate all of the dust." Anha and Matt grabbed the mop and the bucket of water, and they started cleaning the classroom. Anha is cleaning with her mop, and sighs to herself. Anha looks at the clock and said, "This will take forever!" Anha picks up the bucket, and poured the water on to the ground in a huge area. The water poured out of the bucket and splashed everywhere. The water splashed on Ash's desk, and Matt's clothes. Matt growled and grabbed Anha's shirt. Matt shouted and said, "You ruined my clothes, and now I am soaking wet." Matt kicked Anha in the chest. Anha stumbled backward and ran in to the desk. Matt grabbed Anha by her neck, and threw her in to the bookshelf. The books fell on top of Anha. Anha growled, as she got up from the ground. Anha sped in to Matt, and punched him in the face. Matt growled, as he slid backwards. Matt sped in to Anha, and body slammed her in to the desk. Matt held Anha on to the desk, and held her arms behind her back. Anha screamed in pain! Matt growled and said, "Say Uncle!" Anha said, "I will not say it to a crazy psycho like you!" Matt smiled and said, "Oh well, here is a little reward for entertaining me!" Matt took out his knife and cut off some of Anha's hair. Some pieces of Anha's hair fell on the ground! Anha screamed in horror and said, "My hair is ruined!" Matt smirked and said, "Your new hair cut matches you perfectly!" Matt tossed his knife in the air, and caught it. Anha and

Matt refilled the bucket of water and continued cleaning the classroom. Ash said, "Let's torture you guys a bit!" Ash pulled on the chains and spins them in a circle. Anha and Matt spin in a circle. They tripped on the bucket of water, and they fell on to the ground. Anha rubbed her back with her hand, as Matt grabbed the desk with his hand. Ash pulled on the chain, as Matt rolled on the ground, and ran in to Anha. Anha is on top of Matt, as Anha stares in to Matt's eyes and smiled. Matt threw Anha on to the ground, as he gets up. Matt brushes the dirt off of his clothes. Anha gets up, and brushes the dirt off of her clothes. Ash walks over to Anha and Matt, and unlatches the chains off of their necks. Matt and Anha walked out of the classroom, and to the cafeteria. Sally and Fiona walked past Matt and Anha! Sally and Fiona put their lunch gowns on. Sally said, "Serving lunch to these hopeful students is despairful!" Fiona said, "It could be fun!" Sally laughed and said, "You think serving lunch is fun, your head is filled with marbles. Pine Cone Academy is filled with hope and friendship!" Fiona said, "Do you have a plan to tear down the wall of hope?" Sally took out a flash drive and said, "With this flash drive, it lets us upload the Despair video in to any device, and brainwash the students to do whatever we want." Fiona said, "The plan is perfect, this is why you're so awesome, Sally." Sally and Fiona laughed maniacally together, as they walked in to the cafeteria. Students walked in to the cafeteria, as Sally and Fiona stirred the food in their cooking pots. The students lined up to get the food poured on to their lunch trays. Noah and Monica were standing next to each other with their lunch trays. Noah said to Sally and Fiona, "Give us a lunch that is perfect for friends to eat together." Noah winks at Monica, as Sally and Fiona poured the food on to the trays. Monica and Noah smiled at each other, as they walked to the lunch table with their food. The other students got their lunch poured on to their trays, and they sat at the tables to eat their food. Tom and Victoria were sitting together, eating their food. Tom was rubbing his hand through Victoria's hair, as he ate his lunch. Victoria said "Tom, do you like rabbits?" Tom said, "Rabbits are cute and cuddly, and they have soft fur." Victoria ruffles up Tom's hair and said, "Rabbits are one of the greatest wonders of the world." Tom said, "This is why you're a wonderful friend, Victoria! You entertain me with wonderful stories." Victoria blushes, as she continued to eat her food. Jay and Sam were at the lunch table with Tom and Victoria, eating their food. Jay said, "The food is ok, but I expected better effort from a high quality school." Sam said, "The food satisfies my hunger, it is better than eating nothing." Jay said, "You're right, Sam, eating nothing would fill us with despair." Noah and Monica were eating their food next to Sam and Jay. Noah smiled at Monica! Noah said, "What soap did you use in your hair, it smells nice?" Monica said, "I used strawberry soap to wash my hair." Noah said, "Strawberries are my favorite fruit to eat." Monica said, "Strawberries are amazing!" Noah winks and said, "I agree, you are amazing as well." Monica blushes, while she eats her food. Noah and Monica hugged each other! Noah and Monica got up from the table, and threw their lunch trays away. Noah and Monica went back to the table, and sat next to Sam and Jay. The students continued eating their food, as Sally and Fiona activated their cleaning robot. The cleaning robot was named the Cleaning Master 500! The Cleaning Master 500 rolled on to the cafeteria floor. Tom was walking to the trash can, and he tripped on the Cleaning Master 500! Tom fell on the floor! Tom's plate of food flew in the air and landed on Daniel's shirt. Daniel growled as he wiped the food off of his shirt. Daniel got up from his seat, and picked up a pizza slice from the selection of food at the food bar. Daniel threw the pizza slice at Tom! The pizza slice landed on Tom's shirt. Tony shouted and said, "Food Fight!", as he threw a plate of meatballs at Gwen and his soda at Bob. Chris threw a egg roll at Victoria! The egg roll exploded, as it hit Victoria's chest. Tom and Victoria threw lettuce at Chris. The lettuce hit Chris in the face. Chris threw a bowl of soup at Norman. The bowl of soup landed on Norman's shirt. Norman threw burritos at Joey and Abby. The burritos hit Joey and Abby in the chest! Joey and Abby threw a cake at Quentin and Peter. The cake hit Quentin and Peter in the chest. Quentin and Peter picked up a tub of ice cream, and poured it on Daniel's head. Quentin and Peter continued pouring ice cream all over Daniel. Quentin and Peter picked up a bottle of salsa and nachos from the food bar and threw it at Joey and Abby. The bottle of salsa landed in Joey's hair, and poured all over his body. The nachos exploded all over Abby's body. Harry threw a bottle of ketchup at Norman. The ketchup exploded all over Norman's hair. Norman tackled Harry in to the cheese dispenser. The cheese dispenser poured cheese sauce on Harry. The cheese sauce landed in Harry's hair and covered his clothes, as the dispenser continued pouring the sauce on to him. Steve picked up a pot of chili, and poured it on Harry and Norman. Sam poured his chocolate milk shake on Jay. Jay poured orange juice on Sam. Matt and Anha threw a cake at Jay and Sam. Tony poured a gallon of chocolate sauce on Steve. The chocolate sauce covered Steve's body! Joey and Daniel poured a gallon of ice cream on Quentin and Peter. Eddie walks in to the cafeteria and saw all of the chaos, as the students threw food everywhere. Eddie picked up a megaphone and shouted, "Drop the food now!" A breeze of cold air flowed through the cafeteria, as the students dropped the food on to the ground. Eddie said, "Students, clean yourselves outside. The cleaning robot will clean the cafeteria." The students walked outside and cleaned themselves. Multiple cleaning robots cleaned the food in the cafeteria. Sally and Fiona walked out of the cafeteria. Sally and Fiona walked through the hallway! Sally said, "The best way to spread despair is to get rid of the teachers. The students will fall apart, when their mentors can't teach them anymore." Fiona said, "That sounds like a awesome idea, Sally!" Sally and Fiona walked to the teacher's lounge! Sally opens the door, and walks in to the room. Fiona took explosives out of her bag and attaches them to everything in the teacher's lounge. Fiona connects the explosives to her detonator! Ash tapped Fiona on the shoulder and said, "What are you doing here?" Fiona said, "The teacher's lounge needed a makeover!" Ash said, "Oh ok, the teacher's lounge needed a makeover for a while." James came in and said, "The students are probably worried about us, lets head back to the classroom." Ash said, "They can handle themselves on their own." Sally said, "That's right, stay in the teacher's lounge, the students are fine on their own." Sally and Fiona smiled, as they pressed the button on the detonator. The explosives started to beep in the background. Sally said, "We love to hang out, but we are needed in another part of the school." Sally and Fiona walked out of the teacher's lounge. The explosives detonated, and the teacher's lounge exploded in the background. The bodies of Ash and James laid on the ground in puddles of blood. Sally and Fiona laughed maniacally, while they walked down the hallway. The students walked back in to the school. Steve walked to the water fountain and rehydrated himself with some water. Sally and Fiona walked in to the art room. Norman was sitting at the table, drawing in his notebook. Commander Fluff, Norman's teddy bear, was sitting next to him as his bodyguard. A cold breeze flowed through the room as Sally and Fiona walked closer to Norman. Norman was drawing in his notebook. Sally tapped Norman on the shoulder. Norman got spooked by Sally, and fell out of the chair. Sally said, "I am sorry, that I have spooked you!" Norman got up and brushed the dirt off of his clothes. Sally said, "What were you drawing?" Norman said, "I was drawing dragons in my notebook! I want to make people smile with my drawings." Sally said, "Drawings are a wonderful way to express your imagination." Fiona picks up Commander Fluff and squeezes him. Norman said, "Don't hurt Commander Fluff, he is my friend and he helps me survive." Sally puts a knife at Commander Fluff's chest. Sally said, "Commander Fluff's life is on the line! He is about to lay on the ground in a pile of fluff." Norman trembles in fear! Norman puts his finger on his chin, as he thinks to himself. Norman mutters to himself as he said, "Commander Fluff is going to get the stuffing knocked out of him!" Norman tackles Sally in to the wall. Sally kicked Norman in the chest. Norman slid backwards. Sally laughed and said, "Execution Time!" Norman trembles in fear, as Sally laughed. Sally stabbed the knife through Commander Fluff's chest. Sally tears Commander Fluff's head off of his body. Sally threw Commander Fluff on to the ground, as stuffing poured out of him. Norman laid against the wall, and cried in his shirt sleeve. Sally said, "Despair is so delicious, as it flows through the school!" Norman wiped the tears away, as he got up. Sally rubs her fingers on Norman's neck! Sally said, "Every decision that a human makes has a consequence! Despair will take over and squeeze all the hope out of the school like a python." Sally puts her knife at Norman's neck. Norman was shaking in fear as he said, "I don't want to die, I have so much hope to spread with my drawings." Sally said, "Awwwww, the kiddo has a talent that he likes to share with the world to spread hope." Steve walks in to the art room, and threw his science notebook at Sally. The science notebook knocked the knife out of Sally's hand. Steve kicked the knife across the room, as he said "Get away from him!" Steve tackled Sally in to the wall. Fiona sneaks up on Steve with her knife. Steve grabbed Fiona's arm and flipped her on to the ground. Norman grabbed his notebook and walked in to the art closet. Sally kicked Steve in to the bookshelf. Steve laid against the bookshelf, as Sally swung her knife at him. Steve kicked Sally in the chest. Sally flinches, as she gripped her knife. Fiona got up from the ground, and stabbed Steve in the arm with her knife. Steve grabbed Fiona's arm, and threw her at the wall. Fiona laid against the wall. Sally tackled Steve in to the ground, and stabbed him in the back with her knife. Blood leaked on to the ground, as Steve laid on the ground. Fiona got up, and regained her balance. Fiona stepped on Steve's back to hold him down on the ground. Sally stabbed her knife in to Steve's neck. Blood poured out of Steve's neck! Steve grabbed on to a paint bottle with his arm, and hits Sally in the chest. Sally flinched, as she slid backwards. Steve got up from the ground, and roundhouse kicked Sally in the face. Sally sped into Steve, and grabbed him by the neck. Sally smashed Steve in to the art table. The art table snapped in half, as Steve laid on the ground. Blood leaked out of Steve's body. Fiona picked up Steve, and held him against the wall! Sally stabbed her knife in to Steve's chest. Blood splashed on to the ground, as Sally picked up Steve, and threw him on the ground. Steve laid on the ground, in a puddle of blood. Eddie and Twilight kicked down the door to the art room. Eddie shot a tranquilizer dart at Sally and Fiona. Sally and Fiona laid against the wall. Twilight walked to Steve's body, and attached her medical equipment to his arm. Twilight signaled Eddie to come closer to her. Eddie said, "Is everything ok?" Twilight said, "I checked his pulse, and I didn't get a signal from the equipment." Eddie said, "Is that a good sign or a bad sign?" Twilight said, "It is a bad sign! When the equipment doesn't get a signal, it means that they are dead." Eddie said, "We need to clean up the mess!" Twilight nods, as she puts her equipment away. Norman walked out of the art closet, and saw all of the blood. He trembled in fear, as he walked through the room. Norman saw Steve's body, and screamed in horror! Norman broke down in tears, and cried on Eddie's shirt. Eddie said, "Norman, everything will be fine!" Norman cried and said, "I lost two of my friends, the world is falling apart!" Eddie said, "I know, life is rough right now, but we will bring justice to Sally and Fiona." Twilight wrapped a towel around Steve's body! Twilight picked up Steve's body, and carried him outside with Norman. Eddie used the cleaning robot to clean up the blood in the art room. Twilight and Norman walked in to the gardening shed. Norman picked up a shovel from the gardening shed, and dug a hole for Steve's body. Twilight dropped Steve's body in to the hole. Norman filled up the hole with dirt. Norman put the shovel back in to the gardening shed. Sally and Fiona pulled the tranquilizer dart off of their chest, and walked out of the art room. Sally and Fiona walked to the headmaster's office! Fiona kicked the door open! Sally walked in to the headmaster's office, and set up the conveyor belt with the shotput ball. Sally wrapped the rope around the lights, as it hanged in front of the room, waiting for its prey. Fiona set up the spiked trap in front of the door. Eddie walked in to the headmaster's office, while Sally sat in the headmaster's chair. Eddie walked on to the spiked trap. The spiked trap activated, and Eddie limped in to the rope. The rope wrapped under Eddie's legs, and pulled him in to the air. Sally smiled and said, "You fell in to our trap, headmaster. The storm of despair flows through the school, and it will devour the students, and smash their hope to pieces." Eddie said, "Hope will find a way to push back the despair." Sally smiled, as she gripped the knife in her hand. Sally threw her knife at the rope. The rope snaps, and the conveyor belt with the shotput ball activates. Eddie landed on the ground! The shotput ball fell on top of Eddie's head, and smashed his skull. Blood poured on to the ground, as Eddie laid on the ground. Sally picked up her knife from the ground, while Fiona picked up the rope. Fiona took down the conveyor belt and put the shotput ball in to her bag. Sally sat in the headmaster's chair, and loaded up the security system for the school. The computer beeped and said, "Put in the password to continue!" Sally taps on the keyboard and typed in a random combination of letters. The computer beeped and said, "Login successful!" Sally tapped on the security camera system with the mouse, and loaded it on to the computer. The security camera system popped up on the screen, with camera footage of every location in the school. Sally smiled, as she tapped on to the upload button with the mouse. Fiona watched Sally, as she flipped her knife in the air. Sally plugs the flash drive in to the computer. Sally uploaded the Despair video in to the security camera system. Sally plugged the headmaster's microphone in to the computer, and turned it on. Sally said, "Time for the fun to begin!" Fiona said, "I can't wait to see the students suffer." Several students were hanging out in the hallway. Harry and Bob were chugging down a tub of ice cream, while Gwen was watching them. Harry and Bob put their hands on their head as they said, "Ahhhhhhhhhhh, Brain Freeze!" Gwen facepalms and said, "You guys are idiots!" Harry and Bob said, "Even though, we are idiots, it is fun to chug down ice cream, and get a brain freeze." Harry gave Gwen bunny ears with his fingers, while Bob took their photo with the phone. Harry and Gwen looked at the photo. Harry said, "Wow, the photo looks awesome." Gwen tickled Harry! Harry rolled on the floor, laughing! Bob tickled Gwen! Gwen was on the floor, laughing with Harry! Daniel and Tony did a headstand next to the wall. Noah and Monica reenact Sherlock Holmes to each other. Joey shared a bag of pretzels with Abby. Joey said, "I was playing Robot Warriors, and my character was battling a lion. My character defeated the lion with a spinning roundhouse kick, and stabbed it in the chest with his flaming sword." Abby said, "That is cool, Robot Warriors is one of my favorite games." Abby ruffles up Joey's hair! Joey smiled at Abby, while he eats a pretzel. Quentin and Peter have a dancing competition against each other. Peter does the robot, and Quentin does the moon walk. Peter said, "Hey Quentin, I dare you to do a backflip and impress the other students." Quentin agrees to the challenge by shaking his hand with Peter. Quentin backflips in the air, spins in a circle, and lands on the ground in front of the other students. Joey smiled and gave Quentin a pretzel. Joey hugged Quentin and said, "That was amazing, Quentin!" Quentin smiled and hugged Joey back! Sally pressed a button on the computer in the headmaster's office. The TV monitors in the hallways flipped on, with a video of despair. Sally's voice echoed through the hallways as she said, "Hello kiddos, we have a wonderful video to share with you today! Enjoy the despair!" The video played on the monitors!" A group of students followed Sam and Jay in to the janitor's closet. Peter and Daniel said, "Blind your eyes, don't watch the video!" Another group of students followed Peter and Daniel in to the men's bathroom. Tony grabbed Anha's hand, and locked himself in his locker with her. Matt was drinking out of the water fountain, and looked at the video monitor. Sally pressed a button, and a electric chain popped out of the monitor. The electric chain latches on to Matt's neck. The electric chain electrocutes Matt, as the energy flows through him. Matt's eyes turned red, as he gets consumed with despair. Sally smiled, as Matt flipped his knife in the air. Sally said, "Time to hunt down some students!" Matt walked toward the lockers, with his eyes glowing red. He walked over to Tony's locker and saw Tony terrified in fear with Anha. Matt cuts a hole in to the locker with his knife, and pulled it open. Tony is terrified and shaking, while Matt smiled at him. Matt grabbed Anha's arm! Tony grabbed Anha's arm, and pulled her back. Matt kicked Tony in the chest. Tony loses his grip on Anha's arm. Matt pulled harder on Anha's arm. Matt pulled Anha in to the hallway. Anha stumbled backwards! Matt kicked Anha in the chest. Anha leans against the wall! Matt picked up Anha by her neck, and slams her in to the locker. Anha laid against the locker, with blood leaking from her arm. Matt took out his knife, and sped towards Anha. Anha grabbed Matt's arm and roundhouse kicked him in the chest. Matt flew in to the wall, with his knife falling on to the ground. Matt got up from the ground, and picked up his knife. Anha punched Matt in the face. Matt fell backwards, and growled at Anha. Matt stabbed Anha in the chest with his knife. Blood leaked on to the ground, as Anha fell backwards. Matt tackled Anha in to the locker! Matt stabbed his knife in to Anha's neck, and punched her in the face. Anha fell backwards, and leaned against the wall! Matt picked Anha up by her neck, and threw her on to the ground. Matt stepped on Anha's back, and punched her in the face. Matt stabbed Anha in the back with his knife. A puddle of blood formed under Anha's body, as she laid on the ground. Matt flipped his knife in the air, as he smiled and walked to the next locker. Tony looked outside the locker, and saw Anha's body. Tony is terrified in his locker, while crying in his shirt sleeve. Daniel and Norman looked outside the men's bathroom and saw Anha's body. They were horrified, as despair filled the hallway with Matt patrolling outside. Norman sunk down, laid against the wall and cried. Peter and Daniel comforted Norman and wiped away his tears. Peter said, "Everything will be fine, despair will not win." Norman said, "It feels like everything is hopeless!" Daniel said, "Hope will find a way to defeat despair!" Sam looked outside the janitor's closet, and saw Matt! Sam said, "We need a plan to turn Matt back to normal!" Jay pointed to Chris and said, "We will use Chris as bait!" Chris walked out of the janitor's closet, and threw a cream pie at Matt! The cream pie hits Matt in the chest. Sam runs out of the janitor's closet, and tackled Matt in to the ground. Sam held Matt on the ground. Matt threw Sam off of him. Peter tackled Matt in to the ground, and held him down. Matt was struggling in Peter's grip. Jay grabbed the electric collar out of Tom's hand, and tossed it to Peter. Peter caught the electric collar, and wrapped it around Matt's neck. Quentin pressed the button and electrocuted Matt, multiple times! Matt's eyes turned back to normal, as he laid on the ground. Peter got up from the ground, and wiped the dust off of his clothes. Matt gets up and rubbed his head! Joey hugged Matt and said, "He's back to normal!" Matt said, "What happened!" Tom said, "Sally and Fiona brainwashed you, and your actions made you kill Anha!" Matt broke down in tears and cried! Joey wiped away Matt's tears and said, "It's not your fault, Sally wanted hope to be destroyed!" Sally spun in the headmaster's chair, and threw a stack of books at Fiona. Sally growled and said, "Why does hope keep getting in the way of my plans?" Fiona said, "The students are better, and more talented than us!" Sally kicked Fiona in the chest and said, "Despair never gives up! The students aren't better than us" Sally pressed a button and a giant robot smashed through the wall in to the hallway. Sally said, "Lets see the students try to defeat the giant robot." The giant robot smashed through the school's hallway as he said, "Beep, beep, beep, beep!" Harry walked in to the hallway, and threw a tub of ice cream at the giant robot. The giant robot beeped, and chased Harry down the hallway. Harry ran down the hallway, while the giant robot shot missiles at him. Harry dodged the missiles, and tore the water fountain out of the ground. Harry threw the water fountain at the giant robot. The giant robot grabbed the water fountain and smashed it to pieces. The giant robot shot a grappling hook at Harry. The grappling hook wrapped around Harry and pulled him in to the giant robot's hand. The giant robot petted Harry with his hand and said, "Harry, your life will be over soon, Despair will win, beep beep beep beep!" The giant robot picked Harry up by his neck. Harry struggled in his grip! The giant robot threw Harry in to the locker. Harry laid on the ground! The giant robot stepped on Harry's back! Harry screamed in pain, as blood poured on to the ground. Harry took out a nail from his pocket, and stabbed it in to the giant robot's leg. The giant robot stumbled backwards, as Harry used his strength to get up from the ground. Harry pushed the giant robot in to the wall. The giant robot kicked Harry in to the locker. Harry laid against the locker! The giant robot tackled Harry in to the ground, and punched him in the face. Harry growled, and held the giant robot's hand back! Harry pushed the giant robot off of him with his other hand. Harry got up from the ground! The giant robot launched a energy wave out of its body! Harry rolled on the ground, and laid against the wall. The giant robot picked up Harry and smashed him in to the locker. Harry laid on the ground! Spikes popped out of the giant robot's legs! The giant robot stepped on Harry's back! Blood poured out of Harry's body! The other students were terrified in horror. The giant robot patrolled the hallway. Daniel and Peter looked out in to the hallway, and saw the giant robot. Daniel said, "We need a plan to get to the headmaster's office, and take down Sally and Fiona!" Peter said, "We work better as a team, let me call over the other students" Peter walks out in to the hallway, while the giant robot isn't looking. Peter flaps his arms like a bird! Peter said, "Tweet tweet tweet tweet!" The other students saw Peter, and walked out of the janitor's closet to his location. Tony walked out of his locker, and toward Peter. Peter said, "Everyone is together, lets think of a plan!" Daniel said, "We need a student to distract the giant robot, while the rest of us hunt down Sally and Fiona." Chris said, "We could volunteer Joey as the distraction!" Abby said, "The giant robot is scary, and I don't want him to mess up Joey's hair. His hair is so soft, and Joey is the nicest student that I know." Quentin hugs Joey and said, "I won't let the giant robot smash him in to the ground, Joey is my best friend." Quentin squeezes Joey tightly. Joey coughs and said, "Quentin, I can't breathe, you're squeezing me too tight!" Quentin said, "You're my best friend though!" Peter grabbed Quentin by his shirt collar, and dragged him backwards! Joey said, "Thanks Peter, you're the best!" Peter said, "No problem, Joey!" Abby hugged Peter and said, "Peter, you're a life saver." Peter said, "Thanks Abby!" Quentin leans against the wall! Peter said, "Anyone else have a good idea?" Noah said, "One of my friends, Aaron, can distract the giant robot for us!" Noah whistles outside the room in to the hallway. Aaron walked through the hallway, and pushes the giant robot in to the lockers. The giant robot falls on the ground, and smashes the water fountain. Aaron walked in to the men's bathroom. Aaron tapped Noah on the shoulder. Noah said, "He can distract the giant robot for us, while we take down Sally and Fiona." Peter smiled and said, "Sounds like the perfect plan!" Peter and Daniel gathered the other students in a group. Aaron marched in the front of the other students with Daniel and Peter. Aaron threw a cream pie at the giant robot to distract him, while the other students ran through the hallway to the headmaster's office. The giant robot saw the other students, and chased after them. Bob said, "The giant robot is chasing us, we need to run faster." Daniel said, "Good idea, Bob!" The other students ran faster to the headmaster's office, while Aaron stood in front of the giant robot, and hit him with apples, to slow him down. The giant robot swatted Aaron away with his hand, and launched a rope at Bob. The rope wrapped around Bob, as he fell on the ground. The giant robot walked closer to Bob. Peter looked back, and saw that Bob fell in the hallway. Daniel said, "Peter, keep your eye on the objective!" Peter nodded and continued running. Abby said, "I am not leaving a student behind, Daniel." Daniel said, "It is too dangerous, Abby!" Abby said, "I know that it is dangerous, but I am willing to risk my life." Abby and Joey hugged each other. Abby ran in front of Bob, and tried to untie the rope around him. The giant robot walked toward Abby, and grabbed her with his hand." Aaron walked toward the giant robot. The giant robot punched Aaron in to the wall. Aaron rubbed his head! The giant robot shot a missile at Bob. Bob smashed in to the lockers and laid next to the lockers, with blood on the ground. The giant robot kicked Bob in to the lockers with his foot. Bob laid on the ground. The giant robot sharpened the spikes on his foot, and stepped on Bob's chest. Blood poured on to the ground, as Bob's body laid on the ground. Abby was terrified in horror! The giant robot grabbed Abby by her neck, and smashed her in to the locker. Blood poured on to the ground, as she laid next to the wall. The giant robot took out his spiked sword, and stabbed Abby in the chest. A puddle of blood formed under her body. Aaron walked toward the giant robot with his flaming sword, and swung it at the giant robot. The spiked sword was destroyed by the flaming sword! Aaron growled and shot the giant robot with a pie launcher. The giant robot stumbled on to the ground, and exploded. Body parts flew everywhere in the debris! Joey and the other students saw the chaos behind them, as they wiped the tears out of their eyes. They ran toward the headmaster's office. Sally growled and threw knifes at the wall, while Fiona dodged them. Sally said, "I hate hope so much, seeing our work fall apart fills me with so much despair." Fiona said, "That's how life works, it would be boring if despair controlled the world. Hope and Despair keeps everything balanced." Sally said, "Hope and Despair are two sides of the same coin!" Daniel kicked down the headmaster's door. Daniel and the rest of the students walked in to the headmaster's office. Peter said, "You lost, Sally and Fiona! We have you outnumbered!" Sally laughed and said, "Outnumbered, you make me laugh! We are the queens of despair, and all of you have fallen in to our trap." Fiona pressed a button on the wall, and a energy shield formed around the students. Sally said, "Get cozy, we want to have some fun with you!" Fiona grabbed a rope and threw it around Gwen. Sally pulled Gwen closer to her. Sally brushed Gwen with her hand. Sally said, "Your hair is so shiny and wonderful, too bad that we have to cut it off." Sally grinned, as she took out a razor out of her bag. Sally turned on the razor, and shaved all of Gwen's hair off of her head. The students were horrified as hair flew everywhere, and on to the ground. Sally gave Gwen a mirror! Gwen screamed in horror, as she saw herself in the mirror. Sally said, "We're not done yet!" Fiona gave a chainsaw to Sally! Sally turned on the chainsaw, and pushed it through Gwen's chest! Blood flew everywhere, and Gwen's body laid on the ground. Peter growled and shouted," NOOOOOOOOOOOOOOOOOOOO, she didn't deserve to die, both of you are monsters!" Sam put his hand on Peter's shoulder and said, "Everything will be fine!" Sally said, "Awwwwwww, the students are upset at us for killing their friend!" Tony picked up Matt's knife and stabbed through the energy shield. Tony tackled Fiona in to the wall. Fiona kicked Tony in the chest. Fiona grabbed Tony's arm. Tony backflips and kicked Fiona in the face. Tony grabbed Fiona's arm, and stabbed her in the neck with the knife. Tony roundhouse kicked Fiona in the chest. Fiona smashed in to the wall. Tony punched Fiona in the face. Blood poured on the ground. Fiona got up from the ground, and grabbed Tony by his neck. Fiona body slammed Tony in to the ground. Tony got up from the ground, and tackled Fiona in to the wall. Tony picked up Fiona by her neck, and slammed her in to the ground. Fiona stabbed her knife in to Tony's arm! Blood poured out on to Fiona's chest, while Tony choked Fiona. Tony squeezed Fiona's neck, while she was coughing! Tony roundhouse kicked Fiona in the face. Fiona stumbled backwards! Tony put the knife in his pocket, while he walked over and picked up the chainsaw. Tony stepped on Fiona's legs to hold her down. Tony started up the chainsaw and stabbed it in to Fiona's chest. Blood poured out of her body, as she laid on the ground. Tony wiped the blood off of his shoes, as Sally growled at him. Sally said, "Hope is so annoying, despair will not give up!" Tony said, "You killed our friends, your reign of terror will be over!" Sally said, "Despair will consume your soul!" Sally kicked Tony in the chest, and stepped on his back. Sally whacked Tony in the back, multiple times with the electric baton. The electric baton electrocuted Tony, while he screamed in pain. Sally picked up Tony's body, and smashed him through the headmaster's desk. Tony got up from the ground! Sally threw throwing knifes at Tony. The throwing knifes sliced through Tony's body, as blood leaked on the ground. Tony threw a water fountain at Sally. Sally dodged the water fountain, as it smashed against the wall. Sally sped in to Tony, and smashed him in to the wall. The wall made a dent, and the shotput ball machine activated. The shotput ball machine dropped a shotput ball on Tony's foot. Tony screamed in pain! Tony limped toward Sally. Tony swung his arm at Sally. Sally grabbed Tony's arm, and kicked him in the chest. Sally grabbed her knife, and stabbed Tony in the neck. Sally picked up the chainsaw! Sally stabbed the chainsaw through Tony's body. Blood flew everywhere, while Tony's body laid on the ground. Peter growled at Sally, as she put the chainsaw on to the ground. Sally said, "Awwww, did I make you mad for killing your friend!" Peter growled and said, "You are a monster, Tony was our best friend." Peter walked closer to Sally, and picked up a knife from the ground. Peter sped in to Sally! Sally swung her arm at Peter! Peter grabbed her arm, and threw her at the wall. Peter flipped in the air, and did a spinning round-house kick in to Sally's chest. Sally smashed in to the bookshelf, and laid against the wall. Peter grabbed Sally by her neck, and body slammed her in to the ground. Sally laid on the ground, while Peter stepped on her back to hold her down. Peter bent down and stabbed the knife in to Sally's neck. Blood poured on to the ground. Sally grabbed on to a table leg to help herself up. Sally got up from the ground! Peter sped in to Sally, and tackled her in to the wall. Peter punched Sally in the face! Peter growled and said, "You are a monster for killing several of our friends, you deserve to die." Sally said, "That's how despair works! It consumes your soul, when one drop of blood pours on to the ground." Sally kicked Peter in the chest. Peter slid backwards! Sally threw throwing knives at Peter! Peter flipped in the air, and dodged them. Peter landed on the ground! Peter sped in to Sally, and grabbed her neck. Peter body slammed Sally in to the ground. Sally got up from the ground. Peter sped in to Sally, and kicked her in the chest. Sally slid next to the wall. Peter threw his rope at Sally. The rope twisted around Sally! Peter pulled on the rope, and dragged Sally closer to him. Sally swung her arm at Peter. Peter grabbed Sally's arm, and threw her at the wall. Sally laid against the wall. Peter picked Sally up by her neck and stabbed the knife in to her chest! Blood splashed on to the ground, as Peter threw Sally on to the ground. Peter said, "Your reign of terror is over, Sally!" Peter put the knife on the desk, that was next to him. Peter picked up the shotput ball from the ground, and smashed it on top of Sally's head, multiple times as blood splashed on to the ground. Sally's body laid on the ground! Peter set the shotput ball on to the ground, and picked up a towel from the headmaster's desk. Peter wiped the blood off of his body with a towel. The school's alarm system went off! Pine Cone Academy Alarm System said, "Warning! Automatic Self Destruction System has activated, all students must get out of the blast radius immediately." Beeping goes off in the background, as the energy shield dropped around the other students. Aaron walked in to the headmaster's room, and helped the students get out of the blast radius. Daniel and Peter ran out of the headmaster's room, with the other students behind them. The headmaster's room exploded, as the students dived for cover in the men's bathroom. Dust and debris covered the hallway, and filled the air with dust particles. The air returns to normal, while Daniel and Peter walked in to the hallway to check out the chaos. Daniel and Peter were terrified in horror from all of the debris. Peter said, "It was a tough battle, but we have defeated Sally and Fiona." Daniel said, "Yep, the students worked together as a team." Peter and Daniel hugged each other, while the other students celebrated by eating ice cream. The storm of despair has been defeated, and the students have restored hope in the environment of Pine Cone Academy.

Josh Zimmer is an crazy individual with an extreme imagination. He loves to have fun by listening to music, writing stories, and playing video games of various genres such as platforming, multiplayer online games, role playing games, and sports games. His favorite technology brands are Nintendo and Microsoft. They are wonderful role models for the industry. He commands an army of cats to his will with hugs, love, and snacks. He makes the cats purr and meow with happiness.